Legacy (Large Print)

Susan Helene Gottfried

West of Mars, LLC

Copyright © 2025 by West of Mars®, LLC

All rights reserved.

No part of this publication may be reproduced, distributed, or transmitted in any form or by any means, including photocopying, recording, or other electronic or mechanical methods, without the prior written permission of the publisher, except as permitted by U.S. copyright law. For permission requests, contact Susan Helene Gottfried at WestofMars.com

The story, all names, characters, and incidents portrayed in this production are fictitious. No identification with actual persons (living or deceased), places, buildings, and products is intended or should be inferred.

Proofreading by Sue Toth at Sue Toth Editorial Services

Book Cover by Croco Designs

Print only author's photo by Rustbelt Mayberry Photography

Shot on location at Tall Pines Farm, Darlington, PA

Print only author's makeup by the Rainbow Room, Ellwood City, PA

First edition 2025

This one's for you, Mom

Author's Note

A large part of the Tales from the Sheep Farm project is about racial justice. To that end, most of the characters you will encounter do not have their race identified. Only a few must be entirely white, and it should be evident who they are. Likewise, only a few must be other races or ethnicities. It should be evident who they are, as well.

This goes for a character's sexuality and gender identity, too.

The rest? That is up to you.

And if you feel inspired to tell a story of your own in this world, or if there's a character you want to know more about, I want to hear about it.

Your voices matter. Your stories matter. This story, hopefully, continues to lay the foundation for my firm belief in that.

ONE

CHAD

Chad Flaherty had been beaten up before. Twice, in fact, and both times were the fault of Delia Ford, that bitch.

She hadn't even been good in bed.

But she'd been hot, and she'd had an attitude that he'd thought he'd liked—and yeah, there was no way he'd been thinking clearly when he'd asked his dad if he could move her into the condo, do some renovations to keep her around for a while, and flash her around town and let her reinforce his clout.

And that was it: She'd felt like a prize. Like something that should have been unattainable that he'd gotten hold of anyway and made his.

At least until he'd gotten tired of her.

Problem was that she'd gotten tired of him first.

And that, too, was a problem. He was *Chad Flaherty*, the closest thing this God-awful city had to royalty. What was she thinking, stealing his dad's condo out from under him and Dad both and changing the locks? Boy, she'd made it clear that she was done with him. She'd all but come out and said she was on a higher level of existence than the Flahertys.

The Flahertys. One of three families who'd founded Port Kenneth.

All of that was what had resulted in the first beating and Chad's longest-running fall from his father's grace. Dad hadn't been happy to have lost that particular condo. It had been in the Flaherty family since the building was conceived of, although it wasn't the only Flaherty conception to have taken place there, if family legend was to be believed.

The only good thing was that before it had all gone down, Chad had taken out a new mortgage to pay for the renovations he'd forced on her, and she'd been stuck with it all—the mortgage *and* the renovations. He hadn't bothered to hire the best people to do the work. That much, at least, his dad had approved of, especially in hindsight. It hadn't been enough to let Chad back into his dad's graces, though.

The second beating had come after he'd hired a couple thugs to shake her up a bit and put her back in her place. They'd been supposed to talk like they'd been sent by the art thief, who'd stolen all of her ugly pictures from this one gallery in town and left a bunch of them all over the place, like it was funny or something.

They'd been supposed to steal her cameras, not slice her face open.

And he'd thought he'd paid them enough to keep their fool mouths shut about the whole thing.

But as soon as word got out and video got shared and people *cared* about Delia Fucking Ford, the idiots he'd hired had sung. And his father had issued the order to drag his ass back to the basement and teach him a thing or two.

At that point, there was no redemption. William Flaherty was *done* with his only legitimate son.

He'd never had anything to do with the illegitimate ones, come to think of it.

Chad tried to take a deep breath. It wasn't easy; they'd done a lot of damage to his ribs this time, during this third beating, and he was probably a day or two away from his father sending a doctor over to make sure he wasn't about to die. Because William would eventually send the doctor—but only after he'd given Chad enough time to want to die.

He hurt too bad to die. Besides, he'd had enough of this bullshit with Delia Ford, even though his father had made it clear there was no way out from under it. Which was why he was lying in bed, in too much pain to breathe.

This time, he'd tried to say no to the old man. Tried to tell him that fucking with Delia Ford was like going down to the crossroads and selling your soul directly to Satan, except without those months or years where the devil granted you the good things so you got seduced into thinking it was all going to be okay.

"She's friends with Cartieri, who's married to Mackenzie," his father had insisted, slime and dislike dripping over the names, as if Chad hadn't known any of that. At least his father hadn't reminded him for the millionth time that Mackenzie was the ultimate goal. Stopping him from reopening the sheep farm was only the first step, but it was the one William was obsessed with.

Chad tried shifting on the bed, letting out a moan as he did, all of which only made him hurt worse. His place had been stripped clean of any sort of painkiller—even the booze—before they'd brought him back.

The price for actually saying no to his father.

The fact that he was Chad Flaherty was the only reason his bed hadn't been removed. Or that he hadn't been dumped on the street somewhere and told to stay put until they came for him.

This wasn't the life he wanted. Not anymore. Not since Delia Ford had taught him that he wasn't as golden as he'd thought, and his father would gladly turn his wrath on his own son.

Chad Flaherty needed to find a way out.

And God help him, but Delia Ford might be the key.

TWO

Tess

It was a warm evening, even for early June, and Tess was glad to get outside for porch time. The farmhouse never felt overly air conditioned, but it was still always nicer to be able to spend time in the fresh air. If that meant an evening on the porch swing at the rowhouse or what had evolved during the pandemic to be porch time here, Tess didn't care. A day without breathing fresh air was a day wasted.

No wonder, she thought in retrospect, she walked around town as much as she could. She'd never thought about it until they'd been locked up here on the farm and walking to the office or the incubator had become part of the before times, but maybe she was hardwired to want to be outside.

Taylor was already in their spot on the front stairs, Gray in his chair on the far side of the windows of the front room, and Tess had thought Mack had come out already, but he wasn't visible.

She took her usual seat on the near side of the stairs, facing the yard that led to the lower pasture and the old Mackenzie cemeteries. Taylor turned to her. "Are you sure it wasn't my turn to wash?"

Tess waved them off. "I like the way the water feels. You know that." She paused. Her mother and Thomas had dried, and the conversation had, as always with Thomas, been a bit odd and had set her on edge. "But I didn't bring the end of the wine. Should I—" She put a hand down, ready to push off the step and go get it, but her mother came through the door, carrying the bottle and a few glasses.

"Good timing," Tess told her.

"I noticed you'd left it."

"I hate this not drinking business," Tess said, wrinkling her nose as she frowned. "Why can't I be pregnant already?"

"Oh, honey, it'll happen. Give it time."

"It's been a year, Mom." She wasn't looking forward to what came next: fertility experts, the invasiveness, the discomfort. At least they were lucky enough that the cost wouldn't be an issue.

But that had been the deal: They'd had one year after their wedding to not worry about kids. And then one year to either get pregnant or figure out what was wrong. Maybe it was just pandemic stress; this past year hadn't been easy, watching the battles over taking care of each other versus what people called personal freedom, watching hospitals and morgues fill, watching, worrying, mourning, and watching and worrying and mourning some more.

Tess wasn't good at watching. She was good at *doing*, and she was good at succeeding, which made the lack of being pregnant even stranger. She'd never expected to fail at being fertile.

Mack came around the side of the house. "Tink, do you think—"

"No," Taylor said, closing their eyes and turning their face away from him, lips pursed. "We are done working for the day and I refuse to assist you in anything further until tomorrow." They nodded once as if it were settled.

Mack gaped at his assistant. "You don't even know—"

Taylor shook their head slowly. A bit dramatically, even, Tess thought. "Doesn't matter," they said and, in typical Taylor fashion, stuck their nose in the air.

"It's about the records boxes," Mack said, putting his hands on his hips and glowering.

Taylor opened their eyes. "You get *one* sentence."

Tess bit back a smile. This was Taylor playing with Mack more than anything else, but it was also nice to see them enforcing time off. It hadn't been easy to separate work and life when everyone was in the same house.

That went for Tess, too.

Mack took an exaggeratedly deep breath. "Do you think you'll go out looking for the last records boxes this weekend?"

It was, Tess thought, a very short sentence, given that Taylor had allowed him one. She looked Mack over, trying to gauge his mood. It wasn't like him to not try to cram a thousand words into one sentence when that was all he had to work with.

"Now that the rainy season has ended, I see no reason to spend a weekend inside," Taylor said.

"Want company?"

"No."

"Mack?" Tess asked softly. Ordinarily, he would have mentioned something about this idea to her, made sure it was okay. Which meant that either it was a spontaneous question or he was expecting to be shot down.

Mack jammed his hands in the pockets of his shorts. "I just want to be *doing* something. I feel like everyone's locking me up here, keeping me safe, keeping me at stud"—Tess smiled; Mack had listened to more than one rant of her own about feeling like a broodmare—"and Ultimate's not back yet and even if it was, I'm not sure I'd want to be breathing hard in other people's faces, just in case—" He trailed off and turned around, staring down the hill, toward the cemeteries and town.

"We can go into town more often," Tess told him. "While case numbers are down, maybe we should spend some time at the rowhouse. I miss it there." At one point, before they'd had to move into the farmhouse, the house in Woolslayer had been her dream home. Now, she just missed the space—and the privacy.

"Me too," he said over his shoulder.

She got up and went to him, wrapping her arms around his waist and propping her chin on his shoulder. "Let's do it," she said softly. "Maybe a change of scenery is what we need."

He nodded, wrapping his hands around hers. "It might be the best we can do right now."

When they turned around, Tess was surprised to see Thomas was standing on the porch, a wine glass in hand. He rarely joined them for porch time, preferring to plant himself in front of one cable news channel or another, content to have a one-sided discussion with the talking heads on the screen.

"This wine was particularly good," he said to no one in particular—but then again, that was how porch time worked. Someone said something seemingly out of the blue and everyone else just went with it.

"We'll be in town this weekend," Tess told him. "We can pick up another bottle or two then."

Mack nuzzled her. "It sounds hot when you say it like that," he whispered.

"Not if it'll interrupt that," Thomas said, flapping a hand at them.

"Or pick up a bottle just *for* that," Gray said, as Tess had expected he would.

"We've tried that more than once," she said, gently pushing Mack aside so she could see the older man. "It hasn't worked."

"Once a day, at least, for thirty days," Thomas said with a nod. "I guarantee you it'll work."

"That's high romance," she said and noticed her mom's mouth was pinched and she was shaking her head, her arms folded across her lap, her legs crossed at the knee. It was a defensive position, and Tess wasn't sure why.

She hoped it didn't have anything to do with a negative memory about Dan, Mom's previous boyfriend. Or that Gray, who Mom sat beside, hadn't said something to upset her.

"Maybe the idea is to be so busy making sure you don't miss a day that all the stress of wondering if it worked vanishes. Because," Mack said with a glower over his shoulder at Thomas, "you're too busy worrying about making time and keeping it from turning into a senseless, mindless motion you go through, kind of like brushing your teeth before you go to bed."

"Yeah, pass," Tess said, glancing at Taylor to see how all the talk of sex and baby-making was affecting them. They'd come a long way over the past year, but that didn't mean they were totally over their issues.

But Taylor was sitting calmly, looking up at the sky, their face composed. "Mack," they said, as conversationally as ever, "maybe this weekend, I'll go up toward the tip of the north end of the property again. It's been dry, so I'm confident I can get up there before dark if I leave right after work on Friday."

"But . . . " He cut himself off and paused. "We'll miss you at dinner."

"We all have hard choices to make."

Tess bit back a smile at that. Taylor sounded so serious and yet Tess knew it was meant entirely in a lighthearted manner.

"We need those records boxes." It sounded, Tess thought, like Mack was reminding himself of that.

"And maybe you and I will head to the city for dinner Friday night," Tess said, hoping he wouldn't reject the idea out of hand. A quiet dinner, just the two of them, sounded like heaven right then. It was a chance to escape back into the before times, before the pandemic, before their anniversary, before five housemates and worries of killer viruses.

Yes, Tess decided. She needed to go back to what, in retrospect, was a simpler time, even if it hadn't felt simple at the time.

THREE

CHAD

Chad wasn't healed nearly enough yet to join his weekly basketball game. Hell, his father hadn't even sent his goons over with some ibuprofen and someone to check his ribs, but he didn't care. Hanging around, not getting out of bed, wallowing in feeling like he'd been beaten up was exactly what his father wanted him to do. Well, maybe not that wallowing part.

All the more reason to haul his sorry ass out of bed and go sit on the sidelines and jeer at his friends.

"Yo, what happened to you?" Hyron asked when Chad got there. Thankfully the basketball court had bleachers, and thankfully at least three rows were usually open. The gym looked like some public high school, with the bleachers that opened out of the wall for events.

This wasn't a school, though. It was the Y in Larimer.

William Flaherty would have a few more cows if he knew Chad hung out here. And with—horrors—*Black people* and *Latino people*. They might contaminate him so badly, William would have to put Chad out of his misery.

"My dad's not happy with me," Chad said, gingerly taking a seat on the bottom bleacher. A few of the others clustered around to hear the story. "It's nothing," he said, shaking his head. "Go play. I just needed to get out of my house."

The game was hard that day, as if everyone was channeling Chad's mood and working to get aggression out. Chad was just as glad to be on the bench. He didn't consider himself the least bit of a prima donna, but when the games got chippy like this, he often sat out. Larry and Enrique already were.

The guys still on the court were playing too hard, too aggressively to stop and taunt the few on the benches.

Or maybe, Chad mused, they didn't care. Or—horrors—they respected the guys who chose to sit out.

Even though he'd done nothing but sit and watch, Chad's soreness had ramped up by the time the game ended with handshakes and man hugs, like it usually did. No matter how ugly the game got, they always ended it with the ritual.

Chad liked that. It was a lesson his father could learn from. More than one, really.

But just then, he was too sore and exhausted to care about his father.

Go-fer Stanley was waiting, leaning against the trunk of Chad's car, when he came out of the Y.

"What?" Chad asked him, trying to be edgy and nervous but instead, what came out was tired and resigned.

"I won't tell him you're here," Go-fer Stanley said, and Chad took another look at the guy. This wasn't one of William's usual interchangeable go-fer guys. It was Neal, his right hand. Hardly a go-fer at all. "I needed to talk to you."

"How'd you find me?" Chad asked, all alerts on high.

"Don't ask."

Chad groaned. "Where's the tracker planted?"

"Not telling. But listen, this thing with Mackenzie and the farm? It's gonna be his, I don't know what you call it. That thing that's your peak and you go out in flames. You know what I mean."

Neal was known for his loyalty, not his brains.

"What am I supposed to do about it? You know he hates me."

"It's a front."

That was news to Chad's ribs.

"Really," Neal said.

Chad still wasn't buying. "All right. You're here; I'm here. What do you want?"

"Your help."

"Stopping him from his noble quest to end the Mackenzie farm."

"Exactly."

Neal, Chad thought, wasn't long on words. Maybe that shouldn't have been surprising, given that he'd been around for Chad's entire life and Chad didn't think they'd ever spoken to each other before now.

"And *how* am I supposed to do this?" Chad asked, wincing slightly as he tried to jam his hands into his pockets. "I have zero power in this situation. I'm the whipping boy, the one he hates."

"It's a front," Neal said again. He closed his eyes briefly. "But you're right," he went on. "William won't listen if you come at him directly. You'll have to be underhand."

That idea made Chad want to puke. He didn't want to be like his father. He also didn't particularly want to save the Mackenzie farm; he hated that Emerson asshole, and he wasn't big on what the guy's wife was doing to change Woolslayer. Empowering women? That was asking for trouble, right there.

"You helping?" Chad asked him.

He was rewarded with a nod. "Where I can."

"Does that include advice?"

"That girl. The photographer. Use her."

Chad groaned again. Even though he'd come to the same conclusion, hearing it changed things.

And it sounded worse when the words were spoken aloud.

FOUR

MACK

If Mack could add one other thing to the rowhouse, he decided yet again on Friday night, it would be space to properly dance with Tess. The farmhouse had the one front room, the one across from the makeshift PharmaSci office, that he liked to think had been used as a ballroom although it probably hadn't been, and the Mackenzie Manor up in New York definitely had a ballroom. That was where he'd first danced with Tess when they'd gotten back together.

But the rowhouse was too small. Not that it was a small house by any means; it was three floors. It was just that the rooms weren't large enough for a big, sweeping waltz. He'd tried, back before they'd put furniture in. If it hadn't worked when unfurnished, it certainly wouldn't work now.

So instead, he pulled Tess into his arms after they'd eaten dinner and he held her close, swaying to music neither of them could hear, not that it mattered. After so long together, they knew each other's base rhythms.

"We should have done this sooner," Tess sighed, her head on his shoulder.

He pulled her closer, but she winced and backed off, rubbing her chest. "I'm sore."

He frowned. "You're due soon, right?"

She nodded, not meeting his eye.

"Hey." He reached for her again, wanting to comfort her but also just wanting her back in his arms, but she shook her head and left the room.

As much as he wanted to go after her and do whatever she needed in order to feel better, the simple truth was that she wasn't going to let him. The wise thing to do was give her space. When she was ready, she'd be back.

He plopped down on the couch and pulled out his phone, looking for... he wasn't sure what. Certainly not work; that could wait. Maybe friends, but it was still a pandemic. No one was doing much of anything. And Ultimate was still on hold until after the vaccines had been developed and approved.

Taylor had, as usual, sent him a message with the time they'd set out from the house, the coordinates they were headed toward—roughly speaking—and a promise that yes, they had picked up one of the radios, and that Thomas, April, and Gray were all going to stand by, just in case.

Once bitten, twice shy was how the cliché went, although Mack was grateful that there had been no biting the day Taylor had wiped out on an uphill climb and landed not far from a frightened rattlesnake that supposedly had been coiled and ready to strike.

Not that Taylor was the type to exaggerate, and not that Mack had any reason to doubt them. Sima had backed up Taylor's story, saying of course there were rattlesnakes in the area. Copperheads, too—and just over twenty nonvenomous snakes.

Mack wondered how monitoring Taylor's radio was going to work overnight and who would be nearby in case Taylor needed anything. He considered reaching out to April to ask, then decided to trust them all. More than once, Thomas had stood in for Roger with the security stuff—including that day Taylor had fallen and needed a rescue. And it wasn't like Taylor was a novice in the outdoors. Backpacking was one of their top passions.

Mack scrubbed at his face. It had been such a simple idea: Open the farmhouse, take in a few people, get through it together. He'd never expected April to wind up homeless, for Taylor to be carrying such secrets, and he certainly hadn't expected Thomas and Gray to feel so utterly at home, they had moved in permanently. Thomas had put his place up for sale and Gray hadn't done it yet, admitting he was dragging his feet even though he had no intentions of living there again.

And Mack had certainly never expected to feel such a level of responsibility for them all.

Voices seeped into the front room as people walked past outside, and Mack wondered if Henry Mackenzie had felt like this toward the people who'd become his treasure. He had to have; you didn't tell people that you'd take care of them for generations and not care.

Could you?

Tess came into the room, rubbing her arms. "The dishes are done."

"Oh. Did… Did you want me to help you with them?"

"No. Well, at first I did, yeah. But then I figured that even though we're here and we're alone, it's okay to be completely alone, you know?"

"Yeah." He did. They didn't get a lot of time by themselves at the farmhouse. It was a huge amount of space, but there weren't a lot of rooms. That equaled not a lot of privacy.

"Do you think," he asked, "your mother will be okay at the house with Gray and Thomas? I feel like we deserted them up there. We're here, Roger's off, and Taylor's reveling in sleeping in a hammock." He liked to pretend he didn't understand that, but the truth was that he'd fallen asleep in the hammock Taylor had set up near the house more than once. It was the whole *out in nature with the wild animals* part he didn't fully understand.

"If they're going to make a permanent home of it," she said, coming to sit beside him on the couch, "they'd better get used to it. I like *this* house, and if we can figure out how to spend more time here again, I want to."

So did he, and not just because of the privacy issue. This was *their* house. Tess had found it, but he'd agreed to live here, the token rich white guy in a diverse, working-class neighborhood. In a lot of ways, it reminded him of the neighborhood he'd lived in during college, an off-campus house he and his best friend had rented. He'd taken care of the elderly neighbors next door when they'd needed him to change a high light bulb, or on the rare day when it snowed, and he'd done his best to handle their trash cans for them, too. They'd taught him what it meant to be neighbors, not the rich kid and the older couple, and when he and Mary had been gone over the same weekends, or home on school breaks, Sal and Gloria had gotten their mail and kept an eye on their place.

Living in Woolslayer was in many ways like that.

"Jamie asked if we wanted to do anything tonight, but I pushed her off to tomorrow," Tess was saying.

Mack told himself to tap back into the conversation. "Yeah, that's fine," he said. "Do they have ideas? I'm not so sure I want to sit in some restaurant and linger over wine."

"Here or their house. Maybe here, so we can sit on the side porch and they can have her mother babysit."

"Sounds like we're not the only ones who need a change of scenery."

"I think everyone does, after the past year."

He bobbed his head in agreement. The news reports of the 1918 flu hadn't made it seem this difficult. Maybe it hadn't been, but in all honesty, he thought it had probably been harder. They hadn't had the internet and remote work and all the other ways they'd used to connect to others around the world and keep each other sane.

Tess curled up beside him, the remote in her hand. "We have an entire weekend to ourselves," she said, "and no one to fight for the TV. Are we watching anything?"

"Are we trying Thomas' thirty-day plan?"

"Mack…" It came out as a sigh.

"We're not that far off schedule."

"And maybe that's part of the problem."

"Maybe the only problem is the amount of stress we've both been under."

She turned to him. "I really don't want to do this fertility thing."

He took a deep breath, but she was holding a hand up, stopping him, and he let his breath out without saying what she probably expected him to: They needed a new Mackenzie. They needed an heir. "Let's just," he said instead, "wait and see the next week or so." He gave her a long look and she rubbed her chest, above her breasts, and he knew she was thinking what he was.

Maybe they wouldn't need thirty-day routines or fertility experts.

Maybe.

FIVE

Tess

Their nice, mellow weekend alone in Woolslayer was a nice idea, but it wound up being anything but mellow. As soon as they set foot outside—Mack to go running early Saturday morning and the two of them together to pick up more wine and some groceries for dinner with Hank and Jamie—the neighborhood started buzzing. And while Tess had expected it to buzz with the news they were back, she wasn't expecting the other part of the excitement to be about what it meant.

As various members of the neighborhood stopped by to say hello, Tess found herself deflating hopes about the end of the virus until she felt blue in the face.

They were back inside, setting the table before Jamie and Hank showed up, when Tess said, "I can't believe we're trying to bring a baby into this craziness. What are we doing?"

Mack turned to her, grabbing her gently by the upper arms and taking the knives out of her hand, setting them on the table behind him. "Making sure there are fighters on our side when the time comes."

"Oh, that's a *lovely* thought." She considered grabbing him and skewering him with one of the knives for that, but he did have some good qualities, and there was that whole *love of her life* thing—not to mention the end of an entire pharmaceutical company to consider.

Dinner with Hank and Jamie was wonderful. Comfortable, familiar, and totally without pretense. "I didn't realize," Tess said as the meal was winding down and Hank was teasing Jamie about drinking more since her mom had their twins for a sleepover, "how much I've missed just . . . *hanging out*. Dinners at the farmhouse are comfortable and not terribly formal, but they're not like this."

"You have no idea how lucky you are to have five other people you can talk to. It's been just us and the boys, and now Mom and Matthew, and let me tell you, that small group of people gets old fast."

Hank nodded. "Jame and I knew how each other tended to think before the shutdown orders, so a lot of times, it felt like talking to myself, except I'd answer in a feminine voice."

"And from another part of the room," Jamie added with an eye roll.

Tess guessed this too was an old routine. "I can't even imagine," she said.

"You don't want to," Jamie told her. "Just count your blessings that you've had a group of people to get yourself through this mess with. It's made things easier. I promise it has."

Tess didn't answer, wishing it was helping with the whole pregnancy thing. But the truth was that she felt so *watched* by everyone, especially her mom and Thomas. Okay, she told herself, *particularly* her mom and Thomas. Gray was, of course, supportive, and Roger and Taylor both acted like they didn't know anything about it.

Which, oddly, wasn't the gift it should have been.

By the time they said goodnight and Tess stopped to chat with a neighbor who was out with his young daughter, giving their dog one last walk for the day, Mack was busy cleaning up from dinner. "My turn," he said when she carried the wine glasses into the kitchen.

"I'm not sure you're any good at this," she said, waiting for him to back down. He always did—and rightfully so. Mack in the kitchen was still a disaster.

"Fine," he said in his most fake petulant voice. "I'll rinse everything and you can scrub it. Happy?"

That was something he'd never offered before. "Just don't break anything."

"I'm not that—Oh, wait," he said, eyeing the wine glasses. "I am."

"You are." She hated that it was the truth, not something to tease him about.

He turned and winked at her. "It's an act, you know."

"No, it really isn't." She closed her eyes, not in the mood for this. She just wanted to get the kitchen cleaned up.

"Tess. C'mon. Work with me here."

"You *are* better than you were before we moved into the farmhouse. I'll give you that." She paused, considering him. "And you are kind of sexy, standing here and not looking like you're lost and overwhelmed and terrified. Of *dishes*."

"They have sharp edges when they break," he said solemnly, and although she smiled, she used her hip to bump him out of her way.

He kept her company as she washed what couldn't go in the dishwasher, grabbing a clean dish towel and drying the way they had trained him to do at the farmhouse.

"I kind of like this more helpful Mack," she said when they were done and had put away the dry pots and pans. She looped her arms around his waist and looked up at him. "Maybe he'll help put me to bed?"

"He'll take you to bed," he said, holding her tightly and pressing into her waist with his fingertips, a signal to stretch so he could kiss her.

Instead, Tess pulled back and invited him to lead the way.

They were upstairs and clothes were coming off slowly, as if they had all night—which, Tess figured, they did—when her phone rang.

"It's Saturday night," Mack groaned, sitting back on his heels.

"Which means it's important," Tess said, twisting to look at her phone, which was sitting on the night table on her side of the bed. "And it must be, because it's Delia, and she's allergic to anything that's not texting." She picked it up. "Hey, what's going on?"

"Hope I'm not bugging you; Meter wanted me to wait until morning, but I don't think I should."

"Trust your gut."

"Well, then, brace yourself. I got a glimpse of the editorial the *Daily Record* is going to run in the morning, and it's all about how and why you shouldn't reopen the farm."

Tess paused. She'd expected about as much from the conservative yet inflammatory paper owned by part of the Flaherty family. "Is this more than their usual?" she asked carefully, glancing at Mack, who was still sitting on his heels on the bed, watching calmly. He'd gone rather still, and Tess wondered if he could hear Delia.

"Yeah. There's more than a hint that the Mackenzies used to be into human trafficking and are going to get back into it and use the farm as your front."

It wasn't quite a gut punch, but it was close. "Are you kidding me?" She glanced at Mack. He could hear; the dark cloud on his face was proof of that.

"Wish I was."

Tess was still watching Mack.

"Now you see why I didn't want to wait until morning," Delia went on. "I figured you'd want to marshal some troops and have a response prepared, since there's only a few hours until this thing drops. Ashley's already waiting for it."

Mack hung his head and shook it.

"Now?" Tess asked, looking at the general state of undress that had been happening. "We were . . ."

"Yep," Delia laughed. "I've tried to warn you about the Flahertys. They have a way of knowing when it's the absolute worst time to strike."

"It's not the *absolute* worst, but it's not great," Tess said as Mack backed off the bed, still shaking his head as he headed for their closet. Or he was starting to shake it again; she wasn't sure which. It didn't matter. He wasn't happy. She didn't blame him. She wasn't happy about this either.

But she couldn't take it out on Delia. She'd been right to call right away.

Mack came back out dressed in a pair of lounge pants. He tossed a bralette at her.

"Well, have a wonderful, romantic night," Delia chirped, almost as if she knew what she'd interrupted. "May you have the slowest, sexiest of sex tonight, complete with multiple orgasms, and may it be half as good as what we're about to get up to over here."

Tess laughed, thanked her, and hung up, then went to go troubleshoot with Mack. Hopefully they could get this done and get back to the whole baby business—although why she was eager to do so had more to do with Delia's suggestion for slow sex and multiple orgasms than it did with an actual baby.

She thought.

Six

Mack

The promised editorial didn't run.

Mack had spent a sleepless night, pacing the first floor and refreshing the stupid *Daily Record* website until it updated the editorial page. And then he'd run out to Vera's when she opened the café—at seven instead of five because it was Sunday morning—to ask if she had a copy he could look at. She handed it over, holding it between two fingers and with a stiff arm, as if it smelled bad.

Mack understood.

The promised editorial wasn't in the print edition, either.

"I don't know what happened," Delia said over speakerphone when Tess called her. "I *saw* it." She sent over the message she'd gotten.

"Trace the message?" Mack asked tiredly, sitting on the bed behind Tess and smoothing the fabric of the t-shirt she'd slept in. Marriage hadn't changed her, and nor had the Mackenzie fortune. She still slept in crummy, soft, beat-up t-shirts.

"I got it from Ashley," Delia was saying. "I don't know if we can trace who sent it to her, but I'll ask her to try. I hate that we all might be getting played here." She paused. "Fucking Flahertys. This is what they do, you know. They want something from you, so they're fucking with you. And me and Ashley, too."

"Don't feel too used," Tess told her.

"Oh, I do." There was a warning in Delia's voice, and Mack wondered what she'd do about it—but had no doubt she'd do something. Delia wasn't someone to mess around with. It was one of the reasons she and Tess got along so well.

"Well, thanks for being in this mess with us," Tess said softly, hugging herself. She'd managed to sleep, although she said it hadn't been good sleep.

"Sisters in solidarity," Delia answered, surprising Mack with the amount of bitterness she put into those few words. "I wish there was a way to have a better enemy, if we have to have one at all."

"At least you earned it the honest way," Tess said. Mack looked at her. Stealing the guy's real estate out from under him wasn't exactly honest, even if it had been done legally.

"Yeah," Delia said. "You married into it. I guess Mack has to have one flaw."

"I'm right here," he called in the direction of Tess's phone.

"Did I say anything? I did not," Delia said, and her switch to being lighthearted was so complete and genuine that Mack had to smile. "Let me go deal with this," she said and hung up before either he or Tess could answer.

Mack shook his head. "Sometimes, I wonder where we found her."

"If I remember right, I was headed to Vera's to get coffee and ran into the scene outside the gallery when the art thief first struck." Tess cocked her head as if thinking, then shook it. Her hair, long and dark, curtained her face as she looked down and Mack simply stared at her for a long minute, drinking her in.

"What?" she asked him, raising her head.

He started. "Just thinking how amazing you are."

She unfolded her legs and got off the bed. "You tell me that all the time, and strangely, I never get tired of hearing it." She crossed to him, wrapped her arms around his neck, and gave him a soft kiss. "I think I'm going to shower. Maybe you should see what Krista can make of this whole thing. She's always good for ideas."

"And by ideas," he said, frowning as she pulled away and wishing he'd held her tighter while he could, "you mean sources to see if she can learn anything."

"Always," Tess called and disappeared into the bathroom.

Mack debated following her, then decided that calling his mother was actually, surprisingly and uncomfortably, the priority.

"Emerson, really," she said once he'd explained, "if I had foreseen this kind of accusation, I would have warned you."

"You warned me that people wouldn't be happy."

"Happy and… and *this* are two entirely different scenarios."

His mother wasn't one to sputter, and the fact that she just did told Mack pretty much everything he needed to know about her mindset. She'd been caught as off guard as he and Tess had been.

"Let me think," she said, "and see if there's anything to be learned. Unfortunately, I don't have the resources in Port Kenneth that I do here. But Thomas might."

"I'd already thought about that," Mack told her. "Tess and I are heading back over there now." He made a face. "So much for another quiet dinner, just the two of us."

"Take as much time as a couple as you want or need," Krista said, and something in her voice softened, as if her compassion weren't just real, but something she understood. "It'll all change soon enough."

He sighed.

"I know," she said gently. "I am aware of the calendar."

"Mother—"

"I'm not saying anything," she said in her usual crisp, businesslike tones, all traces of compassion gone. Oddly, Mack could better deal with her when she was like this. "I do remember teaching you to read a calendar," she said.

He chuckled, told her he loved her, and said goodbye.

SEVEN

Chad

"For God's sake, Chad. How naïve are you? It wasn't ever going to get printed. Accusations of human trafficking? That's a lawsuit that was probably drawn up and ready to be filed." Sophie snickered. "At least, I hope it was. I hope it cost them a nice chunk of change to get all that in place so quickly. I have yet to meet the lawyer who doesn't charge an arm and a leg for a rush job."

Chad stared at his older sister. Her smirk had gotten so big, it threatened to fill the room they were in. He had no doubt she'd been in on this with their father, and that the whole strategy had been to do exactly what she was saying: waste Mackenzie money and the patience of his lawyers.

An old story about a chicken who ran around screaming that the sky was falling came back to him. It wasn't a strategy he thought was particularly smart, clever, or original.

"If you had a brain in your head," she went on, "you'd know that."

That wasn't worth an answer, and Chad was willing to bet she knew it.

"Right?" she prodded.

He stood up and left, heading out of her apartment and toward the elevator.

"Chad!" She actually chased him down. "Okay, fine. I'm sorry. Come back; we have to discuss this."

"You sure I've got enough brain cells to discuss anything?" The smartest thing to do would have been to not answer and, instead, keep walking, even if it meant giving up on the elevator and jogging down the eleven floors. It wouldn't be the first time, although truth be told, he still wasn't fully over that last beating and it would hurt.

"I truly need your help," Sophie said.

Chad knew better than to buy that. She was every bit as bad as their father, which meant she was as trustworthy as a pathological liar.

"Please? I'm your sister."

With a snort, Chad turned for the stairs.

"Chad! Seriously! Dad's out of control and it's up to us to stop him."

That made him stop; it was too close to what Neal had said to him just days before. Maybe something was legitimately going on. Or maybe Neal and Sophie were both playing him, for whatever reason he hadn't figured out yet. What was there to be gained by doing that? He was the spare; Sophie was the one who'd be inheriting the family business.

"Come inside," Sophie said.

"No," Chad said and walked back toward the elevator. Maybe by the time it showed up, he'd have gotten more information out of Sophie. "If you actually want to talk, we need to do it someplace where Dad's not watching and listening."

She made an exasperated sound and tossed her head, her eyes rolling upward. The disgust rolled off her in waves. "He's not going to bug *my* place. He trusts me."

Chad considered her. She'd been dying her hair auburn and wearing it long. He had no idea how she got the waves into it; maybe they were real but they probably weren't. She'd had her nose done, her boobs enhanced, and her chin chiseled. She said it made her feel better, more attractive, more at home in her body. Too bad she had focused on her looks and not her own brain. Clearly, she'd gotten out of the habit of using it.

"Well, he doesn't trust me," Chad said, "and I don't trust him right back. If you want to talk, we do it someplace he can't listen in."

"I'm telling you—"

She was interrupted by the arrival of the elevator. Chad stepped onto it.

As the doors closed, he heard her snap, "Fine! Wait for me!"

Truly, he didn't want to. But if Neal was really playing both sides, if his dad was truly out of control in his quest to end the Mackenzies, he probably needed to know. His non-life was based on William's generosity—or, more specifically, his need to keep the spare out of the way but under control. It was a crummy life, and Chad was over it.

For what might have been the first time in his life, Chad began to wonder if he could turn this to his favor somehow. If he could use the situation and find a way to get out from under his dad's—and Sophie's, too—control and maybe, somehow, find a better life.

EIGHT

Tess

"I know you'd rather we'd stayed in town," Tess said after dinner that night. She sat on their bed at the farmhouse, petting Scram. The cat's eyes were closed, his head was up, and he was purring so loudly, Mack said he could hear him across the room.

"I thought you needed a change of scenery," he told her, sounding hurt.

"I did. I do." She rubbed her arms. "But we had to talk to Thomas. And you know Mom and Gray won't let us come for dinner and then leave. We're stuck." She made a face, wishing she could thank whoever had started that rumor about the editorial. It would be one of the most sarcastic thank yous she'd ever uttered; she'd truly wanted to spend the entire weekend at the rowhouse.

Scram opened his eyes and gave her a haughty look, as if asking why she had deigned to stop petting him. "Oh, fine," she said with a sigh and got back to work. Maybe if they'd taken him with them when they'd gone back to the house in Woolslayer, she'd have had a better reason to stay there too.

"I already miss our porch swing," she said and shook her head. "C'mon." She kissed the top of Scram's head, dodged his smacky paw, then got off the bed and brushed at some of the cat fur she'd acquired. Of course Mack had wanted a black cat, which had been fine until they'd realized how little black was in their wardrobes.

"Where are we going?"

"For a walk," she said, grabbing a pair of socks.

"Another one? To anywhere special?" he asked hopefully, his whole face lighting up.

Tess had to smile.

It *had* been a while since they'd spent time in that tiny little clearing they'd found, and the weather *was* pretty perfect for heading that way. "I hadn't been thinking that, but yeah, why not?" They stopped and grinned stupidly at each other.

"Keeps our thirty days fresh," Mack said with a wink and a leer.

"I think I should be flattered by how you're acting right now." She paused to cup his cheek, then give it a pat. "But honestly? I never thought turning you into a horny idiot would get old."

Mom and Gray were on the porch when they walked outside. Tess was about to acknowledge them when her phone buzzed. She took a look. "It's Serenity?" she asked, giving everyone on the porch a bewildered look.

Mack eyed her.

Tess, are you available? A few of us would like a word and we heard you are in town.

We are actually back at the farm. Tess sent the message and looked up, considering what to say next, but her phone buzzed quickly.

We would like to speak to you about the farm.

That wasn't what she was expecting—or was she, she realized as she related that part of the conversation to Mack. There was no reason to think others hadn't heard about the editorial; it had probably been extraordinary gossip around town. *Were the Mackenzies really going to support slavery again?*

As much as she didn't want to admit it, she could hear people asking that question—and not just the people who'd thought it would be a good idea to throw a couple of rocks through Vera's café's windows.

"Have them come on up and we'll go to the gazebo," Mack suggested. "Sunset's not quite as nice, but it's better for talking."

Gray nodded his agreement. "May I sit in?" he asked as Tess answered Serenity.

"Of course," Mack said.

Tess noticed he glanced at Mom, but she didn't say anything. Maybe, Tess figured, she was going to stay behind. That would make sense, as she didn't want to get too involved in the Mackenzie family situation, as she called it.

After a bit, Serenity and old Harald came up from the cemeteries, along with two women and a man. Mack took charge, shaking hands and welcoming everyone to the farm. "Or, the farm above the cemeteries, anyway," he added with a conspiratorial grin.

The two women smiled back in a way that told Tess that, once again, Mack's charm had come out the winner.

Serenity, Harald, and the third man were harder sells.

With Gray, they headed to the gazebo, Mack explaining about the sunset. "We watched it every night during the pandemic," he said and paused. "Well, every night that wasn't raining. It's a habit now," he went on as they crossed the parking pad. Plans were being drawn up for a multicar garage on the site.

"So when we're in town," Tess said, "come walk by. I bet we'll be out on the swing."

"I would enjoy that," Serenity said. "I have missed you, Tess."

"I've missed you." She wasn't surprised by how true it was. Serenity was always calm, always had answers and a positive outlook—and a will of iron. "As things keep calming down," she added, "we should plan lunch. I'm only in the office one day a week, though. We're spending most of our time here still. Until the vaccine's ready."

"What we'd like to talk to you about, as I mentioned, is this farm."

"Of course," Tess said, her stomach sinking. "We've talked about a variety of things to do with it, but for the longest time, we kept running into the same problem. Namely that we didn't want to ask the people of Woolslayer to work for us in potentially menial roles, even though we're committed to paying a living wage."

"As I would expect," Serenity said, giving Tess a stink eye.

"That's the minimum," Tess said as they approached the gazebo.

Harald paused. "This place's looking good."

"Thanks," Mack said. "We'd started fixing it up before the virus hit, so it was a matter of finishing it once we locked ourselves in." He gestured around. "Make yourself comfortable."

Serenity and Harald chose to sit on the same side at one of the picnic tables, stepping carefully over the bench seat. Roger had, Tess noticed, swapped out one of the tables for an upholstered bench. The other table had been shoved into a corner, and Tess suspected Sima used it as a desk.

The other three people with Serenity and Harald simply stood behind them.

Mack gave Tess an uneasy look, and then they took seats across from Serenity and Harald, Mack raising his hand to steady Tess as he always did when she stepped over the bench seat. Not that she needed it, but she appreciated the gesture.

"So what's going on?" Tess asked, cocking her head and preparing to listen.

"Word of the editorial has, of course, spread," Serenity said.

Harald bobbed his head. Tess watched him, thinking again how his white hair grew in tufts that reminded her of cotton—and what a problematic thought that was. Or was it?

She'd have to think about it later.

"Who?" Mack asked with a heavy sigh that felt like it wanted to weigh all of them down.

"Who what?" Harald asked, pulling back a bit as if startled.

"Who heard about it?"

"All the ministers and pastors at all the Black churches in town. And down in Knoxville. And probably beyond," Harald answered, indicating the three people behind him.

Tess closed her eyes as she absorbed that. All of them. And three of them had come here to settle this situation.

Mack, though, chuckled. Without opening her eyes, Tess knew he was shaking his head. "What a piece of work," he said softly, then took a deep breath.

Tess opened her eyes and focused on Mack's hands, which he'd spread, palms down, out in front of him on the table. He was sliding them forward as if to meet Serenity and Harald halfway, but he stopped before that point. "Okay," he said and shook his head. "Nice move by the Flahertys; I'll give them that much."

Serenity was watching him carefully. "We need to hear it from your mouth and your lips that this isn't real."

Mack's laugh was brittle. "Of course not." He glanced at Tess, then gave her his attention more fully.

She knew what he was asking. "I think it's time," she said.

"Yeah," Mack said and lifted his left hand off the table. He wiped at his face. "I just hope it's not too late."

"This has been a secret for a century and a half," Tess said. "I think *too late* expired a long time ago."

His smile was wan.

Serenity, Harald, and the other three were eyeing them, suspicious.

Mack took another deep breath, which he let out as heavily as he always did when faced with the legacy of the Mackenzies and this nonoperational sheep farm that spread out all around them. "Okay, so. You know this was a working sheep farm prior to the war and all through it."

"Which war?" Harald asked, his suspicion growing.

"The Civil War," Mack said with a nod. "And you know that my forefather, Henry, was involved in the slave trade." He held up a hand as if to stall any replies, but there weren't any. Just a gentle shifting among the people—the clergy—they hadn't yet been introduced to.

"Here's the thing, though," Mack went on. "Yes, people were bought by Henry and his son Everett. We've been learning that it actually started with Henry's father, William." He held up a hand again, but still, no one was ready with the questions Mack was anticipating.

"The farm was a front, of a sort. Yes, it was a working sheep farm, and the Mackenzies sold meat to the locals. From what we've uncovered so far, they fed both the Confederate and Union troops if they came through, but they were few and far between; this wasn't a hot spot in the war, as you all know." He looked at each of the five.

"The people?" Serenity asked.

"Right," Mack said, giving her a head bob to acknowledge the request. "This is where it's both simple and complicated."

"And what does that mean?" Harald asked, slapping the table with one hand.

Tess thought he looked ready to get up and leave.

"It means that we've found the documentation," Mack said more strongly, his gaze fixed on Harald. "It's all being properly saved and archived and whatever else our historian needs to do so you all can see it. But the short version of the story is that the Mackenzies liked to buy children and teens because they learn faster." He paused and looked at each person again.

Tess could feel the question in his gaze.

"It wasn't legal to teach the enslaved to read," one of the clergy said.

Mack held up one finger. "But you had to catch them and *prove* that they could read. *And* that they were still enslaved. Because once they could read, and once they could do jobs, they were given their freedom. Copies of all the papers are turning up; the thinking was that if they were stolen from the people they belonged to, my family could vouch for them. And they did," he added. "We're finding *all* the paperwork."

This time, when he held up his hand to stop the questions, a few mouths had fallen open. The clergy.

Serenity just sat there, her hands clasped in her lap, watching Mack steadily.

"He also," Mack went on, "tried his best to move them out of the South and into areas where they'd be more welcomed." He grimaced. "As you know, that was a tall order; racism was a problem across this country and still is. But they all left this farm with the promise that no matter what, the Mackenzies would help them."

He stood up and stepped back over the bench; Tess was surprised it had taken him that long.

"And they—we—did. Until my grandfather, but that's another story. Did your local mutual benefit society need a cash infusion? Done. A scholarship to college? Some of those still exist. Or if someone came back to the Mackenzies and could prove they were descendants of the original Mackenzie treasure, whatever they needed, they got."

"For real?" Harald asked.

"We're finding proof of it all. Including the people who, over the years, tried to scam their way into the treasure. Because that happened too."

Serenity, though, was shaking her head. "And how would someone prove they were a relation? This was well before DNA testing."

"Family Bibles," Tess said. "Henry wrote as much of it down as he could. He'd *ask* the people for their history. Near as we can tell, none of what he left behind is a fabrication." She stopped herself there;

Henry wasn't that virtuous. He'd fabricated plenty of histories for the children he'd fathered. They all traced back to the original treasure, but of course not to Henry himself.

In the end, he hadn't been so clever, and Kiersten, their historian, had figured out his code. She said it hadn't been that hard. Tess wasn't so sure.

"This treasure," Serenity said, her voice rippling.

"That was what he called the people he helped," Mack confirmed. He swallowed hard and Tess reached for his hand, giving it a squeeze. His first wife, Kelsey, had been trying to find the treasure. It was, apparently, legendary—just not among the group it probably included.

There was a rich irony in there.

"So as you open the sheep farm back up," one of the clergy said, stepping forward. She was a fat woman in a red dress with a chunky necklace that Tess liked.

"Wait," Mack said. "Can we get proper introductions?"

The fat woman was Reverend Sallie Stevens, a relative of the famous Reverend Sallie Crenshaw. The skinny woman with close-cropped hair, black pants, and a cream blouse was Reverend Sonata Dickens. And the man, who wore jeans and a light gray t-shirt, was introduced as Malakay Dover. He was, he said, a leader in the Buddhist church.

Tess hadn't known there was a Buddhist church in Port Kenneth.

"Back to the question?" Reverend Sallie asked with a warm smile.

"Yes," Mack said and sat back down. "We are going to reopen the sheep farm. It'll be a working farm; we've hired a biologist to handle all the science and to make sure it's all done properly, organically, ethically... all the things that matter on that front. We'll be bringing in an actual shepherd to handle the day-to-day care of the sheep. And," he added, leaning forward to emphasize this point, "it's going to be a place where anyone can come to pick up work experience and new skills. Everything from the business side to social media to doing the grunt work. Priority to anyone who lives in Woolslayer, of course. Kids, adults; we're still working on this part, but the vision is there and it's about assembling the team."

"And," Tess added when he fell silent, "although we can't reopen the butcher shop in its original location"—it was now the Woolslayer art gallery, which had moved into the space not long after the infamous water main burst on New Year's Eve—"we're looking for a location for that, as well. Those plans aren't as far along yet."

"Tess," Serenity breathed. "How do you make time for all of this?"

She smiled. "I have a very good boss."

"So no human trafficking?" Malakay asked warily.

"You are welcome to oversee and be involved as much as you'd like to be," Mack said.

Tess frowned, an idea forming. What if they rented out the gazebo for picnic lunches? They could team up with a local restaurant or caterer and…

"Tess?"

She shook herself out of her thoughts. "Sorry; I'm getting ahead of myself."

"You didn't answer my question," Malakay said, and there was something about the way he spoke that made Tess suspect he'd already said as much.

"No human trafficking," Tess said firmly, looking him in the eye and wondering why Mack hadn't answered for them both.

"I do like the idea of being involved," Reverend Sallie said thoughtfully. She licked her lips, her eyes briefly unfocused.

"Let's do it," Mack said and gave her a warm smile. He turned to the other two. "No human trafficking. Just a lot of good meat and hopefully lessons that'll help others better themselves."

Tess loved how it sounded. The visitors must have, too, because they didn't stay much longer.

She and Mack were able to catch the last bit of the sunset. As they sat on the porch steps, he put his arm around her. "Thanks for that. I had no idea what the question was," he said softly.

Tess glanced at her mother and Gray, but if they heard, they were ignoring them. "Let me tell you about this idea I just had..."

NINE

Mack

The problem with having had that discussion with a bunch of clergy people and Serenity and Harald, Mack thought later that night, was that he was eager to find out *more*. He wanted all the answers and even though he knew he needed to be patient and give Kiersten room to do her work, he also didn't want to wait.

"C'mon," he said to Tess after the sun had fully set. "Let's go take some lanterns and go look at the old cemetery again."

"In the dark?"

She looked dubious, and he didn't particularly blame her. The idea of finding a records box by flashlight was pretty absurd. But what if they managed to...

"Maybe it'll look different by lamplight."

"This isn't foreplay, is it?" she asked, but she was standing up.

"I don't know. I guess it could be," he said, following her inside. The lanterns were in Roger's room. Or what had been Roger's room; of all of them, he and Taylor were the two who'd most fully moved out. That made sense. They both had lives that didn't revolve around the Mackenzies.

"Which headstone do you want to start with?" Tess asked when they were down at the family cemetery. She had helped herself to the gardening trowels April and Gray liked, as well.

His first instinct was to shake his head. "I don't even know. Kiersten found that one reference to the box being here, but we've looked."

"And we have yet to find anything untrue or a false lead in what Kiersten's found so far," Tess reminded him. "C'mon. Something's got to be here." She walked over to the fence around the lower cemetery and looked inside.

Mack joined her. The grass was short, even shorter right up against the few small headstones. Each only had weathered first names on them, and none had dates. For all Mack knew, these weren't people who had been enslaved but babies who hadn't survived childbirth or their first few weeks or months. A life, let alone a long life, hadn't been guaranteed to anyone back then, white or Black.

Hell, in many ways, it still wasn't.

"I still think this is a bad spot for one," Tess said, shaking her head and backing away from the fence. "Everything we've learned of Henry so far suggests he'd have buried it with himself. Or his parents. Where are they?"

That was a good question, Mack thought. "Are they in here?"

"They must be those two weathered stones that we can't read," she said. "But that also doesn't work. Those stones are obviously the oldest, and the notes Kiersten found about records being buried with the family weren't that old." She thought for a minute, jutting out one hip and tapping her toe. She also chewed on her lip.

"Tess?" he asked when she got down on her hands and knees and, grabbing a trowel, dug at the base of first Henry and then Everett's headstones.

"Neither of these feels right," she said.

"Check the wives, too," he told her, content to stand there and watch.

She tossed a look over her shoulder. "You could help."

"I could. But then we'd both be dirty."

"And then we'd both go inside and get clean."

"Or this way, we can both focus on getting *you* clean. Which can be an interesting way to get through this thirty-day challenge."

Tess cocked her head. "Mmm," she said. "Focusing on me. I'd like it, but… we're already focusing on me. *I'm* the one holding up the works here."

"How do you know? Neither of us have been checked out to see where the problem—if there is one—lies." He didn't say it, but this wasn't the first time he'd hoped there wasn't actually a problem. "It could be me."

"I still think you ought to get in here and help," she said as she turned to another grave, trowel in hand.

"I'm helping."

"Oh?"

"Admiring the view. Very important job."

"In the dark?" She snort-laughed. "You're such a jerk."

"But you love me. What did you find?" he added as she rose off her heels and leaned closer.

When she didn't answer at first, he swung around the gate and entered the cemetery. The truth was that something about the two plots of land gave him the creeps. Maybe it was knowing Harald and others in Woolslayer were convinced they were haunted, but Mack doubted that was it. He didn't believe one way or another in ghosts and hauntings.

"Mack—"

He was at her side in a flash, but even from a distance, he'd seen it.

"How do we get it out," she asked, "without disturbing her? And are we even right that this is it?"

He frowned. Those were two of the best questions he'd been asked in a long time.

Tess wiped her hands in the grass right in front of the headstone. It belonged to Jane, Everett's wife. The third generation. Which, if Jane had died before Everett—and Mack would have to double-check the old family journals, but he thought she had, and in childbirth, of course—made a sort of sense.

"I bet that one's got some *good* stuff in it," he said. "C'mon." He stood, extending a hand to help Tess up. "Maybe we should go celebrate. It's still nice out here; why go in?"

She arched an eyebrow at him and he grinned. Their secret spot was quiet. It was private, it was hard to sneak up on, and it was far enough away from the house that noise didn't carry, but it was still close enough that they could get there and back usually without making anyone suspicious.

"Won't anyone ask where we've been?" she asked after the silence had started to feel heavy, like a decision needed to be made. Although, Mack thought, he just had.

"Why would they care? It's *our* land, and I don't think anyone knows about it."

"Sima does."

"She does?" That wasn't what he'd expected to hear.

"She asked me once if she should ignore the spot with the plastic container filled with blankets, and were they all clean or did she need to wash her arms up to the elbows in bleach?"

Mack laughed. He didn't know the farm biologist very well, but that sounded exactly like what he knew of her.

"Let's save that for tomorrow night," Tess said and rubbed at the palm of her hand. "I need a Benadryl or something. I'm getting itchy."

He pulled her into his arms. "Maybe the mosquitos are still out. They love my sweet wife."

She chuckled but lifted her chin, the sign he should kiss her. He did, wondering if a shower would be enough to get rid of the allergen.

Just in case.

He told himself to stop being a hopeful fool, but something felt different this time.

He was both sad and glad it hadn't happened yet. Everyone said their lives would be completely different once the baby arrived, and a big part of him liked things as they were.

Well, he reasoned as they let themselves in the house, saying hello to Gray on the way, it'd be nice to have things settled with the records boxes and the history of the house, the land, and the farm.

But as far as he and Tess were concerned? The year had been a gift.

TEN

MACK

By eight-thirty the next night, there was no sign of Taylor, who had stayed out searching the property for another day, taking some PTO in order to do so, and Tess was worrying. "It's probably dark in the wooded areas," she said.

The sky, Mack had to admit, was coming alive with color as sunset began. And Taylor liked to be back at the house in time to watch the sunset with them. It was what defined porch time.

"Well, going out to look for Taylor by myself is just stupid, and no, you're not coming with me," he told her, giving her a long look.

"Radio?" she asked, giving him one of those looks that told him he should have thought of that before she had to say it.

"They're fine," he said, hoping he was right. "Tink has survival skills we can only dream of." And, he reminded himself, the day they'd fallen down the hill, they'd radioed in immediately. So far, the radio had been silent, other than to announce they were staying out the extra day.

Tess, though, wasn't comfortable, and when the sun had gone down and it was getting seriously dark, she started out-and-out fidgeting.

"C'mon," he said, holding a hand out to her, for the first time glad they were back at the farmhouse. For one, they'd be here when Taylor finally showed up.

And for another, they could do this.

He held the front door open and ushered her through with what he hoped was a grand and suave wave of his arms.

She walked past him, one eyebrow raised.

"May I borrow your phone?" he asked when they were through the vestibule and inside. They needed music to dance to, of course, and he didn't have any on his phone. She did.

"Why?" she asked slowly. He answered her with a large grin and a slow couple of steps into the empty room. "Ahh. I see," she said, biting at her lips. The diversion didn't work; her smile crept out anyway. "I've got it," she said, bowing her head over her phone.

Mack waited, hands clasped behind his back, trying to be still but already feeling like he was vibrating with the beat of music he had yet to hear.

"Why do you like to dance so much?" she asked, still busy with her phone.

He wondered how long the playlist was going to be. "Because I'm good at it," he said, hoping she wouldn't force him to confess that he'd taken lessons in high school because he had to do *something* to be less of a loser, especially in the face of Alyssa Schoenstrom's constant—and constantly escalating—scorn.

"Okay," Tess said, setting her phone on the fireplace mantel and taking a step toward him as she turned to him. Something about her manner told him not to bow to her or hold out a hand in another grand gesture.

Instead, he put a hand on her waist and let her step the rest of the way into his embrace. At first, she was stiff in his arms, almost fighting him for control, but she finally relaxed.

And then the fun began. At least, his did. He led her in more elaborate steps, more whirls and twirls, all the things he'd thought about since the last time they'd danced. And it had been quite some time since they'd last done this.

He wasn't sure when, but Scram strolled into the room and sat by the fireplace, watching as if trying to figure out why he'd been deserted upstairs.

Like any good partner, Mack pointed out the cat and remained attentive to Tess, stopping as soon as she started to turn green.

That wasn't like his Just Tess, and he whisked her over to the window for some air. It was faster to throw it open than to rush through the vestibule and outside.

It was June, though, and the night air that tumbled through the open window was close and humid and didn't offer much relief. Immediately, Mack missed being back home in New York, where a night like this could be downright chilly.

Just as he resigned himself to having to hold her hair while she vomited, she swallowed hard, nodded, and said, "Okay. I'm better now."

He looked down at her. "Do you think you should take a test? I know where Roger hid them."

"We have some?"

Mack nodded. "Roger picked some up right after our first anniversary."

"Well, wasn't *he* the optimist."

"Me. I asked him to," he admitted sheepishly, and Tess gave him a wry smile and shook her head.

"So you're the optimist. I should have figured." She took another gulp of air, tilting her face to the window.

Behind them, something crashed. They both whipped around, Scram hissing, his tail puffed out, his back arched, the fur along his spine standing up.

"I found the third records box," Taylor announced from the doorway. "And I moved it. That's what took so long."

"Moved it? Where?" Mack asked, wondering why Taylor hadn't radioed in for help. Those things were awkwardly shaped and heavy, full of papers.

"Somewhere less obvious," they said, sitting down on the polished wood floor and beginning to unlace their hiking boots. "Wait until you see it up there. If we can figure out how to get you there," they added, pulling a foot out of a boot and stripping off their sock. They sighed as they wiggled their toes. "Living here has spoiled me. Maybe I really should give up on my place." They started unlacing the other boot.

"What's the problem with getting me up there?"

"Well, both of you. Neither of you are in good enough shape to get up there and back in a day. I barely can."

Mack opened his mouth to protest, then decided Taylor was right. He and Tess both were fit, but there was fit and there was going-out-hiking-every-weekend-on-these-mountains fit.

Tess leaned against the window and clicked her tongue at Scram, but the cat strolled over to Taylor and sniffed them cautiously, then smiled and flopped by their knee.

Taylor stripped off the other boot and sock, crossed their legs at the ankles, and stroked the cat. "So there are a couple old wells up there and I stopped and wondered what would anyone want with wells on the farthest, most remote spot on the property—although I'm not sure it is; I think there's more acreage to the east, if I'm reading the maps properly—but I keep coming up with only one thing: They were there for passersby."

"Passersby?" Mack asked, then it hit him who would be passing by in the remote woods and who might appreciate access to a well. "There's no proof of that."

"What if the wells *are* proof?" Tess asked. She had braced her hands on her thighs, her feet planted on the floor, and she looked a little queasy still.

"And why would anyone come this route?" Mack argued, mostly because he needed to convince himself of this idea. "It's rough as hell."

"There's enough bare rock," Taylor said, "that if someone was smart and calm about their path—and knew it was there—they could possibly lose any dogs on their trail."

Tess shuddered. "This grosses me out."

Mack turned to her, afraid she might be turning green again. He understood the feeling, but at the same time . . . She looked okay, though. Better than she had, even. "It's Mackenzie history," he said quietly. "And we know that Henry wouldn't be any more welcoming to search parties than he had to be in order to maintain the various charades—"

"Please," Tess said, her voice thick with disgust. A wave of despair washed over Mack. Already, he was tired of apologizing for his long-dead ancestor. The guy had done a lot of good, but that didn't erase the bad things he had also done. If he had dug wells to signal safe passage and provide for human beings on the run, it was one more tick in the *good job* column.

But he'd feel a lot better if Tess would stop harping on Henry's problematic behavior at every turn. It wasn't like they could change it now. All they could do was *better*—although that felt like a pretty low bar.

ELEVEN

CHAD

The summons came early—six a.m. on Tuesday early. There wasn't time for Chad to put clothes on, either. Thank goodness he'd been alone and sleeping in a clean pair of shorts. Maybe, he reflected as he sat in the back seat between his dad's favorite two go-fers, he'd expected this, even days later.

What he hadn't been expecting was his dad's mood.

"Chadwick Joseph," the man said solemnly. "I had been a bit worried you wouldn't do as expected."

Chad eyed him and shifted his weight, clasping his hands behind him in parade rest, as he knew his dad preferred. It let go-fer Stanley—not his real name—have an easy target if he needed to grab Chad real fast.

Nothing like waiting to be hauled to your own execution, Chad thought.

"Why'd you do it?" he asked. Even though, truth be told, he hadn't been the one who'd spread the word. He wasn't exactly sure who had done it, and he didn't really care. It hadn't been him. He hadn't talked to Delia Ford in years now, which was what made her the perfect person to get him out from under his father's thumb. He wasn't going to ruin that chance, no matter what his father wanted him to do.

"Consider it a warning," his father said, and Chad wondered what William's game had been. Knowing the man, there had been multiple targets. One of them had certainly been Chad himself.

He swore he was his father's favorite target lately.

Ever since he'd lost that damn condo.

The worst part was that his father hadn't known about that law, either. Which was probably the real reason behind Chad's fall from grace. He had made his father own up to not having absolutely everything under his control.

"Well, I'm glad I could play my part."

"Be sure you read the paper this week," his father said, flicking his fingers at Stanley, who put a hand on Chad's arm. "You won't find anything you might be looking for."

The words made Chad's stomach sink. There was more to this than he'd anticipated, although he should have. His father never did anything the straightforward way.

"Is this about more than Mackenzie?" he asked, giving his father a suspicious look.

"Chadwick."

One word, but dripping with derision.

Which meant that of course it was about more than Mackenzie.

As his father sat there and glared at him, Chad realized a couple of things. First was that he truly didn't give a damn what game his father was playing.

Second was that if there was some way he could get to Mackenzie and Cartieri and end this war, he wanted to. Not because his father was out of control, and not because Neal or Sophie wanted him to.

But because he wanted more out of life than this.

Just like that, his goals changed for good. Ford couldn't help him with this one. And neither could Sophie or Neal, since both just wanted help getting William to back off about the Mackenzies.

No. Chad was on his own—and that didn't leave him with a lot of hope that he'd be successful.

At a flick of William Flaherty's fat little fingers—Chad was forever grateful he got his mother's looks, despite the problems *that* created—Stanley and the other go-fer walked him outside.

In the time he'd been inside, someone had swept the front sidewalk, which had badly needed it. Chad stopped and considered that. Maybe this conversation had gone differently than anticipated.

He wasn't complaining. His ribs were still sore from the last conversation.

"C'mon," Stanley said to him, moving to the car and holding the door open.

"Typical Dad, huh?" he asked Stanley but didn't explain: Keeping him barefoot, spreading gravel and broken glass across the sidewalk, knowing he'd have to walk over it. And when his dad was pleased, the sidewalk had been cleaned. The son had behaved. He deserved a clean walkway—but not shoes, and not a shirt; not that he cared—and to be summoned at a normal hour even when he didn't have a job to get to.

He got into the car, letting Stanley close the door behind him, and put his feet up on the hump in the middle, the easier to rest his forehead on his knees.

There had to be a way out. He had to either find one or make it, but there had to be a way out.

TWELVE

Tess

It was so early Friday morning that it might have still been late Thursday night; Tess wasn't sure. All she knew was that she was exhausted down to her bones and what was happening around her was both her worst nightmare and more terrifying than those nightmares had ever been.

"Mack! That's it! We're out of water!" Tess screamed across the clearing. They'd both known it was futile when they'd gone running for the barn, but they'd had to try. Of course they'd had to; the only other option had been to stand there and watch it burn.

But it didn't matter. The farm was too remote, there wasn't enough access to water, even though

Sima had left a few containers around for fires that were less horrible, and whoever had done this, Tess thought, had to have used an accelerant, especially because none of the trees around the barn seemed to be going up in flame too.

She'd been around sites that had caught fire, of course. Usually *after* the situation was under control, the fire extinguished, the cleanup begun.

To be so close she couldn't just feel the flames but had to be careful they didn't jump to her or throw an ember at her was a brand-new experience, and to be honest, it wasn't one she particularly liked.

At least the wind had been blowing away from them, minimizing the amount of smoke she and Mack had inhaled.

He grabbed her, wrapping himself around her. "I can't believe this is happening."

The feel of him, always so solid and strong, made her bite back tears. *Later*, she promised herself.

"Think it's Flaherty?" She wanted to throttle the man. Yes, it was a barn—their *newly built* barn. Yes, there hadn't been anything in there yet, not even a desk for Sima. They hadn't even finished the plans to add an office on the side so that Sima didn't have to have her desk inside a barn.

"Is there another explanation?" Mack asked and scrubbed at his face. "There's nothing here that should have started this, and I can't see it being anything like lightning."

Tess glanced around. The weather for the past few days had been fine. Gorgeous, even. The greenery around the area that had been cleared so the barn could be built was lush—and still untouched by the fire. It was almost as if someone had soaked them with water, so that only the barn would be affected.

Nope, she thought. Not suspicious at all.

They both jumped as a timber fell, a shower of sparks rising even amid the flames.

"We should move back," Mack said.

"We should go back with Mom and Thomas and Gray. They're probably worried about us." She dreaded going back, already anticipating the things her mother would say. They were risking themselves. It wasn't safe. It wasn't *smart*.

But this was the barn, another step toward reopening the sheep farm, and she and Mack had needed to at least *try*, even though she was willing to bet they'd both known it was futile even before they'd run past the gazebo and toward the clearing the barn had historically stood in. Of course they'd had it built on top of what remained of the old foundation; Tess hoped those old bricks and blocks hadn't been damaged at all.

Mack moved away from Tess and took her hand. Together, they headed back down the path, through the gazebo and toward the parking pad, where the family was gathered, just in case this was arson and whoever had done it also had their sights set on burning the house down.

If *that* had happened, Tess thought, she'd have been on the warpath and God help anyone who got in her way. The house was magnificent, and she and Mack had discussed the idea of having it designated historic. There wasn't much benefit to them if they did, though, other than bragging rights, although now Tess had to wonder if there would be harsher penalties for anyone who willingly burned down something on the historic registry.

Her thoughts were interrupted by their arrival at the parking pad and, sure enough, a mobbing by Tess's mom. "Oh, honey, what were you thinking?" she asked, holding Tess's free hand, looking more worried than Tess could remember seeing her in recent years—and that included the night she had joined them during the pandemic, the night she had left her longtime boyfriend.

"I couldn't stand by and do nothing," Tess said, holding up a hand to ward off anything further. "This is our home. It's our responsibility."

"True, but…"

They didn't hear a siren, but flashing red lights alerted them to the arrival of the fire department. Tess was grateful; she didn't want to hear about it from her mother. Not right then. Possibly not at all.

She did stay behind as Mack led the firefighters back to the barn, sinking into one of the chairs in the gazebo, grateful they were there and it wasn't just the three picnic tables like it had been during the worst of the pandemic. It had been Sima's idea to remove the one table and put in actual chairs, and Tess knew her mother and Gray in particular liked to use them. The gazebo was shaded, both by its roof and by the trees around them, so it tended to be cooler and restful.

"How are you?"

It was Thomas, which surprised Tess. He usually steered away from emotions.

"I—" she started, stopping when she realized she didn't know. "It's a barn. It's *my* barn. Our barn, really," she added, chagrined. She felt an ownership of it all, absolutely, but one thing she knew better than to do was to forget, even for a second, that it was *Mackenzie* property and it was only hers through marriage. If she lost Mack for any reason, she'd lose all of this, too.

She told herself to stop being melodramatic. Krista wasn't going to evict her so fast.

"But you need a barn in order to raise sheep," Thomas was saying.

"True, but it's coming up on summer, and we don't have sheep yet. We can rebuild, and I'm sure when Sima hears about this, she'll have more input into the new design; I know she's been learning things because she's given me a list of ways we've gone wrong." Tess took a deep breath. It wouldn't be out of the realm for someone to ask if Sima had been unhappy with the design and had burned the barn herself—until you knew Sima. "In some ways, this is an opportunity."

Thomas nodded. "Glad you are able to see it that way already."

"I deal in a lot of this sort of thing at work," Tess said. "There are some developers out there who love to snatch up a burned piece of property and turn it into something entirely new. It's not my favorite sort of project to work on, but I understand how it goes."

He studied her for a long minute. She did her best to ignore him, tiredly running a hand through the front of her hair. It felt gritty; she supposed that was from the futile effort she and Mack had put up.

But they'd had to do something.

Some of the firefighters must have checked out the house because they told everyone they could go back in. They would, they said, check it for accelerant, and if they found any, they'd hose the house down.

Tess handed Scram's carrier to her mother. "Please take him in. I'm going to wait for Mack."

"Oh, honey, are you sure?" Mom asked, taking the cat. "You've been so tired lately…"

"I doubt we'll be sleeping much after this," Tess told her. "You go on in too," she said to Thomas.

"I'll wait with you," he said, crossing one leg over the other. "You aren't the only one who might find it hard to sleep now."

Tess gave him a wan smile and watched as her mother and Gray headed inside. Mom had a hand on Gray's shoulder and moved close to him, as if to set her head on his shoulder.

It wasn't the first time she'd noticed they had been growing close.

"Is that—" she started, turning to Thomas, but his head was turned toward the path to the barn.

"You might have to dig," one of the firefighters was saying to Mack as they came back. "But if you're going to rebuild out there, you're going to need a way to keep this from happening again."

"A well?" Tess asked, standing up to join them. Her entire body ached, she was so tired. She shook her head and held a hand up. "No. This conversation will have to wait until we've all gotten some rest. We need to be thinking clearly."

Mack nodded agreement and the firefighter eyed them both, as if worried he was being blown off.

"Seriously," Tess said. "Talk to the chief—is he here tonight?" she asked, looking around, trying to find the trucks, but everything was blurring together.

She leaned against Mack, who wrapped his hand around the back of her neck and held her close. Her eyes drifted shut and the fireman said he'd have the chief be in touch.

Mack thanked him and Tess listened to him leave. A heavy firefighter uniform wasn't the quietest.

"I'm so glad it's Friday," she said as Mack continued to hold her.

"Am I going to have to carry you?"

"Maybe," she said. "Are you really going to work today?"

"Later, yeah," he said. "I'll probably grab a nap on the couch and let Taylor handle things."

"These days, they could almost do your job for you."

"Even if Hell froze over and they wanted to, they're not a Mackenzie," he said. "C'mon. Let's go in, you can email Red and tell him you're taking the day off, and we'll try to get some sleep."

"All I can see is fire," Tess said, wondering why her eyes were still closed and then remembering she hadn't been able to keep them open.

"Now that you have the day to yourself," Mack said, urging her to start to walk, "what will you do?"

"Maybe go in for part of the afternoon, but maybe I'll head over to Woolslayer instead and see how things are going in the incubator buildings. It's weird, but being there, especially in the yellow one, leaves me feeling grounded."

"I know it does," Mack said and continued guiding her. The movement helped wake her up enough that she could open her eyes and follow the path by the light of a lantern someone had handed Mack.

"You don't think this is a sign, do you?" she asked as they kept walking. It wasn't usually this far from the gazebo to the house; if he wanted to carry her, she wasn't going to argue.

"Depends on what sign you're looking for," he said, moving his arm to encircle her waist.

"That we shouldn't reopen the farm."

"What? No," he said, pulling away slightly and turning to look at her. "What makes you say that?"

"Well, let's see… Flaherty is doing his best to shut all of this down and, hey, where were the cops tonight, anyway?"

"Well…" Mack scrubbed at his face.

And just like that, she knew. "Because this property's not fully in the city, they don't have jurisdiction?"

"I'll talk to legal about it, but yeah, that's what I think. The firefighter I was talking to said they'd only come as a courtesy—and because some of them wanted to see the land. Meeting with the chief is a great idea. Maybe he'll be willing to help us figure out a fire eradication system, since we're not going to run public lines out here."

"Which is why you were talking about wells?"

"Yeah. It's... it's not a bad idea."

"We'll have to talk to Sima about it and make sure there aren't any biology or ecology reasons why we can't."

"Good idea. What are your other reasons for not reopening the farm?"

"We both have so much going on in our lives. And now this," she said, putting a hand on her stomach. "Are we sure we can handle all of this?"

"Yes," Mack said. "Because we have delegated where we need to, and we will continue to do so. That's the secret, Tess, and if you weren't so tired, you'd be saying this to me." He softened his words with a kiss to the top of her head and a gentle squeeze. "We'll bring in competent people to handle things so all we have to do is sit on our thrones and make sure all the pieces don't get dropped."

It sounded so easy. Too easy. Tess told him that.

"I know," he said and scrubbed at his face again. "But I also have faith in us."

"So do I," Thomas said, coming up behind them. He turned to Tess and gave her a solemn nod, his expression full of meaning. "The secret's safe, but if you're not too tired, go for the thirty days anyway. Might be the last time until you drop the kid off at college."

Tess couldn't help but chuckle, and when Mack joined in, Tess had a sense that it might be okay.

Maybe.

Hopefully.

THIRTEEN

Tess

It wasn't the fire that drove them back into the city, Tess thought. If anything, that had been a reason to stay at the farmhouse. But she and Mack had met with the police in the middle of the afternoon—they'd already caught one of the arsonists, and there were the logistics of dealing with the situation since the farm was on a unique piece of property—and it had been easier to just stay in the city afterward.

They were both exhausted and wound up bringing in a Cheese Cellar pizza for dinner, although Tess didn't have much of an appetite. They were settling on the side porch for their city version of porch time, neither of them having the energy to chat with any neighbors who might be out and about and see them out front, when her phone vibrated with an incoming text.

Rumor has it you're done hiding and back in town. Up for company?

Tess found the energy to grin. Maybe it was just what the doctor ordered. *You want to spend a Friday night with me and Mack and not your fuckboi?* she texted back.

There's plenty of time for both, Delia answered. *Besides, we're at my parents, so we're nearby. Call it foreplay.*

Tess smiled at that. It sounded exactly like something Delia would say. *We're on the side porch, so just come around.*

"Delia and Meter are on their way over."

"Nice," Mack said with a nod and a yawn that he immediately stifled. "Why?"

Tess shrugged. "All she said was that they were at her parents' house."

"Think we can stay awake long enough to have a conversation with them?"

"Fortunately, it's Delia and Meter. We can tell them to get lost and neither of them will get offended."

"True," Mack said, and they settled in to wait.

"I need some *normal* after that," Delia said a few minutes later when she and Meter showed up and had seated themselves, Delia tucking her camera bag under her chair. Mack went into the house for beer.

"What's wrong?" Tess asked.

Delia waved her off. "All the talk about the second wedding. Why aren't I wearing white, and is a vintage dress good enough? Am I sure we've arranged things the way I want them? Should she call the caterer or the florist and handle things? What about this? What about that?" Delia scrunched her face and raised her hands as if to hide behind them.

Tess looked at Meter, who paused, then said, "I got nothing. My mother's not much better."

"They're both forgetting we're already married," Delia said, reaching for a beer as Mack returned with them. She took three long swallows.

"Easy," Meter said softly, and Delia eyed him but didn't say anything. "They're just excited," he went on, turning to Tess and Mack and taking the other beer Mack held out, raising it in a thanks. "When we agreed to have a ritual ceremony along with a more formal reception, they kind of seized the moment. And… I mean, I get it. We're the first of their kids to get married. But it'd be nice if they'd both back off a bit and wait for us to ask them for input."

Tess felt a bit guilty, thinking of her own mother. Mom had been wonderful about helping plan her wedding. Krista, Mack's mother, had been almost totally hands off, but that was because Mack had point-blank told her that if she wasn't, he was sending her the wrong information and she'd miss the whole thing.

Mack made it a habit of threatening Krista with very creative scenarios that he was entirely likely to go through with. And so Krista had become very careful about the advice she offered and the questions she asked. She'd wound up bringing a wisdom to the planning that Tess hadn't expected—but had appreciated. As a result, whenever she'd had anything to say, it had been helpful and had made the night that much better.

Tess put a hand on Mack's leg and gave it a squeeze. Their wedding had been perfect.

"It's all your fault," Delia was telling Meter, giving him a side-eye that bordered on hostile. Tess bit back a smile; Delia could win awards for her bluster.

"It is," Meter said, calm and unruffled. "But you asked what I wanted, and I want the *chuppah* and I want to hold your hand and break that glass at the end of it." He paused, studying the artwork on the label of his beer. "I didn't think that was going to turn them into tyrants, and I'm sorry they did," he said, lifting his head and pinning Delia with his gaze, "and I'm not going to apologize for wanting what I want."

"I'm not asking you to," Delia said. "I'm just asking you to find a way to shut both our parents up before I... go... *ballistic*." Tess watched her friend carefully. There was something good-natured in Delia's complaining, which she hadn't expected. Was it possible Delia was enjoying all the fuss and attention?

That didn't seem right. Delia was the master of hiding in the shadows and not being seen. Then again, Delia's first dream had been to be a dancer, albeit as part of a troupe. Now, she had built a career on social media, which was all about being seen—or, like dance, it was about showing off her art. Maybe the reason Delia hid in the shadows wasn't to hide, but because it gave her a different way to be seen. Maybe it was about putting the focus on what she could create.

As for this wedding, Tess understood the fuss. Delia and Meter's first marriage had happened over a video call that had been even more impersonal than if they'd all been in the mayor's office in person. She deserved her chance to stand up in public and be the beautiful bride. And oh, Tess thought, she was going to be a beautiful bride.

Then again, Tess had helped her find the dress and had already seen her in it.

"What are those things? That first thing, and the glass?" Mack asked and Tess paused, holding her breath. "Something Jewish?"

"It's all custom, not religion," Meter said. "The *chuppah* is a canopy the couple and the rabbi stand under. The tradition began as the couple standing under one of those prayer shawls you see some Jews wear"—Mack nodded—"and evolved into a freestanding canopy instead, probably to spare the people who had to stand there and hold a prayer shawl over a couple's heads for the length of a traditional ceremony without dropping it on them." He smiled and they waited while he took a drink.

"As for the glass, I don't even know. There are a lot of stories about why Jews stomp on a glass at the end of the ceremony, but I don't know which of them are real and which aren't." He shrugged. "Like I said, it's custom, not religion. But I like the idea of it, the challenge of breaking the glass on the first try, like that stomp is the official start of your new life, or you're breaking up any bad vibes that are trying to sneak in, or maybe it's just that it's what you *do*, and both our dads did it and it's part of what it means to be a Jewish man at his wedding."

Delia rolled her eyes and shook her head, holding her beer to her lips for a long second. Meter just chuckled, watching her, and nudged her with a foot. "I don't care that I'm otherwise not the most Jewish man on the planet," he said.

"Me either," Delia said, sounding to Tess like she was reminding him of something.

They grinned at each other and Tess was convinced this was a familiar conversation they were having.

"I definitely need to learn more," Mack said.

"I like your porch," Delia said, staring over the simple wooden railing.

Tess bit back a laugh, although Mack didn't bother to and even Meter smiled. That was as clear a signal to change the topic as she had ever heard. "Me too, even though it's nothing like the front porch at the farmhouse."

"Yeah," Delia said, drawing the word out. "Speaking of that, Sima gave us an earful before we left for my parents.'" She eyed Tess. "It's officially arson?"

"Yeah," Mack said heavily. He rubbed the back of his neck and Tess reached over to him again, rubbing the inside of his thigh. He gave her a bleak smile. "I have the cops talking to the attorneys and bypassing us, for the most part. They can hash everything out and then let us know what we need to know. They've got the power right now anyway, and Tess and I have enough on our plates without having to relay messages between the two."

"I didn't want Snider to make us as crazy as he made you during the art thief," Tess said, feeling apologetic for some reason she couldn't identify.

"Smart. Also, you're not the target the same way I was," Delia said. "I mean, you are, but... it's still different."

"It is," Mack agreed. "Noah didn't try to burn any of your work."

"Have you asked Georgie to get out there and get pictures?" Delia asked.

"I do not want to remember this," Tess said, although she knew her friend well enough to know there was some other, more realistic reason for the question.

Sure enough, Delia was shaking her head. "Not for posterity. The insurance company is going to want pictures, and very few of them aren't happy with Georgie's work; he's been making a killing at it lately."

"So what's the goal with pictures?" Mack asked. He finished his beer and set the bottle down on the porch floor by his foot.

"Clues," Delia said. "Georgie says they'll be able to see patterns. Know how things fell, how in danger the trees were, where the flames ate the wood and where they didn't want to… There's a ton of information you can learn. He's really into it and told me he'd like to learn more about arson and fires and all of it. I can see him going off in a new career direction."

Mack turned to Tess, his eyebrows raised in a silent question.

"Text him," Delia said, raising her chin slightly. "Go on."

Tess pulled out her phone and sent the text. Georgie's reply was fast. *Delia talked to you? I'll go up tomorrow if that's okay.*

Yes, and super. Thanks. Usual fee?

Insurance covers it. Just tell me who you use.

Tess blinked in surprise but then asked herself what was actually surprising about that. Of course insurance would cover it. She texted him the name of their homeowner's insurance and said she'd get him the contact to their specific agent in the next day or so.

Getting Georgie involved was suspiciously easy, but then again, Delia had set it up. Tess eyed her, but her friend gave her an innocent look and finished her beer.

"Do you know anything else?" Meter asked.

"Not that we can talk about," Mack said. "When we can, I'll fill you in."

Meter nodded. "Thanks."

With the help of another round of beer, the conversation wandered from there, covering their various jobs before moving to the pandemic and how it was stretching out, feeling like it was never going to end and the promised vaccine wasn't ever going to arrive, although Mack promised them it wouldn't be much longer before it was approved.

When they circled back to the wedding, Meter shuddered. "I still need a break from it. These next two weeks can't go by fast enough."

"I've had enough wedding talk," Delia said, standing and tugging on Meter's hands. "Let's go home so I can tie you to the bed and have my way with you and make us both forget for a while."

Tess glanced at Mack, whose eyes had gone huge and his face white. He licked his lips.

"Metaphor," Meter said weakly, as if he'd noticed Mack's reaction. He made a show of letting Delia pull him to his feet. "Hey, let me carry these bottles in before we go." He bent to gather them before anyone could say anything.

Mack followed him, although they didn't go inside; the recycling was right outside the back door.

Delia turned to Tess. "Got anything else to share?" She gave her a pointed look.

"Like?" Tess asked.

"Like do I have to worry you're going to puke all over me and my man at our stupid wedding?" She shook her head, and Tess knew the issue was the wedding. Again.

"I have not done that yet," she said, feeling like that was something Mack would say and hoping Delia wouldn't call her on it.

"I know you couldn't puke on us at our first wedding, seeing as how we did it over video."

Tess smiled. "I meant throw up in general."

Delia eyed her. "I thought all pregnant women threw up."

"Apparently not all," Tess said with a smile, wondering how Delia would react to that.

But Delia just grinned. "About time. How far?"

"Not very; I haven't even been to the doctor yet, but Mack and I think the due date will be around Saint Patrick's Day."

"Nice," Delia said, bobbing her head and tapping a foot. She bent down for her camera bag. "Keep me posted and let me know if you want pictures as you grow." She glanced over her shoulder. "I take it you don't want me to tell Meter yet?"

"I know you'll both keep the secret, but maybe not yet. No one else really knows. You, me, Mack, and my doctor. That's it." She hoped Thomas would forgive her for leaving him out—she was sure he would—but there was no reason to tell anyone the circle was growing faster than her waist.

Delia narrowed her eyes. "You mean I'm the first person who figured it out?"

"Yep." The lie was surprisingly easy.

"Me."

"You."

"Wow," Delia said and looked over her shoulder again. The men were headed back toward the porch. "Okay. Wow. Well. Hmm. What do I say?"

"Nothing for now," Tess said with a smile, surprised she'd managed to leave Delia speechless. She'd never done that before.

"Oh, yeah. Right. But beyond that—" She broke off as the men approached, Meter sliding a hand around Delia's waist and nuzzling her neck. She tilted her head to the side and closed her eyes, her hand coming up to cradle his head. "Hi," she said, her voice husky. "Did you miss me or something?"

"You did make me a promise."

Tess glanced at Mack. He was fidgeting, looking uncomfortable again, and she smiled, taking pity on him. "Then you two should get going," she said and yawned. "Besides, after last night, Mack and I need *sleep*. And hopefully not to be disturbed again with more bad news."

"I know how that goes," Delia said. "If you need anything, holler."

Tess was pretty sure there was a double meaning in there and when she caught Delia's eye, her friend nodded slightly.

They said their goodnights, and then Delia and Meter walked around the side of the house, presumably to wherever they'd parked. Tess hoped they'd driven; even with Noah and his crew keeping an eye on Delia, the loss of the barn left Tess feeling like the city was especially dangerous.

She turned to Mack. "You okay?"

"They were serious about that, weren't they?"

"I don't care," Tess said, holding out her arms to him. "I care about *you*, and I think you need a promise that neither of us are going to be tied, or do the tying, to any of our beds."

Mack looked over her head for a long minute. "Is there something wrong with me that I'm not even sure I *want* to find out what it's like?"

"No, and you'd hate it; you'd be too self-conscious."

"But if you…"

"I am quite content with you as you are, Macaroni." She gave him a squeeze. "You're pretty perfect for me."

"Even though I'm the reason your barn got torched last night?"

"The real reason we lost the barn was because the Flahertys took a huge risk that hopefully will come back on them in bad ways. But the silver lining in it all is that we know where security needs to be built up, and we know we need to better protect the property, and a few other things that Sima and I will work on next week. If we treat this as a wake-up call and not some gross attack of vindictiveness, we can come out ahead."

If only, Tess thought, it was every bit as easy to believe as it was to say.

"You hope," Mack said, again staring over her head.

She gave him a small shake. Not that she could move him, but it was the effort, the gesture, that mattered. They both needed her to make it. "I know," she said. "Oh, and one thing I haven't had time to bring up to you yet. Red suggested maybe we should go ahead with having the farmhouse designated historic."

Mack pulled back and ducked his chin. Tess met his eyes.

"Why? And can we, since so much of the interior has been changed?"

"Because if it's designated, the firemen will be there faster and we'll have a measure—a small one—against anything the Flahertys try to do to it. It'll be harder for them to wiggle out of the responsibility, for example, if they get caught. And any fines and penalties will be higher for destroying something of historic value."

Mack frowned, and Tess hoped he was thinking the thing she'd tried to steer him toward.

"We can talk about it," he said. "What if—"

She bit her lower lip and waited.

"No, it's stupid. Probably too late."

"Ask."

"The barn? If we find pictures of what it originally looked like, can that be protected, too, when we rebuild?"

His voice wasn't nearly as weak as she'd expected it to be. Which meant he either saw the benefit to making changes to their plan or else expected to hear her say no.

"You're pretty smart," she said and led him inside where, true to her promise, she did not tie him to their bed.

FOURTEEN

Chad

"Dad," Chad said, glancing at Sophie to see if she'd back him up on this, "you could have killed someone this time."

"One less Mackenzie would be a life well lived. *My* life," William said with a smirk. His eyes disappeared into the wrinkles around them.

Sophie cut her eyes at Chad.

Based on that look, she wasn't going to back him up. She was their father's, bought and sold. Other than the Flaherty empire, Chad wondered what their father had offered her.

"And then you wind up in prison for murder and how does any of *that* work to keep everything together?" Chad decided he didn't care where Sophie had allied herself. This needed to be said.

"Why, Chadwick," his father drawled, sitting back in his desk chair and looking, somehow, like a happy, appreciative snake, "you sound like you care."

Anyone else, Chad would have told to fuck off.

"Or are you worried about that gravy train you fell off when you lost my condo?"

For once, the barb didn't hurt. Maybe, Chad thought, he was growing immune to it. Maybe the scar tissue had finally built up enough.

Or maybe it was the first step to getting out of this madness already.

"I hear she's having a public wedding," William went on.

Chad planted his hands on his father's desk and leaned forward. In the corner, Go-fer Stanley took a step forward, but Neal didn't move. "Ask me if I care."

His father held his gaze and smiled.

Chad mirrored it back to him.

After a long minute, William Flaherty's changed. It might have become genuine. "And here I thought you weren't a Flaherty." He broke eye contact in order to turn to Sophie. "What do you think? Is your baby brother a late bloomer?"

Sophie shrugged, looking at William, not Chad. "Too little, too late," she said, offhand, and curled her upper lip at Chad, who moved away from his father's desk.

"I'm out of here," he muttered.

"No you're not," William said and motioned to Go-fer Stanley, who moved in front of the door to his office. "Not until we discuss what I brought you here for."

Chad let out a heavy breath, all he dared to do. He'd pushed his luck more than far enough already. At least his ribs didn't have a phantom memory thing happening.

Neal produced a piece of paper as if by magic and handed it to William, who set it on his desk, turned it, and, with his meaty index finger planted on it, slid it across his otherwise bare desk. "This."

Chad looked at it. It was a printout about a house that was apparently for sale. "Looks better than that condo ever was," he said with a shrug. Not that he'd looked that closely, and not that he cared. Of course his father wanted to buy more property. The guy, Chad swore, wanted to own the entire city.

He'd have to get in line behind the national corporations who were buying up property all across the country, not just in Port Kenneth. Although maybe that was William's reason now.

"Buy it," William said. As usual, there was a finality in his voice. There was to be no argument. Chad didn't care.

"You want me to *what*?" he asked. He wanted to stick a finger in each ear and make sure neither was clogged, but that wouldn't go over well. It was assumed one's ears were clean when they were summoned to stand in front of William Flaherty.

"Buy it." William glared at him and tapped the paper.

Chad picked it up, shaking his head and looking more closely. No, he decided, it did *not* look nicer than the condo had been. "What the actual fuck?

There's nothing you can do to get me to live in Woolslayer." It was, he thought, one of the few things he could say that his father would respect.

Not that he cared about gaining his father's respect. Not anymore. Burning the barn had ended that.

But he didn't want to live in Woolslayer.

Go-fer Stanley took a swipe at the back of Chad's head. "You sure about that?"

With the wiggle of a finger, William told him to stand down. Go-fer Stanley moved away from Chad, but Sophie came closer and peered over his shoulder at the paper. He tipped it so she could see.

The idea of living in Woolslayer was bad enough, but he especially didn't want to live in a run-down rowhouse. Besides, he liked his place. It wasn't too big, the people in the building were respectful if not friendly, and it was convenient.

It was also owned by his father, which meant he couldn't do things like change the locks or put in a different security system. Keeping the owner out—or denying him access to watch what his son was up to—wasn't the smartest move in the world.

"Doesn't look *so* bad," Sophie said with a shrug. "Dad, what's the game?"

William held up his fingers, a sign to wait.

"And if I do this—" Chad started carefully. He was missing something. He had to be; his father was a bigot and Woolslayer was full of people whose skin color wasn't white.

"Make them an offer they can't refuse." His father flicked his fingers. "Just not a million. That one got turned down immediately. The word came back that they weren't letting people gentrify Woolslayer. So make it market value for *there*, but make it an offer they can't refuse."

The repetition of the phrase was vital, Chad knew. There was no option other than buying an old, rundown rowhouse in Woolslayer. No, not buy *a* rowhouse. *That* particular one.

Chad was willing to bet someone had died in there. Possibly because his father wanted it.

"Why can't you?" Chad asked even though William had just said he'd tried.

Sophie huffed and shook her head. "Don't be dumb," she whispered to him.

"Because now I want your name on it."

"So buy it and put it in my name."

"You need to go through it like any other potential buyer."

"With what cash?" Then again, it was Woolslayer, so he probably had the money.

Again, William flicked his fingers. It was all the answer Chad needed.

"And they're not going to realize my name's *Flaherty*?" Chad let Sophie take the paper from him.

"They might," William said and produced a cigar from a box—Chad figured it was a humidor, not a gun box, although he supposed it could be both—and played with it, turning it end to end and rolling it in his fingers. "Figure it out."

"Do—Do I have to live there?" Chad asked as inspiration struck. Maybe his father just wanted it as a place from which to do surveillance of Mackenzie. After all, the pretty boy lived in Woolslayer, and if

William was as obsessed as Sophie said, of course William would want as close an eye on the enemy as possible.

"Of course," his father snapped, slapping a hand on the surface of his desk, the cigar in his other hand. "What else would you do with it? Let another girlfriend steal it from you? Just straight-up give it to Delia Ford?"

Chad stood up straighter, understanding something for the first time. His father didn't underestimate many people, especially women. But Delia Ford had been the rare exception, and William wasn't over his own failure on that front.

"Buy it. Move in. Live in it. I'll move someone else in where you are now." His father flicked his fingers again. He was throwing Chad out of a place he'd turned into a home, but to his father, things like *home* were inconsequential details, spaces to be filled.

"So it'll be *my* place and you won't interfere with it?" It seemed unbelievable that his father was going to let him do this. "You're not going to wire it so you can listen in?"

His father sniffed and turned his head to the side, and Chad understood. William wasn't going to listen in; for whatever reason, he had finally deemed his only legitimate son irredeemably undesirable, unworthy, a waste of time or effort. *Buy the house*, the message had become, *and then I'll wash my hands of you.*

It didn't escape Chad that his father was abandoning him to Woolslayer.

It made sense. In William's view, Woolslayer was where the undesirables lived.

Behind William, Neal was nodding slightly, his gaze so focused on Chad, it felt like twin little holes were being bored into him.

This could be advantageous to the plot against William, Chad thought. His next thought was that William was probably setting him up for exactly that rebellion. If he was going to work with Neal on this—or Sophie—he was going to have to be very, very careful. And he was going to have to put himself first.

That was a new thought.

"Okay," Chad said with a nod. He took the paper back from Sophie and looked at it—and didn't need to fake the face he made at it. The place was *fugly*. "I think I understand you."

"I doubt you do," William sniffed. "Just see that the house gets bought."

"Am I using your Realtor or finding my own?"

"Use your own." William stared at him, and Chad had the feeling that there was a challenge in there. That his father didn't think he could find someone to sell him a house.

"And you're paying."

"For the house."

"Utilities and taxes too."

William didn't answer.

"Can't have a Flaherty working for *the man*," Chad sneered and then immediately held his breath.

They stared at each other for a long minute, Chad wondering if William would truly cut him off financially—and if this, again, this could be a chance to get out from under his father's thumb.

It still felt too good, too *convenient*, to be true.

Chad was never so glad as he was right then, when go-fer Stanley opened the door and ushered him out of his father's office with something like manners.

"Chad," Sophie said, scrambling after him.

He let her follow him as he made a beeline for Gentry's. They could talk there. Maybe she had insight about what he was being set up for. And maybe she'd even tell him about it.

FIFTEEN

Tess

As the weekend drew to a close, Tess had to admit she wasn't keen on the idea of returning to the farmhouse just yet. "Mom and Gray and Thomas are probably on edge," she told Mack. "They may not want us around."

"You and I aren't back in our offices full-time yet," he reminded her, giving her a look she didn't want to think too much about. "Which is why we're still set up to work from the house." He gave her a look, and Tess felt vaguely guilty.

"I know, but..."

"And it's not as if the vaccine's ready. We can't risk you. Or—" He motioned to her.

"Which is another reason to stay here," she said. She still wasn't sure how Delia or Thomas had figured it out so quickly, but on the other hand, both of them could sniff a secret out of a CIA agent. They could both be trusted to keep the secret, but on the other hand, if Mom had any reason to suspect anything, she'd give Thomas a hard time about his silence.

"I know, but it's not like it'll be secret forever." He gave her another long look. "And you know they'll love fussing over you. So let them fuss," he added with a stern frown that reminded her of Thomas.

That left Tess with only one real option if she didn't want to go back to the farmhouse, so she informed Mack she was going to the office in the morning, at least for a bit. Red had upgraded the office air filtration system as soon as he'd been able, and he'd been focused on helping the firm's corporate and small business clients to do the same. Healthier air was a good defense against more than just the pandemic virus, after all.

A wave of exhaustion hit Tess just after lunch and she decided it was time to give in and head back to the farmhouse for the rest of the week. She'd dodged one night there but had run out of excuses.

"Wish you didn't have to," Red told her as she packed up her things. "But I get it."

She nodded and yawned. The exhaustion was already old, but she'd heard a rumor it only lasted for the first trimester.

She hoped it was an accurate rumor and not some urban tale of wishful thinking.

Red eyed her. "You okay?"

"I haven't been sleeping well since the fire. I mean, it just happened Friday night," she said, hoping he'd buy that. The shudder that followed at the thought of sleeping in the farmhouse was real, though. Maybe she truly wasn't ready yet, she thought, again wondering what would have happened if the house had been attacked along with the barn.

She told herself she had to stop thinking that way, but it wasn't so easy. Not when people she loved could have been hurt.

"Let me know if you need anything," Red said with a nod.

"Just an end to this vendetta William Flaherty has against us." She paused. "I know he's been ruling this town for a long time now, but everything he does shows he's not in the least interested in even seeing if Mack or I are going to threaten him. He just went on the offensive, not caring that we have zero interest in him." She shook her head. "Talk about tilting at windmills."

"You'd think he knows better than to mess with you, since he won't mess with me."

"He doesn't mess with me," Tess said, blinking. "Well, until he went after my barn, anyway." She eyed Red. "If he knows what's good for him, he's going to stop right there. If he comes after that house, he and I will be at war." She had no idea what that could possibly look like, but she wasn't going to take the high road like Mack kept doing. No, she decided. She was going down and dirty.

But only if Flaherty went for the farmhouse.

"I can't see him being that stupid," Red said, "but then again, I didn't see him coming after the barn, either."

"I wish you could look at me and say you're confident he'll be getting a message that he screwed up and had better rein it in, but I doubt that'll happen."

"Sorry," Red said. He looked regretful, not thoughtful, though.

With that, Tess left the office and headed to the farmhouse. Halfway up the private road, she braked hard and fast, sliding on the gravel and reaching for her phone. "Sima? I think I might have figured out how they got to the barn so easily. Can you meet me?" She described where she was.

The farm's biologist must have been relatively nearby because she arrived quickly. Together, she and Tess started down a path that even Tess thought looked recently used.

Sure enough, they came to what had to have been a campsite. Sima picked up a bent tent stake and handed it to Tess. "See what I mean?" she asked. "It's too much land to keep a close enough eye on."

Tess took the stake and tapped it against her palm. "What about fencing along the road?"

Sima frowned. "That could maybe work, assuming no one actually *climbs* the fence, but at the same time, we have to be mindful of migration patterns, which I haven't fully identified yet." She put her hands on her hips and scowled. "I have no idea how to keep out the humans and allow the animals all the access. But you should call the cops," she added. "Maybe they can keep humans out."

She wrinkled her nose, and Tess had to agree with that assessment. It wasn't likely.

"I should call the police. Not that they can do much." She sighed. "Not being an actual part of the city sounds great. No taxes—on the surface anyway. But also no help when you truly need it."

"Yeah," Sima said and deflated.

She was already so small, Tess thought, that she didn't have an inch to lose. "Hey," she said, trying to think through all possibilities, "this couldn't be because Taylor was up here last weekend, could it?"

"No," Sima said. "Taylor wouldn't leave signs they'd been here." She pointed to the tent stake in Tess's hand. "And Taylor sleeps in a hammock." She turned and looked out at the campsite. "This was more than one person."

"It might have been," Tess agreed, following along as Sima pointed out where she thought two different tents had been pitched. She pursed her lips and looked down the hill, toward the farmhouse. "Do you think the barn would have been visible from here?"

Sima turned and looked in roughly the same direction.

"See?" Tess asked.

"I do," Sima agreed. She turned in a circle, her hands on her hips, and scuffed at the garbage again. "Hey," she said and took a few steps forward and kicked at some leaves, first a few kicks, then dragging her foot through the leaves, moving them. "They even built a fire ring. It's not a very good one, but still…"

"How did we miss this?" Tess asked. "How were people camping on *our* land and we didn't know?

And were they here more than once? We had security up here all during the pandemic lockdowns, and they didn't see a single person who shouldn't have been here. How did anyone even know the area's not being monitored?"

Sima shrugged. "Shit happens—and maybe one of those guards talked to the wrong person. Or maybe we all got cocky about how it was going." She kicked at the leaves some more. "You know, Tess," she went on, "I've been through *things*. Maybe the therapists aren't wrong when they say that you can't control everything, you can't anticipate everything, and sometimes, you just have to get burned and take the lessons you learn and be better going forward."

Tess didn't react for a long minute, her mind blank. It was an uncomfortable feeling, but so was acknowledging the level to which they'd been played. They should have been more aware. Somehow. "I know you're right," she said. "Just… *ugh*." She stalked over to Sima and kicked the leaves, sending them into the air instead of to the side, as Sima had done.

"Sorry securing the road runs the expenses up," Sima said.

Tess shook her head. "We can afford it." She took yet another deep breath, grateful for the Mackenzie millions. "I just wish we didn't *have* to."

"Are you wishing you could end the Flahertys?"

"Just their fixation on us." Tess rubbed her arms. "What they do that doesn't affect us—including Delia—is no skin off my back."

Sima looked at her, tilting her head up and scrunching her nose. "What is it about Delia that makes everyone love her?"

Tess arched an eyebrow. "Jealous?"

Sima shrugged and hugged herself. "She's bitchy and a rebel and full of herself when she has no reason to be."

"What's this really about?" Tess asked. It was about more than how Sima felt about her sister-in-law, but Tess didn't think it had to do with the barn. Sima had been angry about that, but pragmatic, too.

"She's so fucking perfect!" Sima yelled, waving an arm in the air and kicking at more leaves.

Tess just chuckled, finally letting go of her own anger at the barn and the Flaherty situation. "No she's not, and you know that."

Sima glared at her, but Tess just kept smiling. "Come on, Sima," she said. "What's really bothering you?"

"Your house almost got torched, Vass and I have a house that's been totally gutted and is being rebuilt, totally custom, but all anyone can talk about is Meter and Delia's new place, like it's so special. Oh, but it's on the *Ridge*, like they haven't been living there for how long now? Delia's been there even longer, but oh, no! We've *got* to make a fuss over their house, which they bought absolutely ready to move into! It's like no one cares about me and Vass! Maybe he was *right* when he said no one gives a damn about him, and maybe now that I'm the family disgrace, it's rubbing off on me, too."

Tess frowned. "Any chance they're waiting for your place to be *done* first?"

Sima glared at her. "They act like it doesn't even exist."

"Well, it does," Tess said. "And you know I have a vested interest in it, so feel free to talk to me."

"But you're my boss. *And* Delia's friend."

"True and true. C'mon. Let's head back down to the house and stake out the gazebo and figure out where to go from here about this security thing."

Sima rolled her eyes. "We call an architect and draw up new plans for the barn? Oh, hey, think you might have one handy?"

Tess frowned. She knew this side of Sima, of course. She'd been nothing *but* this sort of attitude when she'd first started working on the farm. "Do you want handy, or do you want good?"

"I want someone who'll *listen* to what I need."

"I can arrange that for you."

"And a better security system along the road here."

"That's what I just suggested we work on. We just have to come to a decision about what we need to do in order to protect the humans, the wildlife currently here, and the future sheep."

Sima made a wordless sound that Tess took to be the equivalent of a raised middle finger.

Tess just laughed. After a second—and a thoroughly dirty look—Sima joined her.

SIXTEEN

Tess

After dealing with Sima, Tess took a shortened version of the nap she'd promised herself and, around the time she ought to have been conferring with her mother and Roger about dinner, found herself headed for the remains of the barn instead.

"Oh, Mom," she said as she entered the clearing. "You too?"

Mom was sitting on a log, sketchbook on her lap. "I can't help it," she said. "It was just a barn before it burned, and it sat very prettily in this clearing, but right now, there's just absolute beauty in it." She held up her sketchbook and turned pages. "I've been here most of the day."

"You know the fire could still be hot," Tess warned her although she doubted the truth of what she was saying; it had been days since it had burned. She just didn't want her mother... *here*. And to find *beauty* in it? How?

"Sima's been out with more water, poking at things," Mom said. "And your friend Delia is here too."

"What? Where?"

"Up here," Delia called.

Tess craned her head, then took a step back and looked. "How do you do that?"

"Didn't you climb trees as a kid?"

"You grew up in Woolslayer," Tess said. There weren't a lot of trees in Woolslayer.

"Which is why," Delia said, and from the tree came the sounds of leaves rustling and branches creaking, "whenever I'd escape, I'd do it in a tree. No one expects a kid from Woolslayer to climb a tree."

It took her more than a minute to climb down. Mom moved away, along what would have been the side of the barn, and started a new sketch.

Despite her frustration with the idea that the destruction here could be artful and beautiful, Tess couldn't help but smile. Mom had said more than once that the hardest part of being an art teacher was that she didn't have time for her own art; it was all grading and lesson plans, just like any other subject. To see her getting back to it now that she was retired was a good thing.

"I thought Georgie had come out on Saturday and gotten pictures," Tess told Delia when she was on the ground.

"He did," Delia said, adjusting her cameras and her camera bag. "But the drone he ordered for aerial work is on back order, so the options were to buy something not as good or pay me to climb a tree for him." She gave Tess a mischievous look. "Because he too grew up in Woolslayer. Which means if your kids grow up in Woolslayer, make sure you bring them out here. A lot. Teach them to climb trees."

"It's a life skill?" Tess asked.

Delia gave her a grin. "Exactly! By the way, April," she said, projecting her voice down toward Mom, "your art's really nice. Next time I put a show together—and I'm overdue to do one—think you'd want to contribute?"

"Oh, why... thank you." Mom fumbled her piece of charcoal.

Tess winked at Delia. That offer, probably because it was so casual and unexpected, had surely done her mom a world of good. She didn't think anyone had complimented Mom's art in forever. Maybe Dad had been the last one.

She stroked the tattoo on the back of her neck, thinking of him.

"I'm sure Tess or Gray can help me pick the right pictures," Mom went on.

Delia mouthed *Gray* at Tess, who knew her own eyes had gone wide at hearing that. And so casually dropped, maybe more casual than Delia's invitation to be in an art show had just been.

Tess felt, suddenly, surrounded by women with agendas and secrets—and, as another wave of exhaustion hit, realized she was one of those women too.

"Hey, Tess?" It was Sima. She emerged into the clearing and looked at Delia. "Oh. Who gave *you* permission to be here?"

Delia held up the camera in her hand. "Watch it, baby sister-in-law, or I'll point it at you."

Sima put her hands on her hips and glared, throwing eye daggers at Delia, who just laughed and said, "I should get going." She turned her camera, doing something with it. "Here," she said to Tess, handing her something—a memory card, Tess realized as soon as she moved it into her palm so she could look at it. "Your aerial pictures of this disaster."

Tess let out a sigh. "You know I hate to poke at this, but did you learn *anything* about the Flahertys that can help us out here?"

Delia had been putting her camera back in its bag, but she paused and looked over her shoulder at Tess. "Yeah," she said and tilted her head, then got lost in her phone for a minute. "C'mon. Let's sit down somewhere."

They retreated to the gazebo.

"Okay," she said, motioning Tess into one of the comfortable chairs with a wink and a grin.

For a second, Tess regretted telling Delia. Then she reminded herself that she hadn't; Delia had guessed.

"So, here's the thing with the Flahertys. They're not as smart as they think they are. Or maybe it's that their arrogance blinds them; I'm not sure. And it doesn't matter because if you pay attention to the small details and bide your time, you'll get them eventually."

"How long did you have to wait before you got the condo?"

Delia pursed her lips and tipped her head from side to side. "I didn't, actually. As soon as Len told me what to do, I went and did it. But that was a different scenario. Chad and I were definitely over and Len said he'd probably make me move out at any second—and would do it by leaving me basically homeless. So when I say *I went and did it*, I'm not kidding. He walked me over to the office and watched as I filled out the paperwork. I offered to pay him, but he wouldn't let me, thank God." She paused, and Tess had the feeling she was remembering. "That was probably my lowest period. I hadn't been working on the photography as much because Chad didn't like it when I did, and I was worried I couldn't pay the mortgage—up to then, Chad had been putting the money in my account and I was paying it. That was part of how I was able to get away with the whole thing; it was *my* name on those payments, so again, it was his arrogance that he needed to make a show of taking care of me that let him do something I could exploit to my benefit. But as soon as I got word that the condo was mine, even though I had to deal with the mortgage I wasn't sure I could afford—and *that* was a learning curve I'd rather not repeat—everything changed and business picked up again. Go figure." She snorted, gave Tess a dirty look, and then smiled.

"So their pride makes them sloppy."

"Well, it did in that case. And clearly, William wasn't paying much attention to his son, even though he made it clear that he considered Chad a worthless fuckup of a human being."

"Is Chad his weakness?" Tess asked, her brain churning.

Delia pursed her lips again, but not as tightly. "I'm not sure. Chad doesn't think so, but at the same time, he was always coming up with these business plans that he was *sure* William would fund. If only he'd talk to his dad about them. But they had to be perfect first. And they were some *wild* ideas, let me tell you. Our boy may not be the brightest bulb, and he may not be able to finish a damn thing he starts, but he's creative—in some ways. I'll give him that." She paused, wrinkling her nose, but didn't say anything more.

"So it's really a matter of looking for the detail they're overlooking."

"Yep. I'm not an expert in all things Flaherty, but Len is. Ever since Chad messed with his sister, it's been something he's been working on."

"Len?" Tess asked, wondering if she should know who he was.

"Dietrick," Delia said, an inflection at the end of his name that implied Delia did expect Tess to know who he was. "Gay guy in the public defender's office. Wears the loudest clothes you've ever seen and laughs like hell when criminals don't want anything to do with him because of that. According to him, he's got the winningest record in the office and when someone has a fit about being assigned to the flashy gay guy, they hand that person a laminated sheet of his stats. They shut up after that."

Tess paused, wondering if Red knew about this guy. She certainly didn't.

"Thanks," she said after a minute. "Now I know who to talk to."

"Good luck," Delia said, standing up. "You've picked a hell of a war. The Mackenzie-Flaherty thing is almost as legendary as this place." She motioned around her.

"That's the problem. I don't want to be part of the Mackenzie-Flaherty thing."

"Yeah, but you are. Hey, think Sima's still around? I could catch a ride from her if she's ready to call it a day." She looked around, then pulled out her phone.

SEVENTEEN

Tess

It took until the end of the week before security settled the new situation at the farm, and the price tag staggered Tess. Even worse, the cost was for temporary measures until they came up with the right permanent solution. Because, Tess had said to Sima, it wasn't only a matter of keeping predators out. They would be needing to keep the sheep *in*.

That gave way to another discussion about shepherds and how to best manage a flock of sheep.

When Tess tried to fill Mack in, he simply shrugged. "It'd have been nice to be able to give all that money away, but this way, everyone will be safe and—" He paused and gave Tess a sheepish look. "I started running a Flaherty tab. Every last thing we have to spend money on because of them."

She paused. "That sounds…" She rolled her tongue around as she searched for the right word. "Vindictive."

He let out a breath and she knew she'd caught him. "It does," he said, "and maybe yeah, I want to get a pound of flesh out of them for all they're costing us, as stupid as I know that is." He paused and peered at her. "How are you feeling?"

"The same," she said, trying to be casual, but already, she was over it. "The nausea is like waves all day, I'm exhausted, and I just want to *sleep*."

"Porch time in town?" he asked with so much hope, she knew there was no denying him. They'd stayed at the farmhouse for dinner, but they both were itching for the rowhouse.

"You know everyone will stop by to chat."

"Good."

The street was quiet when they got back to town and staked out the swing, although every light in the house across the street was on and a person Tess had never seen before came out of it. She watched a man—who stood straight, chin raised, and who wore a white button-down as if he were some sort of office worker, which wasn't the norm in Woolslayer—leave, then the lights flipped off: third floor, second, first, so methodically that it seemed as if someone was going through each room and turning them off.

The man got into some sort of large dark-colored SUV and revved his engine before peeling away from the curb.

If Mack noticed, he didn't say anything.

Tess sat up, away from him a bit, and pulled out her phone, sending a text.

"Something wrong?" Mack asked, rousing himself from his thoughts. He planted both feet on the floor of the porch and adjusted the way he was sitting on the swing.

She didn't bother hiding her phone under her leg. "It's almost like," she said softly as someone else walked down the porch steps of the house across the street and headed to their car, "that house is for sale."

Mack shrugged and stood up. "Hey!" he called to the person at their car. "Got a second?"

It was a woman, Tess noticed, jumping to her feet and following Mack down their own porch steps, not wanting the other woman to feel threatened by six-foot-three Mack coming at her in a rush. "Wait up," she called, more for the woman's benefit than his.

The woman did look startled, Tess noticed as they got closer. She was white, with darker hair—in the evening light, it was hard to tell what exact color—and business clothes, including a killer pair of heels.

"Hi," Tess said with a friendly smile, slipping her hand into Mack's. "We live across the street"—she motioned—"and, well, by any chance, are you showing this house to a potential buyer?"

If anything, the woman got even more nervous. She licked her lips and glanced around, as if expecting to be attacked.

Tess pulled Mack back a step.

"Yes," the woman said.

"He didn't look like the usual Woolslayer," Mack said conversationally, and Tess blinked. So he *had* noticed. Typical. Taylor was always telling her that Mack was more observant than almost everyone gave him credit for, and while she largely agreed, she had truly thought he wasn't paying attention to what was happening across the street.

"Well, you know," the woman said and took a couple steps closer to her car. "Housing prices are rising, so it's harder to find a bargain."

Tess drew back. "He's not a flipper, is he?"

"Oh, no." The woman said, waving a hand and leaning forward. It was such a cliché move that Tess didn't trust it.

Her phone buzzed. It was Janeesa, the local Woolslayer real estate agent. *Yes.*

People, Tess thought with a mental eye roll, were talkative tonight.

"He's looking for a new start," the real estate agent said. "Somewhere with authentic people and a diverse neighborhood."

"Wood's Ears didn't fit the bill?" Tess asked. "He looked like the sort of person who'd think that was slumming." Which, of course, meant Woolslayer was three more rungs down the ladder of respectability—in entirely too many people's eyes.

Oh, how wrong they were, Tess thought, not for the first time.

Mack gave her a look. He was asking what was wrong with her and to be honest, Tess wasn't entirely certain. All she knew was that something felt *off*.

The woman peered at Tess. "Have you *seen* the prices there lately? It's impossible to find anything in the entire city."

Tess nodded, thinking of Meter and Delia's new place and their search for it. "I know. Corporations are buying everything and turning it into rentals."

The woman eyed her.

Tess introduced herself, but given the way the woman responded, her mouth curving into a smug smile before she recovered and said it was a pleasure to meet her, Tess had a feeling the woman had known exactly who lived across the street. She hoped it wasn't a selling point.

"Well," she said, tugging on Mack's hand, "we'll let you get going. I hope we haven't kept you from anything too important."

"Just a glass of wine and to get these shoes off," the woman said, and Tess thought it was the first genuine thing she had said.

"I hear you, and the shoes are gorgeous. Enjoy your evening." With another tug on Mack's hand, Tess led him back to their porch.

"What was that?" he asked as they got comfortable again.

"Go get a beer," Tess told him. "I'm going to ask Janeesa to sniff around."

By the time he came back, she had an answer. "We have to be the winning buyer. Janeesa's putting in an offer right now. It shouldn't be hard; she knows the selling agent."

"Tess." Mack stopped in front of the swing and held the beer up to his chest. "I own *how* many houses? What do I need another one for?"

"I don't know," she said. "I don't understand any of this. But I trust Janeesa and something about that woman," she said, pointing at the street, "didn't feel right."

Mack was quiet for a minute. He stood where he was and studied her. "Didn't feel right... as in the way the Flahertys make you feel?"

Tess froze, her eyes on him. That was exactly it. And she was willing to bet Janeesa had known it. Offering to put in a bid wasn't like her.

"Put in the offer," he said.

"She's doing it now." It seemed too crazy to believe, but at the same time, it wasn't a bad strategy. Flaherty living across the street could monitor their movements—which meant the rowhouse was in potential jeopardy now, too. "They're really tightening the noose around us," she said, not liking how that felt. She would, like Delia had said, have to watch for the details that got overlooked.

"Not if we get that house," Mack said, a strange note of determination in his voice. Then he sank back onto the swing and scrubbed at his face. "Like I need another house."

"Just one more thing to add to the Flaherty tab," Tess said lightly, but she couldn't shake the feeling that they'd left themselves vulnerable, that maybe they should have listened to Thomas and not written him off as a worrywart.

But then again, Thomas hadn't been expecting an offensive from the Flahertys either.

She pulled up the office's internal scheduler, checking Red's openings for the upcoming week. Maybe he would have ideas. Whenever she lacked some, he always had her back. And right then, she had a feeling she was going to need him to have her back.

EIGHTEEN

CHAD

"Congratulations," William told Chad. He'd even put chairs in front of his desk. Sophie occupied one, and Chad had gingerly taken the other.

William, of course, hadn't moved from behind his desk. Chad was starting to wonder if the guy was stuck there permanently.

"I outbid Mackenzie and Cartieri," Chad said, hoping his father would see the victory for what it was.

But of course he couldn't. Still without leaving his desk or even standing up, he exploded, demanding to know how they'd known to put a bid in, then going on a rant about the properties they owned around the country.

Sophie slid her foot across the carpet and nudged Chad's foot.

He stared at her for a long minute as their father continued his rant. Chad hadn't known about other Mackenzie properties and began to wonder if there was more than a little bit of jealousy involved. While the Flahertys had been focused on Port Kenneth, the Mackenzies had been doing more, expanding across the country.

Yeah, that would rankle his dad's ego for sure.

Sophie nudged him more pointedly this time and then openly glared at his father, who was either still going or had started the rant over from the top. Chad wasn't sure which.

"Dad!" He stood up. He didn't move toward his father's desk at all, he didn't wave his arms around. He just stood there.

"You're going to have an aneurysm, Dad," Sophie said coolly. For a quick second, Chad wished he could talk to William that way. "And over the *Mackenzies*. Come on; they're not worth dying over. You go now and none of your plans will happen because I can't crawl in your brain and extract them. And honestly, even if I could, I wouldn't."

That must have been the wrong thing to say, Chad thought, because William turned a dark red color and Neal stepped out of the corner. Go-fer Stanley came up behind Chad and slipped around William's desk too.

"We'll come back another time," Chad said and headed for the door, not caring if Sophie followed him, but she was hard on his back, all but stepping on him.

They retreated, like they had been of late, to Gentry's Diner.

"Did you *have* to rile him up like that?" Sophie asked after they'd slid into a booth halfway toward the back but along the far wall so they weren't terribly visible through the windows.

"I didn't mean to. It was supposed to be a victory thing. I came out on top over Mackenzie and Cartieri, you know?" Chad slid the coffee cup in front of him closer to the edge of the table so the server would come by and fill it. Not that he wanted coffee, but it was something to do with his hands. "That's not nothing."

"But it means they found out what you're up to, and that's sloppy. If you'd have bothered to stop and think, you'd have realized that."

Chad wanted to punch her for that insult. Instead, he gave the server a polite smile as she filled his coffee cup, then Sophie's. His sister reached for a sugar packet and shook it before ripping it open.

"I thought," Chad said slowly, not sure how to phrase this or where it could lead once he said it, "the idea was to distract Dad away from Mackenzie. Instead, I just bought the house across the street so he can keep a closer eye on them."

"And that's his mistake," Sophie said, pouring whatever was in the creamer into her coffee. She finished and handed the little white pitcher to Chad. "Because Chadwick is about to mutiny."

He eyed her, his stomach dropping as every other fiber in him wanted to root itself to the ground and push her away. "Oh, no. Not if it's going to get me worked over again. That shit *hurts*, Soph."

She narrowed her eyes at him. "Wuss."

"Have you ever been beaten by Go-fer Stanley and his buddies? The last time, it was three of them. Kicking me. I should be dead."

Sophie shrugged.

Chad stared. Was she really that cold?

Of course she was. She was the Flaherty heir apparent, after all. Having no soul was part of the job.

Neither of them said anything until another server showed up. This one was a young guy, maybe twenty, and one of those who was convinced he didn't need to write down their orders.

Sophie must have noticed. Her order became unusually elaborate.

Chad simply ordered a fruit parfait. The idea of giving himself up to Go-fer Stanley and his buddies for another beating stole his appetite.

The server repeated Sophie's order back to her. He didn't even blink when he got to the contradictory request for mayo on the side and double mayo but only on the top piece of bread, and Dijon mustard on both pieces.

"Classy," Chad muttered at Sophie when the server had left. "Fucking with a kid like that."

Sophie shrugged. "Dad says it's our job to make sure no one thinks more of themselves than they're worth."

"And what if that kid's"—Chad pointed in the direction their server had gone—"someone like us, who's trying to build some independence from their domineering parents?"

Sophie closed one eye and arched the opposite eyebrow. "Like I care?"

"You care enough to try to get him fired."

"Are we going to argue about this, or are we going to talk about what we're going to do so Dad gets off the Mackenzie train? This is our best opportunity, although I'll tell you, the security I hear they're putting in on both houses and around the farm is impressive. I didn't think he'd do it."

Chad turned his head and watched the activity around the diner. The place was always hopping.

Their server and his fabulous memory was dancing around tables, talking to people, laughing.

Chad wondered what that would be like. To laugh like that. To have actual conversations that didn't hurt.

Sophie started babbling elaborate plans to shut William down, but Chad kept watching the server. There was nothing dishonorable about the work he was doing, and the best way to derail William's plan to use Chad's new house was to cut William out of anything house-related, even though he'd already put the money to cover the first six months' mortgage into Chad's accounts.

It would be rude and a declaration of war, but all Chad had to do was make a phone call and rearrange that account so his father could deposit, but not withdraw.

And then Chad could get a job and support himself so he didn't need more of William's money—because the old jackass would withhold it as soon as he realized that Chad was making a play for his freedom.

Maybe he'd beat Chad for that. But at least that too would be a lot more honorable than letting Sophie set him up to take one for some team that he didn't think wanted him on it.

Yes, he decided. This was his moment.

NINETEEN

Tess

Tess smoothed the dress over her belly. It was way too early to be showing, but clothes were already fitting ever so slightly differently. She frowned at herself in the mirror and turned sideways. "What do you think?"

"You look beautiful," Mack said and leaned in to give her lips a peck.

Tess put a hand on his chest to stop him because, sure enough, he wanted to pull her closer. "Can you tell?"

"No, but if you're worried, wear something different. Delia said she didn't care if you did." He paused, his mouth slightly open, his brow furrowing.

Tess patted his cheek as she watched it click. "She figured it out. Don't ask me how," she said and turned back to the mirror. Even she couldn't see a difference. "I think," she said slowly, "that I look fine and no one else should be able to guess." She nodded and stepped out of the way so Mack could tie his bow tie.

"Why are you and I standing up with them when Meter's got all that family?"

"So they don't have to choose, of course," Tess laughed. "The problems with having a big family, most of them men." She frowned as her phone buzzed. "That's Mom," she sighed.

Sure enough, her mother had sent her a selfie, asking if she looked okay.

"She wasn't even invited," Tess groused to Mack, shoving her phone at him.

He took a look at the picture and started typing. Tess fought a wave of panic.

"Mack—"

"You look beautiful, Mom," he said in tandem with his typing.

"That had better be what it says."

He showed her. Sure enough, it did, and she relaxed slightly.

"I know a thing or two about dealing with mothers," he reminded her. "You ready?"

Tess swallowed and nodded once, taking one final look in the mirror and sending a silent plea to the busily splitting cluster of cells inside her to let her enjoy the evening. One of her best friends was getting married again. Tess wanted to celebrate, even if she couldn't have more than a sip of Champagne.

They had just gotten to the courthouse when Tess spied Delia. They'd picked Delia's dress out together, but seeing her friend in full makeup, her hair done, and with the perfect shoes, Tess was ready to fight anyone who criticized Delia for not wearing white.

As if Delia would have even if she and Meter hadn't already gotten married. Delia took life on her own terms, and sometimes, she rebelled for the simple pleasure of not conforming.

Not that she'd told Tess that in so many words when they'd started dress hunting. But she might have said something along those lines.

To be honest, it was more like, "I look like garbage in white. Fuck that."

The dress they'd found her was sleeveless, with a deep neckline and tight bodice that swelled into a tea-length skirt that reminded them both of pictures of women in the 1950s. Although it had some white and even some black highlighting it, the dress itself was a lovely dove gray that played nicely, if a bit unexpectedly, with her coloring.

Her hair, recently cut to the middle of her neck, was down in back but pulled up on the sides, and the late-day sun in the courtyard was catching warm walnut tones that Tess thought were new.

She told herself to be glad Delia hadn't gone red or purple again, but she seemed to be intent on being at least somewhat respectable.

"Hey," she said to Tess, giving her the once-over. "Looks good. Very Woolslayer of you to wear a dress more than once."

A man Tess didn't recognize stepped between them and handed Delia a bouquet. "Yeah," he said. "Here."

With a smile Delia took it. The guy vanished and Delia gave the flowers a confused look. "It's a nice gesture and I appreciate it, but…" She raised an eyebrow and swept her gaze around the courtyard, which was filling with people. Someone had put sawhorses up, and Tess knew she needed to get herself and Delia behind them before her friend was mobbed.

"I mean," Delia said, "I *have* a bouquet, and"—she raised the bouquet in her hand and gave it a sniff—"this one's from the homeless dude who sells them over on Center."

"What makes you think that?" Tess asked, taking the bouquet and sniffing at it. "It's nice."

"It is. Whoever supplies him—and I haven't figured it out yet, but I will—has nice flowers," Delia said. "And he's good to take pictures of, too. Very interactive with the people who drive by." She opened her mouth as if to say something else but must have thought better of it because she closed her mouth and started off toward the sawhorses, Tess moving with her.

"Here you are," Meter said when Tess and Delia were safely behind the barrier. "The rabbi's getting restless and has rightly pointed out that we can chat with everyone all night once we get the official part out of the way."

"Oh no we can't," Delia said, giving him a contagious grin. "*I* am dancing with *Mack* all night."

Meter just smiled. "Fine. You dance. I'll chat and the rabbi can go home."

"Good idea," Tess said, turning. "We need to get him out of here before Mack corners him and starts asking him a million questions about being Jewish."

"Is he still thinking—" Delia started to ask.

"Yes," Tess said as Meter put his hand on the small of Delia's back and gave Tess a look begging her to help move Delia in the right direction.

Mack met them under the wedding canopy. They were going to stand together as the witnesses, facing Delia and Meter and the crowd. Which meant a couple things, Tess thought: They were staring at the rabbi's back, and they were visible to the guests.

Again, she sent an appeal to her gut, begging it to let her get through the night without nausea or anything else that would announce her secret to the world. This was Delia's night, not hers.

Someone in the seats just outside the wedding canopy said something Tess couldn't hear, and Delia looked over her shoulder. "What?" she asked, her voice carrying. "You don't think Meter and I are close enough? How's this?" she asked and turned back around, then slid a hand under his tails.

Meter raised up on his toes as if Delia had just squeezed him. Everyone, including the rabbi, laughed. The rabbi made a joke and then got the ceremony under way.

The bride and groom shared wine, and then the rabbi asked Delia to hold out her index finger to receive the wedding ring.

Mack had been fascinated by this when Meter had explained it to him. Because she had to put the ring on the proper finger, herself, it showed her willingness to be married to him.

But Meter's younger brother interrupted in order to hand them custom wedding bands.

Tess touched hers; she and Mack had matching rings and on the one hand, it was just a ring. On the other, it meant everything—and theirs weren't nearly as custom as Meter and Delia's new rings.

Mack put his arm around her and she leaned her head on his shoulder, feeling sentimental and wondering how their relationship was about to change—until Meter's brother turned to the people watching and added a sales pitch for the family's jewelry store.

Delia groaned and Meter gave his brother a good-natured shove and the rabbi wrapped things up. It did seem strange without vows, but Meter had warned them there wouldn't be. "It's not traditional, we've already done it, and honestly? I don't want this to be a big thing," he'd said.

"Get you to that glass," Delia had said, but the look she'd given him was one Tess wasn't likely to forget. Her friend adored her husband, and that, Tess thought, stealing a quick look at Mack as the rabbi picked up the linen-wrapped glass that Meter was about to stomp into pieces, was as it should be.

Life was hard enough, even when you didn't have the Flahertys to fight. Having the right person by your side was the game-changer.

Mack gave her hand a squeeze and Tess decided it meant he agreed.

TWENTY

Tess

After the ceremony, everyone pitched in and folded up the chairs, just like if they were at a house party and not a relatively formal wedding. Meter's brothers helped move the loaded dessert tables forward and the sawhorses came down. It was time to party, drink, and eat too much dessert with Delia's fans, who she'd invited over social media to join her party.

Tess appreciated that the bartenders were supposed to be quick to cut people off. She had no doubt Noah and his team were watching the perimeter of the courtyard, and not for the first time, she was grateful to him and his devotion to Delia, even if he had odd ways of showing it sometimes.

True to their threats, Mack and Delia spent as much of the party as they could out on the dance floor. Mack loved to waltz and Delia's dance background, although it wasn't in ballroom, made them a natural match. Meter, Tess had known previously, was content to stand and watch—that might have been putting it kindly, as he kind of glazed over and maybe even drooled a bit—and Tess herself was feeling a bit too nauseous to try to match Mack's pace. So Delia and Mack it was—until Mack gave Tess's mother a spin, then Delia's mother, then Meter's, and then anyone who looked like they'd let him lead. Six-three Mack and five-nothing Sima made quite a pair, Tess thought, half expecting Mack to simply pick up the tiny biologist and make life easier.

Of course, he didn't. Mack was too kind to strip anyone of their dignity like that. And if he'd tried, Tess would have laid into him about it later.

Then again, if he'd tried with Sima, one of two things would have happened: It would have been a prearranged joke, or she'd have stood up for herself on the spot in a way that would have created a new city legend.

"You're not dancing?" Gray asked Tess at one point. He and Mom had been treated as invited guests, even though they hadn't been issued a formal invitation—meaning they'd been allowed behind the sawhorses during the ceremony.

"He and Delia have fun together," Tess said, trying to be casual but inwardly groaning. "And it's *her* night. If she wants to dance with Mack until the band goes home, I'm all for it."

Gray gave her a look. She gave him her best innocent face in return.

"Is that the *only* reason?" he asked.

Tess told herself that if Delia was going to borrow her husband, she could borrow some of her friend's sass. "Well," she said, lifting the hem of her dress and kicking a foot slightly forward so the toe of her shoe was visible, "these shoes are *not* good for dancing." She faked a wince. "And I can dance with Mack whenever we want," she added. "We *do* have an entire room at the farmhouse on reserve for exactly that."

Gray shook his head and wandered off, hopefully, Tess thought, to find her mother—and not speculate about why Tess was on the sidelines. It was actually, Tess thought, a pretty good place to spend the evening, especially when Sima came to hang out and brought some more of her siblings along for Tess to meet.

By the time the DJ was done for the night and had started to pack up, most of the guests had gone, the dessert tables were all but empty, and even Mack had had enough. He and Tess had pulled a couple chairs out of the stack and were sitting with Delia's brother Leon and some of Meter's five siblings when someone staggered into the courtyard.

His tie was crooked, he looked drunk, dirty, and disheveled, he was all but tripping over his feet—and he was calling Delia's name.

She and Meter had been talking to the DJ and she looked up. "What?" she called, then grabbed Meter's arm, the color draining out of her face.

Meter pivoted and put a hand on the small of Delia's back.

The drunk—who, as he got closer, seemed less drunk and more beat up—staggered over to Delia, his path anything but straight. "Help," he gasped and collapsed at her feet.

She rocked back on one heel. "No," she said and looked around. "Are you fucking kidding me?"

Mack stood up, craning his neck and starting toward them. He didn't need to tell Tess to stay where she was, but after he got to the prone person, she joined him.

The man looked a lot like the man they'd seen coming out of the house across the street from the rowhouse.

"Is this—" she asked Delia, looking from the man on the ground to her friend.

"The one and only Chad Flaherty." She balled her hands on her hips and looked around. "Noah!" she called to no one. "This is *not* a wedding present that I registered for!"

The big security guy bolted into the courtyard. "Dammit," he said, stopping on the other side of Chad and looking down at him. He toed the prone man gently. "We thought we were done with him when we dumped him at the hospital, but the dude's got—"

"A death wish," Delia said. She glared around the courtyard as if expecting someone else to show up too. If anything, the space was even emptier, the party definitely over.

Tess wondered what the head of security meant about dumping Chad at the hospital and being done with him.

"Actually, I was going to say he's got a pretty strong will to live," Noah said, widening his stance and crossing his arms over his chest. "He kept saying they'd kill him if we took him to the hospital." He shrugged. "Maybe he knows something we don't. Hold on—" he said and turned away, putting a hand to his ear.

"Tess," Mack said, putting a hand on the middle of her back. "Maybe we should clear out."

"Go," Delia said with a sigh. "You need your sleep." She raised an eyebrow and gave Tess a meaningful look, then paused and shook her head. "But first," she said and held out her arms.

Delia rarely initiated physical contact—Tess had noticed that even Meter was careful about where and when he touched her—but this was a bit of a no-brainer. "Thank you for doing this again," she said softly.

"Once a year?" Tess asked.

Delia broke the embrace. "No way in hell. I am done with this wedding stuff and not even Meter is worth a third one." She smoothed the fabric of her skirt. "I do like this dress, though." She cocked her head. "If I keep it, do you think I can wear it somewhere else?"

Tess plucked at the fabric of her own dress. "I do."

"Well, so long as Chad doesn't bleed on it, I guess," she said, looking down at the man. He hadn't moved. "Is he even alive?" she asked loudly. "What the actual fuck? A half-dead asshole. I know I said no gifts were necessary, but *this*? And who's willing to check up his ass for the gift voucher? We are *not* keeping this one."

Tess took the performance as her cue to leave. "Let me know what you learn and what you need," she said softly, leaning in to Delia as she spoke, but then straightening and holding a hand out to Mack. With a few waves and goodbyes, they left.

She glanced back one last time. Delia was standing over Chad, her hands back on her hips, her head bowed as if she were looking down at him. Meter stood beside her, his hand again on the small of her back.

Even from this distance, Tess could feel her friends' disgust. And honestly, Tess didn't blame them at all. Any Flaherty was the sort of gift no one needed or wanted. Including herself and Mack.

TWENTY-ONE

MACK

They didn't hear anything about Chad the entire next day, which Tess said was to be expected. Delia and Meter's family were having a brunch that morning at their new house, and they were all probably exhausted.

"I still can't believe all those people showed up—and no one got out of hand," Mack said, flopping on the couch and putting his head in Tess's lap. He was glad they'd stayed at the rowhouse again for the weekend, and when Scram curled up on his stomach, he felt a deep contentment he'd missed the entire time they'd been at the farmhouse.

Here, he wasn't the Mackenzie host holding everyone together—and being held together by everyone. Here, he was Mack, and Tess was Tess, and Scram was their cat, and it was the three of them and no one needed things or wanted him for anything. Here, he could just *be*.

Too bad it would all end in the morning, when they went back to the farmhouse for a week of work.

"Didn't you see the post where she invited everyone?" Tess asked, playing with his hair. She stopped to give Scram a few scritches, then went back to Mack.

He didn't mind sharing her with the cat.

"No," he said, thinking she should have known that. He stayed off social media. Usually, so did she.

"She said anyone who got out of hand was going to star in a Populated Portrait—but it was going to be the rare one that featured the asshole who ruined the party."

Mack smiled. That sounded like Delia. The fact that no one had been willing to test her showed how highly people thought of her—and how they valued the way she kept the Populated Portraits upbeat, positive, and happy.

"I vote we have a meeting of the minds tomorrow night, at the farmhouse," Tess said. "Us, Meter and Delia, Noah, maybe even Red. Let's see if we can figure out what all these pieces add up to. We've got the arson of the barn and the possible threat against the farmhouse, Chad trying to buy the place across the street, and now him showing up at Delia's wedding. *Someone* worked him over plenty good."

It was Mack's turn to give the cat scritches. "I'm going to disagree," he said carefully. "What's going on with Chad isn't our business—and you're the one who's said it. That we should focus on ourselves and our plans because if we get vindictive, we won't come out ahead."

"This is more of a trying to understand what's going on so we know how and where to shore up our defenses."

"We understand what's going on. Flaherty is trying to bring us down."

"Of course, but *why*?"

Mack shrugged, petting Scram, who was now purring. "Who cares? His reason isn't something we can change. It's *his*. We need to focus on this giant Mackenzie enterprise we've got going."

There was a loud thud on the porch. They both jumped, Mack gasping and letting out a small yell as Scram dug his toenails in as he bolted for safety.

"Go get him—" Mack ground out, rubbing his stomach as he shot to his feet and headed for the front door, expecting the next Flaherty-induced horror.

Tess was with him, though, as he opened the door. And he forgot all about the holes Scram had just put in his belly.

Taylor stood there. At their feet was the thing that had thudded: the records box they'd found right before the barn had burned and that no one had bothered to do anything about with everything else that had been going on.

"Shit," Mack said, looking at it. He rubbed the back of his neck.

"I definitely deserve a raise for this."

"Tell me you didn't carry it yourself."

"Oh, I did," Taylor assured him, pushing past him and stepping into the house, saying hello to Tess. "I'll let you bring it inside."

From anyone other than Taylor, Mack would have bristled and pulled rank. From Taylor, he deserved all this—and more.

"Tink—" he said over his shoulder, stepping outside to squat and grab the records box. The things were awful; about two feet deep and three feet long. Every time he encountered one, he wondered when accordion files had been invented and why Henry hadn't used something like that for all this paperwork.

Then again, maybe the point was that the boxes weren't easy to carry. That said, they had done a pretty good job of preserving all the papers inside them. Maybe the idea hadn't been to carry them anywhere but to keep them safe for the day someone decided to look through them.

He glanced over his shoulder, at the house across the street, before he heaved the box into the house, convinced he could feel eyes on him. It was his imagination, he told himself, but to be safe, he perched the box awkwardly on the stairs and pulled his phone out, sending a message to security to keep a closer eye on both of his houses.

Tess and Taylor were in the kitchen; Mack could hear them talking. Giving the records box one final glance and a hand held out to encourage it to stay put and not topple, he went in search of them.

They were looking at something on Tess's tablet, heads bowed over the kitchen table, and Mack paused and looked at them. They were two of the three people most essential for his day-to-day success, and he tried to make sure they knew it and that he appreciated them both.

Tess's hair was long, dark, and thick, Taylor's short and fine and, even though it was only the end of June, already sun-bleached golden from all their time outside. Tess was taller, broader, but that was because Taylor was a slip of a human, narrow and slight. And, of course, Tess was curvy while Taylor was much more androgynous. Tess also had about four inches on Taylor, but looking at them right then, all of that was interesting but not vital to who each of them were and what they did for him. That important stuff was all internal.

"Uhh—" He paused, surprised they continued to be oblivious to him.

"Hi," Tess said, whipping up so she stood straight, one hand going to grab a thin lock of hair that had found its way into her mouth.

Taylor was smirking as they straightened. "I vote yes," they said.

"I knew you would," Tess said, and Mack paused. They were plotting something, which meant he was the target and would find out soon enough. It was either something like the cheesy coffee mugs Taylor and Ellie would pick up at garage sales and make him use at the office, or it was something—usually clothes—that they agreed he'd like.

He knew better than to ask, but he couldn't resist anyway. "At least tell me if this is something that'll make me look good or like a fool."

Tess put a hand on his cheek. "Both, of course. Taylor, if you're going to head out, now's the time. Otherwise, I'm going to cook you something."

They nodded. "Don't put yourself out. I'll see you at work in the morning. Be good to my box! We spent enough time together that I think we bonded." Taylor paused and looked at Tess first, then Mack. "It's hard to tell, since it's not exactly sentient."

Mack groaned, thinking he should have seen that coming, and let Tess walk Taylor to the door.

He waited for her at the bottom of the steps. "If this thing and Taylor are now great friends, does that mean it's creepy if I bring it up to our bedroom for the night?"

"I think it would be strange even if Taylor hadn't bonded with it," she said slowly, giving him a look that meant she found this conversation to be not what she'd expected.

He took a deep breath and confessed to feeling like someone was watching him when he'd brought the box in.

Tess froze, her eyes wide, her lips slightly parted.

"What?"

"This is what the Flahertys are after." Her voice was soft, like she was afraid to speak at a normal level.

"Old Mackenzie records?" He wanted to scoff, but something about that felt... *right*. "But we haven't found anything they'd be interested in," he said equally as quietly.

"Except we're still missing at least two boxes," she said, "and we don't know what they're looking for."

"Tess. We think they were going to burn the farmhouse while we slept in it. Whatever it is, it's bigger than the records of the people Henry tried to give better lives to—and don't start about the women he raped. I know and I agree. Right now, I'm focusing on how the records are presented: as being about the people he helped."

As always, Tess growled low in her throat and Mack tried not to groan or roll his eyes or do anything else that would set her off. It wasn't that he disagreed: What Henry had done was wrong, immoral, unethical, and just flat-out gross.

It was like that part of him balanced out the better part, the part that was almost too good to be true.

"And we're off topic," he said, squatting to pick up the records box. He motioned to her to go ahead. "I don't want to fall backward and land on you," he said, grabbing a breath before she could protest. "And no, you're *not* more fragile than you were six weeks ago. I wouldn't have wanted to land on you then, either."

She only went up three steps before she stopped and turned to look at him. "Back on topic," she said. "There's something in those records no one's found yet, and whatever it is, the Flahertys know more about it than we do."

"You sound awfully sure of yourself."

"Because I am. Mack, I'm not kidding. The root of this whole thing is in one of those boxes."

"I hope you're right."

"So do I. Even though I know I am."

He nodded and motioned her forward, telling himself he admired Taylor for hauling this thing down the hill, even if they'd apparently tied some sort of rope around it—he had noticed the marks in the dirt covering it. Something this heavy, going downhill, would have wanted to create its own momentum and Taylor was strong and wiry, but Mack wouldn't have been surprised if this had been a tremendous hassle.

He reminded himself to do something nice for Taylor. They deserved it—and then some. A raise was pushing it, though; they were already so highly paid that if Mack wanted to give them another raise, he'd have to argue with the board over it.

Maybe a new set of NERF guns, Mack thought with a smile. A shopping spree for either new backpacking gear or clothes or...

He grinned.

There was one thing Taylor had said they wanted, over and over again: a personal chef who'd fill their freezer with premade dinners and show up and do it again when the freezer was empty.

That, Mack could make happen.

TWENTY-TWO

CHAD

It was two days after the last beating, but finally, Ford's personal bodyguard was letting Chad leave. He didn't even know where he was, just that the people had been kind and the bed was soft. The food was even good.

But Chad would have been happier without the interrogation by Ford's people. It wasn't like he'd been able to tell them much of anything. Just that Go-fer Stanley and Go-fer Miguel and Go-fer Luis had been working him over and his father had stopped them and told him if he would show up at the wedding, they'd stop beating on him.

But if he ran, he'd regret it.

Chad had noticed that he wouldn't *live* to regret it.

They'd broken ribs this time. And his nose.

His dad *really* wasn't happy.

As if Chad cared. With each beating, he just hated the man more. He'd told him that, too, when William had called for the first break in the beating. He'd told him he'd changed the bank account with the house funds in it because he wanted to stop being a Flaherty. He'd yelled more, too, spitting blood with each largely unintelligible word, his father's face turning redder and redder, his fists balling and unfolding and balling up again. Not that Chad's wouldn't have been if he'd been able to feel them.

He hoped he had splattered the old man with broken teeth and blood and spit. That it would never come out. That some cop would show up with one of those funky lights and find it. Chad's blood. All over his father.

William hadn't liked hearing that he was a failure as a father. He'd told the goons to have as much fun as they wanted, but to leave Chad alive.

And then the sadistic bastard had stood there and watched, finally telling them to stop so he could make his deal.

Chad's first attempt to get inside the courtyard had been interrupted by Ford's goons. They'd shoved him in some junker of a car and dropped him at the hospital.

He'd called a rideshare and gotten the hell out of there. The driver hadn't been glad to see he was supposed to risk getting blood in his car, but even though Chad told him most of it had stopped, it took a fat cash tip to get back to the stupid party. His father could pay him back for it; he'd never even miss it.

If there had been a point to crashing Ford's wedding, other than to be a dick and try to ruin her night, Chad didn't know what it was. From what he could remember, she hadn't been terribly ruffled, cracking jokes about the gift voucher and complaining she'd specifically asked for *no* gifts.

Chad remembered that. He remembered the smooth and quick way she had changed the focus of the situation away from him. And he of course remembered the way her voice had cut through him and encouraged him to fight the need to slip into unconsciousness; he hadn't been at the hospital long enough to get any of the good drugs. Or any drugs, come to think of it. They had to look at you first before they'd do anything else, and Chad hadn't even been there long enough for *that*.

He'd had to get to that wedding.

She'd always had that effect on him, from the moment he'd met her at o'dark hundred in the morning in Gentry's. He didn't even remember where he'd been before he'd been there or how he got there, but he knew he hadn't been at Journey's End. That wasn't his scene.

Still, it had been some hour in the morning, they'd both reached for the sugar container at the same time—it was one of those old-style ones that poured—and he'd had to look himself over for Cupid's arrows later on, it hit him that hard. She'd made him want to be a better man—at least at first, before he'd realized he was in over his head with her. Then he'd just wanted to get out.

Girl had a kinky side.

She was wicked smart, too. Not in the book smarts way so much as street smarts. The way she'd played him and his father proved that. Delia Ford was more interesting-looking than beautiful, but the real attraction was that she could walk through a nuclear war and figure out how to come out alive and ahead.

Simply put: He wasn't man enough. Not even close.

But once it was all over with her, he had begun to realize a lot of things. That the way he'd been acting wasn't as slick and admirable as his father had raised him to believe it was. That no one looked up to him because he was a Flaherty. That being kind wouldn't hurt and might even help.

Being an ass sure hadn't gotten him anywhere except on a lot of shit lists. It made him wonder how many his father was on—and he promptly told himself to give it up and not ask and not care.

For whatever reason, Ford's goons had put him up for a few days, given him a place to rest, even taken him to have his nose set and his ribs taped and given him the name of a dentist who could fix the teeth that had been broken, and who had done it almost immediately. They'd actually been kind, and he hadn't expected that.

But it hadn't come without a cost.

In exchange, they'd wanted to pump him for information. But he didn't have answers for them. He didn't know why his father had told him to crash the stupid party. "Maybe," he'd said, "he's just that pissed she stole his place out from under me and then sold it a couple months ago—and not to him. That sounds like a grudge he'd keep." It was honestly the only thing he could think of. Good thing they accepted that as the truth it was.

Then they'd asked what he knew about the barn at the old Mackenzie farm. "And *that* whole thing is why I'm trying to get away. Please don't ask me to go back there and suck up to him so I can report back to you." He closed his eyes. Doing that would be torture. Absolute torture.

When Ford's goons didn't ask him to do anything except talk, Chad decided it was the perfect time to officially be done with being a good Flaherty boy. Neal and Sophie had stopped telling him that he had power over his father, Neal refusing to talk to him at all and Sophie changing the subject whenever Chad brought it up. It was, he thought, as if they were telling him he was, indeed, as useless as William said he was.

For the first time, that was a relief.

"I know you said I can go," he said to the main bodyguard when the guy came by. The guy was beyond devoted to Ford, and Chad wasn't sure why. She sure wasn't putting out for him, and if she was, Chad wasn't sure this guy was up to it. Hell, Chad wouldn't have been sure her nerd was up for it, but apparently nerds came with kinky sides, too.

"You can," the goon said, his arms folded over his chest.

"Any chance you've got a place for me to stay for a few more days? Someplace he won't find me?" He gestured to himself. "I'm over this, man. I need out."

The guy pursed his lips and his eyes unfocused, and Chad wondered if someone was eavesdropping and talking to the goon via the earpiece the guy wore. "Stay here. I'll see what I can do. You want to leave PK?"

Chad paused. He hadn't considered leaving town, no.

"You don't have to. It'll just be harder on you if you don't."

"The only thing really keeping me here is that it's the only place I've ever lived," Chad confessed. He was too tired, too beaten up to try to be suave or in control. He just wanted a quiet life, to be thought of as a good person.

Maybe this was a chance. Maybe it wasn't. But it was the opportunity he'd wanted. "Maybe," he said, "once this is all over, I'll leave. But I gotta admit, I'm curious why the old man's suddenly beating me up every time I do something wrong."

The goon raised his eyebrows. "He didn't always?"

"No. And I've done a *lot* of wrong shit up to when this all started."

The goon frowned, then nodded. "A place to stay for a few days is gonna cost you."

"I'm not sure what I've got left," Chad said.

That was one truth that didn't hurt as much as he thought it would.

TWENTY-THREE

Tess

"I know it's not ideal," Tess said to Sima near the end of that week. The biologist wore lightweight field pants, a long-sleeved shirt, and was wearing a brightly colored multiclava around her forehead, holding her curly hair back. And hiking boots, of course.

"Oh, I know," Sima said. "I'm just wondering if we can go ahead and start the flock now anyway. They really don't need a barn until winter, and not at all if we get lucky with the weather, since we're not planning to lamb this year. And we can even make the argument that historically, not everyone had a barn at all." She tilted her head from side to side, as if considering something. "Then again, those little lambs are for *us* to eat, not the local carnivores."

Tess opened her mouth, then realized she wasn't sure how to answer that. She looked Sima over and finally noticed the sparkle in her eyes.

"What if we bring in sheep now but don't have an easy winter, or wind up needing shelter for an unplanned lambing?" Tess asked cautiously. This was something they needed to be prepared for, of course, if they were going to be successful.

Sima shrugged. "I mean, there's that empty front room in the farmhouse, right?"

Again, Tess opened her mouth to answer and realized she couldn't.

This time, Sima started to laugh, a deep belly laugh that was absolutely contagious.

"I'll let *you* explain that one to Mack," Tess said, giving her head a quick shake.

"He doesn't scare me," Sima said, sobering and looking down. It was, Tess thought, a strangely submissive posture. No matter how many times she'd seen Sima do something like this, it still struck Tess as out of character.

"He has his moments," Tess said, telling herself not to pry. Sima was an employee; she was the equal to any of the junior people at work.

Okay, she rationalized, she wasn't quite an equal to anyone in a junior role. She knew more about the farm than Tess ever would. If the junior people at the office knew half as much about how things ran as Sima did, they'd all be immediately promoted.

Sometimes, Tess thought, staring off at the burned-out section of ground and the debris that needed to be cleared away, all that was left of what had once been her barn, Port Kenneth was entirely too small. "What is he after?" she muttered, not even sure where the words had come from.

"Who?" Sima asked, a little more restored to herself. "Mack?"

"No," Tess said with a sigh. "Flaherty. What was he after that made him burn this down? It's a *barn*."

"You don't have the full history of this place," Sima said, and Tess got the impression she'd been thinking about this. "And everyone knows the Flahertys and the Mackenzies and that third family no one ever remembers founded PK. What if whatever it is goes back that far?"

"Oh, I'm sure it does," Tess said. "Mack's the first Mackenzie back in town in forty years. There's no way this is a recent thing."

"If the stories of the Mackenzie Treasure have lasted all these years," Sima went on, "why can't whatever's bugging Flaherty? I mean, beyond people of color and women and access to education and healthcare and..." She stomped over some debris and fallen boards into the middle of the area that should have been the center of the barn and turned in a circle, letting out a wordless yell. "This world is *so fucked up*, Tess. How do you stand it?"

Tess spent a long minute looking at Sima, then said, "I focus on the things I can control, the small little improvements I can make."

Sima let out another yell, not that Tess blamed her. "Don't you ever get *tired*? All you do is *good*. One thing after another. Business incubators. First one, then a second. Now this. And... and... and what else do you do?"

Tess just shook her head, trying to control a flash of temper. "Is that how people think of me? As some do-gooder?"

"You take care of Woolslayer like it's your own!"

"Well, it is," she said, wondering if Sima had processed the question she'd asked. Did people think of her as nothing but a do-gooder? Had she gone overboard with the good intentions? "Woolslayer belongs to all of us who live there."

She knew if she asked Mack if that was how people thought of her, he'd say no, and so would her mother. They'd both tell her she was doing what she thought she could to help make the world a better place. Gray praised her for it. Thomas told her he respected her.

Even though she wasn't due back in the office for another day, she told Sima she had to go, left a quick word with Taylor and her mother, and headed for the office. It felt strange to drive there—and even stranger to walk in after the daily meeting.

Red was free, so she helped herself to the chair in front of his desk.

"To what do we owe the honor? I thought you weren't here until tomorrow."

"I'm more than some do-gooder, right?"

"A do-gooder? No," he said. "A community activist who gets things done? Definitely."

"What's the difference?"

"Who you're doing it for. And why you're doing it."

"But isn't doing it for the Woolslayer community doing it for me since I live there?"

"Okay, Cartieri, what's really going on here?"

A fresh wave of nausea washed over her and she swallowed hard. "Everything," she said, "and you're not my therapist, so maybe we should leave it at that."

"Living through a pandemic isn't easy," Red said and rubbed a hand over the top of his head. Tess wasn't sure, but she thought she heard stubble grating against his palm.

She was immediately contrite. "Says you, whose wife has been debilitated by it."

"Yeah," he said heavily. "So don't fall apart *too* far on me, okay? I need you to bring in income so I can cover some of these medical bills."

"I must seem petty compared to Christine and everything you two are dealing with," Tess said softly, still kicking herself.

"I'm just grateful we hadn't had kids yet," he said quietly. "Maybe it'll still be possible, but who knows? No one knows what this thing has done to us."

"And if not, Mack and I are still working on that kid thing," she said, the words tasting terrible in her mouth. She was almost at the point where she wanted to tell people, even though the doctor had told her to wait until the twelve-week mark, and Mack had told her he thought that was the right move. "You can live vicariously through the little Mackenzie."

"That kid's destiny is *way* above my pay grade," Red chuckled. "Let me know when there's news on that front."

"Of course," she said, immediately feeling even worse. This hadn't been her intent when she'd walked in here.

"You feeling better?" he asked, wrapping a hand around his coffee mug and tapping it gently on his desk.

"No," she said, letting herself be a little petulant. With Red, she could. "I'm apparently some do-gooder, and I *hate* that."

"Yeah, Mackenzie hasn't been as disruptive lately as I'd hoped. Maybe I need to shake him up a bit."

"Good luck with that." It was, of course, the pandemic. And the latest nonsense with Flaherty, too.

He chuckled. "So you're saying I shouldn't even try to plant ideas; I should just come out and say them?"

"Yes, and still, good luck." She glanced around, thinking maybe more time in the office was better than any disruption could be. "He can be clueless, even when you spell things out."

"One of your favorite parts of him," Red said. "You here all day tomorrow?"

"Yeah. Job site on Monday, and then who knows? The biggest problem is that the Piston Building still isn't ready for full density workplaces yet, and that means it's just easier for us to stay at the farmhouse, but it's also harder to come *here*." She looked around again, glancing through the glass walls of Red's office toward the heart of their space. "And I miss being here."

"We miss having you here."

They looked at each other for a long minute, and Tess had a feeling that had just been settled: She'd be coming back to the office more often, no matter how inconvenient the commute was.

Somehow, that decision relieved her more than it worried her that she'd pick up the virus and bring it home to rampage through the family. Or the baby.

TWENTY-FOUR

Tess

Back at the farmhouse after work, Tess found Roger in the kitchen. "It's Thursday," he said when she said she hadn't expected to see him. "You know I like to make you dinner on Thursday nights."

All the tension Tess had been carrying dissolved somehow. "You have no idea how much I appreciate you," she told him.

He laughed. "Yes I do." But he sobered almost immediately. "I know it's the end of your workday and probably not the right time for this, but got a minute?"

"Not if you're quitting."

"I'm not so big a fool that I'd walk away from something this good. But I have been thinking."

"About?" she arched an eyebrow. This had to be big; it wasn't easy for him to talk about.

She pulled out a chair at the kitchen table and sat, but he continued to stand at the counter, prepping dinner. "Okay," he said as if he'd made a decision she hadn't been part of, "you know running these two houses feels a bit too much for me once you and Mack move permanently back into the rowhouse."

Tess nodded, having a feeling where this was headed. He had suggested previously that he might be interested in bringing in a crew specifically to clean the houses, and she hadn't argued with that, even though her mother had taken more than a small degree of ownership in this house. At the same time, while Mom was glad to do the cooking when Roger wasn't around, she had been clear that she viewed the cleaning needs of the farmhouse to be a full-time job.

"I want to incorporate," Roger said and beamed at her the way students did when they knew they were on thin ice but were hoping to charm their way into approval.

"Incorporate?" Tess asked, her thoughts immediately churning. "I thought you just wanted to oversee a cleaning crew here." The idea that he was thinking bigger, in all honesty, excited her and she suddenly felt less tired, more invigorated.

"I did," Roger said with a nod. He turned somber again. "But then I started talking to people in town, and an awful lot of them said they'd come work for me. And I know you're aware that all over, people are quitting their jobs and not wanting to work at all, so I'm flattered that people want to work for *me*. People need jobs, and cleaning and cooking and shopping is as honest a profession as it gets."

"Except," Tess said, holding up a finger, "that it's historically what the Black community does, working for their white employers." She paused and gave him a simpering look, even though his back was still to her and he couldn't see. "Anyone who works for either of us is allowed to use the bathrooms."

"I would expect nothing less." He gave her a sly look over his shoulder. "And a lot more. But it's not just the white folk we'll be working for. We'll work for everyone, Black, Hispanic and Latino, Asian, and Taylor's friends. We'll be the domestic answer to Overwatch."

Tess smiled, liking that idea. Noah was slowly turning Overwatch into an entirely new model of personal security and protection, and she liked that Roger was seeing ways to do the same with his business model.

The end of a pandemic, when the world had changed and contracted so violently and created so much upheaval and opportunity, was the perfect time for smart people to blaze new paths.

"Tell me how far you've gotten with all this," she said.

"I have people who'll do personal shopping and other errands, who'll come in your house and cook for you or who'll cook in their own house and bring it to you, and who want to clean and do laundry and iron. I can put it under one big umbrella and save people the hassle of trying to market themselves by themselves."

"But how many Woolslayers will be able to afford you?"

"I hope any who want us," he said and turned to face her, bracing his hands on either side of the sink beside her. "The idea is to provide affordable help. Maybe a little less than Overwatch, but we're not doing the same kind of work. We're an extra set of hands, a way to make things happen and ease some pressure on your day-to-day life."

It was exactly what Roger did for her and Mack. That was why they called him their house manager, not their housekeeper.

"So a new Black-owned business in Woolslayer," she mused, not bothering to hide her smile. She was known for helping women, of course, but that didn't mean she wouldn't help and support Roger if his business plan was sound. "What are your ambitions?"

"See where this ride takes us. And I didn't finish my reasons for why this will be different. Better pay and health insurance benefits, like I said. And flexible hours, which means time for doctor's appointments and things like kid activities, because that's what the people say they want. Fair wages. Health benefits. And time to be part of their own families."

It wasn't hard to understand, really, Tess thought. Red had always been good about letting everyone at the office have the time they needed, so long as the work got done. Mack had to be more rigid, just because of the nature of PharmaSci, but he'd also instructed his HR department to give grace where they could. And when he'd moved the company, he'd granted most employees the opportunity to stay in Lakeford and work remotely—before the pandemic had demanded the whole world adopt that business model.

"Maybe," he had said to her once, "if Cullen and Tristan had lived in a culture where family was more important than profit, if the board wasn't focused on profit above all else, they'd have been less shitty men. And fathers," he'd added with a glower that Tess understood.

"I just need to figure out how," Roger was saying. "I mean, I found some online business plans and filled in what I can. Can we make an appointment to go over them and you can tell me what I'm missing and where I'm falling short?"

"Of course," Tess said with a smile.

"I know I'm a man and all—"

"You're also my friend and someone I rely on. Of course I'm going to help—" She looked up as her mother bustled into the kitchen.

"Am I interrupting?" Mom asked, and Tess had a feeling she'd been standing on the other side of the door, listening in for the right minute to interrupt.

That didn't irritate her as much as it should have.

"Honey?" Mom asked, peering at her. "Are you feeling okay?"

"Just tired. There's so much going on." She gave Roger an apologetic look. "Don't take that personally in the least and don't think you're piling on; I always have time for you, and you know that. It's more that there's so much stress at work, and then here with the farm. If I had known how hard all of this would be, even before the barn got torched, I don't think I'd have been willing to do it."

"You could bring in an assistant of your own," Roger said, but Tess shook her head.

"There's not enough I could delegate to someone else. Everything needs *me*."

"You've delegated most of the work involved with the incubators," Mom said.

"And I miss them, too," Tess groaned, tilting her face up toward the ceiling. "Why am I so damn ambitious? What's wrong with me that I can't be satisfied with what I've got?" She turned to her mother. "Is this you? Did you mess me up like this?"

"I'd hardly say you're messed up," Mom said lightly.

Roger set a cup of tea in front of Tess. She hadn't even seen him get the teacup out of the cupboard, nor heat up the water. "Thanks," she told him, taking a sip.

It was peppermint.

She caught his eye. He winked.

Well, she figured, he was the man who emptied the trash. And of course, he wasn't a fool.

Then again, no one in this house was. Only her, for taking on so much and always refusing to say no.

She played with the tea bag, making it bob like a buoy. "Roger," she said, "I don't want to lose you if you do this business of yours."

"Oh, you're not. I'm still going to be your chef here on the farm on Thursday and Friday nights, and if April doesn't want to cook or if you and Mack need me at your place instead, you two are going to have to share me," he added with a smile that both Tess and her mother returned. "But the shopping and the cleaning," Roger went on, "I'm ready to turn over to more enthusiastic hands."

"When a baby comes, we may need you more," Tess said.

He nodded. "We'll figure it out. I can always hire more people."

Tess liked the way that sounded, although Roger was definitely high on her list of people she wanted in the baby's life. He had a lot to teach—and that included teaching her and Mack. Roger wasn't only valuable because he ran her errands and cleaned her toilets.

She fought the urge to run a hand over her stomach. If she did, of course her mother would see it, and then she'd pounce. It wasn't the time for that.

"Tess? Oh, good, you are here," Mack said, coming in from the main house, the way Mom had. He carried the cat and set him down on the kitchen floor. Scram, like he did every evening, wandered the perimeter of the room, sniffing here and there. But then he did something odd: He ran off to a spot between the kitchen and laundry room where he had lately taken to scratching. Tess had never thought cats were diggers, and he didn't do it at the rowhouse, but he liked something in that spot.

She added calling Xavier the Savior, the city's go-to exterminator, to her mental list of things the farmhouse needed, grateful she didn't need someone at both houses.

Small favors, she thought ruefully.

"I was coming to check," Mack went on, "if you were back yet. Anything happening at the office?"

She filled him in, Mom and Roger listening, and Gray wandering into the kitchen and sitting next to Mom. She and Mack both asked a few questions, but Roger just kept working on dinner and Gray listened.

"Where's Taylor?" Tess asked suddenly, looking around. She hadn't expected Thomas in the kitchen, but Taylor usually showed up to help cook.

"Wandering the cemeteries."

Tess caught her breath and Mack looked hopeful.

"What is that about?" Mom asked. "Taylor has no reason to be there."

Mack shrugged. "You know Taylor. If they don't get outside at least once a day, they're pretty crabby."

"They wanted to finally check out Jane's grave. I still think there's another records box under her headstone," Tess said, finally taking the tea bag out of her cup and wrapping it around a spoon. Gray had taught her that trick, and he looked on approvingly. "We *have* to find out where the last ones are and get them to Kiersten before the Flahertys manage to interfere again. I'm convinced, and Sima agrees, the reason the Flahertys hate us so badly is in those records."

"Why is Sima agreeing?" Mack asked.

Tess eyed him. "Because it makes sense," she said slowly.

He shook his head. "Why is Sima a part of this discussion at all?"

"Because I asked if she'd seen any signs of boxes as she's been moving about the property. And because we have to design and draw up the plans for a new barn. This directly affects her, you know."

Mack shook his head. Tess tried to ignore him. For one, she didn't owe him explanations; this was a farm matter, and Mack had turned all farm matters over to her and Sima. For another, the Flaherty–Mackenzie feud had swirled to include Sima. She needed the barn more than anyone else, and she needed to be sheltered from the Flahertys and their stupid games.

"Okay," Mack said. "I suppose I can see that."

"Suppose?"

He held up a hand. "I just hadn't thought about it this way, but I see what you're saying." Pausing, he ran a hand over his face. "Everything's a little more connected and convoluted than I think I'd realized. But right or wrong, I think you'll agree we need to find those last records boxes already—which brings us back to Taylor, who's looking at what you thought you found at Jane's grave. Can we please just start there?"

It was, Tess knew, as good as she was going to get. And it did make sense.

Time would tell if she was right or wrong.

TWENTY-FIVE

Chad

"I just want to move in already," Chad told Sophie, hating being frustrated, hating that he had to talk to her, hating everything. "Why is all of this so *slow*?"

She gave him a reproving look. "Dad's doing what he can to speed things up. The closing's already been moved up a couple weeks."

"What happened to thirty days?"

She shrugged, but Chad suspected she knew things. Of course she did. With the same regularity that Chad was starting to have to put up with beatings, she was being folded into William's inner empire. Maybe it was going faster for her, which was fine by Chad. He couldn't handle the beatings coming any more frequently than they already were.

And, of course, he had to be further punished for messing with the bank accounts. Sophie had at least been helpful with that, talking to William and somehow getting him to see something approaching reason. "But you'd better make sure," she'd told Chad, "that you *only* take that money out for the house."

He'd just given her a look.

"So what am I supposed to do once I'm in the house?" Chad asked, hoping he'd have some freedom and could figure out a job situation. Some cash that was his own and not Flaherty family money was definitely a wise idea. He'd never get free if he couldn't support himself.

Sophie shrugged. "He'll let you know."

Chad eyed her, deciding to risk it. Maybe she'd answer for once. "You and Neal still want to rein him in about this Mackenzie thing?"

"Neal?"

Chad froze. How had she not known?

"He talked to you, then," she said, her mouth twisting into a crooked line. She'd cut her hair recently, into a short style that powerful women often wore, the ends hitting just below her chin. It swung as she moved, and it made her look older—and powerful.

If she weren't his sister, he'd be scared of her.

"What did he tell you?" Sophie asked, and now her voice was quiet and rather deadly. Chad told himself to be careful; this wasn't his sister anymore. This was the woman who'd be taking over the Flaherty empire—an empire he wanted nothing to do with.

"Not much. Just that he'd be in touch."

She shot eye daggers at him.

He took a deep breath. "That was a while ago. Now, he tells me he doesn't know what I'm talking about."

"Glad someone around here has sense," she muttered. "As for you, butt out."

"I'm trying, but you and Dad won't let me. Remember?" He stood up. They had come to the park and found themselves a bench. It hadn't been easy;

the park was full of people who'd come out for an Independence Day picnic.

Chad had tried not to think about how much he and Sophie must have looked like a TV show, stiffly sitting on a park bench together, and he hoped no one was going to follow him out of the park and kill him. Or stab him and leave him for dead.

Hadn't he had enough of that at that stupid wedding?

"Are we going somewhere?" Sophie asked sweetly, still seated and looking up at him.

Chad shook his head. "You're turning into him by the day, you know that?"

"Which is why we need to shut him down before he goes too far and there's nothing left for me to take over."

He took his time, thinking. "That's all you care about?"

"Well, yeah," she said, giving him a guarded look and turning away from him slightly. "Once I get my hands on his empire, Chad, there's no stopping us. Think of what we can do."

"There is no *we*, Soph."

"C'mon. You'll be part of things with *me*. I'm going to change things up. No more of this racism shit, no matter how well it sells."

"Really." She'd get run out of town in two days if she tried to take the *Daily Record* to the left. The people into that shit *lived* it. And they weren't going to be thrilled a woman was in charge.

"Exactly!" she said when he pointed that out. "You can be the figurehead and I'll be the brains. We're *perfect* for this, Chaddie. You and me. We can rule the city."

"Except I don't want to. I want out," he said, just loud enough for her to hear. "I want to go my own way and do my own thing." Wasn't this the sort of thing a guy was supposed to say on Independence Day?

It seemed like it should be.

Sophie drew back a little. Her eyes got wide. "You know what he did to Mom…"

"You're not Mom. You have influence over him. And you know I want this thing with the house to be the end of it for me. Give me the house free and clear and I'm out of your hair. Forever."

And then it happened. She tilted her head and narrowed her eyes, just a little bit, and turned all calculating.

"Out, Soph," he said.

"You're my brother. I can't let you do that. But I *can* negotiate something better for you." The look she gave him was pure wheedling, but he wasn't interested, mostly because he had a feeling she'd just told him what that *something better* was going to be: him as the figurehead.

It wasn't appealing, being there only to shut up the people who didn't want a woman in charge.

"Better than getting the shit beat out of me routinely?" he asked, deciding to focus on her ambitions later.

She waved a hand so casually that Chad realized something: To her, the beatings weren't anything—anything worth thinking about, caring about, worrying about. It was zero concern of hers if he wound up like Mom—because she didn't believe he would, no matter how often Go-fer Stanley and the other two were allowed to work him over.

Chad disagreed with that, especially after this last one.

He ran his tongue over his newly constructed teeth. He appreciated how quickly they'd been repaired, but he didn't entirely trust the work. Maybe in time, he would, but right now, the memory of his jagged, broken teeth was too strong.

"I'll talk to Dad," Sophie was saying. "It's pretty obvious that all he's doing is pissing you off when what he's trying to do is intimidate you and make you fall in line. Clearly, he needs another, better tactic."

Chad snorted and turned in a circle, shaking his head. Obvious, huh? "Isn't the definition of insanity doing the same thing and expecting a different outcome?" he asked.

"Who cares? But if you'll work with me, I have more ideas. Maybe you can be more than a figurehead. What would you like to do with your life?" She widened her eyes and blinked a few times, playing the innocent.

It felt like he was exchanging one devil for another. And Sophie was probably going to do something like put an iron collar around his neck and tie the chain to her desk, then make him sit half naked beside her all day, both eye candy and proof of what a ruthless bitch she was. In a lot of ways, she was more dangerous than their father. She knew things about Chad that Dad couldn't even imagine. They had, after all, grown up together. Pampered, privileged, and until everything had gone sideways with Mom, both golden children.

"I'm not sure you're hearing me," he said.

"Chad. There *is* no out when you're a Flaherty. Not unless you want to wind up like Mom, and I refuse to let him do that to you—and he knows it, so save your cynicism about that part. Now shut up and listen to me. Help me solve this obsession with the Mackenzies and put his focus back on the rest of the business, where it belongs, and I'll do what I can for you. But there's no out. You need to make peace with that."

"There has to be."

She took a deep breath. The look she gave him was one of iron and steel. "Sorry."

She actually wasn't.

But he was.

Twenty-Six

Tess

It was a quiet, idle morning so far. Mack had wanted to sleep in, which was fine with Tess. When they'd gotten ready for bed the night before, she'd noticed lights were on in the house across the street, and she wanted to do some spying without Mack teasing her and telling her to just bake some cookies and carry them over to say hello.

She had no problems with that approach—except that Mack would eat at least half the batch. Even if she doubled it.

A group of three young men ran past the front window, throwing something in the yard across the street. With a frown, Tess sat up straighter so she could see over there.

The entire lawn was littered with something or other, and *the entire lawn* wasn't an exaggeration.

Tess got off the couch and called up the stairs. "Mack? You awake?"

His groan didn't fool her. He had probably been awake for some time now and was lounging in bed, scrolling something on his phone. He didn't get a lot of down time—neither did she—so she liked to let him have these few minutes when she could.

But come on. Something was going on. Trash didn't show up on a lawn in Woolslayer, let alone this much, unless the community had organized.

Tess was willing to bet people had found out who'd bought the house—and they weren't happy about it.

She really hoped it wasn't Chad Flaherty. But who else would provoke this sort of response—and who else would be a reason to keep her and Mack out of the loop?

Then again, she reasoned, she wouldn't be willing to be part of this harassment, no matter who it was directed at. Throwing this much trash on someone's lawn seemed cruel.

"Tess?" Mack asked, halfway down the steps. He had his hands braced on the walls and was bent over, sleep still crusting his eyes. Maybe he hadn't been up and on his phone.

"Would you throw some clothes on and come with me a second?"

"Where we going?" He sounded more awake and he'd straightened slightly.

"Across the street. Can you—will you grab me some shoes, please?"

"Any specific ones?"

"We're just going across the street." She smiled, though, touched he'd thought to ask.

"Am I right that you want them to at least match?"

Tess envisioned him rubbing the back of his neck as he looked at one of her shoe piles. At least they always started out with matched pairs. It wasn't her fault that Scram would toss toys in the shoes and turn it all into some kitty play area. He also liked to crunch the aglets on, especially, Mack's various sneakers.

"Yes please."

When he was dressed and she had shoes and they crossed the street together, they discovered that the lawn was absolutely strewn with trash. Fast food bags, bottles and cans, a donut box that may or may not have been empty, a couple of wrappers from Snickers bars, a broken flowerpot, and what looked like an old bicycle chain dangling off one of the porch lights. A broken umbrella, its ribs showing, had been planted in the garden in front of a shrub and three rubber ducks, two with holes in the tails and one that was missing a head, stood on the grass under the umbrella.

"Is that... a tent?" Mack asked, craning his neck to look at something up against the side of the front steps.

Tess looked up at the house. "Someone doesn't like our new neighbor, and I don't even know for certain who it is."

"What?" a tired voice asked. It came from in the house; the windows were open. "You're not exactly dumb, Cartieri. What do you want?"

"We're just standing here, looking at your yard," Mack said.

"It's quite an art show," Tess said, wondering if anyone would view this as art, and what Delia would think of it. She considered texting Delia and asking her to come check it out.

"Know why this is happening?" Mack asked and that easily, Tess knew Mack hadn't made the connection yet.

Well, she told herself, he wasn't quite awake yet. And she wasn't entirely certain, herself. A small niggle of doubt tugged at her.

"Because people hate me," the person said.

"That's... kind of obvious," Mack said. "I'm just wondering the *why* of it all."

The door swung open and Chad Flaherty stepped out onto the porch. "Happy?" he said, spreading his arms out. He was barefoot, wearing jeans and a white button-down, and his face bore signs of fading bruises. "Do I really have to humiliate myself in front of you, Mackenzie?"

"Uhh—" Mack said.

"Chad," Tess said, giving Mack's hand a squeeze and glad she hadn't texted Delia, "why are you living *here*?" Woolslayer was, rumor would have a person believe, entirely too diverse for the likes of the Flahertys.

He held his hands up. "Because my father's making me." He shook his head gently. "And don't ask why he wants me to. He won't tell me and I don't want to be part of it, so I'm not asking. Now or in the future. I'm done. I'm out—or as out as I can be. I'm living here and that's going to have to be enough for him." He turned his head and stared up the street. Another group of kids—or maybe the same group—was hanging around, laughing. They looked to Tess like they were marking time.

She had a feeling she knew why.

"I'd heard you didn't buy the house," Mack said.

"Well, I did," Chad said. "So what's your point?"

"How did you get here, and so soon, too?" Tess asked. "There's no way real estate transactions go through this fast."

His laugh was bitter. "Cartieri, your first mistake is assuming my father does anything the proper, *legal* way. He's almost as loaded as you two are, and he's not afraid to flash it around and make promises he'll never come through on in order to get what he wants. And what he wanted was *me* living *here*." He shook his head as if he couldn't quite believe it himself.

"To spy on us," Tess said, wishing she could walk over to him and escort him anywhere else. To have a Flaherty watching them, especially after they'd burned down the barn...

She rubbed her arms, feeling suddenly exposed.

"Relax," Chad said. "I'm not going to report on your every movement and who stops over to chat, or whatever it is you always-perfect Mackenzies do. Truth be told, I don't give two shits what you do, no matter how many times he lets Go-fer Stanley and Go-fer Miguel and Go-fer Luis work me over."

He closed his eyes and shook his head and somehow, despite herself, Tess believed he was sincere.

"Like I said," Chad continued, touching the bridge of his nose gingerly, "I don't care what he wants. I'm only living here because he evicted me from my last place and left me with no other options. I thought your woo-woo secret boy was going to help me get out from under this absolutely shitty life I'm stuck in, but I guess his woo-woo secret shit only goes so far. So here I am." He held his hands out again, indicating the property, then let them fall.

Tess had to think for a minute. *Woo-woo secret boy*? She wondered if he meant Noah.

Chad was looking around, turning in a circle and kicking at a can. "You know," he said, "people are working *hard* to let me know they don't want me here. And fast, too. I just got the keys yesterday and was out here until midnight, cleaning yesterday's mess up."

"If they were working *that* hard," Mack said, in the blandest, most conversational tone Tess had ever heard from him, "they'd be getting the backyard, too."

"Oh, they are."

"Maybe think about renting a dumpster if it doesn't stop?" Tess asked, eyeing Mack and wondering if he knew things she didn't. It was possible.

"But won't that just *encourage* them to dump their shit here?" Chad asked.

Tess doubted it, but then again, if she rented a dumpster, she'd turn it into a neighborhood trash removal, telling everyone it was her neighborly good deed and asking if anyone needed help carrying anything, or lifting it over the edge.

It actually wasn't a bad idea, she thought, biting her lip. Maybe as summer turned to autumn in a couple months… She'd have to start talking to neighbors now, though, and putting the idea in their minds. Surely they all had collected things during the pandemic that they now needed to get out of their houses. Or maybe they'd just had enough of the generational clutter that was in so many of their homes.

"Tess?" Mack asked softly, and she shook her head. They could discuss her idea when they went inside.

"Great," Chad said, and Tess thought she'd never heard a more defeated human being in her entire life. "Now you're making mental lists of what trash to add to the fun here."

Mack chuckled at that, and Tess had to smile, too. "Don't give her ideas," Mack told Chad. "C'mon, Tess, now that we know what's up, let's go back in and see what we can donate to the welcoming party."

A party wasn't a bad idea, either, and she led with that when they both got inside.

"Wait," Mack said slowly, as if he were trying to digest what she had just said. "You want to throw a block party to welcome *Chad Flaherty*?"

"It's brilliant," Tess said, reaching for his hand. "The message it sends, *again*, is that we're on the high road. We've got a Flaherty living in Woolslayer, so let's pull out the stops and make sure he's confronted with welcomes from the shiny, happy faces of all the diversity that the Flahertys hate the most."

She gave him a fake, brilliant smile and tugged gently on the limp hand she held.

With his free hand, he scrubbed at his face for a long minute, dragging one hand down his face and throat and grabbing his collar before asking, "And *when* are you going to have time to plan it?"

She waved him off. "I'm going to hire Patricia and Ebony and let *them* do it." She waited a bit for that to sink in, then said more softly, "Think of it this way: To some degree, we're still the rich, entitled whites who don't quite fit in. And now we've got the other half of the centuries-old family feud following us here. Who's next? We both know everyone's worried about that, the way real estate around the rest of the city's skyrocketing. Maybe Woolslayer can't help but gentrify itself, simply because no one can afford to live anywhere *but* here."

"We didn't bring Flaherty in, and we're not responsible for the surge in real estate pricing around town," Mack said and dropped a kiss on her forehead. "I know you love it here. So do I. But the world doesn't revolve around the Flahertys and if I have anything to do with it, the world will *never* revolve around the Mackenzies."

TWENTY-SEVEN

Mack

One pre-virus ritual that Mack missed was getting up before Tess on Sundays and heading over to Vera's for coffee and pastries. During the lockdown period of the virus, Mack had paid Vera for any pastry that hadn't sold during the day, something no one in the farmhouse had minded. Day-old pastries from Vera's still tasted good, and together, they'd kept a lot of small bakers in business.

Mack liked being able to have such an effect on a small business. He smiled; Tess had taught him well.

Another thing she'd taught him was that Sundays were her day to sleep in. He wasn't sure how it had evolved, but she got up early on Saturdays and he got up early on Sundays, and they each came up with breakfast for the other.

He was convinced he got the better end of both days: She cooked, like she'd done when they'd come in from dealing with Flaherty the day before, and he got to stop in the next morning and flirt with Vera. And eat her pastries while they were still fresh, which was a luxury he hoped to never take for granted.

He stopped on the front steps of his house, dumbstruck at the sight of Flaherty's. Four camp chairs were set up, along with two broken loungers, facing the front door. The umbrella was still planted by the shrub but instead of three ripped-up rubber ducks, underneath was a broken garden gnome and what had probably been a concrete porch goose. It was wearing a bright orange pumpkin costume, and in keeping with the spooky theme, it had no head or neck.

Neither gnome nor goose fit particularly well under the umbrella.

The yard was, once again, strewn with trash. More bottles and cans, more food bags and wrappers and boxes. It looked like whoever had brought the chairs had been watching a movie. There were even a few old-time red and white movie theater style popcorn boxes.

Mack hoped they hadn't set up a firepit.

Maybe, he thought, that was what they were going to use the backyard for. Flaherty had said the trash extended back there, too.

No one was around, so he set off for Vera's.

As it usually was on Sunday mornings, the neighborhood was quiet. People were just waking up, coming outside with their dogs, many still in robes and pajamas, almost all of them calling a hello to Mack, who waved back and called a greeting and, as he'd learned to do, said hello to the dogs, too.

Vera's was about the same, although the few people starting to trickle in were dressed. That was how Mack liked it: It gave him the best choice of pastry. For Tess, of course.

Vera had a box of their favorites ready and poured the coffees for him, full of the neighborhood gossip that he didn't care about—until she mentioned Flaherty.

Tess had put out feelers about the welcome party.

"Would you go?" she asked him.

He forced a shrug. "It's right across the street, and if it's when we're here and not at the farm..." He also resolved to open that box of pastries the minute he got home and eat Tess's favorite. Maybe while she was watching. Flaherty did *not* need a welcome party.

The man himself was already up and on his porch when Mack got back, a coffee in each hand and the bag of pastries hanging from his forearm and bumping into his thigh as he walked. The big bad enemy had his hands on his hips and looked even gloomier than he had the night before. He was also, Mack noticed, wearing only a pair of athletic shorts.

Guy needed a trainer.

Mack wasn't offering his services. He'd agreed to put together a program for April, but she was family.

Flaherty was anything but.

"Put on a stage show last night or something?" Mack called to him.

Chad waved his arms around, his mouth working. "Help," he finally managed.

"Hold on," Mack said, holding up the coffees, the bag with the pastries going along for the ride. He turned and set everything carefully on the lower steps, then turned back to Flaherty. "What's the problem?"

"Look," Chad said and scuffed at the edge of his front porch with a toe.

Mack hoped he wasn't being invited to look at the guy's pedicure. He'd seen enough grungy feet all those years of playing Ultimate. It was a definite downside to being an athletic trainer.

But as he got closer, Mack saw it. "Chalk?" he asked, giving the guy a confused look.

"It's… I don't know," Flaherty said, scratching at his chest. "Like someone was doing chalk art and left all this dust?"

Mack frowned and looked around. Nothing was immediately obvious. The porch was even free of trash, as if there were some rules everyone had agreed to follow.

"Hey!" Chad yelled suddenly, his attention beyond Mack. "Don't leave that here!"

"Word is you've given the okay to leave it in the"—It was Ezra, Mack saw when he turned, and the man was consulting his phone—"blue bucket near the driveway. Oh, there it is. Sorry 'bout that."

He dropped his dog's full poop bag in the blue bucket that was, indeed, near the driveway. It was at the end of it, next to the mailbox.

"I never said that was okay!" Chad yelled.

Mack motioned to him to keep it down. It was still early and besides, Tess was asleep. Being awakened by a testy Flaherty wasn't the way he wanted her to start her day.

"Tess might have been on to something with that dumpster," Mack said to Chad, whose face had turned red. Not just his face, either, but his throat was flushing, and so was the top of his chest. "Breathe," he said. "Not that any of us would mind if you stroke out, except I'd have to give you assistance, gross as that thought is, because you're not worth losing my license over."

"License?" Flaherty asked, and Mack noticed the guy was already turning back to his normal color. Or something Mack thought was more normal than the flush had been.

Mack eyed him and said nothing.

"I thought you're *the* Mackenzie," Flaherty sneered.

"I am."

"You need a license for that?"

"Yep," Mack said, hoping that would shut the guy up. "You want my help or not?"

"I don't— Hey!" Chad said, looking over Mack's head. "Hey, I don't want that, thanks! Don't leave that here!"

"The blue bucket!" the person called back, and Mack turned in time to see them drop a dog waste bag into the bucket. He couldn't help but admire whoever was behind this. They were organized, they were creative—and they were prepared.

This was next-level trolling.

Mack made a note to make sure he didn't tell Taylor about it.

"I don't care about some damn blue bucket!" Chad screamed and started to turn red again.

Mack started to chuckle but was stopped short by movement on his porch. Tess was up.

In fact, Tess had just taken a seat on the top of the lower steps, correctly guessed which coffee was hers, and was lifting the bag holding the pastry box onto her lap. "Wish you'd woken me earlier for this show," she called.

"Why are they doing this?" Chad screamed.

"Because they don't want you here," Tess called back.

Flaherty let out a wordless yell, his head thrown back, and stormed into the house.

Mack jogged back across the street and sat down beside Tess. He leaned in toward her, then knocked her shoulder with his.

"You're making nice to Flaherty?" she asked, lifting the box out of the bag. With the hand not holding the box, she gathered the bag and gave it a one-handed shake. It fell into something approximating its flattened state, and she tucked it under her leg, then set the box on her lap and opened it. Sure enough, she zeroed in on the apple danish and Mack winced as she closed her eyes and savored the first bite.

So much for him eating it before she could. Maybe, he thought, he'd have to ask Vera to give him two of everything next week.

"He asked for help," Mack said, picking up a pecan roll. "Although I didn't do much more than stand there and take it all in."

She leaned against him. "That's my hero."

He sighed and put an arm around her, looking across the street at Flaherty's house.

That's when he noticed what had been going on with the chalk. It was shaded and hard to see, but it sure looked like someone had chalked some sort of design on the globes of his porch light.

"Hold on," he said and got up to check.

Sure enough, that's what had been going on. The bike chain, at least, had been removed.

The drawing looked like a sunset. Mack hoped that wasn't a sign that someone wanted to sunset the guy. He seemed, so far at least, pretty damn harmless. And, possibly, more inept than Mack felt half the time.

For the guy's sake, he hoped it was just pretty art.

TWENTY-EIGHT

CHAD

"So what have you learned so far?"

Chad wanted to say *don't fuck with Woolslayers* but didn't think that was what his father and Sophie wanted to hear. In fact, he was quite sure his father didn't want to hear that, although Sophie might at least smile. "Cartieri's pretty hot, actually."

William flicked his fingers and Go-fer Stanley showed up with a chair. Chad took it but immediately wished he hadn't. While he'd been standing, he'd been looking down at his father—which was probably why the chair had appeared. No one stared down at William Flaherty.

But now that he was seated, Chad realized he had to look up, just the tiniest bit. Which gave his father yet more power over him. He made a mental note to tell Sophie not to play these sorts of games, although he doubted she'd listen to him. She was too caught up in the power trip already.

"And? How can we use this tidbit of information?" William asked.

Chad shrugged, knowing his father was going to suggest one of two things. Both were bad choices. "I don't think we should. She's tougher than Ford, Dad, and you saw how easily Ford outmaneuvered us—"

"You." The word felt like a brick of iron.

Sophie widened her eyes at Chad. It was a warning to not go there, but he didn't care anymore—and she knew it.

"She's Ford times ten," he said.

William flicked his fingers, waving the warning off. "She could learn a lot from an affair with an older man," he mused.

Chad tried really hard to snort. He was only partially successful.

His father looked at him, one eyebrow raised. "Do you have something to say?"

"I want a job," Chad said. "A real job, one that has nothing to do with Mackenzie."

"And I want the Mackenzies run out of town. One thing at a time."

"You know what Mom would say if she were here?"

His father's face fell as fast as Sophie's went white. It was like a shutter had slammed over William's face, exactly like Chad had known it would. But it was better than sitting here and listening to this garbage. He wasn't going to try to start an affair with another woman who'd eat him alive, and he wasn't going to let his dad think he could, either. If that meant bringing Mom into the discussion, so be it.

"Do. Not. Mention. Her." William punctuated each word by banging his fist on his desk.

Chad stood up. Sophie was still staring at him, stricken, and now she shook her head, her lips pressed together, her eyes wide and begging him not to do this.

"Mom," Chad said and started for the door, hoping he was faster than Go-fer Stanley. "Mom!" he yelled as he pulled the door open. "Mom! Mom! Mom!" he screamed as he flung himself down the stairs, afraid to risk waiting for the elevator.

He sprinted back to Woolslayer, arriving out of breath but also grateful and yet surprised no one had come after him—hopefully that was Sophie's doing. He bent over, hands braced on his knees, and waited to catch his breath and for the fear of being shot in the back to leave him.

"Hey, mister?" he heard.

He looked up. It was a little Black girl, her hair in pigtails that stuck out to the sides, a little brown floofy dog at the end of her leash. He'd seen her around. "You the guy with the blue bucket?" she asked.

"Yeah, sure, kid," he said, still huffing and trying to find his breath. "It's right there by the mailbox." He pointed, not bothering to look, staring at the ground in front of his feet.

She walked over. "It full."

Chad straightened up and joined her, taking one deep breath after another. "It is," he said, marveling at how fast that had happened and at the same time knowing that what he was about to do made him the worst Flaherty ever. He was okay with that. "Here." He held out his hand for the girl's dog's poop bag. "I'll be better about that."

There was, it seemed, a lot he was going to need to be better about.

But it still wouldn't make him enough of a man to sucker Cartieri into an affair.

His dad was on his own with that one.

TWENTY-NINE

Mack

It was the following Sunday, and Mack knew he shouldn't do it. He knew Tess wouldn't be wrong about anything she said when he got back.

But she was distracted and if he was fast, she'd never know.

He slipped outside, the bag in his hand, and darted across the street. The blue bucket was still there.

He put Scram's used kitty litter in it.

"You too?" he heard from the porch. "Of course," Flaherty answered himself. "Why should the Mackenzie be any different?"

Mack couldn't help it; he stiffened. Flaherty had a point.

"Ever notice," he said as conversationally as he could, "that the rules don't apply to us... until they do?"

Flaherty huffed.

"I mean it," Mack said.

"I'm not okay with anyone using the blue bucket, and I'm especially not okay with *you* doing it."

"Exactly. The people who say we live by a different set of rules than they do are right," Mack said, trying to sound like he'd thought about this for longer than the past ten seconds. "It's just that they're wrong about how. And which rules are different—especially here, in Woolslayer." It was a warning, but it was up to Chad to understand that.

"Are you *trying* to be all buddy-buddy with me?"

Mack wasn't sure, but he thought he heard a disdain and entitlement in Chad's voice that hadn't been there any other time they'd spoken. Like Chad was reverting back to being the privileged Flaherty and not the broken man Mack had been seeing of late. He wasn't sure if that was a good thing or not.

"Maybe," Mack answered, figuring maybe a civil conversation would lead to good things. "I mean, we have things in common, even if we're standing on opposite sides of the same fence."

"Well, take your things in common and take your cat shit and go somewhere else with it."

"I get that this isn't easy, but don't shoot your allies. You don't have many of us," Mack said, looking the lawn over. It was worse than ever. More food, more beer bottles and cans; it looked like some high schooler had had a party and this was what was left the morning Mom and Dad were due to come home. One of the shrubs had even been doused in silly string, the can abandoned with the string still attached.

"Some allies, I can live without."

"You sure? Because I don't think you're winning this one."

Flaherty was quiet for a long minute. Mack counted to ten, then turned to go. Of course, as he did, Flaherty spoke. "You need to see what they did out back."

Mack hoped the slides on his feet would be protection enough from anything that had been dumped, that there wouldn't be any needles he needed to worry about. But he followed Flaherty around to the back.

There was a firepit, all right. And it had been used.

It just... wasn't round anymore. He could see the marks where it had sat, and he cocked his head, taking in its new shape. "For real?" he asked Chad and started to laugh at the man's expression. "How do you sleep through all this? They can't be quiet when they're turning your firepit into a dick and balls. That took some serious work. And cooperation."

"I... never mind," the guy mumbled.

Mack gave him a mild look, trying not to assume it was pills or pot, and shoved his hands into his shorts pockets, pretending to think. But the truth was that Tess had been on to something with the dumpster because if this kept up, mice and rats and other animals would find their way to the yard, and then Flaherty would have bigger problems. "Remember Tess's suggestion? It may not be a bad idea." He knew he'd said it before, but he was willing to push a bit harder this time. "If you do it right, you can turn yourself into a good guy, instead of a dick." He tilted his head at the firepit. It looked like there had been three small fires: one in each ball sac and one at the head.

Whoever had done this, they deserved points for creativity.

He still wondered how Flaherty had slept through it. Hell, he wondered how *he* had slept through it, although it wasn't like his backyard and Flaherty's were close.

"No Flaherty has ever been a good guy," Chad said, and his voice was thick with some negative emotion Mack didn't want to get too near.

He forced a shrug. "Be the first. This one's not that hard. Rent a dumpster. Keep that blue bucket there. Empty them both frequently."

"And who's going to help me fill the dumpster with the trash they throw on my lawn anyway?"

Mack gave him a level look. "I hear you don't have a job."

"Ouch."

"Am I wrong?"

Flaherty's shoulders heaved with the breath he took. "No."

"Then get busy," Mack said and raised a hand to clap the other man on the shoulder. He stopped himself before he made contact, wondering what he was doing. Instead, he picked his way across the littered lawn and went back to the house.

Tess was waiting for him. "I thought you were cleaning Scram's pan and taking it out to the trash," she said.

"I did. Stopped to see our buddy," he said, tipping his head and trusting that Tess knew who he was referring to.

"Oh," she said, then did a double-take and peered at him. "Why?"

"Honestly?" Mack said and rubbed a hand over his face, giving her a bleak smile. Why did she get to judge? Last he'd heard, she was funding an entire housewarming party for the guy. "I think he's kind of lost. And your idea of a dumpster was a good one. I told him that." *Twice*, Mack thought, but kept quiet about that. It didn't matter how many times he said anything. What mattered, really, was if the guy heard him or not.

Tess twisted her mouth up. "Think he'll get one?"

"I think he might, just to handle the volume of trash out there. They got his backyard, too."

She looked out the window, presumably across the way to Flaherty's yard. "I like the lawn chairs."

Mack grimaced. "I meant to ask if he'd discovered where the chalk dust on the porch came from."

Tess gave him a look, like she didn't understand what those two things had to do with each other, so he explained.

"Hunh," she said. "Are you ready? As much as I don't want to be at the farmhouse for dinner—or even until after work tomorrow—we need to be there before dinner."

"What's wrong?"

"The nausea," she said heavily, reaching for a bag of cat treats. He took it from her and called for Scram, giving the bag a shake. "The older generation's figuring it out, I swear."

"Oh," Mack said, calling for Scram again. "Where is he?"

"Mack. I think we're going to have to tell them."

"We are," he agreed. "And we will. Just maybe not tonight. Scram! C'mon, buddy! It's carrier time!"

The cat finally appeared, trotting into the room, his tail up. Mack went over to the cat carrier and knelt beside it, bag of treats in his hand.

The cat sniffed Mack's leg and went in the carrier, turning to face the door.

Mack put four cat treats inside and closed the door, leaving it on the floor until Scram had eaten all the treats.

"Can you pay attention to me?" Tess asked. Mack told himself he deserved her impatience.

"I am. You're worried our secret's out. It probably is." He flicked his gaze to her. "Besides, I know you told Delia and Meter, which means Jamie and Hank know, too."

She waved him off. "That was different. And it's only Delia who knows."

"Seriously?"

"Yes," she snapped.

"Okay," said, satisfied that Scram had finished his treats. He slipped the latches and lifted the carrier. "If you're ready, would you grab my laptop bag?" he asked her, but she already had it, along with hers.

They stopped and set the alarm, then moved to their cars. Mack put Scram on the front seat of her car and leaned over to kiss Tess. "See you at the house."

She gave him a peck and a nod that he knew meant she wasn't happy. He was sure he knew why: She was worried about telling the family about the baby and what might happen if they lost it, and she was worried about leaving the house empty again all week while Flaherty was across the street, being tempted to try to break in. And, he reminded himself as he watched her back out of their parking area, she hated the longer drive times from the farmhouse to pretty much everywhere else, but especially the office.

That, he figured, he might be able to do something about. Maybe it was time to propose switching back to their old pattern: spending the week in town and the weekends at the farmhouse. The only reason they hadn't made that switch yet was because Taylor was staying at the farm during the week. And, okay, Mack admitted, Tess was still working more closely with Sima than she wanted to admit. That was two reasons to stay at the farmhouse during the week. Two good ones, in fact.

But maybe they could spend more nights during the week in the city and let Tess and Sima work on the farm on the other days. There were, after all, five work days in every week, not that farming was a profession that let a person take the weekend off.

Mack wondered if Tess would be able to coordinate that with her duties at the office. That was, after all, her primary job. Everything else was supposed to be secondary—emphasis on *secondary*.

Flaherty was in the yard, cleaning up trash, as Mack backed out onto the street.

For whatever reason and prompted by something Mack wasn't quite aware of, he raised a hand and waved. He could imagine his mother saying, "Why would you *not* be kind to him? Emerson, there's a treasure trove of information right there to be harvested."

She wasn't wrong.

But also, somewhere along the way, it had been ingrained in him. Be kind. Raise that hand in greeting. It costs nothing and keeps you on that high road, and the practice to stay there is always useful.

Flaherty just stood in his yard, hands loaded with other people's garbage, staring after Mack as he drove up the street, headed for a week of work and life in the farmhouse with his family. If the guy was jealous, Mack thought, it was fine by him.

THIRTY

Tess

Tess was first to arrive at the farmhouse, which wasn't surprising. Nor was finding her mother alone in the kitchen. The fact that she was cleaning up after baking cookies was a bonus. "I think Mack's got a new playmate," she said, setting Scram's carrier down and evaluating the kitchen, as always. For all that the oven had just been on and it was a hot day, the room was cool enough. That pleased Tess; getting the house comfortable wasn't always an easy task. It hadn't been built for the twenty-first century; hell, it hadn't been built *in* the twenty-first century. Or the twentieth, either.

"Is this wise?" Mom asked when Tess had finished explaining about Chad Flaherty.

"Which part?" Tess asked, crouching to let Scram out of his carrier although he hadn't been meowing or rattling the carrier door. As usual, he began exploring the perimeter of the kitchen.

Absently, Tess opened the pantry door so he could make a circuit in there, too.

"Any of it," Mom said, glancing out back. Tess looked too; Mack usually wasn't that far behind when they were both coming from the house, and she hoped he hadn't stopped to talk to his new buddy again.

Then again, anyone from the neighborhood could have flagged him down, even just to say hello.

It was possible Mack had stopped to be neighborly and instead was getting an earful about how and why he couldn't fight with Flaherty. Not that he would even without the peer pressure.

"If it's smart or not," Tess said and blew out a breath, "depends on who you ask. My gut instinct is that it's never wrong to be kind, and it's never a bad idea to hold the enemy close—there's a reason that's a saying. And Chad does seem... lost." That was the part that intrigued her the most.

If she listened to her gut instinct—which wasn't hard because it was screaming pretty loudly about this—the picture she had of Chad was that he didn't want to be doing whatever scheme his father had cooked up this time.

That was both a relief—because maybe he wouldn't let it happen—and terrifying. What if he was supposed to do something like burn down the rowhouse? And what if he tried?

A wave of nausea washed over her, and she had to wonder if it was from the pregnancy or the idea of what a fire in Woolslayer would do to the entire neighborhood. Her rowhouse was isolated, the houses on either side torn down long ago. Maybe their house would be the only one affected.

Just the thought of losing the rowhouse was enough to make her want to throw up. She loved that house; she had since she'd first laid eyes on it, even before Mack had come back into her life. Every day, she was grateful he'd been willing to live there with her.

Scram trotted out of the pantry, rubbed on both Mom and Tess as he strolled past, and headed for the dining room.

Tess wondered what he was up to. But before she could follow and see, Mack pulled into the driveway.

"I think," he said as he walked through the door, "we need to prioritize finding those last records boxes. The more I think about it, the more I think that's got to be what Flaherty is after."

"Oh, so now you're willing to admit I might be right?" Tess asked, swallowing her nausea and shoving out of her head the lingering thoughts of Chad and his mission. Her indignation, she decided, was justified.

Mack looked properly chagrined. "I should have sooner," he admitted. "But I needed some time to think about it."

Tess grabbed his chin, pecked his lips, and patted his cheek. "I'm always glad when you want to think things through, but please just come out and say so instead of leaving me frustrated because I think you're too set in your opinion to change your mind."

"But then we don't get to have romantic moments like this," he said, catching her around the waist.

She put her hands on his chest. "Do we actually know how many boxes we need to find? And can we finally come up with a way to settle the question about Jane's grave already?"

"So much for romance," he muttered and ducked to give her another quick kiss, but she glared at him, so he straightened and said, "No, we're not sure. She's guessing two or maybe three, but it's only a guess. I think it's based on something she found in one of the records she's been through so far."

Kiersten had, Tess thought, been working pretty darn hard on all the records they were sending her, almost as if she too was caught up in the stories the Mackenzies had left behind. Tess wondered how compelling the stories were—and when she'd get to hear them for herself.

"I wish I knew what she was basing it on," she said.

Mack watched her for a long minute.

"What?"

"She's our employee," Mack said slowly, like he was trying to will her to understand.

"I'm aware," Tess said in equally slow tones, not sure what he was trying to tell her.

"She'll tell us everything when she's ready, and she's not playing games with us," Mack went on, still slowly, as if he was leading her to a conclusion. He widened his eyes and tipped his head toward the kitchen door, and Tess understood.

He was referring to Thomas.

"But," Tess said softly, glancing at her mother, who was busy making dinner, "you've seen how insulted he is that he doesn't know this stuff."

"And according to him, he *should*."

Tess had no real answer for that; honestly, there was too much to say. The issue of Thomas and his involvement with the Mackenzie history was something Tess didn't fully understand. Why had Mack's grandfather Cullen picked Thomas to be the steward of most things Mackenzie but leave him in the dark about so much of the family history? Unless Cullen hadn't known the history, either. From what little Tess had heard about Cullen, that wouldn't surprise her.

"As for Flaherty," Mack went on, his voice still slightly lowered, "I suspect he's figured we're digging up history, and Mackenzie history includes Flahertys."

"But so far, nothing really has involved them."

"Are we sure?" Mack asked. "We've only asked Kiersten to focus on the Mackenzie Treasure. Maybe she knows more about the Flaherty feud than we've thought to ask her about."

Tess opened her mouth and then closed it again, furrowing her brow. "Maybe we should," she said slowly.

"Okay, you two," Mom said. "You're in the way. I need to get dinner moving."

Tess whirled. "I'll help." She motioned Mack away from the fridge and opened it, peering inside. "Or… maybe not," she said, straightening and, a hand on her upper stomach, ran out of the room. Of all the lousy times for the nausea to really kick in, she thought as she flung herself into her home office—for the simple reason that, other than the dining room, it was the closest room to the kitchen.

She sank into her desk chair and leaned her elbows on the desktop, her hands holding up her head, and breathed.

Mack followed her. "Well, the good news is that Mom just looked at me and told me if you're not pregnant, she's a fool. And she's no fool."

Tess swallowed hard, trying not to think about how much saliva was flooding her mouth, or how thick it was.

"Those women who do this more than once or twice," Tess said after the nausea had started to ease. "How do they put up with this?"

"I have no idea," Mack said. He was in the doorway, blocking it, and he leaned out slightly, turning his head toward the kitchen and dining room. "You okay? I think Scram's picking at the floor by the washing machine again."

"Yeah, but..."

Mack shrugged. Before Tess could wonder if he'd known what she was going to ask, he said, "Own it."

"Guess I have to. What's with Scram?" She swallowed one more time before getting up and following Mack into the laundry room.

The cat had gone from scratching at something by the washer and had opened up an out-and-out hole between the floorboard and the floor. He had one paw in it.

"Maybe we need an exterminator?" Mack asked. "Scram, get away from there."

The cat looked up at him and meowed.

"Scram," Mack said, taking a step forward and picking up the cat, who immediately squirmed in his arms with increasing violence until Mack said "okay" and opened his hands.

The cat dove out of his arms and went right back to his hole.

"What is he doing?" he asked Tess, who was watching the cat thoughtfully.

"Scram, that's really not a very good idea," Mack told him. "I think that floor is original, and Tess isn't going to be happy with you."

"It might be original to the room, but the room's not original to the house, remember." The kitchen had actually been built nearby but separate from the main house, either to keep the enslaved out of sight of the main house or, more likely, to insulate the privileged Mackenzies from the heat generated by cooking. The laundry room bridged the kitchen and dining room, a placement that Tess had always thought was awkward and had been derived from practicality—especially since the entire house was a practical house and not a place for entertaining the way the Mackenzie Manor up in Lakeford was.

"So what's he doing?" Mack asked.

"He's found something he's curious about," Tess said, raising a hand in a helpless gesture. She didn't know much about cats; when her dad had been alive, they'd had a dog, but when Dad had gotten sick, they'd had to give it away. And Jamie and her mother and stepfather had always had dogs.

The cat had been Mack's idea. And she didn't regret having a cat, but that didn't mean she understood them, either.

"C'mon, buddy," Mack said, carefully picking him up again and this time, carrying him out of the laundry room.

Tess followed, shutting the door behind her and closing the cat into the larger space of the original house.

Scram immediately began trying to open the door, shoving his paw underneath. He looked at Mack and Tess and meowed.

"Maybe take him upstairs?" Tess asked, hoping Mack wouldn't get bloody for trying.

"I think we have to," he said and reached for the cat again.

Tess reached for her phone. Surely someone she knew would have advice about a cat—advice other than *don't clean the litter pan when you're pregnant*. She'd heard that one already.

She had barely sent the message when Scram came tearing down the stairs. Tess ran over to the bottom of the steps, hoping Mack wasn't lying in a heap on the landing, but he was braced, hands on the wall and feet on the edges of the stairs, eyes wide.

"Are you bleeding?"

"Maybe." He carefully pulled away from the wall. "But we'd better investigate what he's after because I don't think he's going to stop until we do."

It did look that way.

THIRTY-ONE

Tess

"Enough of this," Thomas said at dinner a few hours later, putting both hands on the table and standing slightly, so that no one would ignore him. "Every single one of us at this table knows what a pregnant woman looks like, Tess. You aren't fooling us."

Tess glanced at Mack, who had closed his eyes and covered his face with a hand, adding his second hand the longer the silence dragged on. He wasn't going to be any help.

"Then there's nothing to talk about," she said lightly. "But if we're going to acknowledge it, do we think, Mom, we can change up how we're eating a bit? I... I just can't handle... *flesh* right now." She gave everyone a weak smile. "I figured that one out at the office the other day. And what's weird is that I can do sushi."

Thomas frowned. "Raw fish?"

"Highest quality," Mack said, putting his hands in his lap.

"When's the due date?" Mom asked.

"We think around St. Patrick's Day," Tess said, mimicking Mack's posture. "But it's too soon; we haven't been to the doctor yet. That's in another two weeks."

"Any idiot can calculate a due date," Thomas groused, and Mom shushed him. He winked at Tess.

"It's polite to let the doctors do their thing," Mack said mildly.

Tess turned to him, mouth slightly open but the words too jammed up to come out. Coming from him, that was rich, and he probably knew it. He'd overstepped more than once in this whole *knock Tess up* project.

Not that her doctor had minded, and not that Mack had messed anything up. He *was* an athletic trainer. That had counted in her doctor's mind, even when Tess had discounted it herself.

Gray cleared his throat, putting on an innocent look.

Mom laughed, and so did Tess, who wanted to tell him he was in the wrong branch of medicine, but he was a lot closer than Mack was. He'd at least gone to med school and done an OB rotation. Mack had just asked a lot of questions and read a lot of things suggested by both Gray and Tess's doctor.

"Well," Thomas said, "it's still too early for full congratulations, but I for one am glad a baby's on its way. And that it's time to talk about it," he added with a nod, holding up his fork, a piece of cooked beef on the end of it, in a sort of salute or toast.

Unfortunately, the sight of the beef set Tess's stomach off again and she raised her face to the ceiling, gasping for breath, as if that would calm the nausea. Strangely, sometimes it did.

Most of the time, it didn't. She kept trying anyway, just in case.

"Oh. Sorry," Thomas said with a chuckle and Tess could imagine him sticking the fork in his mouth.

"Me too," she gasped and was out of her chair and running for the front stairs.

Mack took his time coming to check on her, but when he did, he brought a peanut butter and jelly sandwich and an apple, both of which she attacked.

"Oh, you are the best," she moaned, her mouth full and eyes shut. It really was the perfect meal.

Mack moved aside the book she'd been reading and sat down beside her. "Hey, once you've eaten, will you come watch while I dig around at the floor? Scram's doing serious damage in there; he just won't stop."

That was what Tess had wanted to try to problem solve, so as she sat on the bed, one leg stretched out in front of her, she pulled her tablet over and tried to search answers to what the cat was doing; none of her friends had had advice. "Maybe we should call the vet?" she asked after a bit.

Mack, who had been reading something on his own tablet, looked up and frowned. "Why don't we just check the hole and see if there's something he's after?"

"Well, of course, but let's be real. What are we going to find?"

Mack shrugged. "A nest of snakes. Mice. Some toy he's decided he can't live without and has to dig out of the hole it fell into. I don't know. He's Scram."

As if on cue, Scram poked through the cat door, looked around, then trotted over to the bed and jumped up, rubbing his cheek against Tess's toes, purring loudly.

"Yes, Scrammie," she said, tickling the top of his head, "I do feel better. Thank you."

He turned to her and took her hand in his mouth, gently, held it for a second, and let it go.

Tess laughed. "What was that?"

Mack reached for the cat. "I have no idea. C'mere, Scrammie. Tell me what you're doing downstairs, other than ruining a nice floor." He rolled onto his back and set the cat on his chest.

Scram hopped off Mack and strolled away, pausing before he jumped off the bed and went straight for the cat door.

Mack made a wordless sound of disbelief, which caused Tess to laugh. "You know he hates that," she said.

"Are you done eating? I want us to take a look at that floor."

"Fine," she said, biting the last apple slice in half and handing him the uneaten piece. "Lead on."

He waited for her, holding a hand out. She wasn't sure if he wanted the plate or her hand, so she awkwardly shoved the plate into it. He took it with a small nod, as if that was what he'd wanted, then ushered her out of the room.

"I wish we could keep him in here somehow," he said, glancing at their closed bedroom door.

"The whole point of putting a cat door in was so he'd have his freedom—and not bug us to open the door."

"Or ruin the floor," Mack said gloomily, and Tess wondered how bad it was.

It wasn't bad, but it wasn't something they could ignore, either. Tess knelt on the floor and got busy examining what she could see.

"I need a flashlight." She grimaced. "And maybe my yoga mat." She fingered the hole Scram had made, not surprised when the cat showed up and pushed his way between her knee and the hole and started picking at it again, his front paw curled, his claws out. "You want whatever's in there pretty bad, huh, buddy?"

He meowed as if he'd understood her. He did that from time to time, and although Tess knew there was no way he was actually understanding and answering, sometimes, it sure felt as if he were.

Mack handed her a small Maglite; they had them tucked into spots all around the house in case the solar panels didn't provide enough juice to get them through the night.

Tess took it, turned it on, and bent forward to investigate, gently pushing the cat out of the way. He didn't take it well, growling and turning to glare at her.

"Scram," she said, not expecting him to understand, "if you let me look, I can help you get to whatever you want."

"Here," Mack said and, when she leaned to the side, bent down and grabbed the cat firmly, as if anticipating another fight—which he got—and carried Scram to the bathroom, putting him in with a promise that it wouldn't be long.

Tess bent back over the floor. "Well, this is interesting," she said when Mack came back. "This floor's not nearly as old as we thought." She frowned, fingering the splintered edge. "In fact, get me something I can cut a chunk off with, will you? I'll take it to the office and see if anyone has ideas." She frowned and looked more closely at the floor. If she had to guess, she'd say it had been replaced not long before they had learned about the house—which meant Thomas had ordered this floor.

But he continued to say he knew nothing about any flooring renovations.

Tess was starting to suspect he wasn't playing games, like she'd first assumed. Rather, she was growing increasingly convinced he hadn't paid as close attention as they'd all—including him—had assumed. There had been a few other things that had also been changed, as if the caretaker Thomas had hired had slipped a few renovations in and gotten Thomas to rubber stamp them. Thankfully, none of them were objectionable or had been bad for the house. Maybe the caretaker had truly *cared* about the old place.

Tess could understand that. There was something special about this house.

But the inconsistencies made her wonder what had been going on under Thomas' nose—and how to get the old codger to admit that maybe he'd been played. Not that most of the work had been done cheaply, this floor aside. It was a floor in a laundry room; Tess wasn't sure she'd have asked for anything of a high quality if she'd been in charge.

"What do you cut a chunk of floor with?" Mack asked. "And hey, are you going to take the house apart?"

"Why do you sound so scandalized?" she asked. "Or is this one of those moments where you're being reminded that I'm doing something you know nothing about and you hate that?"

"Just Tess." He sounded wounded. She gave him a minute and tried to peek through the hole until he asked, "Will this change if the house can be declared historic?"

"No."

He was quiet for a long minute, then he said, "Maybe we should do this tomorrow?"

"When? I have to be at the office and you have a company to run."

He shook his head, hands on his hips.

"I'll be fast," Tess said. "I bet it's a toy he's shoved down there and we'll get it back, I'll have someone come out and fix this hole, and that'll be it. We'll be done with all of this."

"And how are you going to close off the hole so he doesn't keep digging until we can have it fixed? What if there's some big cellar down there and he falls in and we have to rip up the entire house to get him back?"

"Mack." Tess sat back on her heels and glared at him. "Is this what you're going to be like as a father? Because honey, let's start working out custody schedules." She narrowed her eyes and pursed her lips, strangely ready to rip him limb from limb. Hopefully this was just pregnancy hormones at work.

"A baby won't rip up the floor," he said sullenly.

She sighed and told herself to be kind. "Just get me lights, okay? And as for Scram, we'll put something heavy over the hole, something he can't move. He's a twelve-pound cat; it won't be hard to block this off."

He hesitated, but she could see from the look in his eye that he was going to give in. She pointed at the door and raised her eyebrows.

It only took him a minute, during which both Gray and Mom came to see what was going on. Tess was explaining when he came back, pausing to look for an outlet for the light but handing over a hammer and screwdriver.

She wasn't going to say anything in front of Gray and her mother, but she was quietly impressed he had known where the tools were kept, even if he hadn't made terribly helpful choices.

In a second, she'd popped off a small piece of baseboard and used the hammer to widen the hole, although the pieces of floor she broke off weren't much good for identification purposes. The ring light Mack had brought proved to be good ambient light, but she needed the Maglite to be able to see underneath the floor. She took a minute, pressing against the wall as much as she could to lengthen the angle of her vision and the light, but it was hard.

Still, she could see enough.

"Well, shit," she said, sitting back on her heels and grinning. "Macaroni, I do believe this is the sort of pay dirt we'd been hoping to find."

"The records box?" he asked.

"That, I can't tell, but from what little I can see, it looks like a root cellar." She pursed her lips as she looked around the room, envisioning the house before the laundry and dining rooms had been built and the kitchen connected to the house. It made sense. It absolutely could have been a root cellar.

And that would have made it an excellent hiding place for the records boxes.

"We might have hit the mother lode," she said.

"But it might be nothing?" Mack asked warily.

"Might be. Maybe whoever was around back then removed them. Or, just maybe, they moved the boxes down there." She held up her hands. "There's only one way to find out."

THIRTY-TWO

CHAD

"Chadwick."

"Dad."

"Care to explain?"

Chad swallowed hard, wishing he hadn't answered the phone. His father *never* called; he'd only picked up because thought the man had news of Chad's mom. "I... can't." And he really couldn't. Delia Ford *hated* Woolslayer, hated having to spend any time there, hated everything about it. That's why she had come off as such an easy mark.

But clearly, she'd been back in Woolslayer, and up the street, too, not even visiting with her friend Cartieri, because that was the angle of the picture: Up the street, not across from Chad's house, which would have put Ford on Mackenzie and Cartieri's property.

The problem was that she'd caught him, his work gloves on, standing by the blue bucket and talking to the little Black girl with the pigtails and the little floofy dog. She was beaming up at him like she was telling him something monumental—but really, Chad thought, she'd just been thanking him for keeping the bucket there because Floofy's poop bags were *so heavy*, she'd said with an exaggerated sigh, hunching her shoulders and hanging her head until her fingers all but dangled on the ground, a drama queen of the ages.

The picture was probably from right before she'd gone all drama queen.

And he'd never seen Ford and her damn camera.

Even worse, he'd been laughing. He looked delighted by the kid.

It was hard to believe Ford had even taken a picture of *him*; her rules for her weekly social media post celebrating Port Kenneth clearly said she featured normal, regular, everyday people—and she had a moratorium against including people she knew personally. And as much as Chad wanted to be invisible and a nobody, he was a Flaherty, and Flahertys were Port Kenneth royalty.

Not to mention that he and Ford had shared... something.

His father currently wasn't saying anything. Chad figured it had less to do with the fact his kid was featured so much as his kid was featured *being nice to someone who was Black*. But what did he expect, making Chad live in Woolslayer? The neighborhood was the poster child for tolerance and diversity, and everyone in town knew it. Chad was merely trying to fit in.

The fact that the kid was cute and funny and gave him something to actually look forward to in the daily hell of his life was something else entirely.

"This was a good chat, Dad," Chad said as the silence dragged out between them. "Thanks for calling."

He hung up and, with a shake of his head, went outside to clean up more trash. The dumpster was being delivered in the morning, but even if it wasn't, the trash was already lessening. Almost as if his quiet cleaning had made the game lose its fun. Maybe his dad and his public shows of force weren't always right.

Even his porch lights had been washed, although that had only lasted a day before they'd been decorated again, this time with rainbows and hearts. He hadn't been impressed and had been tempted to tape a note to the side of the house, something about them being late for Pride month. If he'd been able to word it so it didn't sound like... well, a bigoted Flaherty... he'd have done it.

His phone vibrated but he ignored it, taking it out of his pocket and setting it on the top step. His father could do whatever he wanted. And maybe he'd acknowledged that Chad had *some* leverage, since he had backtracked and actually was paying Chad something like a stipend along with the money for the house, but once the garbage situation was under control, he was going to do something he'd never done before: Chad Flaherty was going to find a job.

THIRTY-THREE

Tess

It was three days after the discovery of the possible root cellar, and Tess wasn't amused—because her mother wasn't amused.

Then again, Mom wasn't bothering to hide her frustration.

"Mom," Tess said, "what do you want me to do? Crews are booked out right now, and this is, by comparison, a small project."

"You said you'd pull some strings and get someone in here," Mom said, putting her hands on her hips and glaring.

Tess stood up; she'd been seated at her desk when Mom had walked in. "I'm trying." She swung her monitor around. On the screen was a list of names, each followed by a date. "I've called thirty different contractors and handymen. I've promised premium pay, bonuses—hell, everything but health insurance including vision and dental. It doesn't matter. Between people putting off things they'd wanted to get done around their houses and supply shortages, contractors are booked months out and honestly? I would hate to be the family who gets bumped because someone would rather work for Mack and Tess and be able to brag about getting in good with us." She took a deep breath and leaned against the edge of her desk. "Although I've told them all that if they have a delay or need to fill a few hours to just give us a call and we'll take care of this, no matter how short notice."

"Honey, we all need to be able to get to the laundry. I know it may not seem like a big thing to you, since you and Mack can take your things to the other house, but the rest of us don't have that luxury."

"Has Gray put his house on the market yet?" Tess asked, pushing off her desk and moving behind it again. Distraction was always a good choice with her mother, although there was more to the question.

"Gray is still"—she paused as if trying to choose the right words—"in the pipeline."

Tess sighed, not sure what that was about. "Is he trying to game the market for optimum return?" It didn't feel like something Gray would do, but Tess couldn't imagine any other reason for his reticence. He'd said more than once he hadn't been living there long enough for it to feel like a home yet—and he'd said more than once during the time they'd been shut in together that the farmhouse did.

"I don't think so," Mom said cautiously. "And we were talking about *this* house and what the people who live here need." She gave Tess a strong look.

"I know," Tess said, raising her hands and wondering how the tactic had failed; maybe she had misunderstood how badly her mother wanted this done. "I'd rather not carry laundry between the houses, either; it'll only be a matter of time before we get confused about what's where. But I can't wave a magic wand and bring in people who can rip up the floor. And before you say anything, I really have been trying. I'm about ready to burst into tears and talk about the baby."

Tess couldn't imagine any scenario in which she did that. Cheap manipulation wasn't something she liked to resort to—and given the choice, she'd just as soon wait for the right contractor. It was true they were in a bit of a hurry to find the records boxes and learn if there really was information about Flaherty in there, but honestly, that was a self-imposed deadline. Or a Flaherty-imposed thing, as much as Tess didn't want to give the man that sort of power.

"And you have no idea how tempting it is to just grab a crowbar and rip this floor up and see what's hiding under there," she went on. "I'm holding back out of respect for you and the need to do laundry."

When she didn't get an immediate answer, Tess turned back to her desk. She only lasted a minute with Mom not moving before she said, "Mom?"

"I'm trying to think about what your dad would do. He was handy around the house; I don't know if you remember."

"I do, but this is more than being handy around the house. We have to make sure we don't fall through, ourselves. Our laundry room is sitting over a cave; let's not get hurt in our rush to take care of this."

"I know," Mom said, touching her forehead with her fingers in a gesture Tess knew was a note to herself. "It's just..."

"I know. I want to know too."

Thirty-Four

Mack

"Just Tess," Mack hissed two days later, gesturing wildly between the remote PharmaSci office and the laundry room. "I can't be in two places at once." Why was she doing this to him? She knew he wanted to be there for this.

"So stay and work. There's nothing any of us can do besides watch anyway." She rose on her toes to kiss the tip of his nose.

He closed his eyes as she did, feeling like she was humoring him and hating that she might be. "I'm the Mackenzie," he reminded her, opening his eyes and refocusing on her. "I should be there."

"So you can, what? Bear witness to the removal of a bunch of cheap floorboards? Woo. That's *such* a responsibility. The company you need to run? That's nothing next to cheap floorboards!"

"Tess—"

"Go," she said, turning him and giving him a shove toward his office. "We've got this."

He growled, wishing Taylor would save him—which of course his assistant did, granting him half an hour so he could watch the start of the demolition of the floor. The crew Tess had managed to find was... interesting, to say the least. They were also the last people Mack had expected to wind up hiring.

Delia, of all people, had come through with a contractor, who had suggested they do it today, since it was Friday and he had the time. Tess had been on board with that so they could spend the rest of the weekend in the rowhouse. She'd overruled Mack, who'd hesitated. It felt rushed, and he wasn't happy about that part, although he was grateful to Delia for saving the day—and for letting him spend the weekend alone with his wife. Now that they had the freedom to choose between being alone and being with people, he was realizing how often he preferred being alone with Tess.

As for the contractor Delia had found for them, maybe that was a large part of Mack's hesitation. Tess hadn't known him, either, she said, or she'd have called him sooner, but Saul Ford not only came recommended by his daughter but had a long resume that had satisfied Tess.

Saul was now semi-retired, and Delia and Leon both were with him, dressed in jeans, long sleeves, and work boots despite the summer weather, Delia's hair pulled back in a severe dancer's bun. The sun was pretty merciless outside; Mack imagined the solar panels were working overtime. Good, he thought. Any little bit to help the environment was a good thing, not to mention that all the lights Delia's dad needed would be fully charged. Hopefully that meant the job would get done that much faster.

"All of you," Saul said, turning and pointing at the group who'd crowded the doorway, "stay behind that yellow line on the floor. The three of us will do the work without your kind help."

"Mack, no staring at my ass," Delia told him as she took the crowbar her father handed her.

"Or mine," Leon added, giving his hips a shake.

"What did I say?" Mack asked, turning to Tess, who smiled at him and patted his cheek. He raised his eyebrows at her and she nodded. At least he had permission to stare at *someone's* ass, although at that moment, he'd rather stare at records stored away in their older-than-a-century metal boxes. Boxes he hoped beyond anything were down there. *Soon*, he told himself as Saul started to give directions to Delia and Leon, who nodded and did what he said without any of the usual sassy comments Mack was used to from both of them.

As the three of them worked together, an obviously practiced team, Mack looked at Saul; they'd been introduced so briefly at Delia's second wedding that he'd barely had time to do more than say hello and shake the man's hand. He was built like Delia: compact and strong. Leon must have been built like their mother, Mack figured, as he was leaner and less stocky.

For a second, Mack played with the idea of what the baby would look like. With his luck, it was going to come out looking like Tristan and he'd have *that* reminder staring him in the face for the rest of his life.

He glanced at April, who stood with Gray—closer to Gray than normal, he noticed. But he hoped the baby would look like her and Tess. Or maybe Krista.

Anyone but Tristan. Mack looked enough like him as it was, with his dark hair and broader build.

With a sigh, he put his hand around Tess's waist and drew her close. She'd been handling the almost constant nausea well, he thought and smiled as she leaned against him. And she wasn't vomiting, which was easier for all of them to deal with.

They could do this. They could produce a healthy heir to PharmaSci.

Saul, Delia, and Leon worked in tandem, ripping the floor up. They'd already moved the washer and dryer out to the porch, much to April's dismay; that had been the first thing they'd done. Mack was surprised by how competent Delia was, as though this sort of work was second nature to her, but he hadn't had a chance to ask her or Tess about it.

He went back to his office, sat through the end of a video meeting he wasn't needed for, and escaped again to check on progress, only to find Delia paused, sitting back on her heels. "You two should finish this," she said to her dad and Leon and, without her hands, levered herself to her feet, shaking out her legs.

"Out of practice already, sis?" Leon asked, flashing a quick grin before turning back to look at the floor. Most of it was up; it wasn't a large area.

"We're running out of room," she pointed out. It was true: Leon and Saul were shoulder to shoulder, and their movements were coordinated. Crossing to her dad's toolbox, she picked up what Mack realized was a familiar Hydroflask and took a drink.

"Didn't expect I'd be helping, huh?" she asked, coming over to the doorway.

"No," he confessed, wondering if there was anything she couldn't do. He'd thought she was a photographer who had originally wanted to be a dancer.

"When we were old enough, Dad would take us on any jobs he could; he wanted us to be as capable as possible—that was how he put it, but what he wasn't saying was that it would be a fallback career."

"Was I wrong?" Saul asked, lifting his head. He must have broken rhythm or something because Leon grunted.

"Absolutely not," Delia told him, then turned back to Mack. "He had a deal with the landlord, where he'd do stuff in the building for a rent reduction. We *could* have had a bigger place," she said, narrowing her eyes and giving her dad a look. "And then when I got sick, it was the only work I could get, because I could only work a day here, a day there and no one minded too much." She took a deep breath and shook her head, and when she spoke again, she did so more softly. "This was going to be my future once it was clear dance wasn't going to be. And it's good money, sure, but to work with Dad all day and go back home to living with Dad and…" She took a deep breath and stared up at the ceiling for a second.

Mack waited for her, but she bent down and moved her dad's toolbox into the doorway. "The subfloor's next," she said. "But not all of it, of course. Enough for anyone to get down there safely." She straightened. "I guess if you think about it, I'm just built to be creative. Contracting's a sort of creativity, and dance and photography definitely both are." She turned her water bottle in her hands, her attention seemingly on it, although Mack wasn't fooled. "I picked up a camera more as… I don't know. Something to do. A different way to see the world, I guess. You know: not out of my eyes, just in case things looked better through eyes that weren't mine."

What the proper reaction to that was, Mack didn't know, but Taylor showed up and saved him. As did Saul, who asked Delia if she was getting paid to chat up their boss and waste his money or if she was going to get started on the subfloor.

"He's got money *to* waste, Dad," Delia said as Mack, with a chuckle at that, turned to go back to work. "He may as well waste it on us instead of, I don't know. Handing it out to the homeless dudes who work the corners downtown. The one guy? Who wears the fake Army jacket? He's a raging alcoholic. You give him cash, he drinks it. Give him food, he throws it out. Offer to help him get into a shelter or rehab and have a better life and he threatens to kill you."

Mack paused. He knew who she was talking about; the guy had seemed perfectly nice to him. He'd been meaning to ask Tess if she knew anything about him. "Really?"

"Yeah. You've never talked to him?" Delia grunted as she did something with the floor. "Leon, gimme that—yeah. Thanks."

He wasn't surprised that Delia had spent time talking to the homeless guy. She hid it, but she had a big heart and invested in the people around her. Wasn't that the whole push behind her Populated Portraits, where she insisted she was showing off Port Kenneth at its best? Delia cared a lot more than she let on—which was probably why she and her brother and father were currently ripping up his laundry room floor. For money, sure, but none of them had to be doing this.

As he took his place behind his desk and gave Scram a pet when he jumped up, looked at Mack's camera, and blinked as if saying hello to the person on the other end of the video chat, he hoped that Delia would rub off on his kid in that way.

The world needed more people like Delia Ford.

He reminded himself not to tell her that.

THIRTY-FIVE

CHAD

Well, Chad figured as Sunday morning stretched long, at least someone had used his dumpster for their old couch. And since they had, he now had somewhere to sit. It was beat-up, of course, the springs not cooperative, the cushions sagging. But it was better than sitting on the hot metal bottom—or the trash he'd managed to get into the dumpster before he'd been given a message: Quit acting like the trash you are.

He wasn't sure which he hoped for: rain or a hot, sunny Port Kenneth summer day. Either way, he was stuck out here, exposed until Go-fer Stanley and Go-fer whoever showed up and let him out. He didn't have either his watch or his phone, so he had no idea how long he'd been there, but since it had gone from being dark to being light out, it hadn't been forever. It just felt like it.

"Hey!" he yelled as trash flew over the edge of the dumpster and hit him. He untangled himself from it and investigated. An empty coffee cup and a bag from Vera's Café.

"What you doing *in* there?"

The walls of the dumpster were over Chad's head, so he figured whoever it was also couldn't see in. Which was what made this such an excellent message from his father. Not only was he trash, he was trash that was invisible. And completely dependent on his old man.

That idea made Chad shudder. No matter how hard he tried to get free, his father kept reminding him it wasn't allowed.

"Got any ideas how to get me out?" he asked the voice, wishing he could mention the names of his basketball buddies—Hyron, Larry, and Enrique—and they'd magically appear. Even if they'd never let him live it down, they'd figure out how to get him out of there.

That was what friends did, right?

Although he wasn't sure they were actual friends. Maybe they were simply basketball buddies.

"No, but I know who will," the voice said. "Don't go nowhere."

"Like I have anywhere to go?" he muttered and kicked at some of the plastic water bottles that had accumulated at the bottom of the dumpster. He'd never thought much about water bottles before, but looking at them now—and the way they reflected the sunlight, shooting bright shards of light into his eyes—Chad suddenly understood what a waste they were. He resolved that once he was out of here and had gotten a shower and probably picked up his lawn once more, he was taking an entirely new approach to the meaning of trash.

There was motion by the couch and Chad held his breath, hoping his dad hadn't ordered a few snakes dumped in to keep him company; that was something William Flaherty would do, especially if he was pissed off enough. Chad turned to look at it more closely.

Nope, definitely not a snake.

It was a small cat, orange, maybe not a kitten but maybe a kitten; what did Chad know? What even was the difference between a small cat and a kitten?

Eyeing it, he took a seat on the far end of the couch, away from it. The couch tipped slightly under his weight and the kitten-cat jumped slightly.

It stalked over to him, sniffing and watching him, ears up, something about it wary.

"I feel exactly the same way," he told it.

The wait for the voice's idea of help wasn't long. "Flaherty, that you in there?"

It was, of course, Mackenzie.

"It's the Tooth Fairy," he said back, feeling as tired and drained and defeated as always. Of all the people to come bail him out, it *had* to be Mackenzie? His family's mortal enemy was, once again, coming to suggest solutions?

Or had they put him up to the dumpster, just for this moment? Of being stuck inside, humbled, helpless, and embarrassed?

He thought back to who he'd been before he'd gotten involved with Delia fucking Ford. No one had even *thought* about embarrassing him. He'd been invited to some of the best parties in town, had done some of the best coke a plant could grow, had partied with people whose influence had gone beyond PK. His dad had approved.

And he'd been a major dick.

After that first beating, the one for losing the condo to Ford, Chad had begun to see himself differently.

But all the different views of himself weren't doing him any good. He was stuck in his father's world and desperately needing to get out. Even Sophie wasn't a help; she just wanted him to be what she wanted him to be.

Which wasn't himself.

The cat-kitten thing had run at the sound of his voice. It stood on the far arm of the couch and looked out onto the carpet of garbage. Chad didn't blame it for not taking the plunge and wondered if maybe he should.

"We're a little old for the Tooth Fairy. I think," Mackenzie answered like he'd had to stop and think about it. "What are you doing in there?"

"Do I really need to answer that?"

"Well, you *might* have tried to pull something out and wound up falling in."

"I wish," Chad said with a heavy sigh. "No, my dad sent his goons out before dawn to break into my house and interrupt yet another night's sleep." The worst part, he thought, was that he'd been sleeping really well since he'd moved in—mostly because his father had promised he wouldn't send his goons in. That Chad was on his own out here in the wilds of Woolslayer, with all the *diverse* people. William Flaherty wouldn't lower himself to have even his thugs be in Woolslayer, even though they'd probably grown up here. Or in nearby Larimer, which was worse.

Looked like the old man had lied.

Of course he had. And Chad was the sucker who'd believed him.

"Oh, well, maybe I shouldn't help."

"Oh, well, maybe you should," a woman's voice answered.

Chad closed his eyes, but it figured that if he got one of the power couple, the other was bound to be nearby. All he needed now was Ford to make his humiliation complete.

That was probably a bonus his father had hoped for.

"Tess, if he's in there for a reason, we shouldn't interfere."

"I'm okay if you do," Chad said. He looked down at himself. If the sun stayed out, he'd wind up with some nasty sunburn.

The cat-kitten-thing walked back across the couch and sat down beside him, curling into a ball and starting to lick itself.

Its fur touched his leg. It kind of tickled—but only kind of. It was definitely warm, and there was something strangely comforting about that warmth.

"Go get the ladder and let's see what we can do," Cartieri said, and Chad wondered a bit at the note of irritation in her voice. "Chad, what's wrong with your father that he thinks this is the way to treat his kid?"

"He's a dick." He thought about touching the cat, wondered what it would do if he did. "I thought you knew, Cartieri: This apple didn't fall far from its tree."

"You sound remarkably at peace with that."

"A fact is a fact. It's not like it's something I can change." Because if he could…

"And yet you haven't issued any threats against anyone who has been littering your property, you've kept the blue bucket out and relatively empty for the neighborhood dog walkers, and you rented a dumpster like I suggested."

"What's your point?" He wasn't sure he wanted to hear it. He wasn't trying to be the opposite of William. He was just trying to…

He took a deep breath and admitted it to himself.

He was just trying to figure out how to survive.

It was something he'd never thought about before. He'd always taken it for granted that the money would be there, his father would be there, his life would be there. Even as he wanted to break away, maybe he hadn't stopped to consider what it would mean to *truly* be away from the Flaherty safety net.

The kitten-cat-thing stopped licking and pressed itself more firmly against Chad's leg. It vibrated against him and its front paws stretched out and started pressing at the couch cushion.

He fought the urge to pull away, unsure of what it was doing. Was this normal?

"I'm not sure I have a point. Yet," Cartieri said. "Oh, here's Mack with the ladder."

"Your boy knows how to use one?" He couldn't help himself; this was getting too personal, too nice.

"No, but I do."

Chad shook his head. Empowered women. His father would give birth to a few cows if he were here.

Maybe being in Woolslayer had some benefits other than the diverse people his father hated. It was a pretty good guarantee William would never come visit.

Although that didn't mean much when he obviously had no problem sending his goons in.

There was noise outside the dumpster. Chad, with nothing else to do, stretched his legs out and crossed his feet at the ankles, inspecting the tops of his bare feet. By rights, there should have been broken glass in the dumpster, maybe needles—anything that would royally fuck him up.

But somehow, there wasn't any of that. Or else he'd gotten lucky so far.

Three words that didn't belong in a sentence together were *Chad Flaherty* and *Lucky*.

THIRTY-SIX

Tess

Even with six-foot-three Mack standing on the ladder, they couldn't get Chad out; Mack couldn't find a single angle that would let him haul the other man up and over the edge of the dumpster. Mack was frustrated, and Tess couldn't decide if she was surprised by that or not. On the one hand, Mack had a heart of gold, no matter who was in need.

On the other hand, this was a Flaherty.

He was also their neighbor.

Who was there specifically to introduce some sort of chaos and misery into their lives.

"Call the fire department?" she asked dubiously.

Inside the dumpster, Chad groaned loudly. "You know that in a day or two—at most—the goons will come back and let me out and it'll all be over?"

"And in the meantime?" Mack said, coming down the ladder. "We do what? Throw over a loaf of bread and some water?"

Tess gave him a look. That wasn't helping, even if it was a viable backup solution.

"No," Chad said immediately. "If you saw how many plastic water bottles are in here with us—me—you'd rethink that offer. The water, anyway. I've vowed I'm never using these stupid crinkly plastic things again. Get me out of here and I'm buying myself one of those pretentious reusable things."

"Us?" Tess asked, on guard after hearing that word and not bothering to listen to the rest of his bluster. She wondered if she should have expected this to not be what it seemed on face value. "Who's there with you?"

"An orange cat."

"Oh." That changed things, on many levels. "Where did it come from?"

"What? Do I look like some cat clairvoyant? Someone must have dumped it here. Just like I got dumped. The two of us, and this old couch. No one wants us. I guess we're a team, me and the cat, except I don't think we want each other, either, which means—"

Tess frowned, thinking. Chad could be okay without food or water for however long it took to get him out of there, even if he had to wait for his father's people to come fish him out. A cat, on the other hand, was going to be more stressed by the situation. Not to mention the possibility of dehydration in the summer sun. If nothing else, they had to get the cat out of there somehow.

"Hey, think Scram needs a friend?" Mack asked. He paced the length of the dumpster and then came back to Tess.

"It's mine," Chad protested. "I saw it first."

"You just said you didn't think it liked you," Mack protested.

Tess shook her head. This was getting more absurd by the minute. At least Chad had said one thing that was reasonably helpful. "I think if we move the ladder closer to the dumpster, Chad, can you move the couch closer to the same side and stand on the back to hand the cat over?" The dumpster walls were only eight feet high. It should work.

"I... haven't touched it yet."

"But it's your cat?"

"Isn't that how it works? I see it first, it's mine?"

Tess took a deep breath. Delia had gotten involved with this loser? What had she been thinking? "Let's focus on getting it out first and then decide who owns it, okay? Maybe someone's looking for it." She hoped so. Dumping an alligator you no longer wanted into the sewers was bad enough—not to mention illegal—but leaving a cat to die in a dumpster? At least the alligator had a fighting chance in the sewers, with access to food, water, and shelter. Which meant that dumping a cat like this was also probably illegal.

It took a lot of coaching before they were able to coordinate the couch and the ladder, but once they did and Mack tried peering over, he paused. "Fuck, man, aren't there any *clothes* in there?" he groaned.

Tess bit back a smile. Clothes had often been abandoned on Chad's lawn. She didn't know if they'd made it into the dumpster or what condition they were in, but surely they'd do in a pinch.

"Hold on," Mack said and jumped down from the ladder, then jogged to their house.

"Well," Chad was saying, "there's a dress that looks like it's a size zero, and there's a hoodie with something on it. Oh. *Gimme pussy*. Yeah, whoever tossed that was right on." He made a sound. "I bet the goons left it for me. This sounds like something my dad would do."

Tess didn't bother to answer, and Mack was back quickly anyway. "Here," he said and tossed a pair of shorts over the edge, waiting a minute before he went back up the ladder. He leaned over the side, toward Tess. "Guy's in his boxers," he whispered.

Tess blinked.

"What's going on?"

Tess started, then looked up to make sure Mack was stable before turning to the speaker. She'd been aware of people gathering, but they were keeping their distance and not talking or even calling advice. There seemed to be plenty of snickering, though. And apparently, someone had put the word out on social media because it was Delia who had just shown up.

"Hey," Tess said to her friend, who was with Meter and Sima—and two men, who Tess recognized as Sima's triplets, Nate and Geddy. "What are you doing *here*?"

Delia held up her camera, the strap wrapped around her wrist. "The entire city has been yelling at me, telling me I need to see this." She paused, taking in the huge dumpster, the ladder, and Mack, who was now standing at the bottom. He had an expectant look on his face, but Tess didn't know what that was about.

"Aww, no," they heard from inside the dumpster. "Seriously? Ford? *You're* here?"

Delia's eyes widened and she looked first at Tess, then Meter. "Are you kidding me?" she whispered to Tess. "It's *Chad*?"

"You didn't know?"

"No," Delia answered at her usual volume. "I just heard there was some fool who got trapped in a dumpster and you and Mack are trying to get them out." She paused. "The fire department's ready and waiting, you know."

"No," came from the dumpster again. "They've probably been told to douse me with that foam they use and I bet it's toxic."

Delia rolled her eyes, but she was also giggling, which made Tess wonder.

"This way's better?" Mack asked. "Letting me do this?" He turned his face upward and called out, "You'd better have those shorts on. I'm coming back up so we can see if we can get the cat out."

"Cat?" Delia asked. Something in her eyes and the set of her face changed. Tess knew that look; that camera was about to get a workout. Delia let go of Meter's hand and walked around the dumpster, looking up at the lip and then stopping, lifting her camera. "Okay," she called to Mack. "I'm ready. Let's do this with the cat."

"No!"

"Dude," Mack said, climbing the ladder, "you're not really in a position to complain."

"The last time she used me for her fucking Populated Portrait, my dad had a fit. That's why I'm in here."

"This isn't for that," Delia called. "It's for the *City Central*."

Something banged inside the dumpster. Tess wasn't sure she wanted to know, although she suspected that being in the *Central* would be even worse in William Flaherty's eyes than being in one of Delia's Populated Portraits. Not only was the *Central* the paper that competed with the Flaherty's *Daily Record*, the two were politically opposed.

"Are you *trying* to get me killed? Or do you think this is just the funniest thing ever and so now setting me up for more abuse is your new hobby?"

"Stop being newsworthy," Delia said, lowering the camera just a smidge. "I'll stop taking your picture."

"C'mon," Mack said before Chad could respond. "Let's get the cat out of there. If you pick it up and stand on the edge of the couch, can you lift it up to me?" He leaned over the edge of the dumpster.

Meter and his brothers, Tess noticed, moved to secure the ladder. Sima came to stand beside her. "This is a lot better than listening to your mom complain about the floor," she said softly, glancing at the dumpster as if aware they needed to make sure Chad didn't hear about the situation at the farmhouse.

"I'm kind of dreading going back to the house tonight," Tess told her. "But Kiersten is still scheduled to arrive tomorrow, which means since we'll get down there to look for any boxes, we'll be able to fix the floor sooner rather than later. I hope."

"What do you mean, *how do you pick up a cat*?" Mack was asking Chad, and Tess closed her eyes and silently asked for strength. "You put one hand under its front legs, yeah, in its armpits, and pick it up. It's nice if you'd support its rear legs or its ass, too, but start small." He turned and gave Tess a meaningful look.

She nodded. The issues at the farm were *nothing* compared to the drama Chad Flaherty apparently created without trying.

"That's it," Mack said, then pulled back as Chad bellowed. Mack had a look on his face that Tess wasn't sure how to interpret. Part of her doubted it was anything as life-ending as it sounded.

"What happened?" Mack called into the dumpster.

"Cat bit me."

"It's probably scared. Try again. Maybe be gentle this time?" He turned his head away from Tess this time, and she wondered if he was making a face at Delia, but she didn't move.

"Chad," Delia called as the orange cat body came into view, "can you get your hands higher?"

"Ford, you—"

Mack laughed and did something to get his hand under Chad's and lift the cat. "That good?" he called to Delia. "And since when do you engineer shots anyway?"

"Since I can make a better one and piss Chad off all at the same time," Delia called back, the camera glued to her face.

Tess wasn't exactly sure, but she thought she heard a couple *you go, girls* and even an *amen* from the crowd. "How much of this really is just some big joke?" she asked Sima, who shrugged.

"Hard to say. I'm not hearing a lot of the rumors because, you know, I'm the weirdo antisocial farm girl, but apparently his dad likes Nate's restaurant and Nate's overheard Daddy talking. Chad's only making his own situation worse."

Tess didn't doubt that.

"He should have threatened the garbage dumpers, he should have made it known that no one treats a Flaherty like that, he should have..." Sima shook her head. "He should have done exactly the opposite of what he's been doing."

And if he had, Tess thought, the neighborhood would have found a way to drive him out. A faster, more emphatic way.

This was actually only bringing everyone together—which wasn't a bad thing.

Maybe, Tess thought, Chad was actually smarter than his father—even though, apparently, that was a pretty low bar to begin with.

Meter had a hand on Mack, helping guide him down the ladder because Mack's arms were full of a small orange cat. Tess went over to see it, Sima on her heels.

"Let's get it inside with Scram," Mack said.

"*My* cat!" Chad called from inside the dumpster.

Mack didn't look happy. "It's orange," he said. "And Scram's black. They're perfect for each other."

"Someone dropped it off for a reason, and until we know it's safe around other cats, we can't do that to Scram," Tess said, scratching the cat's head. She looked more closely and frowned. "Mack, it's got fleas."

He held the cat away from his body, and that was when Tess noticed the cat had the side of Mack's hand in its mouth. "Your cat, Chad," he called before she could say anything. "Is your door unlocked? I'll put it inside for you."

"I have no idea, but I hope so," Chad answered, sounding defeated again.

"Mack? Is it biting you?"

"Huh? Oh, yeah," he said, turning his hands and the cat in them. "I guess it is. Seems happy this way, though; it's not biting that hard and it's not squirming. See?" He extended it away from his body again.

Tess shook her head and pointed at Chad's porch. One of Sima's triplets jumped and ran ahead, presumably to open the door.

"It's locked," Mack called from the porch.

An impressive string of curses came from inside the dumpster. And, Tess noted, they weren't curse *words* but actual curses, calling down the wrath of someone or other on his father's head—although based on some of those curses, Tess had a suspicion he wasn't referring to the head on the man's shoulders.

"Tiamat?" Meter suddenly called up, his face turned toward the dumpster. "As in the five-headed dragon goddess or the ancient Mesopotamian goddess associated with chaos?"

"What? I don't know! Who the fuck even *are* you?"

"Me? I'm Dimitry, otherwise known as Mr. Delia Ford. Nice to meet you."

Tess held her breath. Chad's mood was deteriorating the longer the absurd situation dragged on, and there was no way he was going to be willing to engage in a conversation with the man who got his girl.

From inside the dumpster came a lot of crashes. Tess eyed the dumpster, half expecting Chad to pop up over the edge. What had even possessed him to get the largest dumpster made? Why not the small one and just have it emptied or replaced more often?

The dumpster was going to smell royally before it was picked up or replaced, and that would lead to a whole new set of problems: rats.

If William Flaherty's goal was to destroy property values along this stretch of the neighborhood, Chad was accomplishing it for him handily.

Tess wondered if the elderly Flaherty was smart enough to realize that—and what he'd do when he came up against Rheda Salveggio, Woolslayer's councilwoman. She wasn't the type to suffer the sort of nonsense William Flaherty and his son were inflicting on the neighborhood.

Retreating to the porch and watching from the swing was a tempting idea. They might have gotten the cat out, but the situation wasn't over yet.

Not while Chad was still inside his dumpster.

THIRTY-SEVEN

MACK

Mack was still holding the cat when he and and Sima's brother walked back from the porch. Maybe this wasn't such a good friend for Scram, Mack thought. It continued gnawing busily—but apparently happily—on his hand. He tried shifting that hand, hoping the cat would take the clue, but it only dug in. It wanted *that* spot, although Mack didn't know why.

Scram didn't do this.

"It's not ideal," Mack said, wiggling his fingers, which elicited a growl from the cat, "but what if we empty out the blue bucket and put the cat in it for the short term?"

"It'll jump out," Tess said, giving him a look like he was an idiot and should have realized that. In his defense, he was being used as a chew toy, and that had him a little distracted.

"Here," Sima said, taking the cat and touching the top of its head. It let go of Mack's hand and nosed hers but she said a stern *"no"* and the cat settled.

"How—" He rubbed his hand where the cat had been chewing, then checked it for blood. No blood, but the skin was red. He'd be fine.

She smirked. "I'm a biologist, remember?" She held the cat up, looking it over. "Oh, you're a cute man," she said to it. "Natie, have you checked the *back* door?"

The brother took off running.

"Okay, want to know what I'm thinking?" Meter said, calling Tess, Sima's other brother, and Mack over. Sima and the cat came too. "So the problem is that you can grab Chad's wrists but can't heave him up over the side of the dumpster."

"Fire department's still on call," Delia said, joining them. Mack had no doubt Delia would love to see the fire department solve this, but he was still thinking the group of them could—and if not them, someone else from the neighborhood.

Nate came out Chad's front door. Sima looked at him, then the cat, then ran toward the porch. She handed the cat to her brother, he disappeared back inside, and Mack turned his attention back to the discussion at hand. Sima rejoined them, not even out of breath.

Meter suggested they use a bedsheet to help Chad climb out of the dumpster. "There's probably one in there with him."

"You know this how?" Mack asked, but Meter shook his head and looked slightly embarrassed and mumbled something about people at work talking about the trash.

Chad was able to find a sheet. He also thought it was a stupid solution.

"Then we're done," Tess said, raising a hand in what might have been defeat but was definitely disgust. Mack didn't totally blame her.

"I'm out of here," Delia said. "I got my money shot for the day, so I'm going to head over to the paper and hand this one in directly."

"You're not going to stay and get pictures of the rescue?" Mack asked, surprised. How could she leave now?

"If he's supposed to stay in there until Daddy's goons come get him out and we splash *that* in the paper? I'd probably get fired, which isn't the end of the world, but it's also easy income, and I kind of like it. Not to mention what Daddy will do to his favorite kid." She gestured at the dumpster.

Meter leaned over to her and said something softly. She put a hand flat on his belly and blew him a kiss. "Fire department's still waiting," she called over her shoulder and was off.

They moved from their loose circle just enough to let Nate in—until someone else approached. It was Officer Snider. "You had enough?" he asked.

"We rescued a cat," Mack told him, as if that's what the fuss was about, although he doubted the cop would buy it. "It's in Flaherty's house."

Snider turned and looked at the house. "Could be good for him. But if you're done trying to play the hero, I'll go talk to a few of the guys and let them make some calls." He gave them a long look, which Mack understood to mean that Snider knew which cops were on Flaherty's payroll and which weren't. He wondered why Tess hadn't mentioned that to him sooner. "We don't need to leave him in a metal container on a day this sunny and hot," the cop continued. "Kid'll wind up in the hospital, dehydrated and sunburnt."

Mack wondered if that was part of the point. So far, nothing he had seen of William Flaherty's actions toward his son had been anything but cruel. It wasn't totally surprising, given how easily the guy had torched the barn, but if you were going to show kindness to something or someone, shouldn't it be your own son?

And why was Mack's own father a good match for William Flaherty, when it came to being a total dick to your son?

"Do it," Tess told Snider.

"Want to pull up chairs and watch?" Mack asked the Shaikovskys. Sima rolled her eyes but Nate and Geddy decided to, one of them asking for popcorn and the other encouraging Sima to stay.

Meter, though, said he didn't feel any need to stay and wait for Flaherty goons, which Mack thought was wise. He was the winner in the Delia Ford sweepstakes, even if all he'd had to do was sit and wait for Delia to get Chad out of her system and come back to him. Mack didn't know much about what they'd been like before he'd met them, but he thought they were a good couple. A lot better than she would have been with Chad, that was for sure. What he'd seen of Chad wasn't nearly strong enough for someone like Delia—or Tess, Mack thought, glancing at her.

Sima left with Meter, promising to be around when Kiersten arrived at the farm the next day. It wasn't entirely within her job description to handle anything they unearthed under the floor, but she'd asked if she could be there. And if she was, that meant Tess and Mack both were free to focus on their actual jobs, not that Mack wanted to. The Mackenzie heritage was every bit as important as

PharmaSci, Thomas liked to remind him. At the very least, the two were intertwined. And the family history was a good diversion from the corporate world.

Mack settled in with Nate and Geddy, a couple bags of microwave popcorn, and drinks, wondering which set of cops Snider was going to call, and just how they were going to get Chad out of there.

He would definitely have to talk to Kiersten about the records and any mention of the feud between the two families—or anything about the Flahertys. Were they always this entertaining? Or had they at one point been respectable people?

He thought about Henry and his habit of impregnating young women. Maybe respectable was asking for too much from either family.

THIRTY-EIGHT

Chad

Cats were expensive, Chad found out once he was free from the dumpster—thanks to the cops, the fire department, and a lot of jeers and Bronx cheers from the neighbors. Even Mackenzie had pulled up a chair and watched.

He hadn't thought anything could be more humiliating than showing up at Ford's wedding beaten to a pulp, but sure enough, his father had found a way to top it.

Although he'd wanted nothing more than to storm into his house and disappear until the end of time, he made himself thank the cops and wave to the fan club. *Then* he went inside, grabbed a shower, and made himself something to eat, if a couple slices of ham on a stale hoagie roll counted as food. Apparently Go-fer Stanley and his buddies had cleaned out the rest of Chad's pantry after they'd stuck him in the dumpster.

The cat liked the ham. Not so much the hoagie roll.

Thankfully his dad's go-fers had left his car, keys, clothes, and especially his wallet, so he'd showered, gotten dressed, and gone shopping first for himself and then for the cat.

That was where he'd learned how expensive cats were. The thing needed a litter pan, it needed litter, it needed food and toys and something to scratch up, a bed, and a comb. And a vet, but you apparently couldn't buy one of those in the neighborhood pet store.

He was lugging the kitty litter across the yard, making note of the fresh wave of trash, when he noticed movement at his car. Someone was taking his grocery bags out of the back seat. "What are you doing?" He didn't care that he sounded panicked; he was. He'd just *bought* that food and his dad's assholes were taking it already?

"Helping."

"Ford." He stopped where he was, wishing he had something to beat his head against. "Hasn't today sucked enough? You have to come back and make it even worse for me?"

"Yep," she said, one grocery bag of food over each shoulder and one in each hand. "C'mon. I don't know what you have in here, but it's heavy. Get the door."

"It's not as heavy as all this cat litter," he said but started moving, putting the giant bag of litter down so he could dig for his keys. Fifty pounds hadn't sounded heavy.

"Whine whine whine," she said and bounced on the balls of her feet a little as she waited for him to let her in. Which he didn't want to do, but he didn't seem to have a choice.

Why did everyone else get to have control of their lives? And how could he have the same?

He hoped she would beeline for the kitchen once he let her in, but she took her time, looking around. The place still was, he knew, a dump. He hadn't exactly done much of anything with it yet; he'd been picking up the trash in his yard.

"This place is nothing like your condo." She sounded confused by that, like she didn't understand how it could be.

That, at least, made him wonder what she saw when she looked at him. Maybe she didn't see him as the loser he apparently was.

"That place?" he said. "It was never mine."

She wheeled, her eyes big. "You told me it was."

He hauled the litter into the front hall, just inside the door and under the little ledge that he guessed was supposed to be for mail. He'd already developed a habit of leaving his keys on it. "What was Dad's was mine," he said, mentally adding *until it wasn't*.

For some reason, he wanted to shudder and maybe gag. What a fool he'd been.

She headed toward the back of the house, like she had some homing device that told her where the kitchen was.

He followed her, wishing she'd never shown up. He could have carried the groceries himself. He'd been planning to.

But, again, he had zero control of his own life.

She set the first two bags down on the kitchen counter and stepped back to take in the room. It wasn't anything to write home about: only one burner on the stove worked, the fridge was shorter than he was, and one cabinet door hung from its hinges. "So I claimed legal ownership of your dad's place?" she asked. "How am I even still alive?"

"It wasn't easy," Chad said. "I took a nice beating over it."

She had the courtesy to wince. "Sorry."

He gave her a long look. Before, back when she'd been a prize he'd loved to show off, gorgeous and inked and with that smart mouth, he'd have been smug as he said, "No you're not."

Now, he was just quiet as he said it. He stared at the floor.

"I don't know," she said. "Maybe I am. I'll have to think about it." She turned in a circle, one hand trailing behind her as if she wanted to touch him. "You've fallen pretty far," she said.

"I want out."

She paused, looking him over as if judging his sincerity. "Not gonna be easy."

"I know. But—" He stared past her, at the back door. The trim needed to be sanded and painted, but at least that would be easy. Maybe he'd need to add some weather stripping or caulking or something too. But none of the four little panes of glass were broken. That was something.

"This house really sucks," he said heavily.

"It does," she agreed in that happy, sassy voice he'd loved to hear. He'd fallen hard for her, gotten scared of her kinky side, tried too hard to make her into something she wasn't, into his idea of what Chad's Arm Candy was supposed to be, and then in the end had set her up with that bogus trespassing charge in preparation for dumping her in the most ugly, brutal way he could.

Total dick moves on his part. Every last one of them.

"But the good news is that if you try real hard," she continued, and now a note of something crept into her voice, like she was being patronizing, which she probably was, "you can make it suck less."

"Thanks," he said and glanced at her, almost afraid to. Sure enough, she was grinning nice and big. "I hadn't realized that."

"Always looking out for you, Flaherty," she said and chucked him in the arm. He hated that he lost his balance briefly when she did it. "So I can run in the other direction," she added with another grin. Or maybe it was the same one. She had never smiled this much before, when they'd been together. Her nerd must have made her very happy. He sure hadn't.

"Of course," he muttered, closing his eyes. Maybe this was what he deserved. He wasn't sure anymore; if he'd learned anything, it was that the world his father had raised him to believe in was fake and he wasn't all that. He wasn't even a little that.

Women like Delia Ford *should* run away from a train wreck like him.

"Okay," she said. "You've got your groceries, so I'm out of here."

"Why did you even come back? It wasn't to be kind."

"Definitely not," she said and wrinkled her nose. "But I was curious about your cat. Where is it?" She twisted around, looking for it.

"In the bathroom. Someone said I should do that until I got it flea stuff. Which I need to get from the vet," he added, wondering if she too was going to tell him which vet to call.

"Have fun with that," she said and started toward the front door.

"Hey, Ford?" he called after her.

"Yeah?" She stopped and twisted from the waist, like all of her couldn't be bothered to turn and face him.

"We square?"

"Nope," she said and let herself out.

THIRTY-NINE

Tess

They were a nervous bunch of people out on the back porch the following day, waiting for Kiersten to arrive: Mom, Mack, Tess, Thomas, Gray, and Sima—although Tess didn't think Sima was nervous. Excited was more like it, and she was keeping them all amused by spinning wild tales of what was under the laundry room floor. It was the most animated Tess had ever seen the other woman and not for the first time, she wondered what had happened to her. She'd been so sullen, angry, and *hurt* when she'd first started working at the farm.

Mack had been down in the hole with Saul Ford as soon as they'd opened it just wide enough to fit through. Sure enough, there were records boxes down there—and not much else.

Mack had come up the ladder, shaking his head and saying he should have figured, since the first box they'd found was under the floor in his suite of rooms at the Mackenzie Manor back in New York.

Tess was tired of hearing it, and tired of telling him to go easy on himself. They hadn't even thought to look to see if there could be an old root cellar; it hadn't been indicated on any of the blueprints she had found. It had only been Scram's digging that had made things click. And they still had no idea what he'd been digging for.

Kiersten arrived roughly on time. Although she and Mack and Tess had talked over video chat, no one had met her in person, and Tess thought she would be as nervous as they were—and for good reason. Not only was she outnumbered, she was meeting the couple who had been paying her salary since the start of the pandemic, when she'd been laid off by a prestigious museum in Knoxville.

Tess did plenty of meetings, both in-person and over video with various clients at work. There was definitely a different vibe in person versus over video.

They heard Kiersten's giant pickup truck long before they saw it. Roger, in particular, was interested in it. "I haven't heard an engine like that since the army," he said with an approving smile and a nod. Maybe, Tess thought, there was something wistful about him, too, and she was reminded of how successful he was at keeping to himself.

Today, it seemed, was full of surprises.

Kiersten's truck was giant. Gleaming black, too, with chrome accents. And the historian guided it around all their cars like it was a unicycle, stopping near the porch. She sat for a minute, seemingly oblivious to the group waiting for her, and fiddled with things in the truck, then got out, hopping down lightly.

"Hi," she said, wiping her hands on her rear. "I'm Kiersten." She looked around, as if confused about who she should approach first, so of course Tess jumped with Mack to welcome her. "Let me get my things," she said when all the introductions had been made. She turned back to the truck and pulled out a briefcase, which she slung across her body rather than carried, pulling her long—longer than

Tess's—light brown hair out from under the strap and letting it fall in a fan.

Tess liked her already and thought she fit perfectly in the world she and Mack were building.

"I am *dying* to see these boxes in their natural environment," Kiersten said. She started to turn back to her truck but paused, pursing her lips, then shook her head slightly. "Tess, you'll need to tell me how you've been accessing the site, so I can decide if I can go down there or not."

"Why couldn't you?" Mack asked before Tess could.

Kiersten bent and knocked on her right calf. "Amputee, courtesy of defending the freedoms of the United States of America."

She was so matter-of-fact about it that Mom gasped, but Sima took a step forward as if about to ask if she could have a closer look.

"Oh," Mack said and gave Tess a confused look.

"Well," Tess said, "let's start with what I've been able to find so far, and I'll show you where the root cellar is and how I think it was positioned in relation to the house and the first kitchen before the addition was built. As far as the access hole itself, I don't see why you wouldn't be able to get down there. Our crew made it plenty big on purpose." Mostly, Tess thought, because Saul Ford was a portly man and had said that if he could get down there, almost anyone could.

"Perfect," Kiersten said with a nod.

The group moved into the library, Kiersten marveling at the house and asking questions that showed off her rich understanding of the Mackenzie history. In return, Tess shared historical details she'd uncovered about the property and the house itself. As the conversation flowed, Mack ducked into his office for a minute.

"Can you read blueprints?" Tess asked Kiersten as she took them out of the drawer they were kept in. "I know you said you'd like to see them, but I didn't ask how well you can read them."

"As well as any general person. Nothing like I'm sure you can," Kiersten answered. She motioned to the desk. "Go ahead and talk me through what you think I need to know."

Tess did, acutely aware of the woman. She was an inch or so taller than Tess, and even with a button-down shirt and jeans on, Tess could tell she was all muscle—which fit for a military vet. She wore hiking boots, as most people around the house did, when they wore shoes at all.

Mack returned as they were finishing a discussion of where Tess expected the root cellar walls to be, and after a pause for Mack and Tess to retrieve shoes, the six of them moved into the laundry room. A ladder had been set in the hole, and both Gray and Thomas said they weren't going to risk it.

"Mom?" Mack asked. "I'll help you down if you want to see it."

Tess thought Mom looked instantly guilty, but Gray gave her an encouraging nod and Thomas looked a little wistful. Kiersten was looking at the hole, lips pursed, eyes slightly narrowed, and then she nodded slightly. It was almost the same thing she had done outside, looking at her truck.

"You should go ahead of Kiersten," Tess told Mack, but he shook his head and told her to go ahead.

"I've already been down there," he said.

"Want the truth?" Sima asked from the back of the group. "She wants you to be the one bit by anything hiding down there."

"Oh, please," Tess said as Mom took a step back, eyeing the hole. She was probably hoping nothing had come up the ladder over the weekend and was now hiding somewhere.

"There's nothing to worry about," Mack told everyone, then turned to Tess. "Sima and I uncovered it earlier this morning, got the ladder in position and secure, and carried lights down, too. I didn't want anyone falling if they tried to carry a flashlight or lantern."

"Did you look around?" Part of Tess couldn't believe he'd done it without her, but she'd also been in meetings all morning, so the other part of her didn't blame him. If they hadn't spent the weekend in Woolslayer, he'd have been down there sooner.

In fact, he'd tried to convince her to spend the weekend at the farm. But if they had, she reflected, they'd have missed out on Chad's latest spectacle.

She bit back a smile, thinking of Chad Flaherty in a dumpster—and no way to blame the Mackenzies for it. William had tried for about thirty seconds, but the fact they'd been actively helping Chad get out had shot that theory down before it could gain legs.

The picture in the *City Central* hadn't hurt, either.

"Not much," Mack was saying. "I just went down with the lights and flicked them on to make sure they worked and then turned them off again. We may need lanterns with more power, but there's definitely a couple records boxes—three of them that I saw real quick."

Sima was nodding.

"How we're going to get them up here, I'm not sure," he continued with a frown. He rubbed the back of his neck. "Maybe use Taylor's ropes?"

Everyone fell quiet and looked at each other for a long minute, then Sima shrugged. "Time to go down into the bowels of Mackenzie history. Who's first?"

Mack held up his hands. "I'm going to help you, Mom."

She started to protest, but he gave her a look. "Make me happy," he said. "You seem nervous, so let's be safe."

"I guess I'm first," Tess said and moved toward the ladder.

"Here," Sima said and handed her a head lamp.

"I should have thought to grab my hard hat from the office," Tess said with a smile and played with the buttons for a cycle or two before settling it on her forehead. "You ready?" she asked everyone, glancing around at the group.

"Have fun," Gray said.

"One thing I want to find is if there's any sign of a door that used to lead outside," Tess said. "I have suspicions about this old house." She started down.

Sima followed, then called up, asking Kiersten if she wanted her to hold the ladder.

"Yes, please," Kiersten said. "Just until I get down a few rungs. I train on ladders, but when they're positioned like this, I like to have someone hold them, just to make sure I don't knock them."

Tess picked up a lantern and turned the dial. Mack was right; it wasn't enough light. She set it down and picked up a second one, frowning. It still wasn't bright enough.

"What do you train for?" Sima was asking Kiersten.

"Life," Kiersten said as she came into view. Tess turned, surprised to see the historian had climbed down without using her right leg, her movements practiced. "I was on ladders all the time at the museum, where so many things are stored up high," she said. "So I incorporated practice into my workouts, and I just haven't stopped." She shrugged. "Readiness in all things, you know?"

It was admirable.

"Maybe I should do that," Sima said and snickered. "Can you see me doing some ninja course?"

"Why not?" Kiersten asked.

"Hello? I'm a shrimp. What's a normal step for you is a stretch for me."

Mack came down a few rungs, then paused, giving Mom instructions. He came down a few more, leaving room for Mom, then jumped, his hands still in place to catch Mom if she fell.

Tess wondered if he'd gotten off so quickly because of the weight limit on the ladder, but the more Mom came into view, the more comfortable she looked. That made Tess smile; she'd grown up with a mother who wasn't daunted by much.

"Good job, Mom," Tess said. "I honestly thought you'd chicken out."

"I did too, for about two minutes," Mom told her. "But Gray said it's the sort of adventure I should embrace and the truth is that even if he hadn't said that, he's right. I'm not too old to climb ladders."

"It's good for you," Mack said, coming up behind her.

"You're only as old as you think you are, Mom," Tess added.

"Okay," Mack said, reaching for Tess's hand—or the lantern she held. She wasn't sure which, especially because he simply folded his hand over hers. "The boxes. Let's take a look."

Sima and Kiersten grabbed the other lanterns and they moved to the far wall of the root cellar. Three metal boxes, maybe a little bit bigger than the ones they'd already found, sat there—stacked on top of three others.

"Anticlimactic," Sima said and handed her lantern to Tess, even as everyone else drew in their breath. "I'm going back to work. Call me if there's any biology happening here."

"Want to look for any old doorways?" Tess asked.

"Tess. The whole point of a root cellar is that it's built into the ground. The only doors would have been from above. Even if you're thinking something like the Underground Railroad, first off, no one would let someone hide this close to their house and second, I bet that's been closed up for a good hundred years."

"I was hoping," Tess said. With a sigh, she bent down at the foot of the nearest stack of boxes and brushed at the top one. "These aren't as dusty as I'd have expected."

"Here," Mack said as Sima headed up the ladder. He bent and pulled the top box slightly closer and as he did, a cloud of dust rose. "Found your dust, honey."

"Thanks, dear," Tess said and smiled. "What a gift."

"I thought you'd be all, you know, hyper about dirt," Kiersten said.

"Only when in a business suit," Mack said. It was too dark to see his face, but Tess could picture him winking. "Which is one reason I wear them as rarely as possible."

"Really?" Kiersten asked. "Aren't you this billionaire-type? You should be into fast living and fast cars and everything flashy—and hate dirt."

Tess laughed. "*You* have been reading too many romances. Mack is nothing like those guys—but aren't they fun?"

"Sometimes," Kiersten said. "But they're not my type."

"They're not mine, either," Tess said.

"But—" Kiersten said.

"But nothing," Mack said. "She's got the faster car, and don't get in it with her unless you're willing to hold on tight while you brace yourself."

"Mack!" The worst part was that he wasn't exaggerating—about the car, anyway.

"Honey..." Mom said

Tess whirled. "Oh, come on! I am a perfectly safe driver!"

"Safe has nothing to do with whether or not we have to hang on because you also like to go fast," Mack said and leaned down for a kiss.

Tess put her hand on his chest and turned her face away.

He chuckled. "And I am doing my best," he told Kiersten, "to be a good human, which means the opposite of my father and grandfather. Grandpa—Cullen—was into horse racing, as I think you know from reading his journals, and Tristan was just a stain on humanity. Is. I'm pretty sure he's still alive."

"Just absent?" Kiersten asked.

"Hope he stays that way," Mack said. "We stopped getting along when I was fourteen. Well, no," he said, and Tess caught the note that meant he was thinking. "I'm not sure we *ever* got along. He thought I should do nothing but make him look good. I thought I should be outside, catching frogs in the pond and bringing them to the house when he had people over."

Tess couldn't see him in the half light, but she didn't need to to know he was grinning widely, proud of himself for that even now. It was a familiar story, always followed up with that proud grin.

"I always picture Krista when you tell that story," Tess said. It was an amusing mental picture that she drew, of the very proper and often distant Krista trying to be kind about the gift of a frog.

"She was always her usual stoic, cold self," Mack said, "and she always pretended to be disappointed in me, but I could kind of *feel* her laughing underneath, if that makes any sense."

"She's a lot more than she seems at first glance," Tess agreed.

"Hey, what are you finding over there?" Mack called across the room. Kiersten was squatting at the end of the farthest records boxes.

"Nothing," she said, her voice thick with disappointment. "Why don't they have any sorts of markings on them? Not one has had anything on it to let you know what they are."

"I think it's supposed to be in the journals," Mack said.

"But it's not," Kiersten said. "There's no mention of the records boxes. Was this supposed to be some oral tradition, handed down from father to son?"

"Maybe," Mack said. "Or to the caretakers, but Thomas was as surprised by them as we were."

"You know," Tess said slowly, trying to think it through. She felt guilty saying it, since Thomas had become such a father figure in their lives, but what if he'd been playing dumb? What if he knew more than he'd been letting on?

Thomas was a wily one. They all knew that.

But there was nothing to be gained by holding out on them. Not about this, and especially not after the Flahertys had torched her barn.

"Just Tess," Mack said softly, and Tess had a feeling he was thinking what she was. "I can't see it."

"Me either, but what if?"

"As I keep working through it all," Kiersten said, "I'll keep an eye out."

"Have you finished the last box yet?" Mack asked. "Since we're about to dump six more on you."

"Not yet. I'm still cataloging it because I haven't actually had it that long and you keep asking me to stop and look for other things. But once it's all catalogued, I'll go through it again thoroughly and see how many story lines I can trace for you."

"Does any of this make sense?" Tess asked.

"Not the bit about the unmarked boxes, but other things are starting to," Kiersten said. "What we're looking at is a multigenerational effort to make peoples' lives better, under the belief that most of the people in these parts truly wanted that."

"Found anything about the Flahertys?" Tess asked. She was fairly certain Mack had already asked, but she needed to hear the answer directly.

"Plenty. They did everything they could to shut your forefathers down. They believed strongly in slavery and that being white gave them God-given privileges. I think those attitudes, being so different from the Mackenzie attitudes, are what fueled the feud between the families, but at the same time, I can't help thinking there's more to it than that."

"Like what?" Mack asked.

"I don't know," the historian said. "And it's just a feeling, based on zero fact so far. It's just... I've seen too many old documents of people who worked together and were ripped apart first and blamed it on politics afterward."

"As in..."

"All sorts of things. Marriages made for expediency, to tie families together, only the husband beat his wife to death and the very relations they'd been married to fix were absolutely destroyed. Or business partnerships that fell apart." She paused. "If you want to talk about the war years, trading in black market goods, just so families could find food. And that's where the racial arguments really ramped up. Do the slaves deserve to be fed alongside the families? It's..." She shook her head briefly. "Look, one reason I agreed to come work directly for you was because I knew enough of your mindset, and it matches mine. So let's not turn this into a philosophical discussion about race. We're all in agreement."

"Have you found more about the"—Tess paused, like she always did—"*experiments* Henry was so into?"

"Not in this latest box. I know it's hard."

"No one's one hundred percent good," Mack said heavily. "But that doesn't mean this part of Henry's history isn't awful."

"I wish he'd given us ideas about how to get these boxes out of here," Tess said. She needed to change the subject. While they'd been down here, she'd been so absorbed in the situation that the nausea had been relatively tame. But talking about this one part of Henry always upset her stomach, even before she'd been pregnant.

"I have ideas," Kiersten said, and Mack launched into a description of what he thought Taylor had done to haul the one box down the mountainside.

"We'll figure it out," Kiersten finally said, holding one hand up and laughing. "I can't wait; when you add it all up, it does create quite the archive. There are pictures and some artifacts along with the records that I've found so far. I'd be surprised if the total overall value at the end of this isn't—"

"The value is for the family," Mack growled. "This isn't for sale."

"There are scholars—" Kiersten started, taking a half step forward.

"No."

"Okay," Tess said, her voice falsely bright, her temper fraying. "Let's get back to the discussion of how to get these out of here."

Mack looked up. "If we had enough strong backs, we could stick a bunch down here and a bunch up there and work together to hand them up. That'd be better than ropes."

"Strong backs aren't hard to find," Tess said. "But strong backs who can be quiet about what they're doing might be. Especially if Flaherty catches wind of this and starts nosing around."

"I wish we knew what they think is in here," Mack said. He planted his hands on his thighs and stood up, motioning everyone toward the ladder.

"You could ask your buddy Chad," Tess smirked and stood back to let Kiersten up the ladder first. "Oh. Do you need anything?" she asked the historian.

"Nope. Up is a lot easier, especially since it's not dark up there too. I'm really going to have to add ladder climbs in the dark to my routine; I like this challenge."

"Asking Flaherty's not a bad idea," Mack said.

"Do you honestly think he'll answer?" Tess asked, motioning Mom to go up the ladder. She did without any hesitation, and Tess smiled. It shouldn't be such a big thing, her retired mother climbing a ladder, but it felt like it was for some reason. Maybe because Mom seemed so content with her quiet life on the farm.

"Honey," Mom said when they were all up and brushing at some of the dust and cobwebs that had accumulated on them, "do you think we could find a way to use that as cold storage again? It's nice and cool down there."

"I thought you wanted your laundry room back."

"You're the architect," Mom said and patted Tess's cheek. "See what you can do for me."

Mack caught Tess's eye and winked.

FORTY

MACK

By the end of the day, they'd come up with a plan and had started to implement it. Tess had rounded up strong and discrete bodies to help haul the records boxes up: Roger, his sister, Delia, her father and brother, and Meter and his three brothers, as well, although apparently Leon and Nate had to be threatened to keep their mouths shut. It was a bit of a ragtag group, but maybe, Mack thought, they could do it.

Kiersten had offered to put out a call to see if any of her fellow ex-Marines were in the area, and while Mack didn't doubt the discretion of a Marine, he also didn't want to risk crossing paths with someone already aligned with the Flahertys.

He felt strangely paranoid. It wasn't a good feeling.

"I mean it, Natan," Sima warned her younger triplet again when they'd all assembled after dinner. She shook her finger in his face. "You tell anyone about this, I will personally dismember you." She glared at him and said something in a language that Mack guessed might be Russian.

"Why the secrecy?" their other triplet, Gedeyon, asked.

"This doesn't get to the Flahertys," Sima said, giving him a warning look that rivaled anything Mack's mother could hand out. "Not. One. Word."

"Talk to Natie," Geddy said, taking a step back and reaching for his triplet. "He's the one who sees them."

"I just did!" Sima snapped and switched to Russian. The brothers went a little pale, but Meter and the last brother just exchanged a look and a chuckle, then nodded approvingly.

"How serious a threat are the Flahertys?" Saul asked. He moved to the ladder and paused, waiting for an answer before starting down.

"We're not sure," Mack said calmly, returning the other man's gaze. "But we're also not willing to take any chances."

Saul nodded and went down, calling for Leon and Meter to join him. Mack asked where Saul wanted him.

"Come down for now, while I take a look at this," he said.

They all wound up going down, including Tess. The space was barely big enough for the dozen of them, especially with the five records boxes flat on the floor. Saul looked them over, talking to Meter and Leon, but it was Meter's other brother who had an idea about how to hand them up.

"A jeweler," Saul laughed, shaking his head. "What do you know about heavy things? Small and precious, yes."

"I don't think you've met his girlfriend," Meter said. In the dim light, Mack watched him put a shoulder into his younger brother and give him a shove and for a second, he had one of those pangs of longing for a sibling.

"She is precious," the brother—Mack couldn't remember his name, other than it wasn't something familiar—said.

There was a lot of scrabbling on the floor and Mack had a feeling they were doing some sort of wrestling or jostling for position despite the tight quarters.

"Boys," Saul said without looking over. "You want to wrestle? Call a referee and rent a ring. We have a job to do."

"And you thought Deel and I were bad," Leon said. "Hey, Vass, cut it. That's my foot you just stepped on."

That was it, Mack thought. Vassily.

He shook his head, wondering if he'd remember it this time.

"Sorry."

They were, Mack thought, kind of like a bad comedy troupe. He reached for Tess, wondering if she was having the same thoughts about being an only child.

"Okay, triplets upstairs," Saul said. "Tess and Leon, and Kristen. You're the upstairs crew. The rest of us will raise the first box and lift it up to you. We'll see how that goes."

It took teamwork and wasn't easy, but they got two of the boxes up before calling it quits for the night.

Kiersten, who had neither bristled nor corrected Saul when he kept getting her name wrong, was thrilled and had the men bring the first box into the library right away. Saying they really didn't need her muscle and she hadn't come to offer that anyway, she pulled on white cotton gloves and got busy, Gray and Thomas keeping her company while Tess and April apparently bounced between the library and the laundry room.

"How long can you stay?" Mack asked Kiersten with a wince. Saul had asked for at least a day to recover before they brought up the other three boxes.

"I'd like to head back first thing tomorrow to get these secure," she said. "Thank you for offering me a room for the night. I'd much rather start on this than deal with a hotel. It looks like I've got a lot of work ahead of me."

"But if you hang here for two days, you can drive all of them," Mack said, hoping he didn't sound too much like he was wheedling. "It's not like you can't work in our library."

Kiersten gave him a long look. "I appreciate it," she said. "But one night's my limit for hospitality and besides, I have things at home I need to be back for."

Mack's stomach sank at her insistence—even though he didn't blame her and absolutely couldn't ask her to put her life on hold for his history. He only got her during working hours. "How do we get the other boxes down to you, then?"

"I'll drive them down," Gray said at the same moment that Roger volunteered his sister.

"I was willing to come back up, but it looks like that's settled," Kiersten said as she lifted something else out of the records box and held it up. "These are in really good shape, Mack. Much better than many of the others. If you don't mind—"

"I just hope it gives us answers soon," he said, rubbing the back of his neck.

"Let's take a walk," Tess said, "since we missed porch time." She put a hand on his arm and he let her turn him and guide him out of the house. "I know you were hoping to get all of them up tonight, but was that ever a realistic goal?" she asked as they strolled along the path toward the gazebo. Mack suspected they were going the whole way over to the nearest of the eastern pastures; it wasn't far beyond the gazebo.

They'd also have to pass the empty clearing where a barn should have been.

"I was hoping," he said.

"Hey, did you have time for Taylor to get you a copy from the *City Central*?"

"The picture? Yeah." He wasn't sure how he felt about it—except to be fairly certain Chad was going to come outside with more bruises in the next day or so.

The picture, of course, was the one Delia had taken, the hands and the kitten, and the caption had been brutal—to the Flahertys, anyway. *Two of the descendants of Port Kenneth's founding families work together to rescue a kitten from a dumpster in Woolslayer.* Thankfully it hadn't named them, but then again, most people in town had forgotten about that third family, thanks to some revisionist history by the Flahertys and the decades-long absence of the Mackenzies. The subtext of two feuding families finding a way to work together probably wasn't lost on most people, either.

"What do you think it means that we moved here and Chad followed?" he asked. "I mean, other than he's following us. More like… If you were an outsider trying to understand the city and its legacy."

"Hmm," Tess said and surprised him by pulling him down on one of the benches in the gazebo. "I hadn't thought of it like that." She cocked her head, her hair falling between them like a sheet. "That's really… I don't know. A really good thought."

He pulled her close and kissed the top of her head. "I know you hate being asked how you're feeling, but…"

"About the same," she said. "It comes and goes, like waves, but without any real predictability."

They were quiet for what felt like a long time but probably wasn't.

"It still doesn't feel real, you know?" she said.

"Which part of our lives?" he asked heavily. "There's so much going on."

"I meant the baby, but you're not wrong." She sat up and turned to him. "Is this the life we thought we'd have?"

He chuckled and shook his head. "Anything but."

"The stupid pandemic," Tess sighed, and Mack agreed. That, of everything, had changed not only their lives but their expectations, as well. A year and a half ago, back when there were just whispers of a weird virus floating around, he never would have guessed he and Tess would be living in the farmhouse more than their house in the city, that they'd have been chased out of their offices, that socializing would be unsafe—all of it. And that was before he considered the death toll, which continued to stagger him with its always increasing numbers.

And yet, somehow, they were all still living, still caught up in the petty garbage of their day-to-day lives.

He snorted and smiled, shaking his head slightly.

"What?"

"Just thinking of how stupid it is to be so wrapped up in our petty shit, and yet here we are, trying to be kind to a Flaherty."

"*You're* the one trying to be kind. I'm just… I don't know," she said and let out a breath. "Trying to lay low and hope we figure out what he's up to before it bites us on the ass."

"Still convinced it's in those records boxes?"

"Absolutely."

He nodded. "We need to get those last three up and let Kiersten get to work on all of it. I wish we could do it tomorrow."

"What if you and Roger and I try?"

"Tess. You can't lift one."

"Fine. What if I call Red and have him come out. Could the three of you do it?"

Mack considered. Three of them... "Probably not," he said heavily. "The boxes are heavy, and just awkward. You saw how many hands we needed from below."

"What if the three of you *are* below, and maybe my mom and Gray and I help guide the box onto something like a blanket once you shove it up to us? And we don't let Kiersten leave until she adds her muscles to the effort."

She wasn't far off with that idea. They had found the best success with lifting the first two boxes from the bottom and heaving them, pretty much as she described. The crew in the laundry room hadn't really had to do too terribly much other than clear them out of the way once the group below lifted them high enough.

And as for their historian, she'd been a total surprise in person. Mack had a feeling there wasn't a single thing she couldn't do.

"I think we'd need more than the four of us," he said. "We needed all six of us down there today."

"So I bring out a couple more strong bodies from the office. And I could probably help at least steady a box. I'm not exactly a weakling."

"But you're growing one."

She yawned, although he thought she had been about to concede that point.

"Should we head back?"

"I hate to say yes," she said with a nod, "but I'm afraid you'll have to carry me back to the house because I might fall asleep right here, and I bet you've done more than enough heavy lifting for one day."

"Babe, I'll carry you anywhere, at any time." He turned, but she didn't look interested in kissing him; she was standing up and reaching for his hand, as if to pull him to his feet.

He told himself to be happy she was doing so well, and he let her lead him back to the house.

FORTY-ONE

CHAD

Being left dangling was almost worse than getting beat up, Chad thought in the middle of that week as the sun started to set, and he realized he was shifting back into awareness mode. At some point over the next twelve hours, the go-fer goons would probably show up and bring him to his father's office. If he was lucky, he'd get to be breathing when he left.

There were easy precautions to take: wearing clothes to bed. Setting some sort of trap at the doors that would make noise if one or the other was opened, and same for the windows.

All those glass beer bottles people were still leaving in his yard were coming in awfully handy. He was glad he hadn't dumpstered them; a neighbor had come by and asked if they could take them to the recycling center for him and he'd almost said yes.

But still, he had no intentions of sleeping. Not until he knew the goons were going to leave him alone. Or show up and just get it over with.

He was sure this was yet another form of torture engineered by his father.

Problem was, it was a lot more effective than any beating.

This was probably Sophie's doing, he decided. She'd been talking about how, since the beatings weren't working, Dad needed to change his tactics. Next, they were going to have a talk about respect, torture, and what she'd do when he took Ford's goonies up on their offer to leave town—which he'd do in a heartbeat if this torture didn't end.

He wandered around the house, taking it all in yet again. Despite its condition, it was a lot bigger than anything his father had let him live in since he'd turned eighteen, and most of the space was still empty. He'd found a couple things in the trash in his yard that he'd made his, but nothing big: an unbroken set of glass candlesticks—at least, he was pretty sure they were glass—and a couple blankets that, after he'd washed them three times, no longer smelled bad and looked good on the cheap couch he'd bought.

He still needed a better dining set than the card table that had been there when he'd moved in, a dresser… Of course, the kitchen. The list went on, and each time he walked through the rooms, he added to it. The whole damn house needed to be fixed up.

Which meant he needed a job so he'd have a way to pay for it. Being free of Daddy didn't just mean the end of these late-night visits. It meant getting entirely free of the old man. Probably, he thought painfully, it meant working for someone else and abandoning all of his ideas for his own business. Then again, it wasn't like he'd had any idea what to do once he'd drawn up the ideas. His father made it look so simple: Come up with an idea and make it happen. Unfortunately, it seemed William Flaherty had a bunch of people who knew what to do with his ideas.

Chad didn't.

The other thing getting a job meant was walking away from a lot of money. But what was the point of having Daddy's money if he was always afraid that the next time his father summoned him to the office, there'd be plastic on the floor, any money he had would be forfeit, and someone would find his bones in the twenty-second century and wonder what his story was.

"It's not even a good story," Chad muttered, walking around the first floor again, the cat following him like he was dangling a toy behind him, which he spent entirely too much time doing. But the cat liked it, and when the cat was happy, it wasn't biting.

Like Mackenzie and Cartieri's, his place was three stories, which meant it was taller than it was wide—but what did you expect from a rowhouse?

He steered his thoughts back to that nebulous place they'd just tried to go. He had some cash. What if he got a hotel room for the night? Who ever said he had to sit around and wait for his father's summons? He wanted to be free, didn't he?

The cash was where he'd left it and he tucked it into his pocket, hoping there wasn't some tracking device in his clothes or something. He'd already done what he could to find anything on his phone; it seemed to be clean, although maybe some sophisticated software could find something. Besides, his dad had never had Go-fer Stanley and his henchmen take his phone from him, so there really wasn't a reason to expect they were using it to spy on him.

That probably meant his dad was watching him through some cameras or something in the house.

He filled the cat's bowl with dry food, checked its water, and left the house, pausing on the porch and checking the street for the go-fer goons, but his sweep kept being interrupted by the sight of Mackenzie and Cartieri's house. They had security on it like nothing doing, so he knew he couldn't break in, but what if…

He ducked back into the house and grabbed a Sharpie—another gift from the front yard—and then out back, where he'd piled cardboard for the firepit, and did his best to sneak over to the house across the street.

They didn't have a back porch. Of course not.

But they had a side porch, and he shoved his cardboard under the gate, then jumped it and stopped to look for the camera.

They hadn't bothered to hide it. Then again, why should they? They had signs up that the property was being watched—which was what he was counting on.

He uncapped his Sharpie and wrote his message for the security team.

FORTY-TWO

MACK

"You have to be kidding me," Mack told the security team when they called later that night.

"No sir. What would you like us to do about it?"

"Is there a way to tell him to stay there?" He glanced at Tess, who was chewing on her bottom lip as she listened.

"Yes."

"Do that. I'll leave now and see what's going on." After a few more exchanges, he hung up and turned to Tess. "Think it's a setup?"

"I'm not sure," she said slowly.

He tried not to stare at her lower lip. It was swollen and lush, begging him to stay and kiss it.

"Mack?"

"Yeah?" he asked, shaking himself out of his thoughts of kissing her. He'd also missed what she'd said, but he thought it was that Flaherty wasn't smart enough to set Mack up without help from his father. And he had made more than a few random noises about getting out. Maybe he actually meant it.

"Are you going?"

"Huh? Oh, yeah." He leaned forward to give her a kiss. "You are incredibly distracting."

"Still?" But she was smiling, and he knew he'd said the right thing. Best of all, it was the truth.

"Forever," he told her and pulled himself off their bed and toward clothes. It'd be fastest if he ran, and it wasn't like it would be a taxing run. Plus, as soon as he came out into town at the trailhead, Noah's guys would get eyes on him. He was sure they were already investigating, trying to get ahead of whatever this was.

Delia's little private protection service was a handy thing and he appreciated that they kept an eye on him and Tess. Although, he reminded himself, he needed to stop thinking of it as her private service. Noah had launched a subscription service, and it sounded like people were signing up. Women, in particular, liked the idea of being able to walk around seemingly alone, their safety almost guaranteed.

Change was coming to Port Kenneth, whether or not people liked it—and whether or not people pointed to the return of PharmaSci and a Mackenzie as the reason for it. If it was good for the city, it was good for people's lives. What was worth complaining about when the end result was a better life and a more vibrant, safer city?

He didn't hear the whistles until he was past the trailhead and at the playground that was being built on the empty lot that had once, a very long time ago now, been the firehouse.

"I may need you," he said to no one, trusting that he was being heard. "Maybe hang a little close to my house until it's all resolved?"

He hadn't expected an answer and continued his run to the house.

When he got to the house, no one was on the side porch. Mack paused, hands on his hips, his breath a little heavier than he'd intended, looking for Chad.

"I'm right here," Chad said softly, his voice strained. He'd stuffed himself in a shadow in the back corner of the porch.

Mack wasn't sure if the guy was so quiet because he was paranoid or so he didn't startle Mack. Probably the former; the guy *was* a Flaherty.

"What's going on?"

"I've been afraid to sleep since *that* picture ran in the *City Central*. It's just a matter of time before he kills me; I'm not supposed to be making friends with you. I'm supposed to be getting dirt on you."

"We're anything but friends," Mack said, thinking it was nice to hear confirmation of the truth at last.

"Well, whatever. Can you help me get a safe place for a day or two? I have cash for a hotel, but no ID or credit card that's not linked to him."

Mack paused. "Are you making a serious bid for freedom?"

"Yeah." The word came without hesitation. "If I don't, I swear he's going to kill me. Sophie—my sister—can only save my hide so many times."

Mack raised an eyebrow. That sounded like an exaggeration—except maybe it wasn't. Over the past two days, Kiersten had shared some of the information she'd already found about the Flahertys. They liked to throw their weight around and be thuggish. That wasn't exactly enlightening information; it just meant that the present-day Flahertys weren't much different from their ancestors.

"And what do you want me to do?" he asked. "Just trust you and open up one of my houses to you?" Actually, he thought, sending Chad up to New York and letting Krista be his host wasn't such a bad idea. There was no way Flaherty would been able to get near that place, and he was almost sorry he wouldn't be able to see Krista work on Chad and get him to spill any Flaherty secrets. If he knew any; the guy seemed pretty clueless and low in the family hierarchy.

Besides, the only secret he was interested in learning was what William Flaherty wanted from the

Mackenzies. Beyond chasing them out of town, that was. The guy *wanted* something.

"I don't know," Chad said, stepping out of the shadows just a bit. He hung his head and shook it, his hands working. "But I can't keep on like this. I need to be free of him. I'm tired of doing what he wants."

"What exactly does he want you to be doing?"

The other guy shrugged. "Wish I knew, but it's like everything I do is exactly wrong. Even when it's what he wanted me to do. And I'm tired of it. I just..." He stared off the porch. "I just want to run my own life. I am tired of chasing after approval I'll never get."

Mack understood that. It summed up part of his own relationship with his own father. That didn't make their current situation any easier, though. "So tell me, then," he said with a heavy sigh, "what your father's long game is. You've got to know *that*."

Chad pulled one of the chairs into the corner and took a seat. Mack leaned against the railing and waited.

"I don't know," the other man said after the silence had started to stretch. "But it's something that goes back before even he was born."

Something clicked and Mack raised his eyebrows. "The Mackenzie Treasure?"

"Sure. I guess. I mean, I really don't know, but that sounds like the sort of thing he'd like to get his hands on. How big is it?"

"Bigger than he can imagine," Mack said and smiled at the truth of that statement. It also wasn't what Flaherty could ever imagine. Not only would the man never value human life, and not only would he never value Black lives, he'd never expect a treasure to be the descendants of people his ancestors had fought to keep enslaved.

Just that easily, he made a decision. "We'll find you a safe spot for the next couple of days, and if you're serious, I'll get you some official word on the Mackenzie Treasure that you can use to bargain your freedom from your dad."

"My cat—"

"Seriously?" Mack shook his head. *That* was what he was worried about?

Just as fast, he checked himself. The guy had *something* other than his own skin that he cared about. It was a good first step. And if the cat was anything like Scram, Mack did understand.

"Hey," Chad protested, sounding hurt. "I took him to the vet and bought him flea stuff." He swallowed hard and clamped his lips together, his arms crossing over his chest.

"What aren't you telling me?" The cat was *only* a first step, Mack reminded himself.

Chad let out a sigh. "The vet traced his microchip. The first owner paid for the visit and the flea medicine, told the vet to change over the chip to me, and the cat's mine if I won't report him for dumping him."

"What? Why?"

"Well... the guy—the cat," he added as if Mack hadn't known that, "bites. Like, a *lot*. Unless I play with him until he's worn out." Chad sat a little straighter and nodded once, definitively. "The vet told me it was the exact right thing to be doing."

There was something sad about a twenty-something man who was proud of being able to figure out that he needed to play with a cat.

"What's its name?" Mack asked, wondering why he was going down this rabbit hole at all. It wasn't like the cat and Scram would have playdates. Maybe if the cat didn't like to bite, but as things were, there was no way Mack was going to let Scram get hurt.

"I haven't picked a better one yet. What do people name cats? Rover? Fluffy? Cottontail? What does this even matter?"

"Because if I need to have someone look in on the cat, I'd like to know what to tell them to call it."

Chad eyed him, then sighed. "Seriously. What do you name a cat?"

"I'm probably the wrong person to ask," Mack admitted. "Tess doesn't think it's funny that I named ours Scram." Before the conversation could go any farther and they started swapping cat stories, he gave three sharp whistles.

"What are you—"

"Shh. You wanted help. I'm getting you help."

Chad was shaking his head. "You dropped one tidbit of information and freaked out. Notice that?"

Mack gave him a long look and didn't say anything.

"I was thinking of naming him Dumpster," Chad went on casually, as if he hadn't just been stuffed into a shadowy corner and was presumably afraid for his life. "Since that's where I found him."

"Dumpster? That's the worst cat name ever. What will you call him for short? Dumpy? Now you're insulting the poor guy. Give him some dignity, man. He's a cat. He deserves dignity."

"Like Sir Ginger is better?" Chad asked. "That's what his name is now. Sir Ginger the something-something of somewhere-something."

"Marginally," Mack said and turned as motion erupted in the corner of his eye. It wasn't Noah, but it was one of his guys, who radioed in to the big boss and got permission to take Chad—and Sir Ginger, apparently—to a safe house for a few days.

Before Noah's guy escorted Chad across the street so he could get the cat and some clothes, he turned to Mack. "Why are you actually helping me so much? For real. Why?"

Mack didn't think the guy would appreciate being called a dumpster fire—although it fit. He also didn't think he should admit the truth: He wasn't sure.

Instead, he said, "Maybe the Mackenzies aren't as bad as you think."

At least that was true.

FORTY-THREE

TESS

"We should have expected he'd want to know about the Mackenzie Treasure," Tess said the next morning as she and Mack had a rare breakfast together before work. She'd fallen asleep before he'd gotten back to the farmhouse the night before, so he was just now filling her in.

"Everyone wants to know about the Mackenzie Treasure," he said moodily.

Tess understood his crankiness. He was fine with the idea of the treasure, just not the lengths some people were apparently willing to go in order to get their hands on it. "Why should he be any different?"

"Because he doesn't know any better," Taylor offered. They had come into the kitchen quietly and were busy pouring their first cup of coffee of the day.

Tess watched. Their movements, as always, were so careful, so deliberate. Sometimes, it was hard to reconcile this person with the mischief-maker who delighted in tormenting Mack.

"But once he does," Taylor said, turning around, the coffee mug held in two hands, "it's a pretty good bet that he'll back off. *If* that is what he's actually after. But what if it's something less obvious?"

Mack opened his mouth and pointed an index finger at Taylor, but nothing came out.

Taylor smirked and turned back around to toast a bagel.

"Which is what I think is in those records boxes," Tess said, fully aware that no one needed the reminder. "I think the whole idea of the Mackenzie Treasure is the wrong one—especially because no one here in town knows anything about it."

"How do we know Flaherty doesn't?" Mack asked.

"Because he's never mentioned it," Tess said. "He'd have asked Chad something, given him some guidance about what he was looking for, if it was the treasure."

Taylor cocked their head and sipped at their coffee, watching her.

"Dammit, Tess," Mack said heavily. "I hate it when you're right."

"I know," she said and played with her teacup, twirling it on its saucer. It was one of a bunch of teacups and saucers they'd found in the house when they'd first started exploring it; Mack had asked if they were probably expensive antiques but Tess kept saying she didn't care. They were here and she was going to use them.

"But," she went on, pushing herself to view as much of the entire situation as she could, "if Flaherty doesn't know anything about the treasure, what's the point in telling Chad to tell him about it?"

"The idea is that Chad uses the information to bargain for his freedom." Mack closed his eyes for a minute, shook his head, and laughed—all in that very deliberate sequencing. Tess wondered what he was thinking. "He seems pretty devoted to the idea of getting out from under the Flaherty thumb. And get this, Tess. His dad's grooming his older sister to take the whole thing over—and *she's* not so keen to let Chad go, either, although he thinks she might if she gets something out of the deal."

"That's cold."

Mack nodded and drained his coffee. "It is. And ready for this? Chad asked if I'd get him a job in the mail room." He gave her a look; they'd had discussions—more like joint rants—about how neither of them had any say in personnel matters and yet people were constantly asking them to make exceptions.

Scram strolled into the kitchen and jumped on one of the kitchen chairs, sitting down on the seat and peering over the edge of the table. He looked ready for his own breakfast and Tess melted a little bit. She hadn't wanted a cat, but Scram had an innate coolness she couldn't resist.

"We don't have a mail room any longer," Taylor was saying.

"As if I'd let him get near information that wasn't screened first to make sure a Flaherty could see it," Mack said and set a dish with some dry food on the floor near the pantry. "But I have to give him credit for having the guts to ask."

Scram jumped down and flicked his tail, meowed, and went to check out his breakfast.

"Sorry, dude. Cats don't eat at the table," Mack told him.

Tess decided not to bother biting back a smile. They were both cute and she was stuck with them. It seemed pointless to hide how amusing they were.

Besides, Mack knew. Scram probably did too.

"Should we get to the office now?" Taylor asked.

"I can talk to Kiersten if you want," Tess offered. "I've got a light day today. Fucking supply shortages." She made a face, although it didn't begin to touch the depths of her frustration. None of this should have been happening. In an ideal world—which, she had to admit, she'd expected to be living in—they'd have eradicated the virus with the shelter-in-place orders and life would be back to normal by now. Yet here they were a year later, and it felt like things were getting worse instead of better.

"I appreciate the offer, but speaking with her will only take a minute. How about if I suggest she speak to you if she has questions?" Taylor asked. They broke off a piece of their bagel and started crumbling it onto their plate. It was, Tess had long since realized, a nervous tick.

"Sounds like a plan," she said and stood up. "I should log on and see what, if anything, I can get done." Probably nothing, she was willing to bet. But she felt like she had to go through the motions, if only to set an example for the junior people. Red had told her to let herself be pleasantly surprised by news she wasn't expecting—which was code for *check in a few times a day, just in case.*

"Good luck, babe," Mack said, leaning toward her for a kiss, which she was all too glad to give him.

"Macaroni," she sighed, running her fingers down his cheek. He had, of course, shaved earlier and his skin was still soft and not yet greasy or stubbly.

"Just Tess?"

She shook her head. "Just... you know. More of the same."

"Yeah," he said, putting his hands on her waist. "I know, but you've got this."

"Do you even know what *this* is?" She eyed him.

He raised his shoulders in a shrug that he didn't immediately release. "I have a pretty good idea. Take Scram with you and be glad you're not Chad and he's not Sir Ginger, which is better than calling him Dumpster."

Tess closed her eyes. Dumpster. That poor, doomed cat.

By noon, they had paperwork from Kiersten to give to Chad, describing the Mackenzie Treasure and citing just enough of the historical documents to make them hard to dispute without revealing terribly much. Certainly nothing they'd want a Flaherty to know.

Mack volunteered to go out for a run after dinner and find Noah's guys and hand it over, but Tess suggested they just go back to the rowhouse for the night instead. "Mom's hovering over me now that she knows," she said, "and I could use the space."

To her surprise, Mack agreed. "Now that we have the records boxes out of the laundry room, I don't want to hear more grumbling about how we're going to put it all back together."

"We should take some time and discuss it. Maybe a trap door in the laundry room floor so we can go back to using the root cellar for storage?" Of every solution she'd considered and talked over with some of her partners at work, this seemed not just the best, but in a sense the only solution—if they wanted to reclaim the root cellar at all and not move the laundry room.

"Does your mom want to use it?" he asked.

"She's not sure. I described to her how it would work, with a full staircase and handrails, and now she's saying there's currently enough storage, even though this was her idea in the first place. But then she said maybe it wasn't a bad idea in case we ever had a fuller house than we do now, or if she and Gray get the garden running as an actual food source and is more than something to play around in. So I asked Roger when we sat down to go over his business plan, and he agreed he wasn't sure we'd actually use it but voted for the option to have it there, just in case. And he suggested a throw rug over it so it's less obviously there, in case we need it as a hiding place."

Mack paused, as Tess had expected he would. "Who is he hiding from?"

She held her hands up, as clueless as he was. "There's nothing down there to indicate other ways in or out, so if there really was some Underground Railroad action happening on the property, it wasn't in the house."

"Probably the safer and smarter choice back then. You sure you want to go to the Woolslayer house tonight?" He rubbed a hand over his face, which was screwed up in aggravation. "I'm just thinking of the hassle getting Scram into his carrier."

"You're just tired," Tess said, feeling sorry for him—because it was no hassle to get Scram in his carrier. "And the bathtub here is bigger, come to think of it. C'mon. Let's go sit outside for a bit and chat. Hopefully Mom won't hover too much.

Then we can make use of that tub and call it a night."

His smile was grateful—at first. "But I still have to get the papers to Chad."

"Tonight? Says who?"

Scram jumped up on the bed with them, looking at Tess first and sniffing her hand when she held it out to him, but he turned to Mack and gave his thigh a head butt.

"Thanks, buddy," he said, petting the cat and pressing him more firmly against his leg.

Scram raised his head and looked at Mack, blinking once.

"Okay, fine," Mack said, switching to harder shoulder scratches. "We don't have to help Chad tonight. But I gotta say, Just Tess, I feel bad for him. He seems to truly want to get out from under his father and is so absolutely clueless about how to do it."

"Can you blame him?" In so many ways, Chad was following a path Mack had blazed when he was much younger, and for the same reasons.

"Absolutely not. He makes me grateful I got out from under Tristan so early. I mean, that could have been me." He shook his head, lost in thought.

"I'm glad it wasn't," Tess said after she'd let him take a few minutes with whatever was going on in his head. She stood up. "C'mon. Let's go have some social time on the porch with the family and maybe some dessert. Roger said Mom was baking her famous marshmallow cookies today, and I want some before they get stale."

Mack paused and Tess prepped herself. "You mean you haven't had any yet?"

"Only three." She winked at him and left their room, trusting he'd follow.

FORTY-FOUR

CHAD

Chad and Sir Ginger were back in their house the following Monday, which had been somehow untouched in their absence. Except now he was playing host to Sophie, who wasn't hiding the fact that she hated the house.

"I'm so glad this was you and not me who had to do this."

He curled his upper lip. "You're too good to live *here*."

She gave him a mild look. "You could have been too, you know. All you had to do was stay in your lane and—"

"Stuff it, Soph. One thing I learned from that mess with the condo was that I didn't particularly *like* who I was when I was being a full-on Flaherty. I was a dick. Want to know the truth? I deserved to lose the condo to Ford; I was worse than a dick to her. I was *mean*. And I hated it. That's why I stopped going around." He shook his head, remembering back to those days. He wasn't sure if it was something about Delia Ford that rubbed him the wrong way or if it was something about having to walk into his dad's condo and act like the old man would have that got to him so utterly. It didn't matter; he'd had a hell of a wake-up call from that whole experience.

Maybe, he thought now, part of him had wanted her to outsmart him, to make off with the condo, to get out of the situation he'd created to trap her in.

There was still a part of him that was in awe of her.

"But that's what it means to be a Flaherty," Sophie was sputtering.

Chad looked at her. "I guess one of us had to be like Dad, and one had to be like Mom. Hey, have you gone to visit her lately?"

He knew the answer to that. They both did, and they both knew that he knew.

He went at least weekly to see her, always before his basketball game at the Larimer Y. He'd tell her the news, tell her about his latest business ideas, tell her nothing about Sophie or his dad, and then he'd kiss her cheek and leave again. It was one of the most depressing things he did, and it never got any easier seeing her so broken, but she was his mother and she deserved that respect—especially since he was the only one in the family who showed it to her.

"We could both be like Dad," Sophie said softly.

Chad shook his head. "Weren't you listening just now? I hated myself."

"So what's your plan? Going to try to find funding for one of your cockamamie business plans?"

He decided to ignore the insult in her question. But he also didn't look at her as he said, "I'm going to get a job. Learn a few things about businesses and how they're run." Now, he glanced at her. "Legit businesses."

"Please. You know perfectly well Dad doesn't break any laws."

Chad didn't have the energy to point out that was because their father had had a hand in rewriting a lot of them to be more favorable to Flaherty Industries. Which wasn't anything industrial; it was a lot of property, and some other things. Chad wasn't even sure what; he didn't care. He truly didn't.

"Well, I want to see businesses from different angles. Different from Dad's." He hoped that would shut her up. It wasn't entirely untrue.

Sophie clasped her hands behind her back and strolled out of the living room and around the first floor of his house. "Okay, so here's a deal I'll make you," she said when she got to the kitchen and took in its sorry state.

"I'm listening," Chad said, more because he knew he was supposed to than because he cared about what she was going to say. It wouldn't be fair to him.

"I know Dad's funded your mortgage. I'll have him throw in another hundred thou so you can fix this place up—but don't go putting a commercial stove in here, Chad; you'll burn it down and have the Mackenzies screaming about arson again." She shook her head and muttered something.

Chad was fairly certain he made out the word *stupid* in there.

"And?" he asked.

"You have one week to get a job. If you can't, then you come work for *me*. Not Dad. *Me*."

That was probably the death sentence it sounded like. As if working for Dad wasn't, but at least Dad wouldn't chain him to the desk and make him a figurehead with no power.

"Deal," he said. He could do a lot to the place with a hundred thou—and, as Sophie probably knew, the longer he let it sit in the account, the more it would grow.

She was giving him an awful lot, and there had to be a reason why. With Sophie, just like with their father, there always was.

"I'll be back next week," she said and started up the hallway to the front door.

"No sweat," he said and stopped to pet Sir Ginger, who was taking his afternoon nap in a sunbeam.

As soon as Sophie was gone, Chad ran upstairs and grabbed a quick shower, decided not to shave, and pulled on clean clothes. Nothing fancy, nothing that screamed Flaherty. Just a pair of jeans and a t-shirt. Mackenzie dressed like that often enough and Chad decided to ignore the fact that Mackenzie could have worn a plumber's jumpsuit and still looked like a rich snob.

Chad ran up the street, headed for the business district. He knew for a fact there were people there who were hiring.

He wound up in Vera's Café. He hadn't been in there yet, and when he saw that Vera was Black, he knew he'd found the right place.

Vera, though, wasn't dumb. "You willing to work?" she asked him. "Really work? Cleaning tables and doing grunt work?"

"Yes ma'am," he said, not sure where the manners had come from. Maybe it was the need to be the opposite of how a Flaherty would behave.

She eyed him. He hadn't even filled out an application. "You live in Woolslayer?"

He told her where, mildly surprised when she jerked her head back in surprise. "You're the new one," she said. "The one who's not exactly welcome in these parts."

"Yes ma'am," he said because that seemed like the only honest answer. "But I'm here and I'm a homeowner and I want to learn how a real small business runs."

Her suspicion grew. "What did you say your name was?"

He hadn't; he'd just walked in and asked if he could apply for the job. He'd felt like a dork as he'd pointed to the sign in the window. "Chadwick," he said, hoping she'd leave it at that.

Her eyebrows went up, but that was her only reaction. "And that's what I should call you? Chadwick?"

"Why not?" he asked. "I've always been Chad up to now, and that hasn't been good for me."

"This your redemption job?"

"This is my *first* job," he said.

She nodded like she had somehow expected that from a man of his age and motioned him to the far end of the counter, then pointed to a door. "You go get an apron and begin sweeping. You'll see the bins back there. When a table opens up, you take one of them bins and bus that table, putting everything in the bin, and then you wipe the table down. That's it for now until I see how you work."

He nodded. It was grunt work, but part of him thought he deserved to do grunt work. The other part of him thought he'd do it, he'd get paid, and he'd just keep telling himself this was what he needed to do in order to find a better life.

Maybe he'd think about changing his name. Maybe he'd change it to something like... well, not Mackenzie.

But no one had heard anything about the Slates in ages.

Chadwick Slate.

That sounded terrible.

He tied on an apron, grabbed a broom, and set about cleaning a Black woman's café.

If only William Flaherty could see him now.

FORTY-FIVE

MACK

"You're kidding me!" Mack said the following Monday. He laughed. "I just talked to him over the weekend and he said nothing about this."

"Oh, so you're best friends now?" Tess asked, an eyebrow arched and her arms crossed over her chest.

Mack paused. There was something in her tone that made it sound like he was doing something wrong.

She shook her head, her eyes closed. "Sorry. But it does seem like you're investing an awful lot of energy into Chad Flaherty."

He shrugged. "Sometimes you want to watch the train wreck, just to feel vindicated."

"Vindicated?"

"Yeah. That I refused to be what Tristan wanted me to be."

"And you need *Chad* to make you feel that way?"

"Well," Mack said and reached for Tess, who surprised him by stepping into his arms, "he's a good reminder of who I might have been. But you definitely wouldn't have liked me if I'd been like that."

"Definitely," Tess agreed and smoothed his hair at his temples. "You know, I miss Thomas's thirty days."

"Yeah?" It was better than going with his first impulse, which was to ask why she hadn't said anything over the weekend, when they'd been alone at the rowhouse. "But I thought you were feeling..."

"I am, but that doesn't mean I don't miss the closeness. I feel like you've found a new toy in Chad and a new hobby in what Kiersten's learning and..." She shifted her weight from one leg to the other and Mack moved with her, wondering if she was up for an impromptu waltz in that damn empty room. Maybe the reason it was still empty was so they could dance in it more often.

"Just Tess," he said softly, lowering his head to press their foreheads together, "you're not slipping down my priority list." He raised his head and blew out a breath. "I'm just trying to deal with everything and also give you space to feel lousy without any new demands on you."

"There's a million demands on me, you know."

"Which is why I shouldn't add any more to your list."

She played with the front of his shirt. "But you're the one I want on the list." She slipped one of the buttons and touched the skin she'd revealed.

"Good to know," he said and kissed her.

They were interrupted by the doorbell. It chimed softly in most of the downstairs rooms and up here, in their bedroom.

It had also never been rung before.

Almost everyone had gathered in the hallway when Mack and Tess came down the stairs, eyes wide.

Roger had, it seemed, just left and so Thomas was the one checking the video feed.

"If security saw whoever it was coming," Tess reasoned, "and didn't call either of us, they know or recognize whoever it is." She led the group to the double doors that led to the vestibule and opened the front door.

Chad Flaherty stood there.

"What?" Mack asked him. He truly, genuinely couldn't believe the guy was standing there.

"Bad time?"

"Dude. You are at our *farmhouse*. The last time anyone associated with the Flahertys was on this property, they tried to destroy it."

Chad stuck his hands in his front pockets and hunched his shoulders, looking up at Mack as if expecting to be hit. "Yeah, well, that wasn't me. I wouldn't know how to start a fire if you handed me a lighter." He laughed softly. "And I have a firepit. Maybe I should learn how to light *that*."

"Oh, please," Tess said. Mack thought that summed up how he was feeling. He glanced over his shoulder. April and Gray had wandered off, and he frowned. Those two were definitely up to something, but he'd have to worry about that later. Right now, he needed to focus on Chad.

"Hey, uhh—"

"Tess. My name is Tess."

"I know. I just..." He scuffed at the welcome mat. "I think of you as Mackenzie and Cartieri. I should stop that. I know. I should."

Mack glanced at Tess. She looked more amused than anything else and he relaxed a bit. "Anything else you know you should be doing?" he asked.

Chad let out a breath and kept working at the welcome mat until he was able to lift a corner over the toe of his sneaker. "A lot," he said. "But right now, I needed to tell you that my dad said the papers aren't what he wants. He knows the Mackenzie Treasure's not real."

"It's very real," Mack said, bristling. "I can't believe you're standing on the front porch of the house where it was created and spouting that garbage. At me. Who has the proof that it is very, very real."

"But what he wants, he said, is older than it."

Mack blinked. "What does that mean? The Treasure goes back to before the war."

Chad shrugged. "So does what he wants. He said if you're digging through the records, if they've survived, you'll learn it all and if you'll just agree to hand it over to him when you find it like the original agreement says, he'll leave us both alone."

Tess stiffened and Mack wished he had a way to signal to her that he had this. Thomas had finally prepped him for all sorts of scenarios dealing with William Flaherty—and he was standing there, too. All Mack had to do was keep gathering information and see what Thomas thought of it all. "Original agreement? And he has a copy of it?" He doubted it.

Chad shrugged again. "He says he does but if you hold out until he produces it, don't be surprised if he's lying. He's good at that, holding fake paperwork over someone's head. But this time…" He looked up and barely met Mack's eyes. "I get the feeling he actually has it."

"An agreement? From before eighteen sixty-five?"

This time, Chad's hands came out of his pockets. He raised them in innocence; feigned or real, Mack couldn't tell.

"And... I'm supposed to just *trust* the guy? That this supposed agreement is real, it's authentic, and if we honor it, he'll leave us alone? He threw you in a dumpster, Chad. Even worse, he burned down my barn and tried to do the same to my house—*this* house—while seven of us slept in it." He had to swallow his anger. "No. Tell him—"

Chad shook his head. "I'm not telling him anything."

"But you're willing to do his dirty work and deliver a message to us," Mack said and glared at him. "I'm just asking you to be fair to both people you hate."

Tess put her hand on his shoulder, which made him wonder if maybe he didn't have such a good handle on this. Part of him wished she'd take over; she was better in situations like this, where they had to think fast.

"It's not like that," Chad said with a small head shake. He still wasn't making eye contact and for some reason, that irritated Mack. "I delivered the message because it was me or some goon neither of us know, and I figured it was better if it was at least a face you recognize. I can't control what you do once you hear it. And honestly? I don't blame you for not trusting him. I sure don't." He toed the welcome mat again, this time getting it to cover his entire foot.

"Then why," Tess said in the most reasonable voice Mack had ever heard her use, "did you *really* do his dirty work again?" She stepped out from behind Mack and hooked an arm around his waist. "Because by doing it, you're proving you will let him keep asking you to deliver his messages."

Chad's mouth worked for an entire minute before sound came out of it. "It's not that easy," he managed to get out. "And I told you. It was me or a goon. Consider this a sign of respect."

Mack didn't need to look at Tess to know she was glaring. She wasn't on board with the respect part, but as much as he didn't want to admit it, he could see the point Chad was trying to make. And he did appreciate it—to an extent.

Chad let out a sigh, then said, "Because if he's actually acting in good faith, he'll leave us both alone, and if whatever this thing is that he wants is something he wants bad enough, he just might actually do it, and we'll both be rid of him." He jammed his hands back in his pockets and bowed his head, which meant he wound up saying to the welcome mat, "It's just not so easy."

"I know," Mack said, not sure why he was feeling compassion for the guy, just that he was. "And if I can be a dick and say this, it's that you're not angry enough at him. No resolution you make is going to stick until you're too pissed to see straight."

Tess dug her fingers into his side, but he wasn't sure what she was trying to say.

"I've tried being angry," Chad said, switching feet and corners of the welcome mat. "It's just a waste and he uses it against me." He looked up and met Mack's eye. "Maybe I'll never get free of him and that sucks, but so does everything else in my life, so why not this too?"

Tess's grip on him changed. Mack shifted his weight backward, telling her to take the lead.

"You're not going to at least *try*?" she asked, moving her arm from around Mack's waist to his back, as if she were holding him up—or holding herself back.

Chad held up his hands in one of those universal signs of powerlessness.

Tess huffed and disappeared inside.

"Nice," Mack said, not bothering to watch her go. "That's not the reaction you want from her."

"Well, maybe she's got unrealistic expectations."

Mack let himself stare, wordless, at the guy for a minute that dragged on so long, Chad started to fidget.

"What?" the guy sighed.

"You don't get it, do you?" After a quick glance behind him and a nod at Thomas, he stepped out onto the porch, pulling the door shut behind him. He pointed to the chairs by the empty room; he wasn't going to let Flaherty sit anywhere close to his makeshift office.

Chad took the chair closest to the steps. Mack had to stop himself from asking if he was planning to run away; he thought he knew the answer.

"Apparently not," Chad said. He looked out across the lawn. "So just tell me because obviously, I'm too dumb to figure this out on my own."

Mack wasn't entirely certain where to start. "You're giving a lot of lip service to wanting to be free of your father's control, but you're not *doing* a lot to make it happen."

"You don't understand— I tried—"

"Maybe not, but there's got to be more that you can be doing." He thought back to when he was younger and had started squaring off against Tristan and all the stupid things he'd done to get under the man's skin.

Then again, Tristan had never had goons, let alone goons he'd let touch his son. William Flaherty sure was a different sort.

"If there is, I'd love to hear it," Chad said, staring at something. Mack wasn't sure if it was the tree line or Taylor's hammock, or just the grass. Maybe the sky. "I think whoever your friends are convinced him to stop working me over, at least."

"That was probably whoever your dad's cop friends are."

The front door opened and Taylor came out. "Are we having porch time?"

"I honestly don't know," Mack said, watching Chad for a reaction. He was looking at Taylor, his mouth hanging slightly open, his brow slightly furrowed—in short, he looked confused, as if he wasn't sure what to make of Taylor.

Not that Mack was terribly surprised. On top of everything else, the Flahertys were pretty intolerant of anyone not like them.

"Who are you?" Chad asked.

Mack had to fight the urge to slap a hand over his face.

"I'm Taylor Alexander, first executive assistant to Emerson Mackenzie, the CEO of PharmaSci, and it's my pleasure to meet you," Taylor said, and Mack smiled. He hadn't heard Taylor use that phrase in too long; it was how they greeted new people in the office. "And who I might I say I have the pleasure of meeting?" They sat down, not in their usual spot on the stairs but in the middle, in Mack's usual spot.

Thomas came out and took a chair on the far side of the front steps. Mack bit back a smile. So Taylor had broken the dam.

"Chad Flaherty," Chad mumbled, glancing at Thomas and looking even more worried.

"It's a pleasure to meet you," Taylor said, turning to face Chad. "If I may, what prompted you to join the household tonight for porch time?"

Chad turned to Mack, his face slack and slightly terrified. "Don't your employees ever... *leave*?"

Mack gave him a level look. "If I could have brought every single one of my employees—and their families—here to keep them safe during the pandemic, I would have." He wanted to say more, so much more, but Tess had taught him the art of shutting up.

"But it's over."

Thomas shook his head. Taylor turned to give Chad a disgusted look, one eyebrow arched, and it was Mack's turn to be slack-jawed. "Not even close," he said and held up a hand. "If you're going to argue with me, you're going to be escorted off Mackenzie land—by me. The pandemic is *not* over. There's no vaccine yet and we're all at risk. Every single person still alive is at risk. Save your doubting and your made-up claims and all the rest for someone who wants to hear it."

"A lot of people would like to hear it," Taylor said. "I would like to hear it. Unfortunately, it is simply not the truth, and I would much rather hear truths than rhetoric that puts us all at risk."

Chad opened his mouth, then shut it again and, once more, shook his head.

April and Gray came outside, carrying the wine bottle from dinner and two glasses. "Oh," April said. "Would anyone else like a glass?" She leaned toward Chad and paused, then gave Mack a questioning look.

"Chad," Mack said, getting up and moving to the far spot on the porch steps beside Taylor, "I heard a rumor you got a job."

"I told you I'm trying to get free."

"So it's true. You're cleaning Port-o-Johns?"

Strangely, that made Chad sit up straighter. "Actually, I'm doing better than that— although not by much," he added and deflated slightly.

"Gotta start somewhere," Mack said, wishing Tess would come back outside. Porch time wasn't the same without her. "Now that you've delivered your message, are you just going to hang out with us?"

Chad looked around, frowning as he did, and Mack wondered if the guy was realizing he was intruding—and what had taken him so long to do so. "Oh. I... Umm... Yeah." He stood up. "Sorry. It's just nice to be around people who aren't so fast to tell me I'm a piece of shit."

"I did ask if you were working in the shit industry, though," Mack said just as Tess came outside. She handed him an open beer, gave him an odd look, and filled the last open spot at the top of the stairs.

"Yeah," Chad said, edging toward the steps, which were clogged with Mack, Tess, and Taylor. "But you're being nicer about it than anyone I'm actually related to." He frowned and raised his chin, as if looking along the length of the porch.

Mack figured he'd just realized the stairs were blocked. He stood and gestured for the other man to use the path he'd just opened.

"Thanks. I... Uhh... yeah. Hopefully we can end this."

"It'd be nice, but I have no idea what your father wants."

"Me, either." He let out a heavy breath and, again, deflated. The guy was like some blow-up toy with a slow leak. "Hopefully you can figure it out. He doesn't like me enough to tell me these things, and then he complains I'm not helpful."

As he walked across the yard, Chad raised his hand in a goodbye wave, but he didn't look over his shoulder.

Mack wasn't sure what to make of any of it.

FORTY-SIX

TESS

Tess waited until Chad was out of sight, over the edge of the ridge, before she said softly, "Kiersten called while I was inside. She found something you'll want to know about, Taylor."

"Me?"

"Oh, you've dropped the stiff office formality?" Mack asked before Tess could answer.

"Is there any reason to maintain it?" Taylor asked. "I do believe the company's left and we're surrounded by family again."

Mack turned to look at Thomas. "What did you make of that?"

"I'd like to hear what Tess has to say," he said, giving Mack a long look.

Tess bit back a smile. "Well," she said, nodding at him and nudging Taylor. "You ready? Kiersten found the location of the final records box—and that one, apparently, has the bombshell to end all bombshells in it."

"Let me guess," Mack said, an edge to his voice that Tess wasn't sure how to interpret, "it's something Flaherty would kill for."

"It's finally the truth and the story of what started their feud. Be it a dispute over property, a marriage gone bad, a business deal gone sour, or something else entirely."

"I'm glad you didn't let Chad know."

"Don't insult your wife, Emerson," Thomas told him.

Tess turned and smiled her thanks at him.

"I'm not trying to. Are we sure he's gone?"

"No, but he had no reason to stay," Tess said as Taylor stood up and headed down the yard. "Mom?"

she turned in the other direction, but her mom and Gray had their heads together.

They were also, she noticed, holding hands. And her mother had that flush, the one that's common when things are new and fresh and both exciting and unbelievable at the same time.

Pleased to see it, she licked her lips and turned back to Mack, sliding across the top step to sit beside him. He and Taylor had switched positions; he was usually the one in the middle. She wondered if it was in reaction to Chad's visit and decided it probably was. Putting Taylor in the middle probably made them feel safer.

Taylor came back just as Tess was getting settled up against Mack, who put his arm around her shoulders and leaned against the column framing the stairs. "Gone," they said.

"Good. So the final box? Our instincts were right: it's in the cemetery, but we were wrong about where it was. It's underneath Ida's headstone, not Jane's."

Mack groaned, but it was Thomas who said, "We have to dig up a headstone?"

"Apparently," Tess said. "So what's under Jane's, then? A decoy?"

"Who knows?" Mack said.

Tess waited for Taylor to say they would find out, but they only said, "Grave digging is not something I'm terribly comfortable with."

"Are any of us?" Tess asked, but she barely had the question out before Mack was speaking.

"Think we can borrow the crew from the root cellar?"

Mom perked up. "Speaking of which, have any decisions been made about restoring the floor in the laundry room?"

"The plans are drawn up and the materials are on order," Tess said. It was the easiest answer, and it wasn't entirely untrue. "We're just waiting for my favorite contractor to have the time to get over here. Delia's dad said again he won't do it, even once the materials arrive."

"Are we putting in the trap door?"

"Yes, because when I consulted with the Historic Registry of Places, they said they may not *be inclined*"—she sniffed those last two words—"to grant status if we cover up the *historic* root cellar." She rolled her eyes. "These people are drunk on their own power and before you ask, yes, they had a very good time telling the famous Tess Cartieri that she has to play by their rules and not do her urban adaptation garbage that's bad for our historic places in Port Kenneth and yes, that is *almost* a direct quote."

"What I want to know," Mack said, drumming his fingers on Tess' arm, probably to get her attention, "is when we'll start on Ida's gravestone."

"I'm surprised you're not up and headed for a shovel now," she told him.

"As am I," Taylor said.

"Race ya for it?" Mack asked, but Taylor raised a hand in denial.

"You run much faster than I do."

"Probably," Mack said and nudged Taylor's foot with his own. "But I'm probably not nearly as scrappy or familiar with the land."

"I like the idea of calling Meter again and seeing how many family members he can produce, but I can't see his brothers wanting to dig in the dirt," Tess said. "No matter how much Sima loves to."

"Maybe the four of us could do it. You, me, Sima, Roger."

"Five," Taylor said. "I have invested entirely too much into the quest for each and every box to not be part now. And I am confident we can do this with that small crew."

"I thought you weren't comfortable with the idea of grave robbing," Mack told them.

"Oh, I'm not. But I've come this far and so long as there are others the ghosts might attach themselves to, I don't want to miss this."

"Since when are you afraid of ghosts?"

"Since you're asking me to dig up someone's grave," Taylor said.

Mack took a deep breath, his eyes closed. He wore the most satisfied look Tess could remember seeing on him in some time. "Having friends is a really good thing." He opened one eye and looked at her. "Want to invite Hank and Jamie, too? We could use his muscle."

"I should have thought of that sooner," Tess said and smiled. She rubbed the inside of his knee, tracing her fingers over the various bones and ligaments and whatever else was there; he'd know if she asked, but she didn't want an anatomy lesson.

He adjusted his hold on her, pulling her more tightly against his chest. "Just Tess," he said softly, for her ears only, "I never thought it could be like this. With friends."

"April," Gray said suddenly, "you should ask the kids before you take their picture."

"But they look so wonderful like that. The three of you, like you're at peace with the world."

"I think we are," Tess said, looking at Taylor. They exchanged a look and Tess smiled. If it was only for that one minute, it was enough.

Although, to be fair, it did sort of feel like they were soaking in a moment before they had to get up and do battle all over again. The question, really, was which battle to fight first.

FORTY-SEVEN

Tess

Tess wasn't the only one who raised her eyebrows when Mom said she and Gray were going to have dinner by themselves in the gazebo that night. "Like a date?" Tess asked with a grin that felt crooked.

It was about time Mom and Gray did more than what looked like flirting. Even though they hadn't talked about it, Tess was all in on this relationship. Gray was smiling more and Mom seemed less sad.

"On the other hand," she told Mack when they were alone in their bedroom, "they live together. If it doesn't work out, one of them's going to be homeless."

Mack frowned. "I... hadn't thought of that."

"Well, Mom lost her house during the pandemic," Tess said, fully aware Mack had been there for that, "and Gray finally sold his. They are all-in on living here."

"They'll work it out," Mack said with a shrug. "I'm more worried about them having dinner in the gazebo. Last time we were out there, remember how bad the bees were?"

"Yeah, but Sima said she found the nest and took care of it."

"Yeah?"

"She likes to use it for her office," Tess said, feeling crabby that she had to remind him of that. Then again, she reminded herself, it wasn't like Mack got outside during the day as much as he had during the height of the pandemic.

Or did he? Truth be told, Tess was too busy with her own job—and too tired with these early weeks of the pregnancy—to pay much attention.

"Should we send Thomas out as a chaperone?" Mack asked her.

The mental image was enough to make Tess laugh. "It might not be that bad an idea," she said. "Can you imagine any of us going outside for any reason and finding them... Oh, I don't know. Kissing?" She shuddered, which made Mack chuckle.

"I know. She's your mother. But you never saw her kiss Dan?"

"Not like they were about to get it on, no," Tess said, screwing her mouth up and letting it tell Mack the things she couldn't put into words. "They were pretty... circumspect around me."

Her phone buzzed.

"It's Delia, wanting to know what we're doing for dinner."

"Escaping," Mack said, eyebrows raised. As if it was a question; the timing of the offer couldn't have been better. "Ask Delia where we're meeting."

Their friends had a table waiting by the time Mack and Tess got to the Jerusalem Joint. Best of all, it was in the courtyard, which was always shady, although the day's heat lingered and the humidity was up.

"It's always thicker in the city," Tess said, fanning herself with one hand, stopping long enough to pull her hair off her neck and fan the back of it instead.

"I honestly didn't think you two could make it tonight," Delia said. "You're usually stuck at the farmhouse during the week."

"All the more reason to escape," Tess said. "I'm glad you asked."

"Besides, her mom's on a date with Gray and they took over the gazebo and we're trying to not intrude," Mack said.

"Do you have to remind me?" Tess groaned. She put her hands over her face. "Ugh. Maybe I'm not okay with this." She took her hands away and looked at Mack, then Meter, and finally Delia. "Is that okay? It's okay to not be okay, right?"

"Just Tess," Mack said and reached for her hand.

"Don't placate me," she warned, pulling her hand away. Mack, probably to save face, reached for his water glass.

"He might," Delia said, "but I won't. And I say you're allowed to be weirded out, but if they're really going to turn into a couple, you'd better adjust." She smirked. "At least you don't have to worry about having a half-sibling who's younger than your own kid."

Mack choked on his water.

Meter laughed and shook his head.

Tess, though, froze, her eyes wide. "I hadn't even thought of that," she said. "But no. It can't happen. I don't think." She paused for a breath, but it was a short one. Panic was building fast. "Honestly? I don't know. You know my mother. She doesn't talk about these things."

Mack put a hand on her leg. She put her own hand over his; it was exactly what she needed to ground herself and she focused on his hand, the way it felt on her leg and under her own hand. It was warm and solid and the panic fled.

Everyone was silent for a minute, then Delia cocked her head and said, "And let me guess. She's not talking about what being pregnant with you was like."

That was exactly it, and something within herself that Tess had taped shut and tried to ignore broke free. Blaming her sudden tears on pregnancy hormones wasn't something anyone at the table would buy. She really had wanted her mother to talk to her about this, for them to bond over this baby-to-be and the whole experience that the pregnancy was going to be. She had no idea why, just that she had.

Meter handed her an extra napkin that had been on the table. Mack rubbed her leg.

"You know," Delia went on as Tess mopped her eyes and tried to get herself back under control, "I have both a mother and a mother-in-law who'd be glad to fill that void for you." She was less snarky than Tess might have expected. In fact, Tess thought as she wiped her eyes a final time, Delia seemed sincere. "I mean," Delia went on, "it's not as if I'll ever be able to have those conversations, myself." She made a face that Tess wasn't sure how to interpret. Did Delia have regrets?

"Can I—" she started, and Delia nodded, her face now expressionless. Maybe it was a bit guarded, but if so, only a bit.

"Are they both okay with that?" Tess asked.

She felt Mack take a breath in and expected he was afraid to let it out. It was an incredibly personal question.

"Yeah," Delia said, her hands in her lap. "I mean, Mama—Meter's mother—had to make peace with it, but my mom? She knew." It was Delia's turn to pause and again, she made that face, like she was trying to convince herself it was no big deal. Except, of course it was.

Meter put his hand on the back of her chair and Delia leaned back into it briefly. She was wearing a strappy sundress and Meter, of course, had on short sleeves; Tess could imagine how comforting the skin-on-skin comfort probably was. She took Mack's hand and moved it closer to her knee, where her skirt didn't cover her skin.

He gave her a squeeze and she took a deep breath, half-closing her eyes. It *did* make a difference.

"Mom fought for me like I never would have believed," Delia said after a minute. "She called every specialist in the city, into Knoxville, and then wherever else she needed to. Mayo Clinic? Cleveland

Clinic? The hospitals in DC? LA? Hopkins? She didn't care. She was bound and determined to find someone who'd help because she knew the only other option was to outlive me."

Meter, his eyes fastened on his wife, didn't move. Mack shifted uncomfortably. Tess didn't think she was surprised to be hearing any of this.

"And it's not to say," Delia went on, "that I wouldn't fight like that for a kid of my own. But right now," she said, reaching for Meter's hand and pulling it free from the back of her chair, her own arm crossing over her face briefly, "we're happy as we are. If that changes, well, Meter's family's no stranger to adoption."

"The triplets," Meter said, as if anyone needed an explanation, and laughed. "Thank God I'm not blood related to them."

"I thought you liked them," Mack said.

Tess wanted to laugh at his wonder.

"I do," Meter said. "But when we were all little, they were a handful and a half. Three little troublemakers who never sat still, liked to bite and kick and shove, and they may have left me alone and maybe that's because I hid from them, but none of us were really spared, including my parents." He reached for his water glass, took a sip, and grinned. "I'm not sure why they didn't give them back; their extended family came with them and any of them probably would have taken them."

"Then how," Tess asked, hoping she wasn't overstepping, "did your parents wind up with them? You just said there's no blood relation."

"Their parents were best friends with my parents," Meter said. "One of those *if something happens to me, I want you to take the kids* deals, written into both their wills."

"Speaking of which," Delia said, cocking her head and raising an eyebrow. "You two have talked about it?"

Tess opened her mouth to answer, but Mack was laughing. "That's a hell of a back door into the Mackenzie money, isn't it?" He turned to Tess. "Should we offer—"

"No," she said immediately, before he could bring any of the Flahertys into the discussion. "They've done enough to get rid of us."

"I was going to say," Mack said and pointed, his finger moving between Delia and Meter.

"I didn't bring it up so you'd pick us," Delia said. "I just figured that with all you've got in your lives, it was something you were aware of."

"I am," Mack said heavily, and Tess blinked. She hadn't realized that he'd been thinking this way, but it made sense that he had been. Krista had probably prompted him. "We need to talk about it. Both grandmothers have already volunteered."

Tess wrinkled her nose. "I hate that we have to think like this." But Delia was, as always, right. They did need to, and not just because of the whole Mackenzie legacy the baby was going to be thrust into the middle of.

"Welcome to life in the twenty-first century," Delia said. Meter, playing idly with his water glass, snorted softly. "And be sure you have backup *after* the grandmothers. They get old, you know."

Tess eyed Mack. To be honest, her first inclination was to talk to Jamie and Hank, simply because she'd known Jamie almost her entire life. But Meter and Delia were both grounded enough to be able to handle not only the money, but the responsibility that being a Mackenzie brought with it. Were Jamie and Hank?

Of course they were, but would they want to?

"You know what you're asking?" Tess asked, eyeing Delia and Meter.

He swallowed and nodded, fiddling with his napkin. "All things Mackenzie."

"It could actually be fun," Delia said. "The king or queen's regents. Like in your books," she added quickly, watching Meter, who broke into a relieved smile.

"Later," Mack said and patted Tess's hand. "Right now's not the time. We're having dinner with friends and relaxing."

"Sorry not sorry," Delia said with a shrug.

Tess smiled at her; she hadn't expected anything else from her friend.

"Just remember one thing," Delia went on, leaning forward and putting her forearms on the table, her tattoo on display.

"What's that?" Mack asked. Tess had a sense he was playing along.

"If you make the wrong choice, you'll fuck up your kid for life."

"As if losing both parents wouldn't do that?" Tess asked. She shook her head. "As if losing *one* parent won't do that."

"The triplets are largely okay," Meter said.

Delia turned to him. "They were *how* old when it happened?"

He flushed, caught. "Fine. Something like three months. I'm just saying…"

"Meter," Delia said, sitting back and drawing one arm under the table. Tess had no doubt she was grabbing his leg. "That's entirely different from what we're talking about."

"Is there a parent alive who doesn't fuck up their kids?" Mack asked heavily before Meter could respond.

"You two can try not to," Delia said and gave them a big grin, then tilted her head. Their server was hovering with pita, hummus, and some of the other small plates, and everyone adjusted so she could put the food down.

"But do we have a chance?" Mack asked as Tess reached for the pita and scooped hummus onto her plate. Really, she thought, if she could eat only that for dinner, she'd be perfectly happy.

"Probably not," Meter said with a smile. "But no matter what, you've got the two of us to be the super indulgent aunt and uncle."

"We're covered with the indulgence," Tess said.

"Okay, then we'll be the fun ones. The ones the kiddo can run away to," Meter said. "Because you know that's got to happen."

He was met with blank stares.

"Just me?" he asked and chuckled, shaking his head and ripping off a piece of pita, which he dunked in the baba ghanoush. "You all missed out."

"Only children," Mack said, waving a finger between himself and Tess.

"I had Leon," Delia said, "but I also think apartment living changed that dynamic, too. Lots of neighbors would have taken me in, but they also would have signaled my parents. Or maybe it was dance," she said with a shrug. "I had a place to run to. We were always welcome at the studio, even if we didn't have class; it was a safe place, and some of the other girls needed that."

"Do you think growing up in Woolslayer affected that too?" Tess asked.

Delia caught her eye. "Absolutely. I needed to leave, but before I got sick, it was the best place to grow up. Your kid'll be fine."

Tess smiled at her. It was what she needed to hear.

"Just quit isolating yourself at the farm already, will you?" Delia went on.

"As soon as there's a vaccine," Mack said. "The virus is still out there."

"We have to learn to live with it," Meter said. Tess thought he sounded like he was parroting someone else's ideas and wondered what he really thought on the subject.

"Unfortunately," Mack glowered. "Really. April and Gray are falling for each other. We're bringing a baby into the world... there's plenty of good stuff, but sometimes, I wonder if it outweighs the bad."

He caught her eye and Tess had a feeling he was including the Flahertys in the bad stuff.

"Kiersten will figure it all out."

"I hope so," he said with a deep enough frown that he changed the atmosphere at the table, and not for the better.

FORTY-EIGHT

Mack

They weren't an encouraging group, Mack thought as he considered his friends and their siblings the following weekend. He and Tess had been joined by Taylor, Delia and Meter, and all three triplets. Delia's brother Leon and Jamie's husband Hank had come too. None of them had any idea how to properly dig up a grave, although Mack was privately let down that Tess hadn't known. Or maybe Delia and Leon; between the two of them, they knew all sorts of unexpected things.

Gray, Thomas, and April had brought camp chairs down from the house and were sitting outside the fencing, on the high side of the hill, so they were looking down on the group who'd be doing the digging.

Mack wasn't amused by them—and yet, at the same time, he wished Tess would go join them. She had waited until they'd gotten out there to claim she knew how to get Ida's headstone up. Mack both wished she'd told him that sooner and that she'd brought in the people she'd talked to so that they could all pull up chairs and sit and watch.

He was a little tired of needing to rip things up in order to access his family history. Not that it shouldn't have been buried, especially with the Flahertys running around, but it should have been easier to access. Was that too much to ask?

Despite a surprising amount of strength from the women, they failed. The headstone had been in place for so many years, it had settled into the ground pretty securely. Too securely, actually.

"What now?" he asked Tess, who pulled Sima aside and had a conference with her.

Sima's other triplets flopped on the ground. One reached for Delia's camera bag, and she dove at it. "What's the rule, Geddy?" she asked, snatching her bag to safety with a glare that could freeze fire.

"I thought you weren't watching," he grumped.

"I am *always* watching."

"She fought off two guys with knives, remember?" Meter asked, watching Tess and Sima.

Delia put a hand to the left side of her face, then shook her head, her eyes squeezed tight. Mack couldn't imagine what that had been like, but the very fact that Delia's first instinct had been to fight back was pretty darn impressive. Mack had always thought of Tess as the toughest woman he'd ever met, but Delia topped her.

No wonder they were great friends.

"Okay," Tess said as she and Sima ended their discussion and came back to the group.

Delia pulled a camera out and started pointing it around the group. Mack would have been worried about where those pictures would wind up except he didn't hear the shutter snapping—and he knew Delia's rules for family and friends. Anything she took today would be for their personal use only. She was thankfully strict about that.

"We're going to need heavy equipment to get this up properly—and safely," Tess added pointedly. "We are *not* risking breaking Ida's headstone."

Mack rubbed the back of his neck as he looked at it. It didn't look that big, about three feet by four. But as they'd dug, they'd found it was longer, wider, and thicker than they'd realized, and as sunken as it was, they'd have to dig huge trenches around it just to get themselves enough leverage to lift it. That, in turn, risked encroaching on the people buried on either side of her—and no one really wanted to disturb that many graves.

"So what do we do?" he asked heavily. Heavy machinery wasn't the answer he'd wanted.

"Divert someone from the barn, I think," Tess said with a frown.

Mack leaned close to her. "Why don't we try that with the laundry room and make your mom happy?"

"I tried," Tess answered in the same quiet tones. "They weren't interested."

"So what makes you think they'll be into this?"

"For starters, it's outside."

He tipped his head in acknowledgement and heard Delia's camera click. Given how close he and Tess were standing, he was willing to bet the camera was pointed at them, but he wasn't willing to take his attention away from his wife to find out. "Any other reason?"

"It's a more interesting job," Tess said, sounding like she was admitting something. "I can appeal to them on that level—the challenge of the whole thing. Get the stone up without breaking it, get the records box out, backfill where the box was, and get the stone back in so it looks like it was never disturbed. It's a tall order, especially that backfill part."

"But you think there's a chance they'll do it?"

"Who knows? I think it's worth throwing the challenge down."

He noted her word choice. *Throwing the challenge down* wasn't something she used when talking about the hole in the laundry room floor, and he wondered if there was a way to turn that project into a challenge that would excite the crews.

Tess chewed on her bottom lip as she thought.

Mack held his breath, hoping she was thinking along the same lines.

But she let go of her lip, raised an eyebrow, and brushed it all off without a word.

"Well, I promised everyone food if they helped, so let's go get food," she said.

Cheese Cellar pizza—of course—and beer and lemonade, as well as a heaping tossed salad and a platter of cookies and brownies for dessert was waiting in the gazebo. Hank begged off, saying he had to get home to Jamie and the twins, but the Ford-Shaikovsky clan hung out and ate, Leon leading Sima's triplets in conversation that most of the rest of them listened to.

The older generation disappeared inside fairly quickly, but Taylor, Mack noticed, hung out. And it seemed that every time he glanced over, Taylor and Nate were talking about something.

He nudged Tess, who turned to him and wrapped her arms around his neck, pressing close against him so they could talk without being overheard.

"Delia says it's just Nate. He's a born flirt and knows how to work a room."

"He knows how to get Taylor to relax. I've never seen them this chill."

"Enjoy it."

"Hey, you two," Leon called. "The baby's made. No need to try to remember what you did."

"We're reliving the moment," Mack called back, but he did let go of Tess.

"I hope not," Sima said and wrinkled her nose. "There are things I really don't want to see, and my boss and her husband having sex is one of them."

"That would be correct," Taylor said gravely. Mack winked at them.

"You're just no fun anymore," Geddy started. "Not since Meter and Vass had to rescue you from New Orleans." He put a hand up as Sima whirled on him, face beet red, hands balled into raised fists.

Meter was between them before Mack could take that in, let alone react. With one arm around Sima, he rounded on his younger brother, but all it took was a stern glare and a single step before Geddy was apologizing and not quite cowering.

Mack was impressed. Usually, Meter was quiet, easy-going, and chill. The guy rolled with everything—Mack had thought. Apparently not. Then again, he wasn't shy about the fact that he'd always been in charge of the siblings. It seemed this was an example of that.

After a bit, Nate and Geddy left. Sima, still angry, said she was glad she'd brought her own car and was living with their other brothers, the ones who *weren't* her flesh and blood, and the look she turned on the seats her triplets had occupied was almost as withering as Meter's had been.

"That was kind of low," Delia said. "The ones who aren't your flesh and blood."

"It's true!" Sima spat.

"Speaking of which," Leon said, "So who gets baby Mackenzie? Just in case."

"Maybe we should let the baby be born first," Tess said as Mack groaned, wondering why they had to do this again.

"I vote for raising the kid by committee," Delia said.

Mack glanced at Taylor, asking a silent question.

"Absolutely," Taylor said firmly. "I would be a fool to miss an opportunity to send some ghosts to their final rest. Besides, any kid of yours who's born with this much land needs to learn to appreciate it."

"You might have to fight Sima for that," Tess told them.

"She and I can split the duties," Taylor said with a nod. "The more of us who get the kid—and you, too—out here, the better."

"Hey," Mack said. "I like being out here."

"Says the man who spends most of his time inside," Tess said, giving him a nudge with an elbow.

"Yeah," he said heavily. "I do miss Ultimate." It just wasn't safe yet. Not until there was a vaccine for the virus. Thankfully, it was growing closer by the day; he'd seen the latest reports just the other day.

"Soon," Tess said, echoing his thoughts.

"Not soon enough," he said and shook his head. "But anyway, we're all here, and you know what?

When I was a kid, I'd have *killed* for this sort of night." All his friends together, making plans, talking about the future, wanting to be together…

He'd spent a lot of time as a kid dreaming of exactly this.

"Despite the failure at moving the headstone," Mack said to Tess once everyone had left—Meter and Delia and Leon had all cited work in the morning as the only reason they were leaving, although Delia had smirked and told the men they needed better bosses—and Taylor had helped them clean up before heading up to their room for the night, "this was a good night."

"You like any night when you can hang with your friends."

"I like having good friends."

Tess tweaked his chin. He both loved and hated when she did that, but she leaned against him, looking up at him, her eyes sparkling. "I hope when the baby comes, it doesn't change our social life much. Jamie said it might. People without kids have a hard time relating to couples with kids."

"I have a strange feeling we're stuck with Meter and Delia for the long haul," he said. It wasn't a surprise that he was okay with that. They kept things interesting.

But then again, given how Meter handled his siblings, Mack doubted he'd be scared off by a baby.

He chuckled and Tess asked what was so funny. "Is it me, or can you see Meter hogging the baby?"

Tess gave him a side-eye. "Just so long as we don't have Uncle Chad running around."

"Yeah, definitely no Uncle Chads." He shuddered. The guy probably wouldn't know which end was up.

Every now and then, Mack wondered how the guy managed to get dressed in the morning. It seemed like that would be something someone like Chad had to struggle with.

He said a silent thank you to Krista. She hadn't been the most involved parent, but she'd been enough of an influence to have saved him from being like Chad Flaherty.

FORTY-NINE

CHAD

It had been too long since Chad had gone to see his mother. He got lucky and found her on a good day.

"Chadwick?" she asked, her voice as rough as it had been ever since that night. "Is that really you?"

"Yeah, Mom. How are you?"

She shrugged. "I exist." She turned her head toward the window. Chad wondered how much she could see, if she knew the sun was out but the courtyard outside her window was in shadow. "I wish your father had finished me."

"I like the justice in the fact that he has to pay for your care."

"I loved him."

"I wish I knew why." The words slipped out and Chad braced himself for a tongue-lashing, but his mother just sighed.

"Because I was a fool." She fell quiet and Chad let her, not sure how to answer her or if he'd just ended his own visit prematurely. He wanted to tell her about the house and the trash and the dumpster and the blue bucket and Sir Ginger but wasn't sure if she was in the mood to listen. So far since all these changes had happened to him, she had barely wanted him around. As if her circumstances, too, were changing.

"This is your inheritance he's spending on me," she finally said.

"It's worth it. And besides, I have a job now."

She turned her face to him and Chad was, like he was every time he visited, struck by how normal her eyes looked, for all that, by and large, they couldn't see. He *felt* seen by them. Even more, he felt like he'd finally found a way to engage her interest. "You do?" she asked.

"Yeah. Don't tell Dad, although I bet his goons have told him. I'm pretty sure they follow me, or at least check in on me."

"The job, Chadwick. What are you doing?"

Her face had lit up with hope, and he didn't doubt she wanted to hear he'd become an engineer or a lawyer or maybe a doctor who could find a way to cure her blindness or repair her voice box. But he didn't have anything like that to tell her, and that was almost a letdown.

"I'm bussing tables at Vera's Café in Woolslayer," he said, telling himself to own it. It was a *job*. It was money, an income, and Vera had said if he made it past his probationary period and wanted to go full-time, she could help him get health insurance.

He had never even thought about health insurance, let alone wanted it. But now, he wanted it.

"Oh."

"It's more honest than taking money from Dad to get lost," he said. "Although Sophie made sure he's put enough into my account to cover the new house and anything it needs." *Like furniture*, he added silently. There were some things he wasn't going to mention to her.

He didn't know if it was mentioning Dad or Sophie that did it but she turned her face away and refused to say anything else, no matter what tactic Chad tried. She didn't even perk up at news of Sir Ginger, even though when he'd been a kid, she was the one who had loved the zoo. He'd tolerated it, bored. She'd thought it was magical. And now he had his own personal zoo! Okay, it was a stupid orange cat who liked to bite and gnaw on everything, but Sir Ginger was, strangely and unexpectedly, turning into good company.

If nothing else, his constant need to play kept Chad busy.

He left the care facility feeling as empty and lost as ever, but more tempted than usual to stand in his father's office and scream *Mom* some more. The bastard deserved it for what he'd done to her.

If it meant being a busboy and washing dishes and tables and scrubbing toilets for the rest of his life, it beat turning into someone like his father, someone who could do *that* to the woman he claimed to love.

FIFTY

Tess

The plan that Friday had been to meet at Delia and Meter's house after work, cook dinner, and hang out at their firepit as late as they wanted to. The part that Delia hadn't shared was that she was expecting a slew of other friends, plus her brother and more than a few of Meter's brothers and sisters—and it was a weekly event, too. Tess wondered how she'd missed the invitation. Delia said the same thing.

It had turned into a lovely evening, Tess and Mack had agreed when they finally headed home around eleven, Tess having fallen asleep on Mack's shoulder out by the firepit. And it felt good to be part of a large family, even if they technically weren't part of it.

"Do you think," she asked Mack, "that when the baby comes, we really will have this instant huge found family for him or her?"

"Is that what you want?"

"I think so, yeah. Lots of people around to dote on our little one and help raise them… so they know nothing but love and lots of different people, and to *trust*."

"Until William Flaherty walks up to our kiddo and preys on that trust."

Tess paused. It was an important thing to consider and no matter how much she wanted to float in the rosy feelings the evening had left her with, she had to be realistic.

Mack glanced at her and grimaced. "Sorry."

"No, you're right. So maybe we have a lot of people around to get between our baby and the Flahertys. And I know—that's not going to be so easy with Chad across the street." She frowned. "Unless we can find this mystery *thing* that will supposedly get the entire family off our backs for good, and what sort of fools does that man take us for? Even if we find what he's looking for, his grudge is so deep, it's not ending so fast."

"We can hope Chad will be as different as he says he wants to be," Mack said and scrubbed at his face. He dropped his hands and looked at her. "But you've got to admit it's what we want to hear."

"No, it's what we want the reality to be. What I want to hear is the truth."

He pulled into their parking area to the left of the house and parked, giving her an uneasy glance once he'd turned the ignition off.

"I know," she said, holding a hand up while simultaneously reaching for the door handle with the other hand. "Be careful what you wish for. Believe me, I think about that one a *lot*."

She waited for Mack at the end of the car, looking out across the street as she did. She'd meant it to be an idle thing, more a curiosity, especially because the dumpster was gone, replaced by four large trash cans with lids. The blue bucket by his mailbox was still there, and attached to the back of the mailbox was a shelf with bags and hand sanitizer.

Tess was impressed—until she heard, "Oh. Hi."

"You're out here," Mack said and scrubbed at his face. "Of course you are. Waiting for us?"

"No," Chad said. "Sir Ginger stunk up his litter pan, so I wanted to get that out of there." He held up a bag that he put into one of the trash cans.

Tess was so very glad Mack had asked.

"Hey," Chad went on when neither she nor Mack said anything, "have you found anything about whatever it is my dad's looking for? I'd really like to get him off both our backs."

"Nope," Mack said and gestured to Tess to start to head inside. "And I like the garbage cans."

"Umm, Tess, this probably isn't the time—"

"Probably not," she said and gave him a simpering smile.

"But can we talk this weekend, since you'll be gone all week again?"

She froze. "Are you watching our movements?"

He pulled back, licking his lips and jamming his hands in his pockets, then pulling them out, yanking at his shirt, sticking his hands back in his pockets, and fidgeting, shifting his weight and actually picking up his feet and moving them. "Only because I've noticed you're not here during the week, and the other day, someone knocked on your door when I was on my way to work and I talked to them to make sure they weren't casing you or anything. I know you have security and all and they probably saw and heard it all and told you about it, but..."

She wanted to ask if casing the house was his job and he wasn't willing to share, but on the other hand, it had been the kind, neighborly thing to do. Maybe Chad had a shot at breaking away from his father. Maybe.

But it was still doubtful.

"Who were they?" Mack asked, and Tess followed the train of thought inspired by his frown. Why hadn't security told them? Or any of the neighbors—most of whom would have done the same if they'd seen the person. Text chains weren't uncommon, letting each other know that someone was out and about.

"Some door-to-door people. Said they were with some church I'd never heard of. Old Man Johnson two doors down said they showed up on his porch, too. And Mrs. Adelina? The one with the last name I can't pronounce?"

"It's Turkish," Tess told him, impressed despite herself. He was making an effort to meet the neighbors. "I can't pronounce it either."

She immediately wanted to kick herself for offering that. Wasn't she the one always telling people to shut up?

Chad bobbed his head, still fidgeting with his pockets. He even turned one inside out, then stuffed it back in. It made a wad against his hip. "She talked to them, too. And he was the talk of everyone at the café, too. It sounds like they're trying to recruit or something. I don't know; religion's not my thing."

Somehow, that didn't surprise Tess. Not that she was judging; religion wasn't her thing, either, although Mack continued to be interested in learning about Judaism.

"Thanks for keeping an eye out," Mack said and crossed the street to shake the guy's hand.

Tess wanted to ask why. But then again, he *had* done something kind, and that did deserve to be recognized.

She yawned. "Macintosh, I'm going in."

"Huh? Okay." He started back across the street, but she didn't wait for him. "I'm right behind you."

"Tess? Uhh... can we talk this weekend? Maybe tomorrow? Or Sunday?"

"About what?" she asked, trying not to sigh. She wanted as little to do with Chad as possible, at least until she was satisfied he wasn't just saying what he thought she and Mack wanted to hear.

"I've had some people ask me..." He trailed off and she told herself to stop and at least hear this out. "Well, I need your advice in how to handle it. I'll give you all the details this weekend if you're willing."

She yawned again and nodded. "Catch me when I've had some sleep."

This time, nothing stopped her from going in, not even when her key stuck in the lock. Or maybe, she thought as she stepped inside and kicked her shoes into the pile behind the door, she was just too tired to turn it properly.

The worst thing so far about being pregnant was the exhaustion. It was so utter and complete, it was worse than the nausea, which was more annoying than anything.

She didn't believe either would go away when she hit her second trimester. That was still a few weeks away, but it felt like forever.

Maybe, she thought as she called for Scram and headed directly upstairs to the bedroom, they'd start to talk about the two nurseries for the baby: one here and one at the farmhouse. Maybe they'd also talk about the plans to lift Ida's headstone, the progress they'd made clearing out the last of the old barn so they could start on the new one, the lack of progress with the laundry room floor, and everything else that was hanging over their heads.

Not to mention the fact that Red had been contacted by a few developers who wanted to turn some of the city's downtown corporate space into… something else. More companies were wanting to save on rent for office space they weren't using, thanks to the virus. Tess wasn't overly surprised about this new direction; she'd predicted it would happen a year ago. Red had told her to wait and see and not try to predict the future. Mack had shrugged and told her that he had confidence she'd pivot and find a way to make it all work out.

But the simple fact was that Tess loved designing work spaces. She didn't *want* to pivot, but she also wasn't ready to give up her career and focus on all things Mackenzie.

It was *exactly* why she'd dumped Mack back in college. If she hadn't, she'd have been All Things Mackenzie. It would have swallowed her alive and digested her until she'd turned into something unrecognizable.

By the time Mack came inside, she had worked up a full-born anger, which she turned on him as soon as he came in their bedroom and dropped his shoes in their closet.

"This is all some conspiracy, isn't it?"

He paused, his eyes darting from side to side briefly before he frowned, his brow furrowing the way it did when he was utterly confused.

Somehow, that made her even angrier.

"You want me to give up my job and work for you. For the farm. For—" She waved her arms around, words failing her.

Mack grabbed her and pulled her close. "No. Never. What's this about your job?"

She balled her hands into fists and raised them, about to beat on him, but the simple fact that he didn't grab her hands and try to stop her was enough to cause her to pull back, spinning away from him, shaking her head and covering her face with her hands, no longer fisted.

Neither of them said anything for a long minute. Finally, Tess raised her head and took a deep breath.

"Pregnancy hormones?" Mack asked.

Tess nodded, staring up at the ceiling because something inside her was threatening to rip loose and flood the room with tears. "Must be."

The admission felt like a cop-out, though. She didn't want to be one of those women who blamed everything on being pregnant; it wasn't who she was.

But on the other hand, there really wasn't a good other explanation for her moods.

He came up behind her and put his hands on her waist, nuzzling her neck, then brushing her hair aside on the right side. He turned so he was perpendicular to her so he could use his left hand to trace the tattoo on the back of her neck.

She took another deep breath, a cleansing breath this time. "I…"

"Pregnancy," he said softly and, with his right hand, grabbed hers and guided it to her neck. "Everything you need is right here."

She *should* have done the clichéd thing and turned to him and told him that no, everything she needed was right there, in him, but instead she said, "I know. Thanks."

He dropped a kiss on the top of her head. "Get ready for bed before you fall asleep right here."

"I don't think I like being pregnant." Zombie-like, she headed for their closet, where she dropped her pants and pulled her camisole over her head, tossing it all into a pile for the laundry.

"I think you're stuck."

She jammed her bra on a shelf and grabbed one of her favorite t-shirts, grateful it was here at the rowhouse and that it was clean. It had developed a hole under the arm, but she didn't care, and Mack liked to tease her about it. There was a comfort in its softness that made it her favorite, and she pulled it on, then joined him at the dual sinks, where he was brushing his teeth. "Is this what you thought forever would be like?"

"I thought it would have fewer pandemics and historical Mackenzie mysteries." He rinsed and spit.

Tess couldn't stop herself from shaking her head.

"I thought we'd be here more," he went on, turning and leaning against the counter, "that the farm would be our weekend getaway, that your mom and Dan were forever, that we'd be more alone than we are…" He trailed off when she pulled her own toothbrush out of her mouth and pointed at him with it.

"Explain alone," she said through a mouthful of foam, then turned and spat.

"Isolated alone. Instead, we've got a houseful at the farmhouse to help with the baby, and we've got the Ford-Shaikovsky clan, and Jamie and Hank here in town—at least. There are definitely more people we don't know about. Neighbors and the women in your incubators, for instance." He tossed his pants on top of her laundry, then peeled off his socks. "I think we're doing better than I'd thought forever would give us."

"You and me against the world?" she asked softly, then rinsed her mouth.

He smiled and touched her cheek. "We were so stupid, and it wasn't that long ago."

"It was romantic." She screwed her face up. "Or so it seemed back then." She yawned, trying to bite it back. "Or maybe it'll seem that way again in the morning. I don't know," she said through yet another yawn.

"C'mon," Mack said, bending so he could pick her up and put her in bed. She wanted to protest that she hadn't washed her face, that she still had things to do, but the bed was soft, he was climbing in beside her and turning out the light, and even though she knew it was just pregnancy exhaustion, she gave in.

FIFTY-ONE

MACK

Mack wasn't sure what made him do it, but when he actually got up Saturday morning intending to go for a run and, on the way back, stop at Vera's for coffee and pastries, he went to check on their cars. They didn't have a garage in Woolslayer; most people didn't. He and Tess parked alongside the house, like everyone else in the neighborhood.

Tess's car had been vandalized, with colorful lines that stretched from nose to tail.

Why it couldn't have been his, Mack didn't know.

He wandered up and down the street, checking for other vandalized cars. Nothing. Not even to Flaherty's big Range Rover.

And then, coming up the street from the other side, he saw what the colorful lines were trying to lead him to.

I'm still waiting was painted down the far side of her beloved blue Audi.

"It'll come off."

Mack whirled, expecting to find Flaherty standing there, but it was old Harald instead.

"It's just that paint chalk. But it's still chalk," the old man said. He was wearing a baggy white tank shirt and even baggier red plaid pants with black shoes and a brown fedora, his white hair sticking out underneath the brim like tufts of cotton. He looked kind of like a cliché, kind of homeless, and entirely like himself.

"How do you know?" Mack asked, pleased it was him and not Flaherty. Harald could be crusty and hard to get along with, but he was wicked smart. A little odd, too, convinced he could speak to the spirits in the cemeteries near the farmhouse, but Mack supposed that was more superstition than actual oddness.

Harald stepped up beside him. "Because you can see the brush strokes if you look at it the right way." He cocked his head and Mack realized he was doing the same. He took a few steps back, moving to stand where Harald had just been, and he could see it.

In fact, he could see where the *I* had already started to come off.

Glancing at Harald, he stepped over to the car, licked his thumb, and wiped. Sure enough, the stuff came off. Either Flaherty was mellowing in his old age or he wanted attention more than to sow bad feelings.

Mack could work with that.

Harald was chuckling. "Just like every good parent through the ages. Lickin' that thumb and wipin' that face clean." He paused. "When you going to be a father already?"

Mack forced himself to shrug. "Soon, I hope."

"Well," Harald said, joining Mack beside Tess's car and handing over a handkerchief, gesturing awkwardly at the side of the car, reminding Mack of

Thomas, "when you make it, remember I'll babysit. Just me, and not that Prithee woman down the street. She puts too much clothes on a baby in the summer. I done had to unwrap that poor sweaty baby from three layers, and there were still a few more to go when I gave up."

Mack had no idea what any of that meant and made a mental note to ask April about it. That, of course, wouldn't happen until the next day, when he and Tess went back to the farmhouse for the week.

He hated to admit it, but he was looking forward to spending the week in town and the weekends at the farm, just like they'd originally planned.

He turned to say something to Harald, only to see the older man standing there, eyebrows raised under his fedora, waiting for something.

"Sorry. Did I tune you out?"

"You was *lost* in thought. Thinking about that farm of yours?"

"In part."

"And what it'll be like when it's full of babies? That's what it needs, you know. Babies. That'll let those spirits rest. Fill that land with love."

"We're planning on filling it with sheep again," Mack said. "Are baby sheep okay? Will they help?"

Harald leaned close and gestured to the car. "Love is what will help. Don't matter what kind. That land needs *love*."

Mack thought of him and Tess, and now April and Gray. And just the love and family bond they'd created among the seven of them. Plus Sima, who said she loved the land, loved her job, and couldn't wait to love her sheep. "I think we have been. The pandemic's been good for something."

"You plannin' to wash that car?"

"Oh." Mack glanced over at the side of the house. The nearest water was inside. "Hold on. I'll get a bowl of water." He looked at Harald's handkerchief, which he still held, and handed it back. "Here. I'll grab some rags, too."

"I best be gettin' on with my day. You take it easy; it's gonna be a hot one."

"Tess says that's how summer in Port Kenneth just is."

"Tell her old Harald says hello."

"I'm right here," she said from the porch. She had hiked a leg onto the edge of the railing and was watching.

Mack jumped. "Oh, hey. Why are you up?"

"I heard voices." She cocked her head, first one way and then the other, the way she did when she was about to light into him for something.

He held up a hand. "It's a good thing you did. Flaherty left us a message, and Harald was helping me figure out that it's not permanent."

"A message?"

Harald clapped him on the shoulder, gave Tess a friendly wave, and headed up the sidewalk. Mack felt very alone and apprehensive. Maybe even a bit terrified. Tess's car was her *baby*—and he was willing to bet Flaherty knew that.

He whirled around and was on Chad's porch in what felt like two steps but had to be more. There wasn't even time to think about it, as he was already pounding on the door before he realized what he was doing, and when the guy answered, blinking sleep out of his face, his hair sticking up all over the place, again wearing only a pair of boxer shorts, Mack shoved into him and through the door, pushing the other man back into the house.

"Door!" Chad managed to get out but out of habit, Mack had kicked it shut behind him.

When Mack had Chad pinned against some wall—he wasn't even sure what room they were in—he leaned forward to get in the guy's face. "What. Did. You. Tell. Your. Father. About. Tess. And. Her. Car."

He didn't care that he was spitting in Chad's face. Asshole deserved it.

Chad blinked a few times, then gave Mack one of those squinty-eyed looks that made him look like a gopher but also meant he had no idea what Mack was talking about. "Her *car*? What?"

Mack wished the guy had a shirt on so he could drag him around by that. He'd never perfected the really good ear grab that grannies all seemed to know thanks to some hormone or something, and that wasn't violent enough anyway. "Go look!"

He let go of Chad and pointed at the front window. Chad flinched and ducked his head into his shoulders, holding his hands up in surrender and supplication, and went obediently to the window. Mack was more than a little disappointed that all that was visible were the lines across the back end. "What the fuck?" He turned to Mack. "I swear to you on every cell in my body that the only things I told him were to leave all three of us alone and to give it up about the fucking farm already. But you know he doesn't listen to me."

"This is one time where he should have. Where can I find him?"

"Hey. No. You do *not* want to do that."

"Hey. Yes. Yes, I do."

Chad held up his hands. Because he was seriously in Chad's personal space, Mack grudgingly took a small step back. It was that or potentially let Flaherty make contact. "It's a very good way to shorten your life expectancy. Mack, he's got people around him all the time. He'd let you get close just so he could nod at his goons. Trust me on this one; I'm speaking from experience."

Mack had enough clarity of thought to figure it was exactly what the elder Flaherty wanted. Maybe the same could be said for this scene, with him and Chad. "How closely is he watching this place?"

"I don't think at all," Chad said. "Your mystery security man had the place checked for me while they hid me. Back off?"

Mack glared but let Flaherty move away from the window. He didn't even hesitate, moving out of sight of anyone who might be on the street. Something about it felt practiced, like Chad knew exactly where to stand to be invisible. It wasn't the least bit creepy. "What does he want from us?" Mack asked.

Chad raised his hands yet again. "I have no idea, but whatever it is, he *wants* it. And if he's outright bugging *you* now, he's running out of patience."

Mack ran a hand through his hair. This was going down in history as the worst run ever. "And when he burned the barn? That wasn't him running out of patience?"

"That was making sure he had your attention. And if I haven't told you yet, I yelled at him about it. Got the snot beat out of me for it, too." He shook his head. "At least, I think that was one of the reasons. That's been his thing lately because nothing says father-son bonding like letting your goons beat up your only legitimate son."

Mack wasn't sure how to answer that, so he just stared at the guy, whose bitterness didn't last long.

"I don't know what to tell you, man," Chad said when the silence stretched. "Whatever you're doing, do it faster."

Mack glared at him and Chad again raised his hands, this time to protest his innocence. "Look, he thinks he rules everything. Including you."

Mack snorted. "If he wants whatever it is he thinks I've got, he doesn't have a lot of leverage."

A calculating light came into Flaherty's eye. "You willing to go toe to toe with him if you have to?"

If there was a right answer to that, Mack didn't know what it could be. "Not if it's going to get physical, but if you're thinking of going to him and telling him to back off and be patient, I won't say no."

"And you did make good about the truth about the Treasure." Chad nodded. "The idea of talking to him again gives me the willies, but I can work with that."

They looked at each other for a long minute.

"Did you just officially change sides in this fight?" Mack asked.

"I think I did," Chad said, looking away and turning slightly pink with what Mack hoped was embarrassment. "I still wouldn't trust me with anything you don't want him to beat out of me because his goons say I cry faster than a hungry newborn, but yeah. If I get to choose who comes out on top, it's you. No question."

Mack cocked an eyebrow. "And not because I'm in your face?" He was distracted by the arrival of the cat, who rubbed against his ankle.

"Be care—" It was all Chad got out before the cat turned and bit Mack.

"Hey," he said, bending down and picking up the cat, tucking it against his side the way he did with Scram. "Biting's rude. Do you need a toy?"

Chad actually looked grateful. "This," he said and grabbed a laser pointer. "This is why I'm on your side."

Mack took the pointer and put the cat down, then flicked the switch before the cat could bite him again. With a meow, the cat ran after the laser. "Because I'm nice to your cat?"

"My dad would have broken his neck, so yeah."

They watched the cat play with the laser, Chad showing Mack some of Sir Ginger's favorite games.

"I'll take the kindness over the asshole every day," Chad said.

"Exactly why I broke with Tristan," Mack agreed, hating that he understood so completely.

FIFTY-TWO

TESS

It wasn't that the weekend had been so bad, Tess told both Jamie and Delia Sunday night after dinner, when the men went off in search of something or other—probably more beer, but Tess was privately hoping for something chocolate.

It was just that it had been *frustrating*, with the Flahertys chalk painting her car. She knew it was just a car, a thing not worth having a tantrum over, but both friends agreed her anger was justified. Flaherty had sent his goons onto her property again. They might have damaged something she valued—that was Jamie, the psychologist, speaking—and she had every right to be angry and feel somehow violated.

"I've been looking for more excuses to kick some Flaherty ass, photographically," Delia said, giving Tess one of those looks that was both hard to refuse and that spelled all sorts of trouble. "Chad's been fun to troll, but I want the big one already."

"Don't make yourself more of a target for them than you already are."

"Some target," Delia said, her voice dripping with disgust. "They've made a pretty good point of making sure we avoid each other."

"Maybe that's a hint," Jamie said.

"Oh, but it's so tempting to figure out how to steal Chad's house out from under him," Delia purred. "Just to see if I can." She licked her lips, then sobered. "Don't tell Meter. He won't appreciate the beauty of it."

Tess didn't doubt that.

"Do you think," Jamie started, then stopped, pressing her lips together and giving her head a small shake.

"Do I think? Yes, yes I do," Delia told her with a laugh. "But if you're about to ask if it's time to stop thinking about Chad, oh, it is *past* time for that." She looked toward the front of the house, where the men had disappeared. "I am in a much better place, and smart enough to know it—and grateful Meter waited for me to be worth him. But c'mon," she added with a one-shouldered shrug, "admit it. It'd be great fun to make a career out of stealing Chad's houses."

"I just wish I knew what his father wanted," Tess said, tapping her fingers on the table next to her plate. She shook her head. "And then there's this whole friendship with Mack. It's weird."

"From what he's said so far, he sees a younger version of himself in Chad," Jamie said thoughtfully. "Which..."

"But that isn't a reason to be his buddy," Tess said, not wanting to spend a lot of time analyzing Mack and his motives. The friendship, or whatever it was, just felt weird and that was all there was to it. "I mean, we were talking the other day about what'll happen when the baby comes. We'll have all these people around to help, but what if Chad decides since he's now part of the neighborhood, he has to be here, too? And what if he's taking all sorts of information back to his father?"

"Whoa," Jamie said, holding both hands up.

Tess wanted to tell her not to slip into therapist mode. "If you *what if* me or tell me to stop dwelling on the worst-case scenario, I may scream."

Jamie, completely unruffled, looked around. "You have a parking lot on one side of this house and a field that Mack uses for Ultimate on the other. And we're inside. No one'll hear you."

"Chad might," Delia pointed out.

"Exactly!" Tess said. Her impatience drove her to her feet, and she started clearing the table. She felt Jamie studying her. Ordinarily, she'd be relieved. Jamie often knew what she was thinking. Today, though, she was just irritated, but not so much that she didn't acknowledge Delia when she stood up to help clear.

"What does security say?" Jamie asked thoughtfully, which surprised Tess.

"About what?"

"Chad. How often does he come over, how often do they see him looking at the house, how often do they follow him when he leaves—and don't tell me they don't—"

"Oh, they do," Delia said.

"How do you know?" she asked Delia.

"If you're asking if Noah's said anything, the answer is no. But one thing I *have* learned about how Noah runs Overwatch is that he will do all those things if he thinks he needs to. And I guarantee you, Tess, Noah doesn't want to see anything happen to you and Mack every bit as much as he doesn't want anything to happen to me."

"Well, we're paying him for it," Tess said. "Of course he feels that way."

"Don't be so sure," Delia said, "but do ask him about it. He'll tell you every last thing Chad's been doing, including how often the guy cuts his fingernails."

That gross visual aside, Tess made a mental note to drop in at the office in the morning and call Noah from there. She could catch up to Mack at the farmhouse either in the afternoon or after work. But if she called from the city, Noah might stop in and explain things to her more readily than he might over the phone.

The men came back with a fresh case of beer. Jamie eyed Hank. "Some of us—and by that, I mean *all* of us—need to work in the morning."

"There's six of us and twenty-four bottles. Four apiece."

Tess felt Delia's eyes on her. "While I love the engineering talents you're putting on display, I'm not drinking these days. And you all know that," she added, giving Hank a look.

He held up a hand—the one not holding a fresh beer—and said, "I'm supposed to be pretending I don't know."

Tess shook her head. Jamie groaned.

"I grabbed dessert," Meter said, holding up a bakery box tied in white string. Tess and Delia both flashed him appreciative smiles. Tess took it out of his hands, then looked up at him, not sure exactly what it was. "Chocolate mousse cake," he said. "In case you weren't up to anything heavy."

Tess could have kissed him and was grateful when Delia did. She helped Mack serve the cake and took a bite. It was perfect, and she told Meter that.

"I have many talents," he said solemnly, a hand on his chest.

Delia leaned forward and kissed him again. "You certainly do," she purred, the same way she'd been talking about stealing Chad's house.

That reminded Tess of something. "Meter," she said, "the question at hand is how you felt when Delia dumped you for Chad."

"Ouch," Meter said, but Tess thought he was taking it good-naturedly; he smiled and shook his head.

"Is that how you felt or how this question makes you feel?" Delia asked with a sharp, fake smile that told Tess it wasn't welcome.

Well, she figured, it was out there now.

"Both," Meter said and reached for Delia but stopped short of touching her. He glanced at Tess. "Do you want a serious answer to this?"

"Why are we talking about Chad again?" Delia asked. There was something about the way she asked that made it sound rhetorical, or as if she were speaking to the room and not the people in it.

"We're not," Meter said. "We're talking about me, although I'm not sure why." He eyed Tess. "I don't think this is what you really want to know."

She felt Mack's eyes on her and had to admit that no, it wasn't. "I just..." she started but fell silent.

"Okay, well," Meter told her, "here's all I'll say: I never thought she dumped me for Chad. It took a bit," he said, watching Delia steadily as he spoke, "before I realized the problem was that I'd pushed her too hard."

Tess bit back the impulse to ask how. Now Jamie was watching her too.

"And then, when we reconnected and she said she was living on the Ridge, it all made sense." He raised his hand again and touched Delia's forearm, but only with his index finger.

"I couldn't be that poor sick girl from Woolslayer," Delia said softly, her eyes downcast. "Not for you."

Meter laced his fingers through hers, gave her hand a squeeze, and let go.

It was a communication, and Tess wondered what he was saying to her.

Delia, though, was watching Meter's hand, so maybe she wasn't saying anything in response.

"So Chad Flaherty wasn't part of it," Meter went on. "Sorry. I know you're looking to figure him out."

Delia took a breath. "Okay, so I know him better than any of you." She looked up and glared at Tess. "Which, you know, you just ought to come out and *say* already, Tess. This passive-aggressive shit isn't like you."

Out of the corner of her eye, Tess watched Mack turn away, as if hiding his reaction from the group. Which, she figured, he probably was. "Fine," she said shortly. "I'm not being myself. Whatever. Can you just please say something enlightening so I don't have to worry about Chad putting our baby in danger?"

Delia pointed her fork at Tess. "Not so hard, was it?"

"No," Tess said, anger rising. She pushed the last bit of cake away and glanced at Jamie. "But none of you are allowed to tell me I'm dwelling on the worst-case scenario. William burned down our *barn*. That's the sort of thing we should be taking more seriously than we are." She shook her head and held up a hand to Mack. "I'm sorry, but we should be. We're running around, acting like it's no big deal when it actually is. And then the fact that the men he hired said they were supposed to do the *house*, too?"

No one moved.

"And don't give me any of this crap about how it wasn't that big a deal because it didn't actually happen and the house is fine. Weren't you just telling me, Jamie, that I'm allowed to feel things after Flaherty came after my car? Which is nothing like my *barn* and even less like my *house*. And it's certainly nothing like my *baby*."

She stood up and left the kitchen, hugging herself, expecting Mack or Jamie to follow, but no one did.

In the front room, Scram lifted his head from the couch and blinked sleepily at her. She flopped on the couch beside him, started petting him, and let herself cry. She'd tried being okay about all of this, but it was finally too much.

And she wasn't even the reason for it. She was nothing but collateral damage, vilified for being Mack's wife—which was exactly the sort of situation she'd tried to avoid putting herself in when she'd dumped him in college.

She wiped her eyes on the shoulder of her t-shirt, just in time for another wave of frustration tears.

FIFTY-THREE

Tess

Tess heard voices coming from the kitchen, but they were muted, like they were purposely speaking softly so she wouldn't overhear.

After a few minutes, Meter and Delia came into the living room. Mack must have coached Meter because there was no other reason he sat on the coffee table, facing Tess. Delia sat on the floor beside him, legs crossed, back straight. "I'm not giving you some pass for being pregnant," Delia said.

"I don't want one."

"Good. But at the same time," Delia went on, "you're getting one for being the only one around with some *sense*. You two have been through an awful lot and you're right: no one's acting like it's that big a deal when it is. Even if you weren't pregnant, this would still be a worry." She unfolded and stood up without using her hands, then stood over Scram and looked out the window. "And then you've got to look out your windows and see Chad's new digs..." She glanced at Tess and flashed her a grin. "I wasn't kidding when I offered to see if I could get this one away from him too."

"Dee—"

She turned to Meter. "For Tess's sake." She glanced up and Tess followed her gaze. Mack was standing in the doorway, leaning one shoulder against it.

"Jamie and Hank say they love you," he said, "but her mom called and needs a break from the twins, who are also having a tantrum in stereo, so Jamie told us to check the moon and see if it's full."

"I can promise you that Chad doesn't grow fur and howl at full moons," Delia said. She had turned back to the window. "Then again, he got weirded out so fast and stopped coming around almost immediately after I moved in, so maybe he does. Who knows?"

"What did he want with you?" Mack asked. "You seemed fine this afternoon after you two talked."

"Oh, that," Tess said, waving a hand. "That was… I don't know." She took a deep breath, a cleansing breath, and took the tissue Mack was offering. "Tell me I'm going to stop with the tears at some point. This is *so* not like me. I hate it."

"You will. And you're right. I'm not giving you space to process all of this." He rubbed at his face. "It's easier to focus on the records boxes and not on the actual situation."

"But that makes sense," Tess said, mentally adding *to an extent*. "Apparently, they want something in those boxes," she told Delia and glanced at the front window. "And so I don't entirely trust Chad and this whole push to be your bestie," she told Mack.

"Hey," he said, taking a step back, "I'm the one who always talks first."

"Doesn't mean anything," Delia said. "I swear it's some Flaherty mojo, making you think the conversation was all your idea." She shrugged. "I think you're right to be concerned."

"What did he want?" Mack asked again, and Tess paused, realizing she'd never answered.

"Sorry," she said with a shake of her head. "Ready? It's... well, I'd been thinking along these lines, myself, which is what's so weird about it."

Delia pressed her lips into a line and tilted her head to one side.

Tess followed her meaning. Maybe it wasn't so coincidental, but on the other hand, how had Chad managed to get into her head? Maybe the idea was simply that obvious. "A couple neighbors approached him and asked if he'd get another dumpster and if he did, would he help them clean out their houses? He came to me with a list of questions that, honestly, were a pretty good start to a solid business plan."

"Clean out their houses?" Meter asked blankly.

"A lot of families here pass their houses down from generation to generation," Tess said. "That's why it seems like there are never houses for sale in Woolslayer. The downside is that you have generations of collected junk. And some antiques, but mostly junk."

Delia was looking thoughtful, like she was contemplating the photographic value of the exercise. For a second, Tess wondered if Delia had found her way to troll Daddy Flaherty: by showing his son not as a fuck-up but as doing something good—for the very people Daddy hated. Except, hadn't she made that point with the rescue of Chad's cat?

Mack bobbed his head, as Tess had half expected he would. "That's not a bad idea—and not just because I know it's something you'd thought about," he added, giving her a look, which she returned. "And if he can get Daddy to underwrite the expense, he can do it for free or really cheap."

"Get Daddy to underwrite the expense?" she asked, not sure she trusted what she'd just heard. "Mack, stop and think. He exiled his kid to Woolslayer for more reasons than to keep an eye on *us*."

"Bigoted loser," Delia said softly.

"Pretty much," Meter agreed. "And for the record, Dee, I like Woolslayer."

"So do I. I just didn't want to live here."

"I'm glad we're on the Ridge," he said. "But back to Flaherty."

"I have this feeling," Tess said, "that none of us really want to talk about him."

"He's not terribly interesting," Delia said. "Trust me. I know."

"Was he this much of a daddy's boy when you were with him?" Tess asked suddenly.

"Worse. At least now, he's talking about wanting to be his own person. Back then, he was a full-on entitled Flaherty, and he made it at least seem like it would be fun. Now, he seems…"

"Lost," Mack said. "There's not a lick of entitlement in him."

"Maybe his dad beat it out of him," Delia said, her lip curling. She shook her head. "That still goes down in history as the worst wedding present ever."

"Certainly the most creative," Meter said and Delia flashed him a look. They both smiled, although Tess didn't think it felt like something private or between them. It felt like they were acknowledging the joke.

"But what do they all *want*," Tess said, wondering what they would say if she confessed that it was driving her absolutely crazy, to the point she was surprised she wasn't dreaming about it.

"The crew's still on to come lift Ida's headstone, right?" Mack asked.

"They'd better be," she said and checked her calendar and email. Nothing had changed, fortunately; the plan was for the crew to work on clearing away the rest of the barn and ending their day with the headstone removal. "Can you cut your day short and be there?" she asked Mack, half expecting Delia to chime in that she could.

"Maybe?" Mack said, reaching to hook his fingers around the top of the trim in the doorway. "I feel like I should, but I've got a couple meetings to sit in on—in person."

Tess had actually known that; it was another reason they were still in town and not already out at the farmhouse. It was also a trial run to see if they could spend the work week at the rowhouse—which meant, of course, that it was inevitable that she was needed at the farm.

"I don't know how you two juggle everything," Delia said. "And now with a baby on the way?"

"Well," Tess said, giving Mack an uneasy look. "I've had really good support systems. But... I have to be honest, and Macaroni, I haven't told you this yet, but..."

"Go on," he said, eyebrows up and body on alert.

"Serenity and Gerri are asking to take it over. Both incubators. And now that I'm pregnant and getting this lovely firsthand experience... I'm thinking more seriously about it."

"Whoa." That was Delia.

Mack dropped his arms and walked over to her. "Are you sure?"

"It'll free up time I can spend with the baby. And maybe it's time to do something else with Trade Creation anyway. Most of what I do anymore is consult on business plans—and not only with women, either," she said, thinking of both Chad and Roger. "It still fits into the original vision, only with less overhead, which I know Red will appreciate. I need to talk to him about it, but I can put that into motion tomorrow while I'm at the office..." She trailed off, thinking. Truly, she hated to admit it, but deep in her gut, it felt like the right thing to be doing. The right *time* to be doing it. And since Serenity and Gerri were the women who had encouraged her to buy the original building in the first place, they were the right people to be taking it over.

"Are you..." Mack's eyes were a little wild, which concerned Tess. "Are you sure?" he asked again.

She took a deep breath, feeling the truth of the decision. "Yes. Yes, I am."

"Wow," Delia breathed.

Tess eyed her. "Right? But that's the thing: It does feel *right*. If you think about it, by the time the baby arrives, the farm will be well underway, we'll have all this with the Flahertys settled, and I'll have plenty of time to play Mama."

"Your mother won't be happy to hear that," Mack said weakly.

There was truth in that statement and they both knew it, as April had volunteered to be the baby's part-time daycare.

"It doesn't mean something else won't come along," Tess said. "Maybe some mother-child initiative. Or…"

"Or you're not done turning this city on its head," Mack said, giving her a kiss. "I think that's what I most want to hear. That it's time for something new."

"It's time to be a mother," Tess said. She paused, her gaze falling on her phone. "And on solving this thing with the Flahertys already." She looked up at him. "We both know it. It's the only way the baby will truly be safe."

"The baby's got Auntie Delia to protect her." Delia glanced at Meter. "And Uncle Meter, but I'm not so sure what he brings to the table."

"Hey."

"Your super powers," she said, turning to him and touching his cheek, "are best appreciated by *me*."

Maybe, Tess thought, watching Delia and Meter have some sort of private communication in the middle of Tess's living room, Delia would teach the baby how to take risks. She and Mack did, sure, but not the way Delia did, going headfirst, embracing life, and genuinely not caring what people thought.

It was an admirable way to be.

Tess wondered if it could be useful in dealing with the Flahertys and made a mental note to ask—after they'd gotten that damn headstone up, found the final records box, and sent it to Kiersten in Knoxville so she could find the deepest secrets at last.

FIFTY-FOUR

CHAD

"You had to vandalize *Tess's car*?" Chad asked Sophie. On the one hand, he'd have rather been asking their father, but on the other hand, he wanted to yell and stomp around, and there was no planet on which he could do that in front of William. It was also why he'd risked meeting Soph at her place. He still didn't trust that their father didn't have some sort of surveillance on the place and wasn't listening in at that moment.

"Okay, so it wasn't me, and if you were being in the least bit helpful—like you're supposed to be—"

"I made it clear I'm not playing," Chad snapped.

"Well, then how was anyone supposed to know? It's a car. It was parked outside. It was closest to the house, so they'd get the message faster."

"Which was why you put the message *between* their cars." Chad glared at her, wishing for the power to do more. But she was Sophie and she didn't deserve as much hate as their father did. Yet. "To make sure it got seen."

"No one wanted to advertise our presence to the entire neighborhood," Sophie said. She shrugged, but then she ducked her head so she could look up as she watched him. "Who told them?"

"Whoever tells them everything else," he snapped. "I'm not part of the neighborhood network, no matter how bad you and Dad want me to be."

"Why not? You live there, don't you?"

He blinked at her, letting his mouth go slack for a second, just enough to convey his disbelief but not long enough for her to ask if he had problems. Which he did, but they weren't anything that included drooling. "Soph. I'm not just some college-educated white kid; I'm a *Flaherty*. Hell, *I* don't trust myself. You think I'm going to blame any of these people for being cautious when it's the first thing I'm telling them to do?"

Sophie made a face that curled half her mouth and made her eye on that same side squint. "They're just a bunch of losers, Chad."

He spun in a circle, arms down at his sides, frustration level mounting fast. "See? That's the basic problem here. You just automatically assume they're losers. People you've never even met."

Sophie pulled back, her mouth hanging open. "What has happened to you?"

"I got a job. A real job. And that means I'm talking to these people and, even more, *listening* to them all day. They don't like me and I don't blame them and if I were them, I wouldn't like me either. But even more than that, you want to know what I've learned since I moved here? These people aren't losers."

Sophie drew in a breath, but Chad raised a hand and sank down on her couch, beside her. "If you'd pull your head out of Dad's ass and maybe open your eyes, you'd realize how much more you can be. How much more you can make the Flaherty name." He shook his head and stood up. He'd heard and seen enough. She wanted to be a loser just like their dad instead of seeing the possibilities, and that meant he was done here. Maybe for good.

"Chadwick!" she called after him, her voice the same *defy me or else* whip that their dad had perfected.

He flipped her off and stormed out, trying not to let it get to him that her place was nicer than any place his father had let him live since the whole thing with the damn condo. Of course. William played favorites and didn't hide that fact.

Although he'd driven, he needed to walk. He tried going around the block first, but when he came back around to his parking spot, Sophie was waiting by his Range Rover. He still wasn't in the mood, so he took off while her back was to him. He didn't think she saw him, something he decided was confirmed by the time he got to the overpass setting Woolslayer off from the rest of the city, because there was no sight of her. Or his Range Rover, thankfully. He wouldn't put it past her to have a spare set of keys.

The little Black girl and her floofy dog—Aaliyah and FluffMop, he'd learned their names were and yes, she'd named the floofy thing—were walking down the street as he came up it.

"Mister!" she said when he got near. He wasn't stomping nearly as hard as he had been. In truth, it was a longer walk than he'd realized and he was feeling it. The after-rain lingering humidity wasn't helping either.

"Hey, kid." Just because he knew her name didn't mean he used it. The last thing he needed was to be accused of grooming her. Or worse.

FluffMop the floofy dog sniffed his shoe and then looked up at him, tongue out. Chad wasn't sure, but it felt like the dog was laughing at him.

"I went to school today," she told him, just as she had been doing all month whenever he saw her.

"Learn anything?" he asked, like he always did.

She nodded. "But that's not the best part. My teacher said someone paid for all of us in kindergarten to go to the zoo for a day! We get a field trip next week!"

"Wow," Chad said, wondering who would do something like that. He didn't know how big the kindergarten class was, but it probably hadn't been cheap.

In fact, he thought, there was only one person other than himself who lived in Woolslayer and had that kind of money. Okay, maybe not *other than himself*. He didn't have that kind of money anymore.

He looked across the street. It was too early for either Mackenzie or Cartieri to be around, not that they were during the week, anyway. Cartieri's car—now clean and gleaming—was there, but Chad had watched her walk out of the house and head toward the city, and someone on the street had told him that before the pandemic, Tess had almost always walked to her office.

Part of Chad envied that. Walking back from Sophie's had been hard enough, and she didn't live that far away.

"Mister?" Aaliyah asked, looking up at him.

"Huh? What?"

"People say you're not so nice, but you're always nice to me." She squinted at him. "Do you want something from me?"

"Nope," Chad said. "You're easy to treat the right way." He paused, considering, then decided to say it. "Make sure people always treat you the right way." He ignored the twinge that usually came with that feeling. He hadn't always treated his mother the right way when he'd been little, and telling himself that no kid did was almost enough to make him feel better about it. Going to visit her now wasn't nearly enough, although the nurses seemed to think more of him for doing it. And, of course, neither his father nor Sophie visited.

"Now what you thinking about?" the little girl asked, sounding for all the world like she was a grown adult.

"People I haven't been nice to," he said, chasing away thoughts of Delia Ford that popped up without his invitation. "It's not so easy to turn things around when you've been a jerk," he said, this time glancing at Mackenzie's house.

"Well, FluffMop and I need to go home now."

"Have fun at the zoo tomorrow."

"Next week!"

"Sorry." He watched her head down the street, noticing a woman standing on the sidewalk, one hand on her hip.

On impulse, he raised a hand and waved to the woman, acknowledging her. Like her, he stood and watched Aaliyah head to her.

Maybe, he thought, the whole reason his father had demanded he live here wasn't so he could keep an eye on Mackenzie. Maybe it was so he had his nose continually rubbed in all the lousy things he'd done. That sounded like something William would do.

Except at the same time, it meant that William would have to admit that he demanded his kids be assholes. And that they'd learned it from him.

Chad couldn't see that ever happening.

He eyed the Mackenzie house again. But maybe he could talk to the guy, see if next time, he would take some money so some more kids could have a day at the zoo.

Fifty-Five

Mack

Like Taylor, Mack hadn't fully appreciated the difference in the weather between Port Kenneth and Lakeford, New York, where he'd grown up. August days here could be brutally hot when the sun was out, but on rainy days, with the humidity cranked as high as it could go, they were an entirely different kind of awful.

Part of Mack understood why the Mackenzies had left for New York. This was…

He didn't hate it, exactly, but he would take a New York August over a Port Kenneth August any day—and he had spent every summer in PK after he'd enrolled at nearby Kenilworth University.

Despite the rain and resulting mud, Ida's headstone was coming up, and Taylor had managed to free Mack's afternoon schedule so he could be there. Mack was grateful even though he'd told Taylor to make it happen.

When he got to the cemeteries, April and Gray had pulled up chairs underneath a nearby tree, large umbrellas attached to the chairs somehow. Tess and her boss were there, too, as was Georgie.

"I really hope this is what we hope it is," Tess said to Mack when he joined them under the tree, glancing at the situation uneasily. A tree on a rainy day, with the umbrellas… True, there wasn't any thunder—or rain—at the moment, but that didn't mean there wouldn't be any.

"The good news?" one of the workmen said to Tess. "That headstone is close enough to the back fence that we can pull the equipment up outside it and reach on in. That way, we won't have to disturb any of the bodies."

"They're probably nothing but bone by now, but thank you for that consideration," Tess said with a nod. She turned to Mack. "What are the chances Henry designed it all this way?"

"About zero," Mack said to her.

"He was a savvy old bird," Tess pressed.

"Tess. They didn't have an inkling about heavy machinery back then."

"I agree," Gray said. "How could he have even begun to imagine today's technology? Think what he would have done with the internet."

"But," Tess said, more than a little insistently, Mack thought, "they had cannons and other heavy weapons. And the steam crane had been developed by the time of Ida's death, too. It's not such a stretch to think that one day, they'd want to be able to get at that records box from outside the cemetery. They had the technology to lift that headstone; it's only by today's standards that it's primitive."

"She's not wrong," Red said.

Mack knew when he was defeated.

Sima showed up, dressed in weatherproof clothing. "We needed the rain, but ugh, I don't envy the workers. The barn area already looks good, though. It must have sucked hauling all that debris out, but I'm anxious to get the new one built."

That reminded Mack. "That means you've heard back from the Historic Registry?" he asked Tess.

"Sort of," she said. "Since the changes we submitted were actually to restore the façade and make it more in line with the original barn, they told me to go ahead with the rebuilding process. They said they'll either accept or deny our petition; there won't be any back and forth about changes we'll have to make. It's not that historically important," she said, wrinkling her nose. Mack understood.

"I asked if you wanted to fight that," Red said. He was an amiable man, Mack thought. Happy, easy-going—but also as hard-headed as Tess could be once his mind was made up. He'd heard stories of their arguments, thankfully always taking place behind closed doors. Fortunately, as stubborn as both were, they also were willing to back off when they were beat. And as the boss, Red had the final say—and wasn't afraid to use it.

"If they want to be stupid and political and nasty and petty, that's on them," Tess said with a shrug that Mack was tempted not to believe. "We don't *need* historic status for anything out here. It'd just give us protections in case Flaherty gets stupid again. Which I have no doubt he will," she added, glaring at Mack.

He held up his hands. "Don't look at me. And not one comment about us being buddies," he added as Tess pursed her mouth.

"But," she started, holding one of her own hands up, and Mack realized Gray was echoing his grin. "Think about this," she went on, her hand curling so she was pointing her index finger at him. "He led with his biggest move—burning the barn—and then has deteriorated to nonsense, most of it aimed at his own kid… there's a message in there, and I doubt he came after our barn as an attention-getting thing; he *had* our attention already. Maybe he's not the big bad that everyone's making him out to be. Or maybe our lack of response has him rattled."

"Stop thinking about it," April told her, and Mack noticed that Red flashed her the sort of look that usually meant he'd been about to say the same thing. "Whatever his reasons are, they're *his*, and you have enough on your plate right now without taking on someone else's drama."

It was, Mack thought, good advice. Gray leaned forward and, not so quietly, told her so.

"Truth," Sima said.

The workmen had moved into place and were positioning the claw around the headstone. Georgie and his camera were moving around.

"Oh, they'd better not break it," Tess said, turning and watching, one hand near her mouth like she was about to jam it in there in a fit of nerves.

"Like your mother said, enough on your plate," Red pointed out. "You know these guys and you know if it's humanly possible to get that up without breaking it, they will."

"I do," Tess sighed, taking a half step back and dropping her hand. "You're right."

Still, Mack shared Tess's tension as the crew did their thing and began to raise the stone. It was almost impossible to breathe, as first the stone had to be rocked side to side and a crew sent in with shovels.

"Don't you dare damage that stone," Tess told them, only to be met with disgusted looks, which she returned.

She turned to Mack. "I wish Taylor could have been here." She frowned. "I hate that they got shoved out of all this; they've done so much to help us find all the other boxes and I feel like they're as vested in this as you and I are."

"And the rest of us," Gray said. "But I understand what you're saying. This has been a long adventure. Maybe over dinner, we should open a bottle or two of Champagne and toast our success once it's all over."

"We'll definitely wait on Taylor for that," Mack said. "They were hoping to get away, but they had to hold the fort down."

"Where's Ellie?" Tess asked.

Mack shrugged. "Doing her job, I'm sure." He eyed Tess. She knew Ellie had her own set of responsibilities; she wasn't there just to catch Taylor's overflow.

Then again, Tess was so fixated on getting this box up and, given the crowd, having everyone there to witness it, he decided he wasn't terribly surprised she wasn't thinking things through.

He was also surprised she hadn't convinced Thomas to come down, too. He was the long-time caretaker of all things Mackenzie, and Mack was sorry he hadn't left the house. Again. But, he reminded himself, Thomas was happy where he was, which was probably parked in front of cable news, gleefully shouting at the talking heads on the screen.

"Are we sure this is the last box?" April asked.

"From what Kiersten's discovered so far," Tess said. She shook her head. "I still can't get over the idea that we pay her to sit around and read all day."

Gray chuckled. "It's not a bad life."

"She does more than that," Mack said, wondering why he'd been thrust into the role of killjoy. This was his family's legacy, not Tess's.

"Hey!" she yelled as the headstone swung a bit precariously. The crew yelled also, a few of the men jumping to steady it. One tossed an angry look at Tess, and she glared back, pointing a finger at him. "I've made it clear how precious that is!"

Mack hoped there would be an opportunity to get close and really examine the entire thing—and that Georgie would be granted space to do the same. The stone was darker where it had sunk, and he knew Sima wanted to see if it was mud or moss or if it had been stained, and if so, if it made patterns. Mack didn't know why, only that she wanted to do what she called "some biology stuff" to it. He had no idea what that could mean, but Sima had moved closer to the work area, her posture rigid, expectant.

The headstone was set gently down outside the cemetery and Sima scrambled over to it, Georgie hot on her tail—but only for a second. The workmen looked into the hole and reported there was a layer of dirt between the headstone and whatever was underneath, but they didn't know how deep it was.

"I hope Ida doesn't mind that we're doing this," Gray said. "Although I suppose it was all designed to happen."

"Proving yet again," Tess said, "that women just have to shut up and take what their men foist on them."

"Used to," Gray said, eyeing April. "They used to. Times have changed, Tess—as you know all too well."

She looked at him and shook her head. "Times are trying to change. I'll give you that."

"Honey, no one's ever given you a hard time about wearing pants," April pointed out. "I don't know that Ida would have been allowed to wear them."

"Mom," Tess said and gave her a sour look.

"It's just the first thing I thought of," April said. "But don't forget the right to vote, to have a credit card, to own a house..."

"They didn't even have credit cards back in Ida's day!"

April didn't respond. Mack watched them both. Yes, Tess had been touchy over this whole thing with Ida's grave, but it almost felt like April was pushing her, and Mack didn't know why.

"Oh," Tess said and took a step back, putting a hand on her stomach and swallowing hard. "Now? Really?"

"Honey?"

Tess waved her off. "It's just the nausea, choosing right now to annoy me. Like I'm not annoyed enough?" She glared at the workmen. With the headstone out of the way, they were working on digging through the layer of dirt to find the records box, focused on their jobs.

A shovel clanged off the top of the box and everyone froze.

"Can we scratch the exterior of the box?" one of the workmen asked hesitantly, glancing at first Tess and then his coworkers.

"Well, it sounds like you just did," Tess said, sounding resigned. Mack was privately pleased she didn't snap.

"It's most likely fine," he said, following Tess as she approached the hole, hoping he didn't need to assert himself over her. This was technically her show, since she knew more about this stuff than he did, but that didn't mean he was going to let her keep snapping at the workmen for no reason.

She was fanning herself, despite the cool air that had come with the rain.

And then she squatted and reached into the hole.

"Honey—"

Mack was glad he wasn't the only one so concerned.

"It's fine, Mom," Tess said and straightened, addressing the men. "If you can avoid the box entirely, that'd be best. But if you can't, make sure you don't puncture it. What's inside is beyond valuable, so if we can keep it all intact, we need to."

Mack relaxed a bit. She was back to being her usual reasonable self.

It took longer than it had taken to remove the headstone, surprisingly enough, but Tess said she thought it was because they were, as asked, being careful. "The headstone was a matter of getting underneath it, sure," she said, making a cage with her hand. "For the box, because it's thicker, they have to dig out the sides so they can get under it, but that meant first they had to find its edges..." She let out a breath and made a face again.

"Hey!"

It was Taylor.

Mack blinked. "How'd you manage—"

"Thomas sent me down." Taylor had, Mack noticed, taken the time to put some rain gear on. It hadn't started raining again, although the sky was starting to look threatening, but of course the ground was wet. Ida might have been getting a shower—something Mack didn't want to think too much about.

"Tess?" April asked, and there was something in her voice that put Mack on alert. "Honey, do you not feel well?"

"No worse than usual. Oh, maybe not."

Gray scrambled out of his chair. "Tess, here. Sit. Is your raincoat making it too hot for you?"

"I'm a little hot, but it's no big deal," she said, waving him off. She unzipped her jacket and flapped it. "If I delegate to you, do you think the baby will listen and leave me alone?" she asked Mack.

He frowned at her. "I don't think it works that way."

"Well, maybe it should," she said and crossed her arms over her chest, flopping into the chair Gray had just vacated and fanning herself again.

"Hey, Taylor," Mack called. "Do you have a progress report?"

"I just got here," Taylor said when Mack looked at them. "If I am going to walk over there to inquire, you are coming with me." They stopped and looked the scant distance between the hole and the group under the tree. "Although why you don't simply raise your voice and ask politely, instead of making me do it, leaves one to wonder about your character, Emerson."

Mack chuckled.

"Taylor," Tess said, closing her eyes as if suffering, "you're not at work anymore. Relax."

"Just Tess—"

"I do need to relax, Tess, you are correct. Being formal is my coping mechanism and since it is a harmless coping mechanism, I have a hard time telling myself there's anything wrong with it."

"What's got you so wound up?" Mack asked them before anyone else could—and almost before Taylor had finished speaking.

"My apartment is ugly, the new furniture I chose is back-ordered and the victim of pandemic-caused shortages, there is no one else in it, and I truly do not enjoy having dinner by myself."

"Stay here," Mack said with a shrug, flicking his gaze to April. It was still his house, but it did feel like she now made the rules. He probably shouldn't have been as fine with that as he was, but this was *April*. Of course he was fine with it.

"Oh, Taylor, of course," she was saying.

Gray grinned. "If April and I are playing house, you can play the role of our adult child who hangs out because—"

Taylor paled and walked down the hill as if leaving.

Mack gestured between Gray and Taylor, then took off after his assistant.

Until Gray and his mother yelled.

Fifty-Six

Mack

For a second there, Mack had been torn. He'd stopped Taylor in the pasture and was talking to them when the shouts started, and at first, he hadn't wanted to end their conversation.

But Gray was bellowing for him and then he understood that Mom was yelling Tess's name and he and Taylor both were sprinting back up the hill.

Tess was conscious by the time he and Taylor got there. Mack knelt on the ground in front of her, checking her vitals.

"If I go through the trees here, I can get up to the house," Taylor said. "What would you like me to do?"

Mack thought for a minute. "Tess," he said gently, easing her onto the ground, cursing that it was wet but carefully making sure her head was uphill, "what did you have for lunch?"

"I had... oh."

He looked up at Taylor and said, "Bring something to eat? And a lot of water. Maybe some Gatorade if we have any. And one of the blankets with the waterproof backings."

April said there was Gatorade in the kitchen already and went with Taylor, although Taylor took off at a sprint and all April could really do was hustle.

Tess tried to sit up, but Mack stopped her. "Just stay down, okay? My guess is that you're dehydrated despite the rain and you're emotional and it's all telling you to stop pushing yourself so hard."

"I'm fine."

"Fine doesn't pass out. But here," he said, sitting down beside her and letting her put her head in his lap. It wasn't what he'd prefer, especially as the water soaked immediately through his work pants, but sometimes you did what you had to do.

"How's her pulse?" Gray asked, then knelt to check for himself. "I'd like to check her blood pressure."

"Taylor will bring my trainer's bag down," Mack answered. "They'll realize they know exactly where it is."

"I'm fine," Tess protested again.

"Right," Mack said. "About that." He pulled his phone out of his pocket and called her doctor. The conversation was short and reasonable, especially once he mentioned that Gray was there with them. "Her color's already back, too," he added.

The doctor told him to follow his instinct and get her food and especially water and they'd see her in the morning, but if she passed out again or couldn't keep anything down, they should leave for the emergency department and call the on-call doctor on the way. "We've got a couple laboring moms already, so someone will be there," she said. "But I think between you and your other doctor, you know how to handle this."

"Can I let her have it for forgetting to eat?"

The doctor laughed and told him that was between him and Tess.

"Mack," Tess started, but the crew in the hole yelled and started to raise the last records box, and April and Taylor came back with food and drink for all of them. As Mack had predicted, Taylor had grabbed Mack's trainer bag and he let Gray get busy taking Tess's blood pressure.

Gray wasn't happy—and neither was Mack. "But she's lying down," he pointed out.

"Which I can't do if you want me to eat," Tess said. "And stop talking about me like I'm some doll or not here or something. It's gross." She sat up, shaking out her hair and picking at her shirt, which Mack figured had gotten wet and stuck to her—kind of like his pants had.

Nevertheless, he watched her closely for signs she was still feeling woozy.

"Where do you want the box?" one of the crew asked.

Taylor jumped to answer while everyone else fussed over Tess.

"This is not how finding the last box is supposed to go," she said, dutifully taking a few sips of Gatorade.

"It's not how being pregnant is supposed to go, either," Mack told her, leaning in to kiss the top of her head.

She tried to shove him away, but there was no strength behind it. "Tess? Just Tess? Taylor—Mom—"

FIFTY-SEVEN

Tess

Even though she knew what the doctor was going to say, it was still a relief to hear it: Nothing was wrong. A hot, waterproof raincoat on a humid late-August day, lousy nutrition and some dehydration, too much stress. And maybe a bit of a virus, too; no one was willing to rule that out, although her test for the pandemic virus came back negative. Twice.

"You are offloading some of your stress," Mack told her on the way home.

"I think some of it has been offloaded for me," she said, relaxing into the seat of his car. It had an obnoxious amount of room—compared to her car, anyway. It was an executive's car and when he'd looked at it, he'd laughed and asked why not, since he was an executive.

Right then, it felt like the luxury it was supposed to be.

"How so?"

"Well, now everyone knows I'm pregnant, so that stress is done with. The headstone at least got taken out of the ground in one piece, and according to Taylor and my mother, the records box is out and the hole was being backfilled. Once we get home, you can go for a run, take a look at how it all ended, pick up dinner, and tell me all about it."

He eyed her. "I thought we were going to *make* dinner."

"*You* are going to cook?"

"You said you wanted a salad—"

"Oh, Macaroni, I don't doubt that you can rip lettuce, but I was thinking a salad from the Reuben Deli, one of their signature salads, because I don't think you want to be cooking a turkey, just to put a little bit on my salad."

As she'd expected, he paled.

She chuckled and rubbed his arm. "I'm sorry to put you through this."

He eyed her again. "I know you wanted to be in town during the week, but do you think we could have just talked about it some more? This was a pretty drastic way to make your point."

"It was not part of the master plan," she said and looked out the side window.

"Tess—" He touched her leg gently. Before he could pull his hand away, she covered it with hers.

"We've had it easy up to now," she said softly.

"Yeah. And we got fooled into thinking we could just keep piling on."

"Don't start beating yourself up. Let's circle back a minute, okay? You said I need to offload stuff, and I pointed out two areas that have already happened. I've told you that Serenity and Gerri would like to take over the incubators, not that they were particularly stressful anymore anyway. Overseeing the barn reconstruction won't be any different from any project at work I would do ordinarily, and Sima has proven ten times over that she's ready to be the head of the farm—"

"Except she's still making noises about that ATV."

"And I'm still waiting on her to get me all the information about it. I'm not doing her work for her. Not on this one." She took a deep breath and squeezed his hand. "There's really not much else I need to offset."

"Which means you can start taking better care of yourself."

"Honestly, that means we need to be in town more. I love my mother dearly, but she likes to hover, and that makes me self-conscious and then I do dumb things, mostly to avoid her."

"It is time," he agreed.

They passed under the overpass that was the unofficial entry to Woolslayer. Tess smiled. She loved the neighborhood and trusted that once word got out about her little adventure, they'd be inundated with neighbors bringing food and offering to help. She figured she would probably have to explain to Mack why that was easier to deal with than her mother—fewer hurt feelings, for one—but that wouldn't be so bad. Not compared to feeling like she was under her mother's microscope.

Besides, they could chuck the food into the freezer and no one would know when they actually did get around to eating it. Mom, on the other hand, would keep an eye on it all, driving Tess and Mack both crazy about eating it before it went bad, as if the idea of putting it in the freezer was... Tess wasn't sure. A tragedy, maybe, but that felt extreme.

Maybe it was just something her mom wouldn't think to do; she'd have the mindset that the neighbors had brought food and so it had to be eaten.

"But what about Taylor?" Mack was saying. "They've said more than once that they don't want to be alone so much and here we are, leaving them alone."

"Taylor's shown more than once now that they can take care of themself. Besides," Tess added, "it's not our job to fill their social calendar."

"Don't get offended if I talk to them anyway."

"You absolutely should. And when you do, remind them they can come here for dinner too." She waved at a few of the neighborhood women. They, of course, waved back.

The house looked like a refuge when they got to it a few minutes later. Tess knew Mack wanted nothing more than to run around to her side of the car and offer her a hand out and into the house—and she wanted him to do that about as much as she had wanted to have pushed herself too far in the first place.

Thankfully, he didn't blink, otherwise react, or say anything when he came around the car and she'd gotten out and was stretching. "I feel better just being here."

"Good," he said. "Let's go in and I'll order food and check in to see where our records box is and how many pieces Ida's stone is in."

"Oh, don't you even joke about that," Tess warned him, but she smiled and stepped into the arm he held out, an invitation to simply be near him.

The headstone was intact. The records box was in the library and Kiersten had been notified.

"Here's an idea," Tess said, folding one leg under her as she sank into the couch.

"Yeah?" Mack asked, looking up from his phone. Tess guessed he was placing the food order. "Oh, wait. Delivery's backed up an hour and a half. Guess I'll go get it."

"Call Noah. One of his guys will run it over for us." Scram jumped up on the couch and cocked his head at Tess. He gave her a slow blink and collapsed beside her, pressing his back against her thigh and starting to knead the couch cushion, purring loudly.

She gave him his favorite scritches behind his ears, thinking that she must have known they'd wind up back here tonight, since they'd left him here. They never would have done that if they'd been truly planning to spend the night at the farmhouse.

"Seriously?" Mack looked up and Tess nodded.

"Meter and Delia used him all the time during the height of the pandemic shutdowns. It helped keep him in business."

"But is he still running errands like that?"

"For their select few. Send me the order information and I'll send it over."

Mack finished the order, then sent it to Tess's phone. "Now," he said, "tell me about your idea."

"See if Kiersten will spend a few days up here with us, going through this last box right here, in this house, to see if she can find whatever has Flaherty in such a hissy. I'll have the company I need and we won't need to worry about what her silences mean."

He looked out the window for a minute, eyes narrowed, lips ever so slightly pursed. "Yeah," he said. "I'll ask her." Bending down, he gave her a quick kiss and left the room.

The house was quiet and Tess closed her eyes, idly petting Scram and listening to the sounds of the rowhouse: cat purrs, the refrigerator in the kitchen, the air conditioning. She'd been stupid and pushed herself too hard; there was no point in denying that. The trick now was to see if she could turn it into something good.

If Kiersten was willing to come back to town for a few days, she thought she'd be able to.

Scram quit kneading and adjusted himself beside her, then rolled onto his back, stretching his front legs over his head and over the edge of the couch, showing the tips of his teeth.

"I think you're glad we're still here too," she said to him.

He squirmed some more, his eyes drifting shut, his purr gradually stopping.

To be content as a cat, Tess thought and waited for Mack to get back.

FIFTY-EIGHT

Tess

Kiersten was more than willing to come back to town, although she was a little disappointed they weren't at the farmhouse. "I liked it there," she said when she arrived early Wednesday. She hadn't gone any farther than the entry, but her gaze was cool and assessing.

"Me, too, but honestly, I could use less commotion and it's no big deal for Mack to wake up here and end his run over there. Plus, if you were the Flahertys, wouldn't you expect the records box to be at the farmhouse and not here?"

"I can't get a good read on anything about the Flahertys," Kiersten said. She looked around again. "This place is cute, too. Post World War II?"

Tess smiled at the historian. "Maybe, if I'm out of work since no one wants new corporate spaces right now, I should go into business with you. We can be history nerds together."

She got Kiersten settled in the guest room—the other woman again having turned down the offer of a hotel room—and showed her to the records box, which was on a couple towels on top of the dining room table.

Tess took the box's top off while Kiersten got her archival things ready. And then she took a seat at the far end of the table and pretended to work from home while Kiersten started sorting.

Mack and Taylor showed up right before noon, carrying bags from the Jerusalem Joint. "Anything?" Mack asked as Tess helped Taylor unpack lunch.

"If so, I wish everyone else was here," Tess said, although the idea of having Mack free for lunch was enough to tempt her to drag him upstairs. Taylor wouldn't mind; they'd done it often enough during the early days of the pandemic. Well, through the entire pandemic, she corrected herself. Which was technically not over yet.

"Yes," Kiersten said slowly, looking at all of them in turn. Something about the way she did made Tess think she knew what Tess had been thinking.

She told herself she was being stupid. She was married. She was *pregnant*. Of course she had a sex life.

"They had a business deal," Kiersten went on, looking at whatever was in her hands as Mack set four dinner plates on the kitchen table. "As I told you they might. Mackenzie, Flaherty, and Slate."

"We have heard next to nothing about the Slates," Mack said and motioned her into the kitchen. "At some point, I'd like to know why."

Kiersten smiled. "Because when the deal soured in 1860, they left town. Run out of town, actually, thanks to those Flahertys. That's all I know about them so far, but I'll keep looking."

"Is there a chance," Tess asked, "that they weren't run out of town so much as put in the ground somewhere?"

Kiersten paused. "I wouldn't be surprised," she said.

Mack grabbed a plate and a chair, in that order. Once seated, he started scooping food, as did Taylor.

"Do you two have to be back by a certain time?" Tess asked.

"One o'clock meeting," Taylor said. They rolled their eyes. "The meetings resume, and I will never have my boss to myself again." Now they shook their head and spooned tabouleh onto their plate. "Just when we get the NERF guns back, too."

Tess caught Kiersten's eye and winked.

"You haven't asked what the business was," Kiersten said, taking a plate of pita and passing it to Tess. She had put the document back in the box. "Because that's where it gets fun."

"Sheep?" Mack asked.

"The sheep were a… bonus," Kiersten said. "First of all, do you know who Henry's father was?"

Mack shook his head. "Some dude lost to history?"

"William, just like the Flaherty who's currently giving you a hard time, only *your* William is important because he's the son of the man who first came to America. The Mackenzies have been here a long time, Mack. Longer than some other, better-known founding families, if you follow me. And in keeping with Mackenzie legacy, they were kind to the people around them—meaning the native people. William and a very young Henry fought to keep them from being displaced, but the government refused to budge.

"That was when the Flahertys and the Slates saw opportunity, and the idea for Port Kenneth was born, and so was this business."

"Quit playing and tell us," Mack said in a mock growl. His smile undermined any hostility.

She gestured. "This is Tennessee. What else is the state known for?"

"Whiskey," Tess breathed. "But..."

"It may not have been what became official Tennessee Whiskey, and it was even before there was such a thing, but yes, at least according to that," Kiersten said, gesturing to the records box and, presumably, the document she'd been reading.

Tess frowned and glanced at Mack first, then Taylor, and finally Kiersten. "This is probably what Flaherty wants."

"I don't think there's a *probably* involved here," Mack said. He crossed his arms over his chest, his lunch abandoned. "Can he seriously think a recipe this old, this many years later, is worth all he's put us through?"

Taylor speared a piece of chicken with their fork and quietly ate. Tess wondered what they were thinking, what insights they would have.

After living together for a year and a half, she knew to keep her mouth shut and wait. Taylor would share it once their thoughts had coalesced.

"It gets better," Kiersten said, ripping a piece of pita in half and setting it on the edge of her plate. She reached for the green salad and helped herself to some, putting the lid on the dressing and shaking it a few times before pouring it over the greens. "Prohibition started here before it did across the rest of the country. And what do you do with all the rye and barley and corn and everything else you'd been growing on your hundreds of acres"—she gave them all meaningful looks—"so no one will suspect you're bootlegging?"

If Tess had been holding anything, she would have dropped it as all the pieces fell into place. "Sheep!"

"Which the Mackenzies had farmed back in Ireland."

It all fit. Every last piece, including the feud with the Flahertys and what William Flaherty was after now. Even the fact that it had been William *Mackenzie* who had kept the whiskey recipe and it was now William *Flaherty* who wanted it.

Mack was grinning at her.

Tess couldn't help but grin back.

FIFTY-NINE

CHAD

"Hell no," Chad told Mackenzie when he showed up later that day. "I am not giving you anything on blind faith."

"I'm asking for information. That's it."

"No."

He watched the guy start to twitch. Maybe the great benevolent Mackenzie wasn't any different from William Flaherty. Not when it came to expecting to get what he wanted, no matter what, just because of who he was.

"Okay, fine," Mackenzie said, turning away with a shake of his head. "Maybe you *are* sincere about getting out from under your father's thumb after all."

Chad stared after him as he took a leap off the porch and headed across the street.

Sir Ginger was waiting inside. The cat rubbed against his legs, then promptly bit his sock, pulling only the fabric away from his leg.

It was an odd sort of progress.

"C'mon," he said to the cat and reached for the most beloved wand toy, the one with the strange red squiggly thing on the end. "We have to play fast. I have to be at work soon."

It was still a new feeling to be at work, even though it had been a couple of weeks now and Vera said she was pleased with him. He'd never worked so hard in his life, doing whatever she needed him to, including some chores he swore, to judge from the way she chuckled as she watched, she invented just to see how far she could push him.

He wasn't going to be a typical Flaherty.

In fact, he liked working for the Black woman, liked her customers, and even liked the exhaustion that chased him home after a shift. He liked being able to eat his meals there so he didn't have to cook, and he liked that she would let him run home so he could keep Sir Ginger on a consistent meal schedule, like the vet had suggested as a way to help some of the biting.

He was standing on the couch, one foot planted in the middle of each cushion, laughing and encouraging Sir Ginger to jump higher after his squiggly thing when the doorbell rang.

He figured it was Mackenzie and ignored it. Sir Ginger was more fun.

The bell rang again.

They repeated that pattern twice more until Chad couldn't take it. He didn't barge in on Mackenzie like this. Mackenzie could lay off.

"What?" He flung the door open and bent to catch Sir Ginger, who looked ready to bolt.

The cat squealed and dug his toenails into Chad's stomach, taking advantage of that moment when Chad let go and yowled at the pain to escape up the stairs to the second floor.

Chad didn't particularly blame him.

"Chadwick."

It was his father.

Chad turned away from the door and walked back into the living room so he could put the toy away. It was time to get ready for work.

"I needed to speak to you." William followed him into the house, closing the front door quietly behind him.

"I didn't answer the door for a reason."

His father just gave him a withering look. "Don't forget who pays your mortgage," he said softly.

"Not for much longer," Chad answered in the same low, almost threatening tone.

"You are my son," William said. "Do you think I'm going to let you go so easily? To turn into"—he motioned all around him—"*this*?" It came out in a sneer, which didn't surprise Chad. If anything, he'd expected it.

"Yes to the last, no to the first. Which is really stupid, Dad." He shook his head. "Look what you did to Mom when she wanted more control over her own life—"

"If that's what you think that was about—" William started, his face turning red.

Chad held up a hand, not sure what to say. He didn't care what had happened between his parents, or why. He'd crushed Mom's voice box, she'd gone blind... he didn't know the whole thing, and he didn't care to. All he'd ever really cared about was that he couldn't talk about her, he had to hide his visits to her, and the problem wasn't that she'd survived so much as her survival continued to be proof of what a failure his father was—when he didn't hide behind Go-fer Stanley and all the others.

"How little you know, Chadwick."

"Don't make me start screaming her name again, Dad." It may have been the only leverage he had, but it was effective leverage.

William snorted and looked around, wandering deeper into the house. Chad trailed him, glad when Sir Ginger showed up. Hopefully he'd bite the old man.

Sir Ginger growled, the hair along his spine standing up, his tail puffing out.

William turned and Sir Ginger hissed, started to charge, stopped, and ran out of the room.

"What. Was. That?"

"My cat."

William's mouth worked, but nothing came out.

Chad had to admit he was... amused. It was a new sensation. "Tell me something," he said and barreled on before his dad could say anything. "Do you even know what you're trying to get out of Mackenzie?"

"Just tell me what they tell you."

"They tell me only what they want you to hear. Which means they tell me nothing you'd find interesting. Or," he added, trying to resist the temptation to look at his dad and watch him have a stroke as he said, "Tess is telling me how to set up my own business helping the people here. It wasn't even my idea; they came to me and asked if I'd do it."

He glanced at his father, but he didn't look ready for his head to pop off.

He did, however, look greatly constipated.

"I've got to get to work, Dad. Thanks for coming by," Chad said, lunging for his shoes and heading to the front door. He'd walk to Vera's barefoot if he had to, but he wasn't going to be late. He hadn't been late once yet; it wasn't the day to start.

William sat down in an armchair.

"Oh, no," Chad said. "Dad. I'm leaving. That means you are too."

"Not without knowing what Mackenzie's up to."

Chad held his hands out in frustration. "Mackenzie's up to running his company and opening his farm back up. That's it. Now you know. Goodbye." He made a shooing motion at the door.

His father narrowed his eyes. "That had better be all it is."

"Good to see you again, Dad. Thanks for the housewarming gift. Oh, wait—"

That got a growl out of his old man. "I'm still paying your mortgage."

"Yeah, and thanks. I'm glad you decided to listen to Sophie about that."

"And your credit card."

"Might want to check that statement," Chad said and motioned, again, to the front door.

This time, his dad left.

SIXTY

MACK

"So, we should, as the group who's been involved with this from the start, decide what to do," Mack said. Everyone was there: Thomas, Gray, April, Taylor, Roger. Of course Tess, and even Sima. He'd hoped Kiersten would stay, but she had said it was family business and as much as she was involved in the family history, she didn't much want to be involved in the family's present.

In a sense, Mack didn't blame her.

He'd even patched his mother in via video. Krista's longtime lover was with her, and Mack thought they looked cute together, sitting closer than he could remember seeing them. Maybe having him out of their hair was good for them. "Emerson," she said, "what are the options?"

He eyed Tess. "Well, anything we want. We go into the whiskey business. We bury it back under Ida and forget it's there and let Flaherty have an aneurism over it. We give it to him."

"We could find other partners," Tess said. "That's an option, too. Or we could just sell it outright, but it could still fall into Flaherty's hands that way."

"I—" Mack said, glancing at the others to see if they had any early input. No one looked like they wanted to say anything. "I kind of feel like we got a reminder earlier this week that we should think about scaling back. My vote's that we do nothing. Well, not do nothing." He looked at Sima. "Maybe we grow some ryegrass and barley for our sheep. Just in case."

She grinned, mischief glinting in her eyes. "Copy that. A lot? A little? And some corn, too." Her grin got bigger and she actually quivered with her excitement. "Oh, this can be *fun*."

"It's crops, Sima. For the sheep," he told her, but when she fake pouted and caught his eye, he grinned at her. They were on the same page. If whiskey wasn't getting distilled, they could pretend like it was.

That might get Flaherty's goat more than if they were actually doing it.

"Anyone got another idea?" he asked the group, looking at everyone in turn, but all he got was nods of acceptance and a lot of laughter.

"Emerson," Gray said, shaking his head and laughing silently, "I think you might be on to something here."

"What about your friend Chad?" Tess asked, somehow keeping the sneer out of her voice as she said his name.

Mack shrugged. "He's not our responsibility. I mean, he is as far as he's our neighbor, but that has nothing to do with the farm."

"What are you going to tell him?" she pressed and for a second, he wished she'd let it go. But only a second; he reminded himself that her tenaciousness was part of what he loved about her.

"Nothing," he said. "We don't owe them anything. William can make all the noise he wants; he's not going to get anything from us. Even if he burns our houses this time. Which he won't," he added with a glower. The security was amazingly expensive, even for someone who was used to big expenses.

"The problem you're establishing for yourself, Emerson," Thomas said, leaning forward and capturing his attention, "is that sooner or later, you'll have to give him what he wants."

"Oh, he can have the recipe," Mack said. "It's not hard to find the official guidelines for Tennessee Whiskey, and this?" He raised the piece of paper. It was a copy of a copy of the original. Kiersten had, of course, taken the original back to Knoxville with her. "This doesn't have enough corn in it. Corn's not good for the sheep," he added with a wink. "Don't grow too much of it, Sima."

She tittered and he couldn't help himself. He grinned back. Between her and Taylor, he and Tess were in for a lot of trouble. Okay, mostly him, since Tess often teamed up with Taylor.

"How do you know all this already?" Tess asked him, eyeing him suspiciously, like she hadn't expected him to be this prepared. Part of him thought he should be insulted by that.

Taylor coughed and reached for their water glass.

"Seriously? You two are at it already?" Tess glared at Mack. She should have expected that efficiency from Taylor, he figured. It was, after all, why Taylor was paid so well.

Sima just grinned. "I like people who are proactive," she said. "And just so we're all clear here. They can eventually have the recipe but will need to get their grains from…"

Mack kept grinning, pleased Sima was figuring out his long game.

"This may not go the way you'd like," Thomas warned. "I'd go so far as to say it definitely will not."

"Oh, it probably won't," Mack said. He wasn't sure he even cared. Flaherty could do what he wanted, even down to getting his grain for his precious whiskey from another source. He and Tess had enough to deal with; he'd said so and would continue to say so until everyone else believed they truly were going to slack off a bit. They had a baby to occupy themselves with.

Or, they would.

After a few minutes of chit-chat, everyone drifted away. Krista and Logan said goodnight, leaving Mack and Tess staring at each other.

"So," she said.

"So," he said.

"I think we've done it. I think we've unraveled all the secrets now."

"I think we have."

Sixty-One

Tess

The following weekend, the Saturday Ultimate Disc lessons and scrimmages were in full swing in the yard to the side of the rowhouse, and Tess had needed to see them to realize how badly she'd missed them. It wasn't just the simple beauty of watching the disc fly through the air so much as it was the atmosphere. All were welcome, lessons were given freely, there was a lot of laughing, and anyone who didn't want to play or learn was welcome to hang out on the side porch. People brought munchies and cookies and it was a couple of hours where people just got along and spent time getting to know each other. It was Woolslayer at its best.

And strangely, anyone present who wanted to play in the wider city leagues but couldn't afford it often found themselves taken care of.

The day was winding down. Most of the players had gone home, so Hank had brought the twins down into the yard and he and Mack were working with them, as much as you could teach five-year-olds. Mack knelt on the ground with Tim and was helping him hold the disc properly, while Hank was telling Ryan to get ready to run and pointing in the direction he wanted the boy to go.

Mack was going to make a great parent, Tess thought, watching him. Tristan might have been a lousy role model, but Mack had picked it up somewhere. Maybe he was only following Hank's lead. Maybe it was innate. Tess decided she didn't care where it came from. All that mattered was that their baby would benefit from it.

Meter was in the yard with a couple of Mack's former teammates, trying to learn but mostly, to Delia's chagrin, getting tangled up in himself.

"He says he can play softball just fine, but watching him out there, you'd never imagine he's got mad sex skills," Delia said, her camera in her lap for the moment.

"I'd hope he doesn't try to fling you across a grassy yard," Tess said.

Delia just winked and flashed her saucy smile.

Jamie laughed and shook her head, then turned to Tess. "Have you hit that second trimester need for the constant O, or was I the lucky one among us?"

Tess caught her breath. She and Jamie had never really talked about their sex lives in detail; this felt exposed. And even a bit rude to do it in front of Delia, who simply raised her camera. Tess figured there wasn't much else to do because it wasn't a conversation her friend could join.

"You have, haven't you?" Jamie asked with a knowing nod and smile.

Tess covered her face with her hands, fighting the urge to duck and cover her entire head. She figured she was blushing, too. "Why is it like this?" she moaned. "Everyone said the second trimester was the *good* one, the *easy* one, but this is not easy!"

"Look," Delia said and Tess peeked between her fingers. Delia had lowered her camera again. She had, like usual, perched on the porch railing and was turning to face the women more fully. "It's all about communication, right?"

"What is?" Tess asked, dropping her hands and staring at her friends.

"Great sex. I mean, sex *is* communication. And the best sex happens when you get off on giving pleasure as much as receiving it. But for most people, it's work to get to that point. So if you're needing him all the time, make no apologies but remember that part of needing him is giving *him* more pleasure than he can stand."

Tess knew her mouth had dropped open and she forced herself to shut it.

Jamie, though, looked thoughtful. "I'm not a sex therapist," she said slowly as Delia looked from Jamie to Tess and then raised her eyebrows as if expecting a response.

"But," Jamie went on, "that sounds like the best advice I've ever heard." She paused, looking over at Hank. "And to be honest, Hank and I have been married eight years now and I don't think I've *ever* thought of it that way."

"There's a real power rush," Delia went on, "when you look at him and realize *you're* the one responsible for him making... whatever. Those noises. Move like that. Touch you there. Kiss harder and deeper. Thrust more slowly. Whatever." She attempted a shrug, but Tess didn't buy her casual air. "I mean, think about it. We're all monogamous, right?" She waited for Tess and Jamie to nod. "That means *we* are the only people on the planet with *that* power over them. That's something else. Totally next-level stuff—and you get, what? Three months to have at it?" Delia cocked her head. "Maybe I am sorry I can't have kids." She winked, and Tess knew that last statement, at least, was a load of hooey.

"I am going to have to try that," Jamie said slowly. Tess agreed; even after the attempt at thirty days and how that had altered things with Mack, they hadn't achieved anything close to what Delia was describing.

For a second, Tess felt a pang at what she'd been missing out on. On what she'd been making Mack miss out on, too.

"And then think about the power Flaherty's chasing," Delia went on and smirked. "As far as I can see, there's no contest. He gets to be flashy. We get intimacy, a real bond with our men, a stronger marriage. We win every single time."

The three women straightened up as the men approached with Jamie and Hank's twins. Ryan—Tess was pretty sure; the twins were identical and sometimes it was hard to tell them apart—was in Hank's arms, his head on his dad's shoulder, his eyes closed as if the day had worn him out. It very well could have, Tess figured. They'd been playing pretty hard.

"You look smug," Meter told Delia, coming to stand between her knees, putting his hands on her legs gently, as if afraid he'd tip her off the railing.

"Always," she said and smiled him.

"Jame?" Hank asked. He jostled Ryan. "I think we're being given a sign."

"Looks like it," Jamie said, standing up.

"You know," Mack said, rubbing the back of his neck when Jamie and Hank had said their goodbyes and chased Tim to their car, "this finally feels like the right time."

"The bottle?" Tess asked. It had been sitting in the kitchen since the discussion and revelation about the recipe. Tess hated it. Hated the idea of it, hated that it was going to be a gift to Chad, hated what it represented.

But Mack, despite being the one who'd said they were going to do nothing, was convinced it'd be fun.

"Yep. Delia, you might want to have the camera ready. Or not, since—" Mack pointed at what Tess assumed meant Chad's house.

"Are you embarrassing him again?"

"He doesn't need my help for that," Mack said, sounding a little confused.

"True," Meter said.

"You can't tell me that living across the street from him doesn't suck," Delia said.

"It's not my ideal," Tess said, thinking that was a bit of an understatement. Of course, on the other hand, he'd been a respectful neighbor so far, and quiet. And he'd kept the trash cans and the blue bucket out for anyone in the neighborhood to use. A lot of neighbors were telling Tess they were pleasantly surprised by that, and one or two had even come to her, asking if she thought Chad would help them empty their houses with the proper amount of reverence and respect.

Maybe having him as a neighbor wouldn't be so bad.

Maybe.

But a lot possibly hinged on how he was going to react to Mack's little gift.

"Meter? Delia? You in?" Mack asked, eyebrows raised, a hopeful expression on his face. He had drawn his chin in toward his chest slightly, which made him look somehow paternal.

They exchanged a look, then Delia let out a long sigh and said, "Sure," jumping down from the railing. Meter reached for her camera bag and handed it to her. She took it with a smile of what Tess thought was thanks. "Let's do this. How awful do you think it's going to be?"

"Hopefully not," Mack said.

"Then where's the fun exactly?"

That was Tess's question, too.

SIXTY-TWO

MACK

The first thing Mack noticed was that Flaherty didn't say *what* in that tired voice when he came out onto the porch. "Something wrong?" he asked instead. He also seemed to have more energy.

"Brought you a present," Mack said and leaned forward, setting the bottle of whiskey on the porch between them.

The guy eyed it. "You spit in it or something?"

Mack rubbed the back of his neck, a bit confused by the question. "I hadn't thought of that, but if you want me to, I guess I can." He'd feel stupid doing it, with everyone watching him, but if that's what was going to be needed here, he'd do it.

"Why would you think I'd want booze you spat in?" Chad asked, shifting his weight onto his right foot and crossing his arms over his chest.

"It's not for you. It's for your father. That's my answer to what he's looking for."

Chad bent down and picked up the bottle, reading the label. He glanced up at Mack, his mouth open for a second before he said, "You're telling me this whole Mackenzie-Flaherty feud is over cheap whiskey?"

"I don't know what it would cost if we produced it today, but yeah. Our families have hated each other because of some sort of whiskey." He watched Flaherty carefully.

"And you know this how?" The question was asked slowly, as if the guy were thinking as he spoke.

It was Delia who sighed. "Because they found the recipe, Chad. How else?" She shook her head. "This isn't hard to understand." She took a step closer to the porch. "It's about *whiskey*. All this stupidity, and then your dad burned down Tess's barn. Because of *whiskey*, and not even Tennessee whiskey, apparently."

Flaherty was still studying the bottle; he hadn't stopped since he'd picked it up. "When you put it like that..." He turned the bottle in his hands as if to read the back label but then set it down almost exactly where it had been. "What else did you find out?"

"That's it," Mack said, although that wasn't entirely the truth. But it was all he was willing to share, at least for the moment. According to Tess, he was sharing too much already. She was probably right about that and they should have stayed home.

"So..." Chad eyed him. "Should anything be stopping me from handing this bottle to my old man and telling him that's all he's getting, and that you and I are going into business?"

"Like we'd have a better outcome?" It was, Mack thought, a ballsy suggestion, one the guy probably wouldn't survive once his father found out about it.

Flaherty eyed Delia. "Probably not."

"Smartest thing you've said in eons," she said, widening her stance and adjusting her camera bag. "So what *is* the plan, Mack?"

"Just what I said," Mack answered as if Chad had been the one to ask the question. "Take the bottle to the old man. That's all he gets. I don't make the whiskey, he doesn't make the whiskey, we live our separate lives and if we fight, it's over what's best for the city."

Flaherty raised his eyebrows at that, and Mack wondered if his father knew how much of a running start he and Tess had. Probably, he decided. They hadn't been quiet about... well, most of it.

"Peace," Chad said. He motioned with an index finger, drawing a line between Mack and himself. "Peace?"

"We're neighbors," Mack said, as if it were that simple. In some ways, it was—but only some. Everything else was probably messy, complicated, and waiting to bite him in the ass if he wasn't careful.

Thankfully he had Tess and Delia in his corner. And hopefully they wouldn't let him screw this up too badly.

"One condition," Flaherty said, looking dubiously at the bottle and then back at Mack.

"No."

"It won't hurt," the guy said. "But you promise me here and now that one day you'll tell me the full story behind all this."

Mack shrugged. "That's a pretty open-ended request—and it's assuming we ever discover anything worth telling."

"Whatever you know. One day, we'll meet at my dad's grave, pour some of this cheap shit all over it, and raise a toast to the Flakenzie whiskey we've been distilling without his knowing."

Tess shook her head. Mack could feel Delia shaking her head. Meter stayed quiet.

"Mackerty," Mack said with a grin, impressed the guy had figured out that part of things so fast. "I think of it like that."

"Are we *really* going to fight over whose name comes first?" Flaherty asked.

Mack caught his eye. "You tell me."

"Get off my porch. All of you."

It didn't seem right to point out that none of them were actually *on* his porch. But they left anyway.

SIXTY-THREE

CHAD

Chad had thought about repeating Mackenzie's schtick with the presentation of the bottle of cheap whiskey. A couple problems had cropped up with that, though, beginning with the fact that it was his only bargaining chip with Sophie.

And after Mackenzie and Cartieri had taken Ford and her nerd and left, he'd broken open the bottle and had a celebratory sip.

Cheap whiskey, Chad had learned, wasn't good.

He'd poured the bottle out. Shit was *vile*, and if this was what the families had been fighting over for more than a century now, the fight was even more stupid than he'd first thought. They'd also deserved to fail, and if the quality of the whiskey was the reason the Slates had vanished from town and memory, that maybe had been the smarter play.

Instead of the grand presentation, Chad decided to meet Sophie at Gentry's. Even though Chad got there five minutes early, Sophie had beaten him. Thankfully Gentry's wouldn't seat anyone until their whole group had arrived, so she was standing in the waiting area, looking peeved, and wouldn't say much until they were seated, which was fine with Chad. Gentry's seating didn't allow a ton of privacy, but it was more than he'd get standing in the waiting area, everyone right there and probably pretending to be lost in their phones but actually listening in.

"So what's so important?" Sophie asked.

Chad didn't buy her standoffish manner. He stared at her. "You mean you can't guess?"

She tilted her head slightly and looked at him from the side. It wasn't quite a side-eye, but it was close. "So they found it," she breathed. "And?"

"And what? They're keeping it. Keeping it hidden, too."

"Chad— You know Dad's not going to be okay with that. He wants it."

"And now you have the leverage you want over him." He didn't add that he had the leverage he wanted to get free. Wasn't that a given? The whole world, it seemed like, knew he wanted to stop being a Flaherty.

Sophie, of course, knew that. She brought it up.

"That hasn't changed," he told her, surprised she even had to ask.

"Chad," Sophie said but was interrupted by their server. She ordered cheesy bacon fries; Chad just wanted a chocolate-covered-strawberry milkshake.

Sophie shook her head. "You're still so much like a little kid. You know that, right?"

He shrugged. "Ask me if I care. I'm done, Soph. I'm out."

"I need you," she said, actually glancing down at the paper place mat in front of them. "I can't dethrone Dad without you. We have to do it together."

That pained her, he could tell. She wanted to do it alone as much he wanted her to.

Realizing that surprised him, although he told himself it shouldn't have. Part of why he was so desperate to get away was because he wasn't valuable. No one *wanted* him.

"What do you need?" It came out as a resigned sigh which he attributed to habit more than anything else because hearing those words made him want to punch himself in the face.

"If Dad thinks you and I have teamed up with Mackenzie to do whatever this surprise is, to work together, but only if it's the three of us, he'll give us—me—more room to run things."

"He'll give up the feud?" That was mostly what Chad wanted. Well, that and to be left alone, but he wasn't so sure he was about to find that. Not so fast, anyway; he might have to shift to the long game.

"I'll find a way to make him," Sophie said and while Chad knew the intent was real, he wasn't certain she'd be able to. When William fixated on something, he didn't stop until he'd gotten what he wanted.

Then again, Chad figured, if he thought his kids had come together, that the loser disappointment had fallen into line at last…

He froze, staring at Sophie.

"Something wrong?"

"He's not going to buy it. That I'm your partner in this."

She smiled sweetly. "Yes, he will. When I tell him I know how to get through to you more effectively than any of his beatings ever have."

That was probably true, but Chad narrowed his eyes, not trusting her. "And just how can you get through to me?"

"By promising you that," she said in a sotto voice that put Chad on edge, "so long as you do what I want, no one's going to lay a finger on you again. Unless you can manage to get someone willing to get naked and give it up to you."

Her voice was so smooth, so silky, so... *menacing* that Chad shuddered.

Sophie's smile threatened to turn his insides liquid.

"So there it is," Chad said, but Sophie's demeanor changed immediately and she was his sister again.

"So far as Dad's concerned. Me, I don't care if you want to keep your little job with the Black woman. In some ways, it's a good look. The younger Flahertys *are* different! They're better! They're"—she leaned forward and hissed—"infiltrating so they can wage war from within."

The idea sickened Chad even as he understood where she was coming from.

But Sophie wasn't done. "No one needs to know that it's all bullshit and you're the first independent Flaherty in generations. Maybe ever," she added thoughtfully and sat back as their server arrived with their food.

Chad played with his straw before taking a sip, mixing the chocolate fudge sauce into the strawberry ice cream, getting a little bit of whipped cream in there too and watching the cherry tilt to one side.

"I'm serious," Sophie said after she'd eaten a few fries. Despite the mess, she was using her fingers, licking them with a smile that was as childlike as Sophie ever got. "I'll put it in writing if you need me to."

Mackenzie, Chad was sure, would tell him to do exactly that. Get it in writing.

"Done," he said. The only other better deal he was going to get was from Overwatch, and that was a new identity and a one-way ticket out of town.

Not that he had much in Port Kenneth. A blue bucket. A couple neighbors. A crummy job bussing tables in a coffee shop owned by a well-respected Black woman.

And yet somehow, it was enough. Not for the long-term, but for right now. For the building blocks to something else. Something he hadn't figured out yet.

"One more thing?" Sophie said and Chad wanted to kick himself.

"What?"

"Write up a business plan for me about how we're going to be working with Mackenzie."

"But… we're not."

She smiled, and it was that predatory one that made his hands shake. "Dad can't know that. Remember?"

Maybe, Chad thought, that one-way ticket to parts unknown wasn't such a bad idea. He could find a crummy job somewhere else. Neighbors were a fact of life. And he could buy his own blue bucket.

"Of course," Sophie went on, lifting a fry that immediately went limp in her fingers. A piece of bacon fell off and she frowned at it, then shrugged and put the fry in her mouth. "Dad'll never see it. Maybe you and Mackenzie are fighting over it, each trying to get the most favorable terms. And of course, you and I are going to screw him in the end. Dad'll love that little touch; he'll think it's real."

Chad caught on. "So Dad has to let go of all things Mackenzie so you can handle them."

She beamed at him. "See? This isn't going to be so bad."

Chad doubted that.

SIXTY-FOUR

He'd been sitting on his porch for so long, the neighbors had begun asking him if he'd locked himself out. "Waiting for someone," he said. She had to come by sooner or later; she couldn't stay away any more than he could.

Aaliyah was convinced he was waiting for her. "I done *told* you, mister," she said, one hand on her hip, the other jutted out. The kid was five or six, and she had the attitude of a mother. "I have *school*."

"And you'd better not fail out," he told her.

"Like you did?" she asked.

He laughed, one of those laughs where you throw your head back and laugh straight out of your gut and for a second, life feels amazing.

"Look at you," someone drawled.

When Chad lifted his head, it was to see Aaliyah running away and Delia Ford standing at the bottom of his steps.

At last.

"I've been waiting for you to show up," he told her.

"Oh?" she asked, raising an eyebrow. "And why is that?"

"Maybe," he started but then licked his lips, suddenly nervous.

She pursed her lips but waited.

He found himself staring at those lips. He'd wanted her so badly, it had hurt, even when they'd supposedly been together. He'd never been sure if she'd been aware she was in love with her nerd even then, but he'd known. She'd never talked of him, but she'd held back parts of herself. Big, important parts.

Guy was lucky.

"Maybe?" Delia asked, ducking her chin toward her chest. Her eyebrows came up higher.

"Maybe it was a good thing you stole my dad's place." He paused, thinking, trying to sort through his words. "We both came out ahead."

"He beat you for that. *Before* the beating that was my wedding present." She made a face, and Chad was willing to bet she was thinking *strangest wedding present ever*.

"Yeah," Chad said. "But no one ever said freedom came easy."

They stared at each other for a long minute.

"We square?" he asked her.

"No," she said, turning her back to him and walking across the street.

Chad watched her go, wondering how or why he'd ever thought he'd needed her at all. *Want*, sure. But *need*? And to settle the situation with his father?

Nah. He was doing just fine on his own.

Or… he would be, if he could figure out the whiskey thing.

He stood up and went inside. Beyond the fact that the business plan needed to exist just in case, convincing Mackenzie to put it back into production would give him needed leverage over Sophie and his own future.

He didn't need Delia Ford after all.

Note from Susan

I hope you had fun with Mack, Tess, Chad, and *Legacy*. I'd like to take this moment to thank you for the support… and ask you for a bit more.

Please leave a review online! Be it the store where you bought the book or a site that lets you talk about books, it's a simple way to say thanks to an author for the hard work they do bringing their book, their world, and their vision to life.

Second is more of an invite. And that invite is to join my mailing list: http://westofmars.com/newsletter You'll want the one marked "Susan Helene Gottfried Author Newsletter," of course.

I try to send it out monthly, with news of freebies—I write a short story every year for my newsletter subscribers—and sales, some of which are for newsletter subscribers only. I try to not flood your inbox because I'd rather have you reading my books!

Thanks in advance. These small actions help raise my visibility, which means more people can join in my fictional worlds.

(Also? Are you missing the sample chapter at the end of this book? So am I, but wait until you see what's coming next! Be sure you're on my newsletter to get the early word!)

About the Author

Susan Helene Gottfried is the heavy-metal-loving, not-disabled enough divorced Jewish mother of two. A freelance line editor to authors of fiction by day, her select roster of clients tend to hit bestseller lists, and more than a few have quit their day jobs. It's not entirely her doing, but like does attract like. As an author, she focuses on contemporary fiction, loving the challenge of creating great characters who find themselves in situations that force them to grow and change.

Susan holds a BA (University of Pittsburgh) and MFA (Bowling Green State University) in English Writing and Fiction, respectively. She lives with a couple cats in the Pittsburgh suburbs, just West of

Mars. She's a member of the Editorial Freelancers Association and Pennwriters and is the recipient of a 2024 Greater Pittsburgh Arts Council Creative Entrepreneur Accelerator grant. Visit her at westofmars.com or talesfromthesheepfarm.com

Also By

Tales From the Sheep Farm

Maybe the Bird Will Rise (2023)

Populated (2023)

Safe House (2024)

Saving Sima (2024)

Legacy (2025)

Collected short stories

Permission to Enter (2023)

Broken but Undaunted: Collected Stories (2023)

The Trevolution (short story collections and novels)

ShapeShifter: The Demo Tapes (Year 1) (2008)

ShapeShifter: The Demo Tapes (Year 2) (2009)

Trevor's Song (2010)

ShapeShifter: The Demo Tapes (Year 3) (2011)

ShapeShifter: The Demo Tapes (Year 4) (2013)

King Trevor (2012)

Short stories

Mannequin: A Short Story (2011; out of print)

Guitar God Numero Uno (With Love Anthology 2011; out of print)

The Taste of Pink Snow (Pink Snowbunnies in Hell Anthology 2011; out of print)

Make a Wish (Bestseller Bound Short Story Anthology—Volume 2 2011)

The Ghost of the Dresser (Bestseller Bound Short Story Anthology—Volume 4 (2012)

Broken (2014; out of print)

Undaunted (Running Wild Press 2018)

Siren Song (Hard as Steel Anthology; 2024)

In Search of Culinary Excellence (To Appalachia, With Love Anthology, 2024)

www.ingramcontent.com/pod-product-compliance
Ingram Content Group UK Ltd.
Pitfield, Milton Keynes, MK11 3LW, UK
UKHW040737200225
455358UK00003B/121